To Jerom

THE
DOG HEAD
DAWN

Hope you enjoy my book !!!

L P DUNCAN

Lots of love

Lorraine x

WULVER PUBLISHING

Published in Great Britain by Wulver Publishing
23, Fallow Court Avenue, London N12 OEA

First published by Wulver Publishing, 2014
Text © L.P. Duncan
Illustration © L.P. Duncan
Front cover © Diane P George
The right of L.P. Duncan to be identified as the author and
illustrator of this work has been identified by her.

Printed by CPI, 38 Ballards Lane, London N3 2BJ

www.lorrainepduncan.co.uk

For my family, especially my son, Laurie. Grateful thanks to my mother, Diane, for the use of her original oil painting for the cover of the book, to Timothy Clifford and Vanda Harvey for their help on the book cover graphics, to Frankie Fihlebon for agreeing to be my model for the Morgar illustration and to my kind friends for all their support.

MORGAR OF THE UNFATHOMABLE FOREST

CHAPTER ONE
Fair Isle

The Wulver slips from the rock shelf in his grotto into the heaving, dark water inlet and swims a short distance to the open sea and poking his head above the surface looks up to the night sky shimmering with the ever changing hues of the Northern Lights. Lower down he views the red, burning flames and black smoke from the funeral pyres.

Momentarily, he breathes in the stench of the burning flesh from the dead Humans and sickened by it, dives deep down into the dark water, his eyes becoming like torches where he swims amongst green turtles and sleeping fish.

Crabs and lobsters emerge from rocky crevices, lured out by the light from his eyes and begin voraciously feeding on the spiralling clouds of plankton. He picks each crustacean up one by one and places them in his netted bag tied from around his waist, swims upwards and back to his rocky retreat.

He is sad for the Human natives of this island, sad that the foreign ship had been swept here by the storm, sad that the islanders in their kindness had tried to help the dying, plague ridden Humans aboard it, sad that all are now dead, but what could he do? It has never been his way to involve himself in the affairs of Humans.

Yet there is one that still lives, but how she has managed to survive mystifies him? She has lost all her family, including her three small children; he has watched her admiringly, tirelessly, pulling the dead onto the funeral pyres, until she is the only one left.

1

He hears her crying uncontrollably for her young, wandering along the beach, crying up to the sky for help and he is puzzled that she believes that the sky can help her?

He is moved to such pity for her plight, realising that she must be starving, hence his dive into the deep for these delicacies that he knows the Human's love, but he worries how he can give them to her without distressing her any more than she is already? And so he sits on his rock seat, his webbed feet dangling in the water, ruminating on what he should do next.

The young woman looks up at the Northern Lights as she makes her way down to the beach following the old familiar path, so familiar to her that she could find her way even in the darkest of nights.

She pads over rounded pebbles until the foam edged incoming tide seductively creeps over her naked feet, so very cold that she shivers involuntarily. The sea retreats with a heavy sigh but rushes back fiercely, now up to her ankles, and she knows it is calling to her, wanting her and she resolutely wades in. Soon, the water is up to her waist and she gasps when the brutish undercurrent tugs at her skirts, it moves around her with a swirl of vicious intent and pulls so violently at her lower legs that she loses balance and is dragged beneath the water.

She attempts to fight back in her panic and then angry at her cowardice for wanting to still live, she closes her eyes and yields to the all, encompassing power of the sea.

Webbed feet still dangling in the sea, the Wulver feels the underwater current momentarily shift, there is something in the water by the shoreline, something not of the sea, caught in the thick green fields of kelp and it is trapped and dying and he knows it is her.

Slipping back into the sea, he swims rapidly underwater to the shoreline and pulling her lifeless body from the strangling, tendrils of moving weed carries her to the stony beach and lays her gently down on her side.

There is no movement from her at all, quickly he bends down lifting her up from under her arms and holds her up from behind. Her head lolls forward, he lifts her chin, until her body jerks spasmodically, she bends over and retches out the sea water and when done, leans weakly back allowing him to support her.

"Do I know you?" She asks quietly, but she knows who it is, it can be no other. She had seen him two years before in the deep rock pool, his head raised up from the still water, watching her, eyes dark and limpid, like the eyes of a seal, his face covered with fine, slick, hair, water dripping down like beads of oil, she had detected his kindness and smiled at him and after, when she had told her people of the sighting they said for her to have seen the Wulver was such a privilege, that he had not been seen by any of them, and she would be blessed with good fortune.

"You know me well enough." He answers.
She sobs out.

"But I wanted to die, why did you save me?"

"Because it was not your time. It was the time for the other Humans, but not for you."

"But I'm all alone, what will become of me?"

"You will not be alone any longer."

3

She turns and looks up at his dark seal eyes' and his bestial features, knowing that as he has chosen to help her, she would always be safe.

The years pass, no longer do Humans from the other Northern Isles bother to come and view the wreck of the plague ship, flying even now, its ragged yellow flag of quarantine. It had spread far and wide, even to Mainland that the desolate Fair Isle was ridden with disease and so they were left completely alone, happy and content in each other's company. Lomond, their son is born and already, not even in his third year of life is adept at the skills of survival on land and sea. From the high cliffs on the west coast he stands with his father and views southwards to the far distant, Orkney Isles and he knows beyond that is the vast mountainous country of Scotland where his mother originally came from and vows when he is old enough, he will make his way there and climb the high mountain called Lomond, his namesake, simply for that reason.

CHAPTER TWO
Mahayla

"How could they, how could they do this to me...why should I and why would I want to...he stinks...why does he stink like he does?"

Because he stinks of rotting flesh like his banished father before him replies her inner voice, and then aloud, "But why are they making me to do this...I can't, I will not."

She sobs as her path takes her further away from *them*, anything to get away from *them*. She wanders blindly through the Unfathomable Forest, accompanying bouncing balls of mosquitoes hover just in front of her path as the terrific hot August sun beams through the trees and burns her head.

She growls up to the sun to stay forever, never to be hidden by the clouds, never to slip below the tops of the trees, because before long she will be hidden away, under the ground with *him*, lying with *him* in the darkness for the hibernation, trapped with *him* forever more.

She comes across the small stagnant pool, so very close to the boundaries, but she doesn't care anymore.

"Why do we always drink from the underground springs, why can't we drink from the surface?" The birds trill loudly in agreement from the trees.

Rebelliously, she wades into the stagnant pool and swimming down into its filthy depths begins furiously digging with her hands into the soft mud bank until she comes across the first rock, she then unrolls large rock after rock, clawing viciously away, rising every few minutes for a gasp of air. It's of no use, she realises on the final dive down, she'll never get through, when in front of her eyes, through the lifting silt, the released underground spring explodes through with such force that she is knocked ferociously back. She swims beneath the surface, swirling and twisting in its turbulence, exalted that this sunken warm pool, now full to brimming, has turned into something so gloriously cold, so vibrant and so clean.

The day light animals come in all forms, drinking gratefully from the clean fresh water; a hawk flies over and drops, in its shock, a small fish into the water from its talons. All morning she swims, until finally exhausted she slips out and lies on the dry bank when she hears them from far away.

"If they kill me, I wouldn't mind, anything is better than the future." She omits a low whistle.

The horses come at her command, thundering towards her, the Humans unable to control them.

She stands up and turns to face them as they come streaming through the trees, the wolfhounds bounding through first. They growl at her apprehensively, the five horses rear up snorting wildly. She whistles, a small whistle, the giant horses calm as the dogs lie on the ground in submission.

The mounted Humans stare at her in complete shock, never have they seen anything like her. One of them whispers,

"What is this witchcraft?"

Arrogant, undaunted, her irises so piercingly blue they looked like the sky above, eyelids rimmed in black, tumbled tawny long hair, red gold in the sunlight, a close fine covering of downy hair from cheeks bones down, they feel they are in the company of a wild animal, she snarls softly, they are fearful of her yet she looks back at them with no fear. They contemplate unsheathing their swords and running her through, so nervous are they of her and her control of the dogs and horses.

Apart from one. The youth climbs down from his horse and walks slowly over to her, his eyes never leaving hers, and hers never leaving his.

"My Lord..." One of his men calls out warningly.

"Leave me."

But they stay, unsure of what to do. Without looking around, he says again.

"I said leave me."

Reluctantly they turn their horses, one reaches for his mare's reins but she tosses her head away aggressively.

Another calls for the wolfhounds but they refuse to budge, the strange female creature whistles low and instantly the dogs rise and follow after the retreating men.

His men are frightened as they ride away and talk in low voices,

"We shouldn't leave him...But what can we do, it's a direct order?...But what if she slits his throat with that dagger at her side?...I'm afraid she is a witch...No, not a witch, stupid, a Dog Head, to see one is apparently good news, if you treat them kindly; they repay you with great wealth...I've never heard of them...That's because there are few left...But I'm a' feared of her, what if there are others that will come and slaughter him...He told us to go so what else can we do?"

They make their way to a small glade where the sun shoots down arrow heads of piercing light through the trees.

"We'll stay here and wait, he won't be that long."

Taking refuge under a close leaved Lime tree, they snigger then, knowing his notorious way with women, their laughter makes them happier; the horses pull strips of bark from trees as a lone Song Thrush warbles as soothingly as a lullaby, the dogs roll onto their sides, happy for a rest in the sun after the miles they had crossed since dawn, until they all fall into a deep slumber.

Hours pass, the sun slips low when he appears through the trees, leading his mare quietly through. The wolfhounds rise from the ground and whimper loudly waking the men from their deep slumber.

He mounts the mare and rides swiftly away, groggily they follow behind, but when they see his extreme speed, they force their horses to catch up and stare in fascination at his wild animated face, never have they seen him like this before. They arrive back at Elsynge Manor and slumping back in his throne he looks only upwards at the dark coffered ceiling. They drink wildly, trying to enliven him, but nothing takes him from his deep mediation.

In the early hours he slips away and they don't see him or his horse for days but they guess where he has gone to. Finally he returns, the mare trotting head down as they appear together on the seventh dawn.

After that he is a changed person, furious, battle after battle, ignoring his heavy stallions, he chose instead to ride the white mare and at the start of every conflict, he would scream out, "She is the arrow, follow her."

For in his mind the horse was the embodiment of *her,* his lucky talisman.

All enemies were vanquished in his endless passion, because the only other time he had felt such passion was when he had been with *her.*

The last time they had lain together entwined as one, she had whispered in his ear, "You cannot be with me and I not with you." He argued back, "But why could you not come with me?"

"We are from completely different worlds and neither will be accepted in either, you know that, but I promise you one day you will have such wealth from our union, trust me, one day it will be yours."

He reluctantly understood her words, she was right, the Church would never agree to their union, they could never be together, but nothing on earth would ever be like her, ever.

He gave her his pendant seal to remember, he said, their union and watched her hang it from around her neck and she gave him in return a long thin tube of metal decorated with embossed markings.

"What is this?"

She smiled.

"This is from me to you, to seal our union. See the inscription I have inscribed for you. This Star Gauge will allow you to see forward in your life, to such great distances and to see ultimately the great wealth that I bequeath to you."

He looked at it briefly, still not understanding what it was and tucked it in his boot, being much more aware of staring at her sadly, so that he would never forget her image.

After he left that dawn, she felt such sadness too, strange that she found she had loved the youth, it was never her plan. She removed any evidence that Humans had ever entered the Unfathomable Forest. She fed the wild boars with truffles, they willingly trampled the earth so every sign of horse hooves, the smell and essence of the Humans and dogs were trampled to nothing. She returned to the deep pool, glistening in its freshness and went for her final swim. The Swallows dipped down, skimming the water's surface in an endless display for her, because they knew she would soon be gone and they too. She then left and disappeared further into the deep depths of the Unfathomable Forest.

The next dawn the male Dog Heads were about to embark on their yearly pilgrimage to the far side of the forest, when it was noticed she hadn't returned. They whistled to the birds and animals to tell them what had befallen her but they remained silent. They searched and searched, but all of them knew it was pointless, she was completely adept at hiding herself and would not be found unless she chose otherwise.

Exactly twelve full moons to the day she disappeared, distressed birds screamed through the forest, telling all of her reappearance, and there lying by the deep pool they found her quite dead. The Elder knelt down, his grief almost unbearable and pulling back the deerskin hide she had covered over her body, he reveals a lifeless baby still latched to her nipple and bending over her body, he shudders with grief.

The Dog Heads come closer and crowd around anxiously, he can no longer hide the child and in the midst of raising himself up he pulls the hide further down and head bowed, moves back silently. They take in the scene and the scent in disbelief, realising instantly that the child is half Human.

Morgar howls up to the skies in his anger, his mother joins in, until the Elder growls at them to stop. His daughter, his only daughter is lying dead in front of his eyes, but inwardly, he thanks the spirits she would not now be married into that bad strain, but at such a cost.

But before she could be stopped, Morgar's mother bends down and with vicious intent grabs the lifeless baby by its ankles and swings it wildly through the air growling in her anger at its treachery to her son. But the lifeless baby, filled now with oxygen from her swinging actions begins to mewl weakly, Morgar growls viciously, "Throw it to the wolves, mother, where it belongs."

The Elder grabs his arms with crushing force from behind, something from his dead daughter still lives and he roars in his rage.

"This male child will not be hurt by anyone of you; he is half of our blood regardless, so therefore he is protected until he is of age as our law stipulates...our law also stipulates, which directly applies to you personally Morgar, which I'm sure you can't have forgotten...*that the son will not suffer for the wrongdoings of his Father before him.*"

They all turn and look accusingly at Morgar, who abruptly ceases his low growling. The Elder strides forward and takes the dangling baby into his arms and glares at Morgar with dangerous eyes, "Your father was banished from here for his wrongdoings, but you and your mother were allowed to stay and, as my daughter had not consented to her enjoinment with you, there is not a case to be answered to, so I do not want to hear another word."

The others cry out, "Hear him, hear him." The Elder continues in his rage.

"And if the Human father, whoever he is, had forced the union with my daughter, then the wickedness will be upon him and, he will be judged accordingly by the spirits, but not by us as earth bound creatures."

But he knew that it had not been a forced union, without the others seeing, he had already secretly hidden the strange pendant that had hung from the baby's neck in his clothing.

In Dog Head custom, they left her body for nature to dispose of. The wolves fed first, then the foxes, followed by the weasels and stoats, bones disappeared down burrows then the rats and mice took away her long hair to line their nests even the wood ants carried away small triangles of flesh to their underground nests until finally all that was left, was her nearly bare skull. But no animal dared to take that last remnant of her body away as the birds from the Unfathomable Forest guarded her revered head ferociously by day and night.

But a pair of goshawks from the north unexpectedly soared down just before dawn; one grabbed it up in his talons and soared upwards, the other attacked, intent on snatching away the gruesome trophy. In the bitter battle of their airy acrobatics, the birds from the Unfathomable Forest flew at them outraged. The skull was released in fear and dropped into the deep pool where it spiralled down to the bottom.

The seasons rolled by, the skull stared up through empty sockets to view the sky above, being either lit by the sun or by the changing phases of the moon and stars, or darkened accordingly depending on the position of the earth as it continued its relentless orbit around the sun.

In the autumn, decaying leaves fell onto the surface of the deep pool, blanketing the celestial view momentarily until they sank below, followed by the snows of winter, then ice, then the spring sun again, followed by the burning summer sun until four years had passed, when the small, moon face of a child looked down into the water and dropped in fat, white grubs. The image left and again the seasons changed relentlessly until fourteen years had passed since her death.

The Dog Heads viewed the star formations daily, as they had always done over the centuries, gauging the weather by the gaseous emissions that created the aura around them.

Just before the sun rose that dawn, the sea blue face of the Dog Star ascended from the dark tree line. Its reappearance after so many months heralded the dog days of summer were coming to a close and that cooler days were rapidly approaching.

They had never seen the Dog Star shine as powerfully as it did now, but even stranger still, its small accompanying star companion, Little Pup, barely discernible for centuries, shone just as powerfully.

A most fortuitous sign for their autumn pilgrimage to the far side of the forest, but none of them remembered that it was exactly at this time fourteen years before that she had died. But one did remember and he growled happily at the significance to him personally, because the fierce light from the two stars proclaimed the preferment of a king.

CHAPTER THREE
Elsynge Manor, Enfield

Isabel, the fourteen year old, new Queen, from the sunny regime of Castile in Spain, now in her third week of being in this most freezing of English manor houses, makes her excuses to the King and leaves him with his brutes of drinking, shouting men and quickly strides off.

The Spaniel trots tightly at her side, her two Ladies-in-waiting follow rapidly behind, shocked, yet still grinning at the shenanigans of the wild men. The King glares after them, having all evening barely disguised his dislike of his new wife and her spoilt dog to everyone present.

The new Queen makes her way quickly up the grand, sweeping stone stairs, feeling so unwell that she almost faints when she reaches the top tread. Her two Ladies-in-waiting grasp her from under her arms and almost bodily lift her to her rooms. They steer her to her bed and gently lay her on top of it as the Spaniel leaps up and lies at her side.

"Please leave me." She calls out weakly, wanting to lie quietly alone with her dog; they flutteringly leave, their silk dresses making the most irritating noise as they shut the door behind them. She hears their suppressed giggles outside the door and then the sounds disappear off into the distance until she can hear nothing.

She has no doubt they are making their way back down to the banquet. How annoyed she is with them, ever since their arrival in England, they have changed from such good friends into such weak, giggling, disobedient fools.

She closes hers eyes, not quite understanding why she feels so ill, a terrible heaviness is creeping all over her, becoming inexplicably heavier by the second, the Spaniel presses against her side and licks her cheek softly.

"I fear my beautiful dog, that you and I..." For a brief second she struggles to continue and then slips into the darkness as the Spaniel follows swiftly behind.

One hour later, the door to her inner chamber is quietly opened and three men enter. They silently walk over to the bed, all appraising the still form of the beautiful girl for a brief moment. The King, conscious of his right hand man's extreme disapproval, abruptly rolls the lifeless Spaniel onto its back. He knows what he is doing is entirely wrong but regardless takes a knife and prises out one of the jewels imbedded in the dog's collar. He hands the stone to the younger of the men.

"Test it." The youth pulls out a small phial from within his robe. The jewel lying in the palm of his hand reflects shards of rainbow colours from the light of the flickering candlelight and the King begins to grin. The jewel is placed on the stone floor; a drop of the brown fluid from within the phial is dripped onto its flat surface. They watch intently as the jewel turns to a fizzing lump, the youth looks up nervously at the King's face.

"I'm afraid, my Lord, that it is completely and utterly worthless, nothing but a piece of cheap glass."

The King growls deeply in anger.

"Test the others." The youth takes the knife from the King and prises out one more and the test is repeated.

"Again completely worthless, my Lord, and studying the rest of them, they are all equally as worthless, so where could she have hidden it, her Ladies-in-waiting have searched everything? I felt certain that these stones would be real, whilst I know so obvious...but what better place, blatantly right under our eyes."

"Test the rest of them." Each stone is tested but still with the same result.

"Take it and get rid of it, I never want to see that dog again."

The King strides from the room, his anger almost unbearable, to have been convinced of this final nonsense by his nephew. He already has Isabel's large dowry, the only reason he had agreed to the marriage, his coffers practically bare after too many wars of his own doing, but it is not enough, not nearly enough. He had heard the rumour from her two Ladies-in-waiting, that she possesses a diamond of such worth that he would be the richest king in Christendom. Only a few hours before, he had summoned her advisor, ambassador and had gone through all the documents relating to her dowry again, but nowhere was the diamond mentioned.

"I have been led to understand," he asks delicately and diplomatically, yet staring down in revulsion at the bowed head of Le Marques de Draq, never having met anybody quite as odious as this man before, "that part of the dowry would be a diamond, a diamond called Le Diamante Azul."

The Marques lifts his head quickly, black piercing eyes staring into his, but immediately drops his head again in obedience to the King of England.

"I do not know where you have got this information from, it is completely untrue...but is my Lord saying that he is not happy with the vast new wealth that he already has?"

For a second the King stares menacingly down at the bowed head of this most repulsive of men, his men angrily muttering at the advisor's insolent reply.

"I am more than happy, but..." He now looks down suspiciously at the lowered, balding head.

"If I find that I have been lied to, heads will be severed from bodies and yours will be the first, so be warned." The balding head sinks lower.

"I can assure you, my Lord, there is no such diamond."

Head bowed still, he backs away, internally fuming.

So the English King is not so stupid as he had thought, how does he know about the diamond? Only he, Isabel, and of course, her father knows of its existence. But, Isabel has no idea that he knows...it then dawns on him, of course, it can only be her Ladies-in-waiting, her inseparable friends from childhood. There is nobody else that she trusts, the stupid, stupid, girl.

As he continues to back away, he sees from his bent, posturing position that the King is still watching him like a hawk even when he disappears into the shadows.

Back in Castile, the girl's father, so old and sick now, has no power left, and in his absence in the supposed role of ambassador, accompanying Isabel to England, his men have completely taken over the kingdom. He had chosen this role, the role of her advisor, not just to find the whereabouts of the diamond; he'll easily take that off her when the time is right, but much more as a spy, to see how strong the King of

England's army really is, and, to ultimately prepare for invasion. But even though he is now the ruler of Castile, he must have the diamond to be able to afford vast armies and then the English King will find that he has a deadly adversary and it will be his head that will be severed from his body and then he, *Le Marques de Draq,* will marry Isabel, but just for such a short time, the poor child. He realises he must move really quickly now and take possession of Le Diamante Azul from her, by fair or foul means, before it's too late.

CHAPTER FOUR
The Unfathomable Forest

The soft, cool dawn, the late summer intoxicating smell of rich, green foliage, heralds that all species had reached their dizzy heights of fertility and growth and with the clue of the dew drenched leaves, heralds also that before long the furnace of August would be over and soon after that, all would shrivel and die.

In the airy theatre of the sky above, full with the dipping and swooping of swifts and swallows, snapping up the buzzing insects, they know too that their days are numbered here and they must soon head south to Africa. But for now, all of nature embraces their holiday from the freezing winter that will soon be upon them.

Under the canopy of that rich foliage, the thundering of the two horses' hooves, muted by the soft forest floor of moss and decades of layers of countless acorn shells, still sends heavy vibrations shockingly into the ground like deep drum beats, warning all the creatures of the forest to conceal themselves, no matter how large, how vicious, how timid and how small.

The two riders pull their horses to an abrupt stop in the small glade. They are now at the start of the Unfathomable Forest, already looking impenetrable, the trees standing so close to each other, that a man on a horse would struggle to ride through and the bracken in places higher than a man's head.

"Time to release it."

The sack, tied with rope at one end and slung over the youth's saddle is thrown to the ground where it lies completely still on the leafy ground

"Ha, ha, it's dead already, probably died of fright, useless, stupid creature."
The two grey wolfhounds, however, sniff around the sack and begin growling viciously.

"Damn, it's obviously still alive. The question is this then my friend, shall we allow the dogs to kill it now or shall we release it and see what fate chooses for it within the forest?"
The older rider sits quietly, staring down at the sack, deeply unhappy with the whole situation.

"I think it should be allowed a sporting chance."
And without waiting for an answer, he dismounts and pulling away the two growling wolfhounds, unties the rope at the one end and opening up the sack looks directly into the eyes of the Spaniel that stare directly back at him. He's surprised there's no look of fear, just almost acceptance that it's here, in what must be the most terrifying situation that a dog could possibly be in.

He pulls the Spaniel out by its ridiculously over ornate, jewel-less collar. It immediately sit's, obediently looking up at him with its soft, brown eyes, completely ignoring the savage growling of the two other dogs that are desperate to be given the order to kill.

The mounted youth sneers, "Look at that stupid cur, it's so stupid that it doesn't even realise what's going to happen to it next."
 The older man walks back to his horse and remounts.

"Just leave it. I've got plenty more important things to be getting on with other than killing a small dog, besides it will be dead within a short time when we ride off."

He is completely aware that the forest is teeming with wolves and even now they are probably only a few yards away. He looks back down at the Spaniel as it still sits looking directly up at him. The youth laughs out loud.

"I swear it thinks that you're going to help it, look at the way it's staring at you."

In response, the older man turns his horse's head away and pressing his knees gently against its sides slowly trots away. The youth glares at his retreating back and then quickly pulls out an arrow from the quiver, takes his bow and fixes the Spaniel in his sights. The dog stares up at him now with deeply, unhappy eyes.

"My friend said to give you a sporting chance, so I will, so run dog, run as fast as you can, because if you don't, I'm going to kill you and, if I miss which I certainly won't, my dogs are going to rip you up anyway, you stupid, dumb animal, because you don't have any idea what I'm talking about do you?"

He unleashes the arrow, but to his utter shock the Spaniel darts to one side, so quick, that the arrow slams into a tree trunk behind with a sickening thump. The Spaniel speeds back and sit's obediently again, staring back up at him, the wolfhounds now besides themselves in growling anger.

"Kill it." He shouts, and quickly pulls out another arrow. The two dogs tear over, but the Spaniel darts away, running in a wide circle, so very fast as they snap after it in hot pursuit, but back it comes and again and sits staring up at him with pleading eyes as if to ask for quarter. He quickly aims the arrow, when the wolf hounds rebound clumsily back, their claws stirring up the debris of the forest floor in a wild flurry, insane with anger, but yet again, it effortlessly squirms away from their jaws in another wide circle and sit's once more looking up at his face. The string of the bow is pulled tautly back when the older man gallops back through the tree's and shouts at the two wolfhounds to stop and then to the youth.

"What are you doing? I told you to leave it."

He pretends to look down angrily down at the Spaniel but he had almost grinned when he had turned back seconds before to see its surprising turn of speed.

"So dog, you have surprised me, there's more to you than meets the eye."

His comrade, behind him, jealously hearing the older man's words of praise towards that imbecilic dog, raises his bow.

The Spaniel, detecting the hatred on the youth's face, knows his death is now imminent and there is nothing else he can do but run. He tears away and dives headlong into the bracken, hearing the whistling arrow streak after him, he twists, turns, leaps, when the head of a strange youth suddenly pops up from within the bracken right in front of him. He twists awkwardly away, changing course, when the arrow abruptly slams into his flank, he squeals in pain, drops down, and finds he cannot move with the unbearable pain.

He hears the excited shouting from the youth back in the glade.

"Did you see how fast that thing can run and how scared it was and then how it screamed out in pain? I got it, can you believe that I got it, without being able to see a thing through all that bracken, you've got to admit that I am nearly the very best of all the archers!"

The older man speaks angrily; he can hear the Spaniel whimpering in agony a short distance away.

"Why did you have to do that? Sometimes you're stupidity and cruelty shocks me, I'd better find it and put it out of its misery, there is nothing I can abide less than an animal suffering in pain."

And all around, sudden shrill scream of a bird pierces the silence, making them both spin around, the horses snort furiously, rearing their front legs and smash down their front hooves as the men struggle to rein them in. Both are unsure where the source of the unearthly screech has come from, but obviously something has stirred within the forest. The two wolfhounds whine and abruptly lie down on their stomachs as the horses continue to stamp and snort.

The older man looks down in surprise at the strange, submissive behaviour of the two hunting dogs; so out of character from their normal viciousness. He hisses angrily to the younger man.

"Stay here with the dogs but I'm warning you now, never, ever do anything like this again."

He dismounts, whispers in his frightened horse's ear to stay still and pushes his way gently through the waist high bracken, hand grasping the hilt of his sword, his eyes quickly looking from left to right and over head.

The early morning sun rises above the trees and already it is unbearably hot. He walks slowly and carefully in the direction of the low whimpering, making as little noise as possible. He is trained in the warfare of massive battles on the great plains; that is why he is the King's right hand man, but in the deep forests, he is not so sure.

The Spaniel abruptly stops whimpering, now shaking uncontrollably when he picks up the scent so close to him, a creature smelling of the rich aroma of the forest, mingled with a scent of an animal that he doesn't recognise but also with the sweet smell of a young human. He hears a slight movement in the bracken next to him, a head appears, peeking through; the strange youth, but with such feral eyes that he whimpers again apprehensively.

"I'm sorry dog, that was my fault," the youth whistles softly and quietly creeps over to his side.

The youth whistles again, a change in his dialect, causing the birds to shrill angrily from above and all around. The soldier stops and looks all about and above him, the birds warning cries tell him that something is approaching or is already close to him, but yet he has the strongest impression that he is being distracted to put him off the location of the dog.

The youth strokes the dog's back gently, quite taken aback by its rabbit soft hair, certainly nothing like a wolf or a fox. As he continues to stroke downwards, he stares at its strange saddled back of brown and white patches and the freckling of brown spots spread liberally around until he reaches the wound.

He examines the arrow, gently touching it all around its entry point into the dog's flank when suddenly and quite unexpectedly yanks it out, the Spaniel squeals in agony, the older man turns quickly, even above the screaming of the birds, he had still heard it, and unsheathing his sword quietly moves forward in the direction of the noise. The youth spits into the wound in the Spaniel's flank, pulls up a clump of sphagnum moss, deftly pokes it in and whistles softly,

"Now dog we run." He leaps away into the foliage, the Spaniel hesitates, but realising that the pain had miraculously gone chases quickly after him.

The older man, hardly any distance away, sees for a split second, before they disappear from sight, a glimpse of the dog and a boy running in front with long, straggled, fair, hair, bizarrely interlaced with a profusion of pheasant tail feathers.

He looks in wonderment, a boy living in the Unfathomable Forest; no humans have ever managed to survive in here?

He moves forward quickly now and a few yards on sees the discarded arrow, the bloodied tip already swarming with flies. So the dog had been injured and judging by the pool of blood, badly, but then how was it possible it could run away like that? He now runs swiftly to catch up with the fleeing boy and dog, but then he stops abruptly. Why is he being so stupid? He could so easily be being led into a trap.

He stands completely still, the birds still screeching above and stares at the dense foliage in front of him wishing he could see through and beyond, when the boy with the straggled hair rises up from amongst the bracken, head half turned and stares defiantly at him, like a challenge, but then with an enormous smile, ducks down and is gone. He is faced again with the wall of bracken, but the vision of the strange boy remains vividly in his mind; the boy's eyes were so piercing, like that of a wild animal.

He finds himself turning away and walking back in the direction of the glade, questioning himself why he had not lunged out with his sword and killed the boy who had stood literally just in front of him? It would have been so easy. But what could he do, kill an innocent boy, simply because the dog ran with him?

He thinks again of the boy's extraordinary, startling yet unsettling eyes, he looked like he was about maybe thirteen or fourteen years of age, about the same age his son would have been if he had not been taken away by the sickness all those years ago. Is that why he didn't kill him?

He pauses, the birds have abruptly stopped screeching, and then a thought comes to him; the boy had on no upper garments, is it possible he could be one of the legendary tree people or Dog Heads? He had only ever seen ink drawings of the strange species but he recalls their heads had a fine covering of hair and pronounced canine teeth, but this boy had no hair covering on his face at all, and his teeth when he had smiled were just like those of a human and yet, his eyes were so strange.

He wonders then, what had been the fate of the Dog Head female all those years ago? He hadn't gone on the hunt that day, his son had been too ill but he had heard afterwards from the King's drunken entourage that the King had not just captured one of the illusive creatures, but had forcefully known her intimately. In those days he had turned a blind eye to the King's wildness, thinking of it as only as what young males do...but now a strange thought comes into his mind, is that why ever since then, that he hunts everywhere else, but never close to the Unfathomable Forest and why does he always refuse to have any fields of crops grown anywhere near its boundaries?

He shakes his head, as if to dispel a bad vision and continues on, muttering to himself, "If the boy is a Dog Head, it will eat the dog anyway, probably already doing it."

But deep down, intuitively he knows that he won't and at some point in the future he feels that he will meet the boy and the dog again.

A small part of him is happy that the dog has strangely survived, in all, such a bad business. The King's judgement on most things having become more awry and more ill judged the older he becomes instead of vice versa and the only reason he stayed at his side was because of the promise he had given firstly to the Queen before she died and then to the old King on his deathbed.

He wades quietly through the bracken and enters the small glade, as his comrade visibly jumps in his saddle and cries out, "Why have you taken so long I was getting worried, there have been so many strange noises, is it dead?"

He looks up at the frightened face of Sir Stephen, the King's only nephew.

"You had indeed got it with your arrow, you should feel proud of yourself with your superb archery, I will tell my Lord how well you have done today."

The youth looks at him anxiously, checking for sarcasm in his voice, but detecting nothing, smiles with the realisation that he has for once been given praise and from him, the man that only gives men praise if it is truly deserved.

"I left it with many wolves circling around and then one took it away into the bracken and so I decided, just as you had said so wisely earlier, to let it face its own fate. Now let us go back."

He mounts his horse, calls to the wolfhounds who rise immediately from the ground and who now run in front of the two horsemen in a bid to put themselves ahead and further away from the Unfathomable Forest.

CHAPTER FIVE
The Peregrine Falcon

Isabel, her consciousness rising like light from the darkness, struggles to open her eyelids. She lifts her left arm that feels so strangely heavy that she can hardly raise it and without understanding why, spits onto her fingers and smears the saliva onto her eyelids. A small moment of relief as the cool fluid sinks in.

Blinking her eyes, she slowly becomes aware that there is a cacophony of birds singing outside and realises it must be the early morning. She blinks more rapidly now, the fog lifts from her eyes and finds that she is lying on her bed looking up at the ornate awning overhead. She looks down to find she is still wearing her garments from the night before and frowns in confusion and even though she is fully clothed she realises how deathly cold she is and turns to look at the fireplace and cannot quite understand why the fire is not lit and, more importantly where are her Ladies-in-waiting?

Something is badly wrong and then the memory of last night floods back to her and with it comes the shocking realisation that she and the Spaniel had been drugged.

Anxiously turning her head from left to right, the fear rising in her chest she tries to whistle for her dog to come to her, but her mouth is too dry. She sits up, but then wishes she hadn't, the room jumps up and down alarmingly, reminding her of the voyage over from Spain, the ship being tossed about in the heavy sea's causing her to vomit so much that she thought she would die.

The panic rises more, where is he, where is her dog?

Slowly swinging her legs over the side of the bed, the room still rising up and down, she places both feet on the ground and tentatively stands up as the room now swirls all around and slumping to the floor, she cries out desperately, "Where are you Archie?" But there is no sound of the familiar pitter-patter of his paws and it dawns on her that she's completely alone in the room as tears begin to trickle down her cheeks.

She lies then in a shifting state of consciousness until finally in a more lucid moment, she whispers out loud,

"You must, must get up."

With extreme effort she manages to crawl over to the table set against the far stone wall and stretching up grabs the handles of a pitcher of water. With shaking arms, she lowers the heavy weight to her mouth and takes huge long gulps aware that she must wash the drugs from her body.

The water makes her feel marginally better. Grasping the table she pulls herself up and realises then that her whole room had been overturned, all her clothing, all her books, everything she possesses are strewn all over the floor and then she knows she has been betrayed and it can only be by them, how could she have had such weakness to have told them on the voyage over?

It then dawns on her; she is in a perilous position.

Faint voices in the distance, coming closer, she picks up the pitcher of water, replacing it on the table and totter's weakly back to the bed, barely managing to climb up and slowly positions her body in the exact way she had found herself in earlier.

She decides her best course of action is to pretend to be still unconscious until she can work out what to do, the most important thing being to find out what has happened to her beloved dog.

And then, quite unexpectedly, she hears the sudden rapid sweeping of wings coming into the room from the open window. She lies completely still, eyes shut, the familiar voices of her Ladies-in-waiting are almost at her chambers, but she mustn't call out, mustn't move.

Shockingly the bird alights on her chest with a heavy thud, she gasps, feeling its pacing talons nearly piercing through her bodice but manages to stay as still as death, when to her horror she feels a small hard object like a pebble roll down her sternum and nestle in the hollow at the base of her throat.

The bird is now completely and strangely motionless and she has the strongest feeling that it's studying her intently. Barely opening her eyes she is confronted with the strange sight of a Peregrine Falcon staring at her with gold ringed, dark brown eyes. Her eyes widen more to meet its and to her shock, she sees it has on an intricately, plaited, leather harness and from the centre of the cross section on its chest the skull of a small rodent dangles down.

How very strange, she has never seen such paraphernalia on a bird before?

The falcon continues to stare at her intently. Never in all her life has she been so close to a bird, just literally a few inches away from her face, but instead of fear she finds to her astonishment how strangely calm she feels. It cocks its head from side to side, still staring at her face and then apparently satisfied with its hard eyed appraisal, abruptly lifts its wings and flies swiftly across the room and out of the open window.

31

Isabel fumblingly picks up the small stone from the hollow in her neck and holding it up studies it between index finger and thumb and whispers in disbelief.

"One of my diamonds."

She breathes in deeply, what can this possibly mean?

The outer door to her chambers opens, she puts the diamond into her mouth, closes her eyes and then remains completely still realising her very life depends on it.

Her Ladies-in-waiting loiter outside the inner door; she senses they are too terrified to walk in. Finally they enter and pushing each other forward they both stop at the foot of the bed. The younger sister whispers fearfully.

"She looks like she's dead, I cannot go any nearer, you go and check!"

Isabel hears soft footsteps coming towards her and then warm fingers pressing on her wrist, a few seconds pass.

"She has a very faint, fluttering pulse, barely there."

"I think she's soon to die, look how white she is and her lips are so blue!" Deep sobbing ensues.

"Let's talk outside."The older says harshly. They leave the chamber and shut the door quietly behind them, but Isabel can still hear their whispering voices.

"What have we done? I fear that what my Lord's physician gave us to administer to her and the dog was too much; I told you she was too thin, but you wouldn't listen to me and even if she does ever awake again she will find that her dog has gone...and if she were to find out that it had been taken to the Unfathomable Forest and slaughtered, that would surely kill her off quicker than if she had actually been poisoned?"

"Who really cares, I certainly don't. And what does any of it matter anymore anyway? Judging from the weakness of her pulse she will soon be dead and well before sundown. The diamond has not been found, my Lord has lost interest in it, so I say let sleeping dogs lie."

"But shouldn't we at least tend to her, perhaps light the fire to make her more comfortable?"

"Why? She's practically dead, or soon will be."

More sobbing begins, Isabel lies completely still, comforted that one of her diamonds lay safely on her tongue and her treasure is not in the King's hands but whoever the owner of the Peregrine Falcon is certainly has them in their possession and that someone is trying to help her.

But who could it possibly be? But more than anything she knows intuitively that her dog is still alive and somewhere in the Unfathomable Forest.

"We should tell my Lord how she lies so still and near to death."

"Tell him, what does he care about what happens to her? He hates the sight of her, the only person he's interested in is me, or soon will be and it's all his doing anyway...I'm beginning to wonder now if the diamond even exists, we've searched everywhere. I'm sure she has lied just to make herself so much more important than us, like she has always done all of our lives."

Isabel cannot believe all that she has just listened to. She had believed that they were her truest friends and to find they had resented her for so long was more shocking than being betrayed and drugged by their hand now.

A strange chill wind rushes from underneath the door making both sisters shudder, they turn nervously to look at its closed face, both seeing in their minds eye the spectre of a dead Isabel rising up from the high bed.

"Anyway shush now, we are talking far too openly."

The older sister hurriedly pushes the younger as they leave the outer chamber without shutting the door and run down the dark corridors as the chill wind follows behind, ruffling their skirts, exciting and lifting dry leaves to fly through the open apertures of the cloisters and skittle after them in a wild headlong flurry.

"The King." Isabel whispers, picturing then his sneering, sardonic face. When she had first met him, she thought him handsome yet cold, but the perpetual sneer on his face that he had worn continually in her presence, had made her realise that he couldn't bear the sight of her and even on the wedding night he had made no attempt to come to her chambers. It dawns on her now that all he had ever wanted from her was her dowry.

She vows then, she will get her vengeance for his cruelty towards her and the Spaniel.

But she cannot think anymore as a fresh surge of the drug sweeps over her. Removing the diamond from her mouth she pushes it down the front of her bodice, positions her arms as before and plunges once more into the darkness.

In the Unfathomable Forest the Peregrine Falcon swoops down through the trees and settles on a branch as the youth looks up and whistles softly.

"Thank you Elsu."

The late afternoon, her inner door opens silently; Marques de Draq stands in the threshold studying firstly the upturned room and then studies Isabel for a long time, his eyes never leaving her still form. He had been told that she had been struck down by a mysterious illness and the King's personal physician had said she was not allowed any visitors, for fear that she may have the black death and that her dog had already been killed as a precaution, hence he had found the immediate corridors to her chambers completely abandoned and no one to question him.

He did not believe any of it for a second so he had come to see for himself how the land lay. He knows the King and her Ladies-in-waiting are somehow responsible for her condition and judging from her upturned room entirely evident of what was being searched for. But, he smiles inwardly; the diamond can't have been found judging from the King's filthy raging temper today.

He continues to watch the slight, barely discernible rise and fall of her chest and listens for the intake and outtake of her breath. Finally he approaches and taking her pulse notes how thin, reedy and almost nonexistent it is, obvious to him now that she had been overdosed with an opiate, a practise he is well acquainted with, having dispatched many of his enemies in the same manner. He bends down and whispers quietly in her ear.

"Isabel, my poor Isabel, if only I had known what the King planned to do to you; I could have helped you, my poor child. I made a vow to your father that I would care for you always. He has told me about the diamond, with instructions that if anything bad were to happen to you here, that I must take possession of it and use it accordingly."

He pauses, to see if there is any reaction to the blatant lie, yes, he had made a vow to her father to care for her always, and yes, her father had told him about her diamond, but that was all.

But annoyingly, there is still no response from her, just the same barely palpable breaths in and out, in and out. He finds his anger rising and struggles to keep his voice calm.

"If only you would speak to me, I could use its wealth to buy huge armies to destroy the King of England and restore everything that is truly yours back to you, if only you could tell me my dear, where it is, before it's too late."

But there is no answer, just the same weak, shallow breath whispering in and out.

He exhales in anger at the lack of response, now what's he to do? All his ambitions thwarted by this stupid girl. He glares down at her for a second and then it strikes him how incredibly ill she looks, he places his palm on her forehead to find it so shockingly cold that he removes his hand quickly as if somehow she would taint him with her closeness to death.

"Why are English buildings always so freezing and damp, even in August?" He mutters irritably and striding over to the fireplace quickly places the kindling on top of the half burnt logs. He blows carefully; a breeze through the opened window joins in with him as if to help, when a small flame licks up from the remnants of yesterday's fire.

The fire picks up more. He quickly shuts the window as the cold room heats up by degrees and picking up a heavy cloak from the floor, covers her carefully over with it. He sits on the bed and reaching under the cloak holds her cold wrist, checking for an increase in the blood flow through her veins and looking at her pallid, but still beautiful face he shakes his head.

"Poor, poor, pious Isabel, your very godliness has brought you to this unhappy consummation, if only you had bent just a little from your unwavering devotion to him above, I doubt you would be in the position you are now in."And he sighs at her stupidity.

But becoming bored after awhile, a thought crosses his mind; there is one thing he can do that might create a proper reaction knowing how much she is repulsed by his physical presence.

He begins to trail his index finger down her forehead, down the bridge of her nose, over her top lip, his finger rests on her bottom lip for a second, it pulls down softly, he stares intently at her small, white, perfect bottom teeth, shuddering with emotion as he does so, and then controlling himself, proceeds to trace his finger down the rounded contour of her chin, tracing down her neck until finally resting it in the hollow at the base of her throat. He viciously pushes his finger in but still there is no reaction at all.

Strangely moved, he sighs heavily, he should return to Spain while he still can, realising how dangerous it is for him to remain in England. He begins to walk away when he hears a small gasp, he turns back and feels her forehead again, her temperature has marginally picked up. Elated, he picks up her wrist and takes her pulse, still weak but stronger and more regular than before and bending down hisses softly into her ear.

"Remember Isabel, I am your only salvation."

But his words fall on deaf ears. She is in an entirely different place altogether, a place of utter darkness where there is nothing to be seen and no sound to be heard.

He leaves the room quietly, he had better show his presence again to the King, no doubt he will have already noticed his absence, but later he'll sneak back and then Isabel would be conscious! He almost skips away in his excitement down the quiet corridors. Filled now with joy, he contemplates his position; he is now the ruler of Castile, Isabel is not dead and when she is conscious, she will obediently hand over the diamond, because what choice does she have?

Dusk falls, Isabel opens her eyes slowly, her chamber glows with the soft, orange and yellow hues of the dying fire, but she doesn't notice.

"Time to leave now," she whispers firmly to her body to will it on as if it were not part of her. Slowly climbing down from the high bed, she stands still for a second to judge her stability; she is still incredibly light-headed but she has no choice but to go and as quickly as possible.

Picking up her voluminous dark, wool, cloak and wrapping herself within its warmth, she weaves over to the door, determinedly whispering.

"I must be strong, I must be strong."

She leaves her chambers into the dark corridor, there is not a soul to be seen anywhere, but the very absence of any humans, even her enemies fills her with more fear than she thought possible.

"Please God, please help me in this, my hour of need." She whispers feverishly over and over again, as she totters weakly along, leaning against the corridor wall every few steps for support. Down the winding back stone stairs she comes to a landing and stops for a second gasping for breath, viewing apprehensively the next flight of stairs going down into almost pitch black. Down and down, another flight of stairs until finally, at last, and thankfully, the heavy wooden door is open to the outside and still no one, not one single guard is to be seen. And then she understands why, hearing now the wild shouting and laughing of the King's men from the main outer concourse, wilder than she has ever heard before and something tells her they are celebrating her imminent demise.

The welcome fresh air fills her now with more strength as she falteringly wends her way to the stable block. She slips in, grabs a bridle and then along to the enclosed pasture where the immobile form of the old mare stands so still that it could almost be a statue cast from white alabaster.

She had seen the old mare in the pasture when she had first arrived, she couldn't risk taking any of the King's prize horses and she felt certain this old horse would not be missed by anyone. But what she doesn't know that not only is the old mare the mother of the King's two top stallions, but also his most revered and most favourite of horses and by his command to be treated royally until before too long, she dies of old age.

Isabel clucks to it anxiously, the old mare turns its head and picking up on her emotion, trots over skittishly, the first cool evening for months having already filled her with such unaccustomed energy.

Isabel opens the gate as the mare approaches, snorting out white misty clouds from her nostrils in her excitement. For a second Isabel strokes her nose to calm her and then stretching up, slips on the bridle and then weakly climbing up the perimeter fence, clucks again. The mare stands stock still as Isabel slips onto her broad back; and without any further command, the horse carefully carries the weak girl away to the Unfathomable Forest, the place she remembers so well from fourteen years before.

CHAPTER SIX
The Deep Pool

Earlier that day, the youth and the Spaniel had ducked, dived and jumped along a diverse hidden path that twisted and changed through the foliage, commanded above by birds that were loyal to him alone, as they flitted from tree to tree above and had whistled down their cautionary instructions. Stop, wait, go left, go right, until eventually they had reached the Deep Pool surrounded by the treacherous shifting mud flats and to an unknowing eye looking deceptively the same as the forest floor.

"Now dog we will remove it."

The Spaniel sits quietly as the youth kneels down and carefully manoeuvres the collar around trying to find how to unclasp it. He comes across a small keyhole, and stares at it in surprise having never seen anything quite like it before. Removing two long thin hooked bones from a selection housed in a small pouch hanging from his belt, he inserts them in and wiggling them around hears the lock turn as the thick collar falls to the ground. He picks it up, he's very keen in fashioning apparatus himself, but never has he seen anything quite like this.

"Far too thick for your neck, not a good design at all, I wonder that you could have stood it in all this heat?"

He looks at the front leather face, noticing the imbedded empty sockets, and then pinching its thick rim between finger and thumb, turns it over and studies the band of leather neatly stitched in place all along the outer edges. Picking up one of the bones, he deftly unpicks the stitching

41

at one end and then rips off the leather band to reveal nine, small, imbedded, flat faced stones.

"What are these things?"

He picks one out and lays it on his palm, intrigued by its transparency but yet with a deep blue hue like the Dog Star at dawn.

He looks in Archie's eyes and whistles liltingly, "So these are the things you have been guarding, alright, we'll give her one so she knows you still live but you have to accept that you cannot return to her for they will surely kill you outright if you do."

Picking up the collar again, he prises out the rest of the diamonds and slips them into a small leather pouch hanging from his belt.

He looks up to the high branches of a sweet chestnut tree whistling softly, the Peregrine Falcon swoops down and deftly picking up the diamond from the palm of his hand in one grasping talon rapidly sweeps up and disappears through the trees. He turns to the Spaniel, whistling softly.

"Elsu will find her, now we need to get rid of the collar."

Cannin knows that the dog stands out far too much as it is with his unusual brown and white markings, but if any of the Dog Heads were to see the ornate, heavy, collar around his neck they would instantly know that he was not just some random cur that had wandered into the forest, but a dog of importance and knowing Morgar's hatred for anything to do with Humans, he would be the first to order its death and the first to eat it. And so the only place he can think of hiding the collar forever is in the pool of deep water in front of him.

He bends down, rolling over rocks until he finds one that is suitable in diameter, takes the collar, wraps it around and holding it steady between his knees, locks it again. He looks over at the Deep Pool and wonders how his old friend that lurks in its dark depths is after all this time.

This was once one of his most favourite places in the Unfathomable Forest, his secret place, and more importantly, a place which the Dog Heads kept away from.

When he was very small, when they first allowed him to wander alone, they had warned him to keep away from the area. They warned him of the vice like grip of the mud that surrounded the pool, warned him of the thrashing animals that had been sucked down to their death and that it was the work, many years before of the Spirits who had deliberately released an underground spring to pour directly into the pool to keep the surrounding mud in a constant wet state for ever more, as a warning to them all that it was an evil place and a place of wrong doings and death.

So, of course, that's where he went. He felt positive they were just being overly melodramatic, after all, they generally let him do what he wanted and roam where he chose, being firm believers in learning by your own mistakes.

He knew they liked him to a certain extent, but he also knew, even back then, that he was different from them and on that first occasion the Deep Pool had showed him how different.

He hadn't known why he had been drawn to stare down at its surface, but he had felt at the time that it was important and had crawled along the fallen ancient oak tree that partially spanned the start of the mud flats until he had reached the thinner branches that stretched over to the Deep Pool, alarmed somewhat by the terrible creaking, imagining himself toppling headfirst into the sucking mud and die with not one of them to even had noticed. But finally, he had got there, and looking down at the surface of the water, he gasped at the image that looked back up at him and had never been so shocked.

His base instinct was to bare his teeth in a defensive snarl, the head below bared it's teeth back at him, he closed his mouth abruptly, scared by its ferocity and the reflected image did exactly the same.

There was now no movement from the water below and as he waited, he studied the small face looking up at him, it seemed quite a nice, but strange little face until finally he couldn't resist the grin, the face grinned back and then he laughed, of course, it was him, and contemplated himself in wonder.

Never had he imagined that he would look like this. There was no hair on his face at all...but maybe that was just because he was so small...maybe the hair would come later, and then as he got older his teeth would grow just like theirs, but please, he had whispered to the Spirits, not as big and grotesque as Morgar's.

He had found himself wishing that he could stay just as he was; he turned his head from side to side, checking out his child profile, when his watery refection rippled away and instead of his face it was replaced instead by a ghoulish mask with black soulless eyes. He watched spellbound as the mask mutated into a giant open mouth equipped with rows of jagged teeth that had leapt from the pool to bite off his head.

He had pulled back in that instant, the fish diving back down into the green water soundlessly and in a graceful watery swirl had disappeared into the dark depths. The attack had been so fast and so vicious, that he had rapidly shinnied back along the tree to solid ground.

He contemplated his next move and decided that he would make friends with the monstrous fish; the study of his reflection was far too important and the only gage he had to see if, as time went by, he was going to change horrifically into Morgar.

He gathered large white grubs from under logs and dropped them onto the surface of the pool, the fish would rise up from the depths, eyes as dark as night and in a great flurry of activity would snap them up, dive down, but without warning would leap back up at his face again and again. Each time he pulled back until one morning the giant fish stopped its lunging attacks and from then on it would lurk just beneath the surface patiently waiting for the fat grubs.

How often, over those long hot and languid summer days, he would return to the Deep Pool to study his reflection, but eventually they had found out where he had been going to, their anger had been terrible and they had warned him that if he ever returned there again he would be banished to the world of the Humans. The threat of the unknown Human world had been so terrifying that he had never returned to the Deep Pool until today.

But, ironically, this very dawn, he had seen his very first Humans, the young one with the cruelty, which he had been told about by *them*, but in the other he had seen surprisingly there was no cruelty.

45

He suddenly stops his thoughts when the Peregrine Falcon swoops down through the trees and settles on a branch overhead. He looks up and whistles softly, "Thank you Elsu."

The dog, he notices, is in a deep, exhausted sleep at the forest edge, an old fox vixen appears and lies on her side a few feet away. She too falls into a deep sleep as the sun beams down through the green foliage onto their still bodies.

Flitting over a Blackbird alights on a branch over head, tail raised and warbles melodically and when she finishes, another further away repeats the song back like an echo but Cannin notices the very last note drops subtly lower in key, warning him that trouble is approaching.

In that very second all the other birds abruptly stop their dialogue, everywhere becomes deathly silent, which means that one of *them* is very close by, a slight breeze wafts by his nostrils carrying with it the scent of Morgar's breath and he very nearly cries out in his exasperation.

Out of all of them, it would have to be him. But how very strange, he was sure that he had left with the other males on the yearly Pilgrimage to the far side as usual?

A chill, impending feeling of doom sweeps over him and he immediately throws the rock and attached collar into the dead centre of the Deep Pool. Impossible to be traced now but he feels sorry for disturbing the monstrous Pike in this way, especially having thrown in something inedible into his watery larder.

But he has no choice, if caught; he knows he will be in more than serious trouble for returning to the forbidden area and especially with a dog of the Humans and quickly darts into the bracken.

The Spaniel sniffs in the air deeply; he too has picked up the rotting scent and anxiously follows the youth, knowing his only hope of survival is to remain with him and that the creature closing in on them is a serious threat.

The silence of the birds is palatable; the forest seems now to be full of menace as frightened squirrels run along the branches above them. A pair of tiny wrens sweep back and forth, wings fluttering warningly by the youth's head, as Green Woodpeckers drum on tree trunks from all around to mask any sound of their flight.

With glimpses through the bracken the dog notices that even the wild boar have stopped their noisy foraging in the undergrowth and stand completely still as if rooted to the ground.

The youth stops abruptly; staring directly in front of him and suddenly disappears, the Spaniel follows and finds himself disappearing down a deep tight hole into a larger space of cool darkness underground, just as the enormous figure above appears from behind a tree.

The Spaniel growls apprehensively, he senses immediately the stinking creature above is to do with the youth but also picks up on his bad intentions towards him as a growling deep, menacing voice follows.

"What have you done Cannin bringing a domesticated dog into our territory? You could bring the Humans here with your stupid actions. It has no place here, kill it now or I shall."

Cannin mentally pictures Morgar above, grinning his perpetual ghastly grin. The only one out all of *them* that cannot close his mouth properly because of his heavy protruding jaws and over abundance of yellow, pointed teeth and he knows that the Dog Head seethes inwardly at this cruel trick of nature that sets him apart from the others.

Ever since the Deep Pool incident years before, Morgar had self appointed himself as Cannin's guardian and from then on had spied on him continuously, telling tales to the others so more and more *they* thought of him as a nuisance.

But as Cannin had got older he now watched Morgar from the safety of the tree tops.

If only Morgar knew that on so many occasions he had witnessed the Dog Head's disgusting habit of rolling in rotting carcasses and then more worryingly devour the decomposing flesh, an act that was strictly against the law.

He had tried to hint to the other Dog Heads, but they wouldn't listen, saying his breath wasn't his fault, he had turned when he was younger, that a terrible thing had happened to him, and Cannin detected from the ones that were not so enamoured with him that somehow it was to do with him.

"You know the law Cannin, animals do our bidding not the other way around, never let an animal have the upper hand, and now it thinks it has. Look how calmly and arrogantly it has made you do its will. It has been ruined by the Humans and can never be trusted. Next you will have all the other animals telling us what to do, and to what end? Anarchy and rebellion will then ensue."

With the dog following anxiously, Cannin crawls along another fork of the tight dark tunnel until he sees a faint light spilling down from another air hole further along and calculates he's now behind Morgar.

He calls up.

"I will not kill him, nor will I hand him over to you; you'll slaughter him, leave his body to rot, then you'll slobber and roll over his remains and only after that will you partake of his flesh."

Morgar swiftly turns in the direction of the accusatory voice that comes from below the ground, visibly taken aback; the Mongrel has found out his dirty secret. If the others know, if he tells, he himself would be banished forever like his father. He hesitates before answering and then angrily retorts,

"Why do you call it *him*, it is not him, but *it*...it is an animal and nothing more, destroy it now or I shall do it myself."

"No, he is under my protection; I will speak to the Elder and only to him. He will decide about the fate of the dog, not you."

Morgar bristles at his rudeness.

"But Cannin, you can't stay under the ground like a rat until he and the others return, I want to speak to you, I want to help you."

Cannin crawls off again along another of the ancient flint tunnels, the Spaniel running directly behind.

But Cannin is worried, what he has done, does go beyond anything he has done before. It was okay when he was small, but he senses more and more that *they* are tired of him and tired of, in their view, his strange antics. No longer do they pander to him, all of the female Dog Heads in particular now favour Morgar and the older and weirder he becomes the more they stand by him, but the Elder is always aloof and fair, he must speak to him.

Morgar kneels, sniffing down into the small open air hole, large rats having already gravitated to the vicinity by the stench of his breath. They hungrily wait in the bracken all around for how often has this Dog Head generously left the remnants of his rotting meals for them.

But this time they can tell something strange is afoot, the Dog Heads males have gone on their yearly pilgrimage to the far side of the forest as usual but for the first time in their memory, Morgar is the male that has been left behind, an odd decision as he is of the hierarchy.

But now they nervously realise he wants them to go down in the tunnels, he glares down at them, they hesitate, they can attack the dog but they cannot attack Cannin, he is of the Dog Heads, and the revenge would be catastrophic for them.

Morgar grins down, just for a small distance, he squeaks convincingly in their tongue, only to flush them out and then he will give them the spoils of his meal. They peer down into the air hole, sniffing fearfully; they are also terrified of the underground creatures that live below and know as a species they are particularly revered by them as a delicacy and particularly in the winter months.

Morgar growls angrily now, reminding them that the tunnels in this part of the forest were abandoned years ago.

They still hesitate, but as they can only smell Cannin and the dog, they abandon their fears and hungrily stream down into the old flint mine tunnels in hot pursuit.

Further on, both Cannin and the Spaniel know what is following behind them and by the sound of their excited squeals how many of them are following. Cannin pushes the Spaniel into a small cleft in the flint wall and crouching low turns to face the giant rats. The rats see his piercing lit eyes, stop and sniff intently, picking up on his anger and realise that it isn't going to be quite as easy as they had thought.

Growling viciously, Cannin removes his catapult from his shoulder, he knows he can only kill a few at most when he hears a sharp, scraping sound from behind the rats and the tunnel is suddenly alight. He catches the sight of a small, dark figure illuminated by a fiery torch setting fire to the rats and realises the small figure has to be one of the Minors; he quickly scrambles away, the Spaniel on his heels until he sees a shaft of light coming from an air hole just above. He reaches it and hesitates, sniffing upwards, but the fumes from the burning rats' hair fills the tunnel and he finds it impossible to detect anything else.

Slowly he pokes his head upwards when Morgar's giant hand grabs his head and bodily pulls him out; the pain so unbearable that he feels his skull is going to cave in and he cries out in agony. The Spaniel immediately barks furiously below, such a strange and unaccustomed noise in the Unfathomable Forest that all the birds' screech wildly and he's instantly dropped to the ground.

"Tell it to shut up."

But Cannin holds his head with both hands as the Spaniel keeps up its wild, echoing barking, nearly grinning in his agony, because he realises then that Morgar has absolutely no power over the dog.

But abruptly the barking stops, all is now quiet from below the earth and the birds immediately cease their screeching.

"Well Cannin it appears that the dog is being devoured even as we speak, how stupid of you to have gone into their tunnels."

"And how could you have been so cruel to have sent your rats to their deaths."

"My rats, what rats? I have no idea what you're talking about Cannin."

Morgar circles around the small crouched form below him. He has trouble controlling himself, how close he was, how wonderfully close to crushing his skull, and how lucky for the Mongrel that the dog had barked, otherwise all his and his mother's plans would have been ruined after all the years of plotting.

"I'm afraid you have crossed the border to no return. When it is known that not only did you return to the Deep Pool after having been warned never to do so again, but to also bring with you a domestic dog of the Humans to that forbidden area, it will not be banishment that you face this time, I fear you will be tracked down and killed outright."

Cannin unclasps his hands slowly from around his head and looks up at him angrily and resentfully.

"What if I tell them about you and your nasty habit? And anyway now there is no proof, the dog is dead, and so it's your word against mine."

He puts his head down, clasping his hands around his skull waiting for the kill, but strangely nothing happens, apart from Morgar circling around him, his deep, stertorous stinking breath burning his head.

Cannin knows precisely what he is doing and closes his emotions about the Spaniel to Morgar's penetrating mind search so all he can register is his physical pain. On the other hand he can tell that Morgar is building himself up into a frenzy of passion and deliberates about facing his chances with the Minors below, he has got his weapons after all and rather them than a crazed, gigantic Morgar, three times his height and strength, and at least he would never be able to follow him into the small tunnels below.

The pacing stops.

"Cannin, Cannin, I'm afraid you totally misunderstand my intentions towards you. I have only ever tried to keep you on the straight and narrow." He says this in a new soft, placatory tone that Cannin has never heard him use before.

"Why do you think I call you Mongrel? It is not as a derogatory term but as an honest one. The others have always tried to hide it from you, being as you are the Elder's grandson. It is time that you know that your mother was a Dog Head and your father a Human, which is why I call you Mongrel, because you are neither one nor the other. Why do you think the Elder said that you would be banished to the world of the Human's if you ever neared the forbidden area again?"

Cannin unclasps his hands again and looks up at the grotesque face above him in surprise, because only two dusks ago the Elder had told him of his parentage and had pressed a small, leaf covered package into his hand.

"As you are almost of age, it is right that I pass this on to you. I never knew your Human father, but I do know that he gave this to your mother as a keepsake, they parted before your birth and he has no idea of your existence. I would suggest that you do not show the others what I have given you, they will not like it and keep it hidden otherwise I worry for your safety here, there are some that would like to see you dead."

Cannin had unwrapped the package and stared at the small gold disc, one side showed a seated Human male in strange attire and on the other side was the same Human but this time astride a rearing horse and brandishing a long sword and all around the edges of the two faces of the disc were strange markings unlike anything he had ever seen before.

"I may have made a mistake in giving this to you Cannin, but it is yours nevertheless, and if you choose to seek out your father I will not stop you, because what will be, will be." He had smiled down at him and walked away. Cannin would liked to have asked him more questions but he knew that it was not the Dog Head way and he would not be given anymore answers.

"And so, I have a way out for you." Morgar's growling voice continues, cutting through his thoughts.

"To the far north lives the Dog Head King, he is the ultimate ruler of all. Seek him out, he will give you his patronage and then you will be able to go anywhere you like, without fear from either race."

"But why would he help me as a Dog Head, considering my half Human blood?"

Morgar feels the excitement building up in his chest, for the Mongrel to except his words so readily and to be so gullible is almost laughable.

"Because it is told that he is the same as you and born under the same circumstances, half Dog Head, half Human." What an invention! He nearly laughs out loud at his cleverness, if only his mother was here, how she would love this dialogue. He is thoroughly beginning to enjoy himself and warms to his craft.

"He had to fight many hard battles for his supremacy, but he is of the new ways and would like a path that mixes with the Humans, for trade, commerce, expansion, et cetera, et cetera. The old days are behind us, these are the new days. Long gone are the ancient forests of Doggerland, from where we originally came, sunk below the Great Water so long ago. We are a dying breed, there are so few of us left, one third of the females as you would know from personal experience, die in childbirth. We must embrace the Humans and join in with them and you above all others, with your mixed heritage can see it is the only way forward and your role from now on is to be our ambassador and that is why you must go to him. These Dog Heads here are so behind the times and so primitive in their ways that I have despaired of them for years. The only reason I stay is when your grandfather passes shortly to the other side, I shall become the next Elder as my birthright decrees, and then Cannin I can assure you, we will follow the new ways. But for now it is incredibly unsafe for you to remain here, the others will kill you and your grandfather nor I, governed by our laws, will be able to save you."

Cannin takes in his words, he didn't know any of this.

Morgar, taking the initiative at the worried look on Cannin's face, bends down and open mouthed whispers conspiringly in his ear as Cannin again recoils at the stench.

"It is said that he lives in a castle of such wonder, that the nobility of the Humans bow and scrape for an audience with him and shower him with gifts."

The Dog Head King must be incredibly powerful for Morgar to speak so warmly of him; in fact he's never heard him speak so much. Part of him feels strangely moved that he has for the first time spoken so much to him and so forthrightly, but the other part of him is still hugely distrustful.

"But would I have to give the king a gift?"

He remembers the times when other Dog Head tribes from forests far away had gathered here, and he had been in awe at the rich gifts that had been swapped over.

He then thinks of the stones in his pouch but they are not his to give away.

"I feel he would be happy just with the gift of you."

How hard Morgar struggles not to explode with laughter, his mother was right, the ultimate revenge. Circling again, he studies the small head below him.

"But I sense your apprehension, I have something else you may give him, something from me, as the next Elder, that will most certainly make him welcome you with open arms."

The small face looks up at him, almost gratefully, he notices with amusement. He unties a leather pouch from his belt and hands it over to Cannin.

"Open it and smell inside." He opens it up and smells the overpowering pungent smell of a dried fungus that nearly makes him gag and not one he recognises that *they* use.

"He cannot get this in the north, it only grows here, but it is something I know he cherishes beyond anything. This will be the ultimate gift, nothing of course apart from you as the kind gift giver."

"How long have I got?"Cannin asks quietly.

"You need to leave immediately, you know well enough that they will be back by mid morning and you must put many leagues behind you." Cannin looks back up at him but now with worried eyes.

"But do I have time to pick up my winter provisions?" Morgar restrains a frustrated growl.

"Yes, but you need to be quick."

"Okay I'll go now."

He quickly jumps up and sprints off.

"Wait I'll accompany you." But he had already disappeared into the bracken and gone. Morgar roars after him.

"Go quickly now Cannin and be very careful, so very careful." And as an afterthought, roars out again,

"And always remember to use the stars to guide your path."

He growls softly in his happiness, the fool. He'll probably not even make it out of the Unfathomable Forest; the black Dog-Wolves will be stirring soon. He's always been far too protected in his short life time, safely guarded when they begin their hunting and he laughs inwardly, he'll never be able to fight them off.

But what if he does manage to get through, he muses, what next, how will he be able to cope with the wayfarers, robbers and murderers in the land of the Humans going to the North? They'll kill him...he laughs inwardly, but he frowns suddenly and heavily at the thought that he might have even reached that point, but then he begins to laugh inwardly again, because if he ever does reach his final destination he will meet his father, the so named by him as 'The King of the Dog Heads' who will eat him alive, because the next king of the Dog Heads is Cannin himself through his mother's royal blood, but he has no idea, no idea at all.

His father will then challenge him to the 'Fight of the Death', as the only two true contenders to the legitimate role of 'King' and the only Dog Head alive that can call Cannin out, and knowing his father's prowess in weaponry, well then he will ultimately die but if he dies in the meantime, after all there are so many insurmountable obstacles in his path, mission accomplished anyway and he laughs out loud.

But then he frowns, he doesn't know the exact date but very soon the Elder will be at the end of his three hundred year lifeline, he who could have been the King, but who chose to simply call himself the Elder, that weak old fool, with his grovelling and subservient ways towards the Humans.

Trade, commerce, sharing? It is his fault that they are in decline.

He then reflects angrily, as always, on what Human it was that had deflowered Mahayla, hating the thought it could have been one of those shambling, unkempt, ragged wrecks of Human males seen on the peripheries of the

Unfathomable Forest. Humans who had either fallen from fortune, grace or who would always be desperate criminals, born innately within them and if they made the mistake of wandering too far in, he would slaughter them with relish and feed them to the Dog-Wolves or on special occasions he would allow them to kill the Humans themselves. But on two occasions only just recently, he had been interrupted by the Elder who had appeared as if from nowhere and insisted on giving the Humans an audience.

He spoke to them in his perfect Human tongue, offering them clear spring water in bronze bowls which they would gratefully gulp down and then he would question them in depth about their personal and intimate lives and when satisfied with their answers, would reach in his pouch and hand over to the bewildered, yet so grateful Humans, large lumps of copper ore, enough, he explained, to feed their families for a long time and to return to them and forget the path to fortune because in these dark days of now, it would never be. The condition of their release and good fortune was also on the strict understanding that they never speak of *them* and never to return because he could not guarantee their safety in the depths of the Unfathomable Forest.

Morgar loomed behind with his three lieutenants and the Humans saw that it was no idle threat, as he stood there seething with his foul breath blowing out like a tortuous storm from inflated nostrils. But as they were escorted out of the Unfathomable Forest by the Elder, the only thing the Humans could ever remember afterwards was of trees and leaves blowing in a warm wind, a place of bliss but yet with dark, menacing shadows in the peripheries of their minds.

Morgar would often reflect begrudgingly afterwards, how the Elder knew which of the Humans to trust, because they never did return.

But these things are in the past now, he reminds himself, he will ultimately join his father and wage war on the Humans for their constant clearing of great sections of their forests for their endless ever expanding fields of crops. The other Dog Heads here, who he and his mother had worked on for years, would join in but not all, there were still amongst them ones who had not been swayed, but they would succumb especially when they see all the other tribes from within the forests on this island joining in too, but only if is seen that the true royal line has gone.

He then growls loudly in his exasperation, if that bitch Mahayla had married him fourteen years before, he would have been in such a strong position, the undoubted birth of a son who would have been the King and he as his advisor, and then he wouldn't have needed to join his father in his madness. How he hates her for what she has done and how he hates her son.

CHAPTER SEVEN
The Minors

Cannin springs through the foliage as lightly as the accompanying small roe deer that had hidden in the bracken, the two wrens buzz back and forth above his head until both settle on a low branch ahead. Walking over to their perch he sees the air hole below and squeezes down and back into the Minors' private, dark tunnels.

No Dog Head has ever been permitted to enter their underground world, other than in the designated hibernation caves, an understanding that both races have always had. Certain tunnels of theirs lead to the hibernation caves; the Minors stoking their underground furnaces day and night to keep the Dog Heads warm in the two months of hibernation and in the spring when they awoke they would find beautifully crafted weapons of new and ingenious design. The Dog Heads in return hunted through the other months, supplying the Minors with abundance of fresh meat, fish and the fruits of the forest and in the autumn with fallen branches for their furnaces. The Dog Heads were also their protectors, keeping their existence a secret from the outside world.

"A very happy alliance; and one that has not changed for centuries."

The Elder's voice echoes sharply in his head, he grimly acknowledges the words, but regardless, he senses the dog is still alive but not for much longer unless he moves quickly and tries to stop the slaughter, after all if he hadn't interfered in the first place none of this would now be happening.

He crouches low on his haunches, the daylight from above shining down, illuminating his head like a beacon. He is now their target and from what he has always heard about them, whilst no higher than his navel, are the most formidable of warriors. He has never seen one personally; none of the Dog Heads had; that is apart from the Elder, the only one permitted to do so because of his high rank and he had often tried to imagine what they must look like.

He once asked the Elder, who quite confusingly said that if he behaved righteously, then one day he would meet them, but only if *he* behaved righteously, he had reiterated again. He continued on to tell him that they were slaves brought over the great water by the Latin people that had lived on the land many centuries before, and it was the Minors that had created the mines for their masters, supplying them with an endless supply of flint and other precious metals.

When the Latin people left they also left their slaves behind having no further use for them, and being only used to living in the dark of the tunnels, that is where they remained. It was said that their fear of sunlight, whilst always small of stature, had diminished them even more and as the centuries rolled by, they had become smaller and smaller.

"And so today," Cannin whispers as he returns in the direction where he had left the dog, "I have not behaved righteously in any of my actions for not only have I returned to the Deep Pool, but I also took a domestic dog of the Humans there and now I'm in another place where I shouldn't be and no doubt on a fool's errand."

But as he breathes in deeply he is rewarded with a mere scent of the dog and a sense of his energy in tiny air fibrillations. He chases forward until he reaches the air hole where he had been pulled up by Morgar and looking down at the floor of the tunnel, picks up one of the dog's long white fine hairs. He sniffs it and bending down follows the scattered trail of one more, then another.

He passes the blackened, burnt corpses of the rats and continues on half crouched until he comes to a tunnel that forks to the left and downwards. He sniffs again, the scent of the dog has picked up marginally in strength, they obviously haven't killed him yet and senses that he is being led, and as so weak an animal, probably willingly and naively, not realising his fate at their hands.

Urgently now, he half scrambles, half runs as the tunnel roof dips and rises wildly, his ability from his Dog Head ancestry of being able to see clearly in dim light kicks in as he is led further downwards.

The scent of the dog, always illusive but always just there, makes him go ever deeper; he follows the walls of the tunnel where veins of precious metals glitter and reflect off the luminosity of his eyes.

The snaking tunnel continues relentlessly on and in what seems an eternity since he started out; he begins to wonder how far he is from his original starting point. He passes other tunnels leading off from the one that he is in, the only thing keeping him on this path being the scent of the dog and shudders at the thought of it disappearing and of getting lost, never to find his way out to the outside and then he panics, the very thing he had just thought becomes reality, the scent completely disappears.

He takes the air in again, there is an expanse of water ahead and going steadily downwards in what can only be the way forward, he stops and sniffs again and is relieved when he picks up the stench of wet dog in the far distance.

He slips into the dark, freezing channel of water and swimming beneath the surface, glides through shoals of tiny fish, the luminosity off his eyes illuminating their skeletal, translucent forms. They stare directly at him, the excitability of seeing his lit eyes sends them into a paroxysm of delight as they dart, swirl and cavort in front of him and when finally the waterway ends and he clambers up the rock shelf and out, he turns back and half smiles at the myriads of tiny glowing eyes reflecting back up at him.

He continues onwards. The air is getting thinner and thinner, increasing his anxiety, especially as he feels quite distinctively he is now being followed by tiny feet. Every few seconds he looks back but there is nothing to be smelt or to be seen.

The dark deepens to inky black as the stored daylight fades in his eyes. He can only now just about see the twisted contours of the tunnel, abruptly the tunnel roof rears up and he feels his head swathed in a cold, still darkness. The unbearable silence in this underground world begins to grate on his ragged nerves; he begins to wish something would happen, anything at all, when with a start he takes in the smell of burning tallow. He rounds a bend and then another, where now the tunnel is lit dimly from low wall mounted metal vessels.

Flashes of moving white shapes high above makes him look up, he nearly shouts out in fright, swooping skeletal owls, with skeletal rats hanging rigidly from their dead beaks, wings outstretched, glide above his head. He stands completely still until realising that it is only the exhalation of his breath that moves them and he nearly laughs out in his relief. But then he wonders at the Minors' masterly skill in hanging the skeletons with no visible signs of support.

He continues on, when he finds himself entering into a large cavern. At first he cannot quite understand what he is seeing, strange, lurking shapes are all around him, he gasps out loudly in fear causing the tallow to flicker alarmingly. He holds his breath, but the tallow vessels continue to burn and sway their flickering beams erratically all around, giving him the distinct impression that he is not the only living creature in this space.

He crouches down instinctively and crawls forward then cries out to his soul when he sees the rearing, bared boned skeletal forms of rutting red deer males, interlocking antlers in a fight to the end, tens of wild boar, heads down in varying charging stances, tusks highlighted in the burning tallow light, snarling wolves, teeth bared, and amongst them, all manner of smaller animal skeletons in varying positions of fleeing or in attacking mode. His fear subsides; he stands up and wanders amongst them all, completely entranced by the accuracy of the creatures' skeletal interlocking, without sinew and muscle to hold them together and he wonders again at the Minors' ingenuity.

So many he wanders past, that he becomes sadder and sadder, and sickened by the starkness of death all around him he immediately walks back to the lit tunnel and follows again the smell of the dog, the only living thing that he can detect and he is now more desperate than ever to find him.

He turns a bend into the next section of the tunnel and for the first time, a new and unexpected sight meets his eyes, high straight walls to either side rear up into blackness and as far as he can see, darkened niches are cut at regular intervals into the rock walls and at the very far end, like the dark pupil of a tiny creature the tunnel continues on, seemingly into infinity.

Between each of the niches there is a tallow burning vessel, casting the recesses into shadow. He approaches the first niche apprehensively; he instinctively knows that what is hidden within is something that he is not going to like. He pauses and peering closely in, recoils at the sight of the small, standing skelcton of a Human form, its dark grey skin still stretched tightly over the bones, and its face set in a grim, close lipped grimace. Each niche he passes houses another and another, so many of them on either side that he is shocked at their numbers.

"But at least I now know what you look like." He says unthinkingly and out loud.

He continues on staring at their dead, yet so alive, stony faces that he becomes even more morosely depressed from what he has discovered in this subterranean world, he pities these poor people marooned beneath the ground for so long, still even now, shackled by the tyranny of their old masters. He is in awe of their beautiful attention to the detail in immortalizing all the animals above that had been thrown down to them over the centuries but saddened beyond

66

anything that they hadn't walked above and seen all the creatures for themselves in all their living glory, but fated instead to die down here.

Leaving the catacomb, he passes into a low, unlit tunnel when all of a sudden; the still air is disturbed by a small charged wind that races towards him, indicating that he will soon be among them. Removing a stone from his pouch, he prepares his catapult and then sighing deeply, changes his mind, he has no inclination to fight these people, remembering then the Elder's words from two dusks ago, "What will be, will be."

Fatalistically he puts the stone away and slings the catapult back over his shoulder.

His legs are now so heavy with fatigue that he can barely walk, but he carries on through the dark low tunnel until he finds he is in another high vaulted cavern. He struggles to see as the light from the burning tallow vessels send out weird flashes of light until blinking rapidly he sees the sitting dog staring directly at him from the other side of the dark cavern, surrounded by motionless shadowy, small figures, so still and grey they could almost be rocky out crops.

He stands rigidly; his heart hammering in his chest when one of the small figures disengages itself from the mass and comes towards him, he inhales sharply; it looks so precisely like one of the dead Minors in the niches that if it hadn't moved he would have thought it a corpse and then comes the shocking realisation that he had been surrounded by them all along and at any time they could have attacked or even killed him.

The Minor comes closer still, lifting an arm horizontally, palm down...Cannin breaks into a wide, shaky smile...he is being given the unquestionable Dog Head salute of friendship.

This is so entirely not what he had expected, that he lifts his arm immediately and salutes the Minor back, when he is suddenly aware that he is completely surrounded. He is astounded at their stealth with which they had crept all around him, the dog whimpers for him to be calm when small, tiny frozen hands begin pinching his legs and arms painfully.

A small part of his mind feels they are sizing him up and calculating how much flesh they can strip from him and with their fevered sniffing how succulent he will taste, but the dog continues its low whimpering and he realises that all they are doing is judging his physical size and he is filled with the strongest impression that they are pleased with him, even proud.

They push him forward and prod him along into another tunnel, there are no burning tallow vessels here and everything is again inky black and their voices, unlike the Dog Head's use of the Human tongue, mutter the same words over and over again.

"Hic est filius eius, hic est filius eius" (he is of her). And then more prodding small fingers propel him along. In the distance he is aware of the dog's scent in front of him when he realises they are steadily going up, his vision increases in its luminosity when ahead a vertical oval of light appears from the gloom.

They halt him with their tiny pinching fingers, clasping on tightly as if not to let him go and then with a final mass of hard pinching, he is shoved violently up towards the lit hole where the sitting Spaniel waits for him. He strokes the dog's head and looking back he can just about see their small forms in the shadowy tunnel.

He enters into a high space and realises it's a hibernation cavern, but not one he had been in before and by its emptiness, obvious that it had not been used for years. He looks up to the air hole, an ancient ladder leads up to the outside, a warm draught flows down, he hears the birds above sing their usual calm evening songs, as butterflies of different hues flutter in and out.

He's shocked at the time that had passed in the freezing tunnels, the light is muted, indicating the sun will set soon and he realises he will have to leave immediately. He turns back to see they've crept forward almost to the mouth of the tunnel, he points upwards to the air hole above, indicating he must leave. In response they point their wizened, stone grey fingers in the direction of the far right hand corner.

One moves closer even closer still, at the very mouth of the tunnel, shaking a head like carved stone in what Cannin realises is a negative and points again to the dark corner.

He walks forward, an abundance of forest flowers cascading down from the air hole, loop through the rungs of the old wooden ladder as thick, hairy ivy branches entwine down to the ground and moving like opening curtains in the warm breeze, he glimpses through to a bed of dried heather that lies so invitingly. The intoxicating scent of the flowers combined with the warmth from the dying sun in the cavern and his utter exhaustion makes him yawn loudly and he looks wistfully at the bed.

"I wish I could lie down right now and sleep but I can't." He turns to look at them," You need to understand that we have to go."

All shake their stone like heads negatively and point at the heather bed. He looks at it again, feeling drowsier and drowsier.

"Would it matter?" He whistles to the dog, because who else can he ask, realising now there is nobody else that he can ask in this strange new world that he has become part of.

"If we have just a small sleep, after all we have a long way to go?"

In response, the Spaniel trots over to the bed in his relief and falls into a deep sleep. The grinning stone like heads nod creakily up and down and point encouragingly at the dog for him to follow suit.

He smiles wearily back, they're right, he's far too tired and lying down next to the dream ridden twitching dog, he closes his eyes, opening them again suddenly, but the warmth from the dog, the warmth from the heather, the soporific scent of the wild flowers makes him feel so relaxed, the most relaxed he has ever felt.

He looks over once more at the small, dark silent figures in the shadows and sensing their goodwill towards him he closes his eyes, because deep down he doesn't ever want to leave the Unfathomable Forest, it is the only home he has ever known and the thought of the outside world of the Humans terrifies him.

He whispers to the still dog, "Perhaps we could just stay here with the Minors. After all, hibernation comes soon and then when I wake up again, I could hunt for them in the summer months..."

His voice fades away as he falls into a deep and dreamless sleep.

The Minors stand silently like stone sentinels in the shadows until the air hole up to the outside shows the sky is dark apart from the Dog Star and Little Pup glaring down and while Cannin sleeps his innocent sleep in the deepest of slumbers, they gather around remarking on his similarity to *her*, as he lies on the bed of heather that was his mother's bed for the months she had carried him in her womb fourteen years before.

When she had left them that dawn carrying the baby they knew they would never see her again. They worried for the child but she assured them repeatedly that she had to give him to her father to look after, that he above all others would keep him safe, that he would understand.

She had the illness that so many of the Dog Head women suffered from, that is death soon after a child was born and there was no cure, hence their ever diminishing numbers. They knew that's why she had enjoined with a Human, to ensure the royal lineage would continue and not with the hated Morgar.

It was they that had released the underground spring into the stagnant pool for her, hearing her distress and understanding it totally. Out of all them, they had liked Mahayla the best, she had always been kind to them. Long before as a very small creature she had collected fresh

71

woodland flowers, berries, crab apples, and would lower the gathered items down the air holes in intricately made reed baskets that she had fashioned herself. She soon learned to speak their language as they whispered up to her. They were her councillors and she theirs, if only in her child like way. When she got older she would slip down special plants that would soothe their ailments as she whispered of her small troubles, simple events, like been chased by Morgar, but as the years passed by, more of his bullying and his and his mother's cruelty to the animals.

But they were not stupid they had already witnessed long before she was born, of the bad strain, of Morgar's father, Luthias and his evil influence. His incessant screaming down at them to produce more weapons, more weapons with evil ferocious barbs and slicing slivers of metal to cut through any living beast and particularly of Humans and as they were of Human origin themselves, they were frightened of how far he would go with his madness.

They knew and could hear above of his incessant intake of the 'bad fungi', and so his crazed behaviour increased until finally he had gone too far, and even though he was of the next high born family after the Elder, all the Dog Heads finally rounded on him and he was forcibly banished.

They had sighed with relief at the time, but not for long, when they found out that Morgar and his mother, Malita had begged to remain and they knew that the decision to allow them to stay would be a costly mistake with serious repercussions in the future. And so it was, as they had predicted, the trouble had now started. But they would help

Mahayla's child, the true and the last of the royal line of the Dog Heads.

CHAPTER EIGHT
The return of the King's horse

The mare trots to the outskirts of the Unfathomable Forest, and then plunges through the overgrown foliage. The path had long gone, but she knows exactly where she is. Snorting with excitement with the barely conscious girl clinging around her neck like a limpet, she barges her way through and whinnies loudly, but nothing happens, she calls again. She pushes through the foliage more, calling for *her* to answer, but all she can hear is the sighing of the lush trees' moving foliage above. Two wrens swoop down, studying her intently and then call out with their shrill piping voices, "*She* is gone, gone, long ago."

But the mare is not convinced, she continues through, smashing her path heavily forward. She awakes more roosting birds, their shrill calls pierce the hot, dark, sultry, air, warning her, "Go back, go back, *she* is long gone."

She stands still then but snorting wildly when she picks up the scent of the Dog-Wolves tearing towards her.

The Spaniel wakes up and leaping from the heather bed, stands on his hind legs sniffing the breeze from the air hole and begins yelping with a mixture of excitement and fear. Cannin opens his eyes groggily, still smitten with the sleep inducing scent from the wild flowers but hearing the dog's cries, sniffs the air in intermittent deep breaths, jumps up and climbing the wooden ladder is up and gone into the night.

Further away Morgar quietly sits cross legged on the ground looking up at the two stars' powerful light ferociously burning down through the trees, shining, he believes, on his head alone. The nine females recumbent with heavy sleep from the hot day, swing gently in their deer skin hammocks tied from the tree's all around him as inwardly he rehearses his lines for when the male Dog Heads come back in a few hours.

He hasn't told his mother yet of the Mongrel's departure, he can't take the risk, knowing her unpredictable mouth, but still he looks over at her fondly as she snores happily like a fat, old, female boar, one long hairy arm hanging limply down, but with her fingers curling and uncurling in her usual angry fashion even when she's asleep.

He sniffs in then, picking up the scent of the Dog-Wolf before she appears, he waits until her head nervously pokes through the ferns, very clearly scared of disturbing him.
He snarls at her.

"What do you want?"
But looking into her eyes, he reads instantly what is afoot and picking up on her excitement chases off in hot pursuit.

What immense joy, another Human has stupidly entered into the Unfathomable Forest!

He runs, deftly following the wolf until finally through the trees, a stark vision of white and black meets his eyes, eerily picked out by the Dog Stars' light, the vision of a white horse glaring out from the darkness in stark contrast with a black cloaked Human female clutching wildly on its back.

His pack of black Dog-Wolves circle around the old mare, she stands still but her head turning wildly, watching for the first sign of attack, she cannot do anymore with the girl on her back and she snorts wildly in her anger and frustration.

Morgar watches from his hidden position, his favourite of the male dog- wolves, the strongest and most powerful he has ever nurtured, approaches her head on. She now stays completely still, head lowered, eyeing him dangerously. He skulks over, stomach close to the ground, ready for the kill as the other wolves close in at the rear.

"He is the master of the game!" Morgar cries inwardly and grins hideously with excitement, his stinking breath attracting a wild abundance of insects and he chews happily as they flit haplessly, like fools into his mouth.

The Dog-Wolves emboldened with courage from Morgar's patronage, have already surmised that the old mare is weak with age and with her intent on protecting the Human female astride her is incapable of defending herself and grinning, yellow toothed with hunger they eagerly close in.

A tearing sound fills the air, the mare trembles violently at the searing pain, but remains stoically still, fixedly staring at the alpha male, knowing him to be her most serious threat. The female Dog-Wolf tries to gulp down the strip of skin and flesh torn from the mare's rump, but the rest of the pack turn on her, snarling with fury and try to rip the vestige of flesh away from her.

Morgar chews more, his excitement growing out of all bounds at the smell of the drawn blood. The alpha male crouches ready for the spring at the mare's head when a shadowy figure appears from the foliage.

The Dog-Wolves are startled at the sudden appearance, they retreat a little but glare angrily over at the figure for halting their kill.

Cannin looks at the pale face of the girl, her black eyes wide in terror, her mouth muttering silent words, she suddenly sees his dark form and screams out," Please, whoever you are, please, please help me."

The alpha male glares over at Cannin with unconcealed hatred, Morgar had already informed them that they had full permission to kill the Mongrel, that he is a renegade and a traitor to the Dog Heads and so head high, tail wagging he trots over as if to welcome him as an equal and a friend.

The Human female cries out in warning, but already Cannin growls low and dangerously, refuting his position. The alpha male stops in his tracks and backs off slightly, cocking his head from side to side, listening intently to the Mongrel's verbal offer of violence.

And then the youth breaks into the strangest and the most ominous low screeching noises that she has ever heard, like some primeval, reptilian ancestor of birds, so menacing that she shudders, coming from now, she realises as he steps forward from the shadows, from a semi naked long haired youth of possibly the same age as her.

The mare, understanding the youth's warning to the Dog-Wolves, snorts wildly and rears up with Isabel clinging tightly on in abject fear, the alpha male backs off even more, omitting low yelping noises and looks over his shoulder into the dark bushes for further orders, but Morgar is strangely silent.

 The youth calls out softly to her.

"Get off the horse and come to me slowly."
She whispers up to the sky,

"Thank you God, thank you for sending me a saviour whose tongue I can understand." Her fear when she had first caught sign of him was that he would be some kind of wild, forest barbarian.

The youth whistles low, the mare immediately quietens and stands with quivering limbs as Isabel shakily slips off and walks slowly over to him. When she is at his side, the youth now whistles a piercing sharp note, the mare immediately kicks out her back legs wildly at the Dog-Wolves, catching two in their heads with her hooves and then stomping and rearing in her fury, she unexpectedly speeds forward, teeth bared and grabs the alpha male by his snout, swings him wildly in the air and flings him into the undergrowth as the rest of the pack with frightened yelps, turn tail and disappear into the darkness.

The mare, sleek with sweat trots immediately over to the grinning youth and whinnies her greetings in high excitement, knowing intuitively that he is of *him* and he is of *her*. Cannin strokes her nose, breathing softly in her nostrils and then trailing his hand over her body makes his way to her rear and studies the wound on her rump. He spits into the wound and pinch's the flesh together, all the time whistling a strange low tune.

Isabel, in spite of her fear, is astounded at the old mare's behaviour, not just with her instantly obeying the youth's command in attacking the Dog-Wolves but also in the way that she greeted him afterwards, as if she had been trained by the youth as his battle horse. She follows behind.

"Thank you, thank for your help, but you know this horse?"

"I have never met her before."

He answers quietly, hoping she would follow suit, not at all happy with her loud shrill, high pitched voice and walks back around to the mare's head and continues to stroke her nose as Isabel follows behind and shrills out again,

"But it is as if she recognises you?"

"I cannot think why."

But she can tell that he seems darkly disturbed by her words.

She stares at his shadowy profile intently and aware of her scrutiny, he turns to face her and half smiles. She half smiles back but her attention is fixed completely on his eyes, never has she seen eyes so disturbingly blue, so penetrating, and even more peculiar, shining as if lit eternally. She looks immediately downwards in embarrassment, and in a quieter voice asks,

"You are the one that has my dog aren't you?"

In response and to her enormous surprise, he lifts her high in the air and places her on the mare's back.

"I'll take you to him but from now on you must be very quiet."

All this Morgar has watched, firstly in shock at Cannin's appearance, secondly, in more shock that he has warned off his Dog-Wolves, he didn't know that he had the power to be able to do so, thirdly that the old mare fought like a stallion half her age and had thrown his top wolf into the foliage and fourthly, he is completely surrounded by a conglomerate of stinking male boars, who somehow without him having detected them, had angrily surrounded him in their hairy corpulence. He watches as Cannin, the girl and the white horse disappear through the dark trees and then he growls down at them furiously.

"Move off pigs before I slaughter you all."

They stare up at him with small dangerous eyes, tusks raised with evil intent and jostle him more and even though he is so huge, he realises that unless he stops insulting them, they'll rip him to shreds. He contemplates unsheathing his gladius, but changes his mind, he may cut a few throats but then the rest will rip off his gonads, drag him down and rip out his entrails whilst he still lives.

He realises that the only way forward is to remain calm when he sees more and more arriving until he is surrounded by the largest contingent of mature male boar that he has ever seen. He stares down at them in confusion; this is the time of the year when they are at their most dangerous but normally only towards each other, so why have they amassed together like this?

For the first time in his fortieth year of life he begins to feel nervous and risks a low whistle to his Dog-Wolves and is rewarded with hard shoving and angry grunts from the boar, but in the distance he hears the alpha male whimper quietly back, the pack are also corralled in and they too are not allowed to move.

He cannot understand what is going on, but as he contemplates the situation, he laughs inwardly.

Of course, Cannin is now truly a renegade; there can be no coming back from all the traitorous deeds he has committed today and especially after this last outrage. He allows himself to be moved on, but towards what weird destination the boar are pushing him onto, he has no idea. He cannot read their minds, no matter how he tries, but as such unrefined, angry, stupid creatures he doesn't care, before long they will give up on this nonsense and run off and kill each other as usual, their only passion at this time of the year being to rut females. But he will not forget their insubordination and when the time is right and when they least expect it, he will track all of them down, no matter how long it takes and kill each one individually.

"What an extremely strange day, full of so many events...but it couldn't have gone better even if I had planned it myself."

And he grins his perpetual, hideous smile up to the Dog Stars' glowing presences.

CHAPTER NINE
Sagar's destiny

It is a strange silent walk through the forest as Cannin leads the mare and the girl onwards. Hidden deep in the foliage and to either side he is aware that he is being flanked by the wild boar and a short distance behind he can hear their rear guard are trampling over his and the mare's tracks to happily leave no evidence of their path. He grins at the strange behaviour of the wild boar, but why they have chosen to help is a mystery, particularly as they refuse to engage in any form of dialogue with him.

He knew at the time that it hadn't been just his threats and the subsequent help from the old mare that had got rid of Morgar's pack, he had already detected the boars' mighty presence all around and if it hadn't been for them, he doubts that he would be alive now.

But one thing is for certain, there is no choice now; he, the girl and the dog must leave the forest immediately, his crimes are now so enormous that he'll not be forgiven, and he thinks sadly, not even by the Elder, the one that he will miss the most out of them all.

Isabel stares constantly at the slim figure walking in the dark shadows in front and even though he can only be of her age she notices that his muscle formation is more like a full grown male and she prays to God again, thanking him for sending this wild youth to her aid.

Cannin in turn, knows there's something wrong with her; her nervous, high excitability one moment, and then falling practically asleep on the mare's back a moment later, is disturbing to say the least and whilst she is exquisitely beautiful, the most beautiful creature he has ever seen, he wonders if she is perhaps touched in the head.

Finally they reach the air hole; he pauses and omits the purring chirr of a night jar, his message to all below that everything is as it should be. Immediately Isabel hears the responding low whimpering of the Spaniel, she slips off the mare, her face so flushed with excitement and uttering such, loud, high pitched squeals that Cannin cautions for her to wait.

He climbs half way down the old ladder and quickly looks down to the low dark tunnel mouth leading to the Minors underworld and he's relieved to see they are no longer there.

"Come down now, but slowly." He whispers up, but to his surprise, he is forced to jump down from a great height to the stone ground below as she climbs down the ladder at great speed, somehow managing to do so despite the encumbrance of her long garments.

The Spaniel is equally beside himself with excitement; yelping and jumping up to lick her face. Isabel kneels down, clasping the dog wildly and between kisses, cries out, "My dog, my beautiful dog!" Finally, tears unashamedly coursing down her face, she smiles up at Cannin, "Thank you for saving Archie, thank you for saving me and thank you for saving the old horse, because without her I would never have got here."

She stands up and rushes over to him, he steps back apprehensively; she moves forward even more and offers her hand so urgently to him that he is forced to take it. She cries out, her high pitched voice almost now to the point of hysteria.

"I am indebted to you for the rest of my life, whatever I have is yours, for however long I live and may it be long, but I fear possibly not, when they find that I have gone, I fear they may try to find me and I worry that I ask too much of you, if you would just help us one more time?"

"You owe me nothing." He answers quietly.

He is deeply embarrassed by her high emotion and her gratitude towards him, never having witnessed or experienced anything quite like it before in his life and most certainly not the way of the Dog Heads. He begins to feel more and more that she is out of control, her delicate white face, her wide black, staring eyes, her masses and masses of black long hair, her timidity and weakness in her movements, apart from surprisingly and so nimbly ascending the ladder after him, unnerves him too such a degree, that he feels he does not want the responsibility for such a strange creature.

He quickly removes a pouch from his belt and hands it over to her.

"These are yours."

She eagerly, feverously, tips the diamonds into the palm of her hand. The constant light from the Dog Stars beams down through the air hole and shining on the stones, enhancing their hue, makes her look up into his eyes, realising then that is what they are like, they are like the blue shining hue of her diamonds! She cries out,

"No, no these are yours to keep forever, I still have the one you sent me, it is enough, I only ask of you one thing, if you would, if you wouldn't mind, showing the three of us the way out of this forest and onto a safe road so we can get far away."

She pours them back into the pouch and hands it back to him; he takes it extremely reluctantly.

She cries out again.

"Put them away, they are yours to keep, but promise me, promise that you will help us?"

He ties the pouch back onto his belt, with the sole intention of returning it to her when she is in a better state of mind.

"I will help you."

She sways precariously on her feet and he realises then that she is dangerously overwrought; the dog runs to his side and sits next to him anxiously as they both watch her crumple to the stone ground and he wonders what he's supposed to do with her next?

Further away, Morgar now knows where the wild boar are taking him, but he cannot understand why would they bring here of all places and for what possible reason?

He can see the Deep Pool just ahead, its surface glowing with a strange ethereal light from the two stars' above, but all around everything else is cast in warm blackness. There is no sound apart from low grunts from the wild boar until; from directly over head, the shrill shriek of a Peregrine Falcon pierces the night air. He immediately looks up, confused why a falcon would be flying around at night. He becomes more and more disturbed with the uniqueness of it, but then of course, he reassures himself, it's simply taking advantage of the unusual light from the two stars' to hunt.

But in that very next second the wild boar in their heaving, stinking masses begin to trot off and quickly dissipate into the darkness until he is left completely alone.

His senses are now on full alert and he begins to feel more and more uneasy, the weird silence is almost unbearable; he feels something is about to happen and unsheathing his gladius crouches down, staring wild eyed all around for what he feels intuitively will be an attack.

"Well Morgar, here you are."

He leaps to his feet in utter shock, swings around and points the short sword up to the throat of the gaunt, tall figure of the Elder.

"What are you doing here?" He growls, feeling angry and frightened in turn, but noticing straightaway that the Elder for the first time ever is not only not wearing his Pendant of Office, but is weapon less and almost semi naked apart from a deerskin loin cloth.

The Elder smiles serenely at him.

"Calm, Morgar, calm, is that any way to greet me? But I apologise if I have startled you."

"So was it you that commanded the wild boar to bring me here?"He demands angrily, his sense of power rising at the Elder's strange appearance.

"Not I, you know they are the masters of their own destiny and choose their own path."

Morgar stares at him incredulously.

"But of course there was one you may remember that could command them and that was my beloved daughter, Mahayla. Did you know that her name comes from the Celtic people of this beautiful island and means guardian? An apt choice because it seems even in her death, she is still her son's protector."

Morgar snarls angrily.

"Such mumbo jumbo, your dead daughter has no power, you delude yourself."

But, nevertheless the Elder's words have a profound effect on him and he swivels nervously around to look at the Deep Pool to see a massive dark shape rise up out of the water. He gasps involuntarily, the shape rises higher, metamorphosing into a dark crescent. It twists mid air, exposing a speckled underbelly and then dives back into the water with a loud plop.

"Just a fish, that's all it was, just a fish." He cries inwardly in his relief.

"But of course you are right Morgar, what nonsense I speak. I expect the real truth is that Cannin has inherited his mother's abilities."

Morgar swings back around, his temper rising again, hot and vicious at the thought that Cannin could control the wild boar and that he couldn't.

All of a sudden, the harsh rattling noise of beating wings disturb the night air as a Peregrine Falcon descends from the rich darkness of the trees behind to land effortlessly on the Elder's shoulder. Morgar recognises it immediately by its ridiculous tackle as Cannin's bird and he menacingly raises his gladius again.

"Calm Morgar, you know Elsu well enough, I am only here because she flew to me earlier to report such strange things, so very strange that I left the others to make their own way back and as you were left in charge I would now like to hear your version of the events that have happened here today."

Morgar lowers his gladius, this is now his opportunity, regardless of everything, the Elder is always fair and always listens. He hesitates before he speaks though, his attention momentarily caught by the sight of blood trickling down the Elder's chest from Elsu's talons piercing his skin and wonders that he allows the bird to wound him in such a way. He breathes in sharply, the sight and smell arouse his blood lust and with an effort to retain control he finally speaks.

"Cannin has committed many great sins today, all traitorous and against our laws..."

He tries to speak more but the Elder lifts his hand for silence.

"Where exactly is Cannin now?"

"I do not know, for he has fled with a female Human riding a white mare and..."

The Elder lifts his hand again for silence.

Morgar feels his temper rising out of all proportion, to be stopped when he is trying to explain about Cannin's treachery is beyond vexation.

"Good, I am glad he has left and that you persuaded him to find his father."

His father? Morgar thinks inwardly, nearly laughing out loud in his scorn, no, not his, you old fool, but mine.

The Elder's voice continues,

"No, Morgar, I mean *his* father. He will meet your poor, deluded father first as is destined; but then afterwards he will meet his father, which is also destined."

Morgar is now uncontrollably fuming that he speaks of his father in such a way...poor, deluded, how dare he? But the thought of Cannin meeting his natural father afterwards can only mean one outcome, that Cannin will be the King of the Dog Heads.

The Elder quietly walks away; the falcon swoops off with dark beating wings as he makes his way to the start of the treacherous mud flats and gazing at the Deep Pool where the two Dog Stars reflect down upon its surface like father and son moons, he sighs deeply and in a low voice whispers,

"This is where it all began and this is where it now ends."

Morgar, hearing his words, and beside himself in rage, leaps two giant strides forward and viciously stabs the Elder in the lower back, and pulling the glasier out, he growls out,

"Did you know that this was to happen then, you old fool?"

There is no answer, the Elder drops to his knees; Morgar kicks him brutally between the shoulder blades, he falls forward and flat onto his face. Morgar rolls his body over with his foot until the Elder is face up but lying on the surface of the treacherous mud.

"So Sagar, was this foretold too?" He screams out.

The Elder opens his eyes and quietly answers him.

"Yes, it was foretold."

"Then this is your destiny."

He puts his foot onto the Elder's chest and pushes downwards as the body begins to sink into the clogging depths. But to his astonishment the Elder smiles up at him benevolently.

"Thank you Morgar for your kindness to me in my dotage, you know I always expected great things from you that is why I allowed you to stay with us after your father was banished, and now you have."

"How is this kindness?" He cries out, now in anguish.

"You were not to know poor Morgar, that when the dawn rises in a short while, it will mark the end of my three hundred year life line. I didn't tell any of the others the exact date; you know how I hate fuss, so I thank you for the privilege of your company alone as I go to join my daughter and her mother, something I have wanted to do for so many long and lonely years and, with my passing coincidently, this very dawn Cannin will come of age and as he is now on his travels my duty here is finally done."

The stark enormity and yet the futility of his crime hits him and as he looks down at the Elder's face, he realises for the first time how much the Elder had meant to him, his kindness, his attention to him, always listening to his bitter complaints about Cannin, never siding against him, always fair in all his decisions, always fair.

He wildly clutches his arms around his body, trying to crush the anguish, to get rid of the pain, to rid himself of the Elder's words echoing in his head, he rips great clumps of hair from his head and in his grief whines so plaintively that his pack deep in the undergrowth join in.

The Elder continues to smile back up at him as the thick mud oozes into his mouth and then Morgar, weeping profusely, kneels down and so gently with his giant arms pushes him beneath the surface.

When there is nothing to be seen anymore, he pulls his arms out from the sucking mud, staggers up, weaves over to retrieve his gladius and weaving back, stabs it over and over again into the wet mud as if it were its fault.

Finally, sated, he pulls it out and grabbing the great clumps of his hair scattered all around, wipes the blade clean, replaces it in his sheath and then punches the giant hair ball deep into the wet mud with his fist.

He staggers back, falls down, caked with the drying mud and curls in a ball on the solid ground conscious that only a few feet away and a few feet below him, lies the body of the Elder and he whimpers inconsolably of what he has done.

His Dog-Wolf pack skulk out of the bushes and quickly lick up the Elder's blood from the ground until there is no evidence left and then drop all around him in their dark forms, whimpering with him, as all the watching animals and birds hiding in the darkness know that with the passing of the Elder, bad and dangerous days are ahead now that Morgar rules supreme.

But not one will tell Cannin what has happened here, the Elder's last and final command will be obeyed to the letter, until he reaches his destiny.

CHAPTER TEN
The coronation

Cannin picks Isabel up at the dog's barking order, and lays her fragile body on the bed of heather. Archie jumps up and lying at her side looks up to him so beseechingly to help that he find himself placing his palm on her forehead and finds it strange, in the hottest month of the year that she's as cold as ice.

He has absolutely no idea what to do with her, the forest animals he understands and can treat, but her condition is like nothing he has ever come across before.

He turns to look at the dark tunnel mouth wishing the Minors would appear and as if on cue, two come forth from the shadows and in the hand of one them, he, she - he still can't work out which is male or which is female - carries a goblet of elaborate design.

They bow their heads deeply to acknowledge his presence but without looking at him approach the girl, muttering incomprehensible words and shoo the dog off the bed. One lifts her head from behind with both hands, whilst the other puts the goblet to her lips and pinches her nose, which seems to work as the girl, eyes shut, begins to gulp down the fluid greedily until the goblet is drained. Her head is lowered carefully back down and they solemnly return to the dark tunnel, as more appear carrying a strange array of items which they carefully stack one on top of the other. They then walk over to him, heads bowed. To the fore of the approaching group, he recognises the Minor who had saluted him earlier; who he now realises must be their equivalent to an Elder.

In front of him and to his complete surprise, they all kneel down on one knee and lower their heads in deference. He looks down at them in bewilderment; surely they cannot be bowing to him?

The Elder begins speaking.

"...John...Cannin...Mahayla...Sagar..."

He recognises his name and his grandfather's but the words in front of and between and from then on are completely unintelligible to him, the Minor's voice drones on and on and to his ears, is an incantation of something so dark and forbidding, that he feels something momentously bad has happened and his heart begins to pound erratically in his chest.

Suddenly they all rise as one and surround him, the Elder stretches up and places his hands on his shoulders gently at first, but then with surprising strength pushes down and Cannin realises that he is being asked to kneel. He lowers down on one his knee, not knowing what else to do when the Elder gently places his hand on his head. More of the dark incantation is uttered as one by one the other Minor's bring over the stacked articles.

Isabel lays quietly, aware of the low repetitive words, reminding her of her old life in Castile when she would listen daily to the old priest muttering his ancient Latin in the small chapel when she realises that what she is listening to is a coronation of sorts and opening her eyes she views the strange sight in front of her. A large group of small, grey people surround the youth, she immediately recognises them from Spain as the Pygmaei from the dark country, but with such a difference, the people in front of her are half their size and their skin colour so strangely muted that they look as grey and as lined as the surrounding rock walls.

As she watches, two of the small grey people bring over a tunic and slip it over the youth's head, two more bring over a leather chest plate and hold it against his chest, whilst others scurry all around him and deftly fasten the leather straps.
She watches his bewildered face and realises that he has no idea what they are doing and why.

A dark cloak is brought over and swept over his shoulders and clasped to the left with a jewelled brooch as two more from behind fold the cloak back from his shoulders.

The Elder raises his hand from his head indicating he must rise and so he rises and stands tall as two more run over with a short sword and belt, they try to remove his belt with the many pouches hanging down and for the first time he growls quite decisively, "No."

They bow their heads to his command, but buckle the sword belt anyway below his own belt. The light from the two stars shine down on him and as he his lit from above, he reminds her of a young king warrior from an ancient time long forgotten.

She thinks back, and only such a short time ago to her sumptuous wedding to the King, the pomp and the splendour to suddenly leaving London the very next day with no warning, only a few of her people were allowed to accompany her, no courtiers were invited and the escort was made up with a group of rough soldiers, because the *King* wanted to celebrate his marriage by hunting.

She should have guessed then that her marriage was doomed.

As she stares at the youth, mesmerised by his physical appearance, a thought crosses her mind, why is it when she looks at him now that he conjures up painful memories of the King? But then she puts the thought out of her mind when another of the small people brings over a small, handheld object, bows and passes it to the Elder who turns, bowing low to the youth and hands it over to him.

He takes it, looks at it with confusion and then with suspicion. She cannot tell what it is, but she can see by his face that the object deeply affects him.

"But this is Sagar's Pendant of Office?"

The ancient Minor speaks out again in his flat, monotonous voice with Cannin staring down at him uneasily.

When the Elder finishes his sentence, all the Minors bow their heads again, but there is now such a chill silence that follows that she finds herself nervously calling out,

"He says that it is not Sagar's Pendant of Office but yours, it is your birthright."

At the sound of her voice they all spin around and stare so starkly at her that she finds herself blanching in fear with Cannin looking at her with deep suspicion.

"How is it that you understand their language?"

Quickly the Spaniel runs from the dark shadows and jumps back to her side and presses close, the atmosphere has become so charged with Cannin's agitation that he fears what will happen next.

"I understand because the language that I speak in my own country was derived from theirs."

"Ask them this then, where did they get the pendant from?"

But abruptly he looks up to the air hole, something has obviously caught his attention from outside, a second later the mare whinnies from above followed by the loud, beating wings of a large bird that swoops down and perches on the top rung of the ladder. It screeches so raucously, that she sits bolt upright in alarm and looking up recognises it by its strange apparatus as the falcon in her bed chamber.

She watches the youth cocking his head from side to side listening to the bird's calls when he abruptly hands the pendant over to the ancient Minor and calls over to her.

"We have to leave immediately."

His sense of urgency frightens her.

"Why has something happened?"

"My tribe are coming back earlier than they usually do and we cannot be caught by them."

Cannin whistles to the dog who immediately jumps from the bed and picking him up by the scruff of the neck, carries him under one arm and quickly climbs the ladder as the falcon flies up into the night when the ancient Minor walks solemnly over to her, takes her hand, pulling her gently up to find that she now has the Pendant of Office in her hand. She looks quickly at its gold, tubular shape engraved with strange markings, one end looking like the head of a snarling dog or wolf, and somehow she knows that it is as old as the hills.

"Avete vos." (fare you well) He says quietly.

"Avete vos." She replies and slips the pendant into the deep, inner pocket of her cloak. He moves back a few steps as Cannin quickly descends the ladder and frowns over at her.

"If you wish for me to still help you, climb up and wait for me above."

She bows to the Minors, climbs the ladder quickly, surprised at how suddenly she feels so well and clambering out at the top bends down to stroke the waiting Archie and then rising she strokes the old mare's nose and looks at the deep, dark forest surrounding her and wonders why God has led her on this strange path and closing her eyes she tries to suppress the hot tears of uncertainty.

Cannin bows his head to the Minors and in response they kneel down and lower their heads.

"I thank you for your kindness, I now know that many things have always been hidden from me for a reason and I must follow the path of my fate to find the answers and, perhaps that is for the best, for I have no pre conceived ideas or expectations of anything and no doubt my journey from here will be my penance for having been born half Dog Head and half Human, though through no fault of my own."

He knows they don't understand a word he is saying just as he couldn't understand what they were saying earlier, but he felt regardless it had to be said and by him.

He turns, climbs up the ladder and when he reaches the ground above, he picks Isabel up and seats her on the mare when he hears the Minors' voices crying out from below.

"Ave Imperator, ave Imperator, ave Imperator."

And even when they disappear into the trees heading to the north with the grunting, legion of wild boar, he can still their voices crying up from the bowels of the earth directly beneath him and he vows that if he ever returns they will be released from their dark world and live on the surface with him.

CHAPTER ELEVEN
The Dog Stars

Morgar lying on his back; opens his golden eyes to view the two Dog Stars still burning eerily in an almost pink dawn sky; he smiles up at them and quietly utters the words,

"Cannin may now be of age but before too soon we will celebrate his death."

The black Dog-wolves rise up from all around him, stretching and yawning happily at clearly his better state of mind; he kneels up, yawns and stretches in the same way, leaps to his feet and then growls out,

"Get out of my sight."

They quickly lope off and disappear into the foliage; he begins his way back to the camp, at first walking tall but after a few strides decides that it would be better to appear grief ridden and adopts a peculiar, half bent tottering run, and whimpering loudly, he too disappears into the dark foliage.

In the murky depths of the Deep Pool, the giant pike glides restlessly to and fro above the intriguing red collar strapped around the round rock lying in the debris at the bottom. Every now and again he dives down, sniffing the familiar scent of the boy that had long forgotten to visit him and wonders why he has sent this inedible offering to him.

Caution finally turns to frustration and he begins to nibble at the leather collar and then voraciously rips it from the rock as the deep water begins to thrum with the strange energy from the skull of *her.*

He hates it when she does this, only a few hours before she had filled him with such anger that he had leapt out of the water in a frenzy of passion.

He rapidly pushes the collar up to the surface with his nose, knowing that she wants it gone and with a giant switch of his tail he flicks it up and there it dangles from the old lichen branch that many years before the boy had looked down at him from.

The thrumming tension in the water immediately subsides, she is now happy but he is not, not one edible morsel has dropped in since yesterday, bar two dragonflies, his hunger is now insatiable and to take his mind from it, he again begins to broodingly circumnavigate his watery realm, eyes periodically rotating to the surface, watching darkly for any sign of movement from above.

The King lying on his high bed awakes from his drunken stupor with a terrible cry, the ghastly dream still prominent in his mind, of fleshless skeletal wolves with red eyes like fiery torches emerging upwards from the deep realms of hell, trotting, bleached boned towards him, brazenly, with no fear, to rip him to shreds and no matter how much he strikes out with his sword they continue to circle him and even now he can still see them lurking in the shadows of his mind.

"My Lord, has something upset you?"

"Oh God, how did you get in here, I don't remembering asking you?"He turns to stare at her, wide eyed with shock and then with such loathing that she nearly sobs out.

"I thought you wanted me to, do you not remember I helped you up here in the early hours?"

He turns his head away from her, sickened by his drunkenness and weakness to ever have allowed her to have even crossed the threshold of the door to his private chambers, let alone in his bed.

"You mock me, I would never ask you to join me in bed, why would I? Your younger sister perhaps, but not you, you're uglier than sin itself. Go and see if the Queen still lives."

She cries out.

"But my Lord, surely that is something that a servant should do? I am the eldest of the Ladies-in-waiting and should not be treated in such a way."

"You are the Queen's servant and nothing more, so get away from me; I detest the sight of you."

She clambers off the bed, wailing loudly and gathering her scattered clothing attempts fumblingly to put them on. He snarls at her in disgust and leaping from the bed he walks to the window, stares up to the pink sky and, for a second views the Dog stars strange presences above, wondering why he hadn't noticed them during the night of wild frivolity outside on the concourse and then, quite inexplicably, he suddenly feels such a blast of happiness at the sight of them that he decides to visit his old mare for the first time in years and completely stark naked turns and leaves the room with his two wolfhounds bounding in front.

Every servant on route averts their eyes, bowing as he passes, each one wishing to view his famous, battle scarred, muscular body, but know they can't be seen to do so, on pain of death. The two wolfhounds bound ahead, happily turning every now and again to bark loudly in their excitement at his good mood.

Two servants rapidly open the massive front doors, he doesn't even seem to notice as he steps out into the open and smiling broadly he lifts his arms to the sky and shouts out in a deep, booming voice,

"Welcome the dawn!" And padding down the long gravel drive, grinning widely, oblivious to the sharp stones hurting his bare feet, he passes the stable block and makes his way to the pasture, his eyes still transfixed by the two stars above.

He stops and stands quite motionless caught by the beauty of the scene in front, the two blazing stars set in a pink sky, while lower down the yellow haze of the sun creeps up over the jagged black panorama of the tree tops beyond, highlighting his long, fair, straggled hair and in turn, turning the high shroud of white mist covering the flat pasture to gold. And to him it is like heaven has come to rest on earth. The two wolfhounds begin excitedly barking, prompting a flock of Lapwings to rise up through the gold mist with blue, black, purple wings and as they swoop overhead he sees their strikingly white under bodies and hears their calls shrieking out, pee-wit, pee-wit, pee-wit reminding him so vividly of that dawn from many years before and he smiles at the memory.

The wolfhounds bark more sharply and it is only then that he notices the gate further down is wide open. The sun lifts higher, burning quickly through the mist and then he sees that the paddock is completely empty.

His happiness disappears, replaced with a pang of sadness, guilt and desolation that he had not often enough come to visit her, his most favourite of horses, and now because of his neglect she has left him.

The two dogs sniff excitedly by the open gate and then speed off with huge bounds away from the pasture into the deep meadow and then he knows precisely where the mare has gone.

He calls to the wolfhounds who streak back to his side and walking back, so deep in thought, that he doesn't even notice two of his men running down the gravel drive towards him until one of them shouts out,

"My Lord, the Queen has gone!"

He looks up as if startled and then collecting himself, growls out.

"I know, get Sir Clifford and Sir Stephen to join me in my chambers immediately."

He strides on, back to his now empty chambers and darts a look of disgust at the dishevelled bedclothes where that bitch, Lady-in-waiting had dared to enter his bed. He curses at his servants who follow after him into the chamber telling them to run far away or he will cut their heads from their bodies and dressing himself quickly, sits on the window seat ruminating on what has occurred.

The face of Isabel angrily looms in his mind and he hisses out loud.

"How she sickens me with her pernickety, finicky, feeble little movements, fluttering like some accursed little coat tit, so weak, so inconsequential and then aggravating me beyond reason with her reproachful, judging eyes, judging me, judging my men, the sanctimonious, little baggage of nothing, with no substance, no strength, her vile black clothing hiding, no doubt, a repulsive, skeletal form and now, on top of all her insults to my being, she has stolen my horse, and for that she will now truly die."

He quietens his violent diatribe when he hears footsteps approaching along the corridor until finally a knock at the door, and he barks out.

"In."

They both enter, shutting the door behind them and bow low, he sits casually on the window seat, one leg up, his booted heel resting on the window sill, seemingly absentmindedly staring out of the window at the fading stars in a now perfect blue sky. But as they both know him so well, they both know it is now when he is at his most dangerous.

"You both told me that the dog is dead so where exactly did you take it and kill it?"

The older man and the youth quickly exchange glances; this is not what they were expecting. There is a prolonged silence until finally.

"Sir Clifford?"

"We took it to the Unfathomable Forest, my Lord, with the belief that with its remoteness, you would never be bothered with it again."

He appears to take in the words, but still stares out of the window; the loaded silence in the room becomes so intense that both men look out to see what he seems so interested in and become as engrossed by the strange stars in the sky as he is, until finally he speaks out.

"And exactly how did you kill it?"

The youth eagerly cries out, anything to alter the King's dark mood.

"I wounded it my Lord with an arrow and then Clifford..."

The King now turns to stare at his nephew with such contempt at his lack of respect for his right hand man that he lowers his eyes and remembering the praise he had received from his accomplice in arms the previous dawn, he now lowers his tone.

"I beg pardon, my Lord, I mean Sir Clifford went to finish it off, but he didn't need to because a company of wolves dragged it off into the undergrowth."

The King turns his head and again looks out of the window.

"So Sir Clifford, tell me, do wolves eat collars generally?" They glance again at each other, wondering where this is all leading to.

"I think not my Lord; flesh is the only thing they are interested in."

"May you be right. I want ten men mounted and ready to leave at my command, in the meantime go to the Queen's chambers find something from the dog, hair would be ideal, and a personal garment from the Queen, some garment that would have been close to her skin..."And under his breath, he mutters, "God perish the thought of that and as long as I don't have to touch it."

He continues to look out of the window as they bow and leave, quietly shutting the door behind them and then he paces around the room his heart hammering in his chest, he is being forced, driven to see *her*, and pray God, he cries internally, that he will see Mahayla again.

CHAPTER TWELVE
The Pendant of Office

Morgar stumbling and whining, staggers through the trees, but so far his performance has not brought any of the females running to his aid from the encampment, not even his mother, and then he realises, of course, they would still be fast asleep and nothing would stir them out of their laziness until the dawn chorus begins.

He then considers perhaps a more dignified approach would be more appropriate; after all, he is now semi-officially the Elder.

He now walks in an upright stance but head bowed silently in grief, until nearing the encampment he hears to his surprise the low, muttering voices of the much earlier than usual returning males as they approach on the other side of the clearing. He crouches down behind the bracken, his heart thumping heavily with the thought of how he's going to pull off his acting debut convincingly, especially now that he sees their grim faces.

The nine females stir, three quickly clamber out, while the others fall out of the hammocks when they realise the males are all back much earlier than usual and that nothing is prepared. But Malita in her usual bad temper takes her time to clamber out until she too stands to attention.

"Where is the Elder?" Lonan growls.

Morgar bristles that the younger Dog Head is assuming the role of leader and more worryingly the other nineteen males, even the ones loyal to him and his mother seem to accept his position without question...but not for much longer, he growls inwardly.

As always, Malita as the eldest of the females; is their spokesperson.

"He hasn't returned here, why has something happened?" She asks this in her usual, bombastic way but Morgar notices her voice quavers slightly in fear, or is it perhaps in excitement?

"In the midst of the ritual, he just completely disappeared without saying a word, we have searched everywhere, there are no tracks, no clues at all to his whereabouts and all the creatures are silent and refuse to engage with us. Something has happened, something bad."

The females all look around nervously, there is indeed a strange atmosphere, all of them realising that the Blackbirds that usually begin the dawn chorus long before the other birds are strangely silent. None of them say it out loud, but the situation is almost identical to when Mahayla disappeared all those years ago. Lonan glares around the encampment.

"And why are you all on your own, where's Cannin and more importantly where's Morgar?"

"My beloved son," Malita cries out indignantly, "Was with us when we fell asleep at dusk and Cannin, well you all know what he's like, he's a law unto himself, I expect Morgar has only gone to find him."

Morgar realises this is now his cue to join them; he cannot leave it any longer and stumbling forward, tears streaming down his face he emerges through the trees, drops to his knees in front of them and bows his head.

The tribe stand silent and immobile staring at his mud splattered body, but not one comes over to help him, including his mother. He knew this was going to be hard, his mother's face so studiously impassive that he realises this is going to have to be the best performance that he has ever done. He begins to wrench more clumps of hair from his already sore head and howls convincingly in agony,

"The Elder has gone, gone, I couldn't stop him, I tried, I tried, so hard, but he wouldn't stop!"

He now whimpers inconsolably, such a heart wrenching sound that Malita rushes over, and not seen by the others, smiles happily at him for a second and then holds his wrists in a vice like grip to stop him wrenching out more hair.

"Stop my son, stop, what do you mean, where has the Elder gone?"

He sobs now.

"I caught...I caught Cannin at the Deep Pool with a Human female, he fled from me with her, just as the Elder suddenly appeared as if from nowhere. He told me to forget about Cannin, that he is a traitor to the Dog Heads and a traitor to him and he shouted out, let him join the Humans and good riddance and then he just walked over and waded into the treacherous mud."

He howls even more at this, prompting the females to join in with even more ghastly howls.

"Shut up!" Lonan shouts out, they all immediately quieten, "Continue Morgar, but this time without all the dramatics."

With an effort to keep his temper under control at Lonan's affront, he continues on in a low and pitiful voice.

108

"He said he could not bear the shame of Cannin's treachery and of his daughter's treachery any longer, and that he couldn't think of a more fitting place to end his life, he said...he said, that this is where it all began and this is where it all ends and then he thanked me for being with him in his final hour. I tried to pull him out, but he struggled violently, the sucking mud took hold, pulling him beneath..."

He lifts his arms to validate his words as they all stare at the caked on mud.

"But he screamed at me to leave him be, that it was his choice and that you would all understand."

He hangs his head as if completely drained of emotion. The females whimper quietly, but as Malita turns to face them all, she sees the majority of the males are sullen and hugely suspicious and the ones she thought she could rely on hang their heads down and will not meet her eyes.

"If the Elder chose that he wanted to die in the mud flats, near to where his daughter died, I, for one cannot blame him, I understand his sentiment and who are we to question his judgement or his final wishes? As we all know he only ever did what was right and correct, and lest we forget, it was his time anyway, so enough of this undignified whimpering, he would be ashamed of your behaviour."

The females immediately quieten; being completely terrified of her and Morgar.

"And as Cannin has obviously chosen to relinquish his position of being the next Elder by his treacherous acts against us and to join with the Human's and as my son is the only one amongst you that is of the next correct blood line, I vote he stands in as Elder, temporarily of course, until my husband can return from the North to take his position."

The look of horror on all their faces is a sight to behold and she has to try and suppress laughing outright, because there is nothing that any of them can do, not a thing. Morgar rises to his feet, still trying hard to appear distraught, when he is surprised that the ever silent Modin moves forward.

"But what of the Pendant of Office?"

Morgar stands completely still, but his heart pounding angrily in his chest, so nearly there, why hadn't he remembered the importance of the pendant? And then he realises the Elder had deliberately played him along and then another horrible thought comes him, what if the Elder had already given Cannin the pendant?

Lonan grins.

"Of course, Modin is correct, there has to be the Ritual of Passing Over, where an Elder physically hands over the Pendant of Office to the next Elder, which he too has to accept physically in his hand for the ceremony to be legal and there has to be a high born or royal blood line witness present. So I'm afraid, Morgar, you are the same as the rest of us, even with your high standing; you cannot lead us even temporarily."

"What does it matter about the pendant, some, ancient, archaic, folkloric symbol of what? We are leaderless until my husband can get here." Malita screams out in her fury. Morgar glares over at Lonan as angry as she.

How does he know all of this information about the ritual, he is of the low born? It is almost as if he had been tutored, and when he looks at their faces, he realises they had clearly

110

discussed it all before hand, no doubt on their way back from the far side and when they all nod their heads in agreement, even his so called allies, his suspicions are confirmed. Lonan grins even more.

"I'm afraid that the majority of Dog Head tribes on this island would not see it that way, as far as they are concerned, the Pendant of Office that was Sagar's, is the only and real symbol of the King. He may have chosen to call himself simply an Elder, but all the tribes know he was truly our King."

The females begin weeping at the remembrance of his modesty, his piousness, his kindness. Morgar walks forward in his frustration.

"But he wasn't wearing it, he was almost naked and weapon less, and if he chose to just simply called himself Elder, surely that shows that his pendant is simply that, the mark of an Elder, not of the King?"

Now Modin calls out again.

"Regardless, it is our law and it is to be passed onto Cannin with the usual ceremony, if he chooses not to accept it that is his right, or if he chooses to be the Elder or indeed the King, again it is his choice. Perhaps Sagar had it hidden secretly on his person, not wishing to hand it over to you Morgar? Clearly he was not in his right mind to do what he did, I suggest we exhume and search his body."

Morgar growls internally in anger, wishing Modin dead too, the stupid, interfering, fool, they will all see clearly where he had stabbed the Elder. He growls out in his fear.

"No Modin, it would be sacrilege to disturb him in such a way, how could you even consider such a dreadful act?"

He falls to his knees again.

"I could never witness such a thing, leave him, leave him where he lies!"

He weeps out loud, not with tears of remorse but at his failing, all his and his mother's dreams squashed to absolutely nothing because of his own greed and stupidity. Lonan nods his head.

"Morgar is right, it would be unseemly at this stage. I suggest we all sleep, we have run hard and fast during the dark hours and then we will find Cannin, not only to find out his version of events, because after all Morgar, we have only heard your words and as the animals are choosing not tell us what has actually happened says to us all there is more to this than you are actually saying. But we also need to find Cannin to see if he has by chance the Pendant of Office. And if he doesn't, well then we'll have to exhume the Elder's body, because then we will have no choice."

They all turn away, the males removing their weapons, Morgar considers to shout again of Cannin's treachery but realises then that there's little point when Malita walks over to him and places her hand lightly on his massive shoulder.

"Come my son, walk with me through the cool of the trees, you are overwrought... would any like to join us on this saddest of dawns, where our Elder has left us to fend for ourselves?"

Not one answers, but she had expected no response. He staggers up as both silently disappear into the dark shadows of the trees. They make their way to the scene of the crime; she has guessed what he has done and leads him to a fallen log where they sit companionably enough, looking through the dark of the trees to the Deep Pool beyond.

Morgar stares over at its glittering surface, hard and dry eyed, as she holds his giant hand tightly, not daring to say a word, aware that every tree, every bush hides a multitude of animal informers against them.

She rises and walks around the fallen oak until standing behind his giant form and begins to carefully undo each of his many long plaits, grimacing at the bloody, bald patches all over his scalp and spitting onto each accordingly, she re-plaits his hair gently.

Finally, she sits back next to him, a small branch in her hand and brushes the dry leaves off the sandy soil in front of their feet and then with the pointed end begins to make markings on the surface. He takes the stick off her with a growl, wipes the surface clean with a sweeping movement of his foot and responds with deep, ugly, scoring marks into the sandy soil with such viciousness and malice that she quickly takes the stick away from him, looking up and all around and then falls to her knees clawing away to hide the evidence of their correspondence that they had always done together.

She then sweeps the dead leaves of August back over the ground when they both hear in the way off distance the unexpected thundering sound of horsemen coming in their direction, as the Dog-Wolves watch silently from the shadows beyond.

CHAPTER THIRTEEN
Morgar's vengeance

Marques de Draq, peering out of the first floor window, bleary eyed with lack of sleep and too much wine after the revelling of only a few hours before, watches as the ten horsemen noisily ride up the long drive. The sharp, clicking of the horse hooves on the gravel, combined with the harsh sound of the various metal components of their tackle clinking and clanking together, jar his frazzled nerves to a point of agony and he wishes them all dead.

But as they approach he recognises Sir Clifford as the forefront soldier holding the reins of the King's impatient, chestnut stallion and guesses that the gathering is something to do with Isabel. They stop and wait outside the massive entrance doors as the King's horse continues to half rear and paw the ground aggressively.

He dresses rapidly, tearing down the flight of the stone stairs; two servants open the doors as he rushes out.

"Has something happened?" The King's men pay absolutely no attention to him; he runs to the stable block and points to his horse.

"Prepare it for me immediately." The youths' rapidly do as he asks, he mounts quickly and pushing his horse into a fast, clipped trot quickly makes his way to join the soldiers at the rear when the huge, entrance doors open again and the King marches down the five stone steps, his two wolfhounds trotting soberly at his side. He mounts quickly and whirling around on the rearing horse laughs wildly when he sees him.

"Marques de Draq, I do not remember asking you to join us, what is this outrage? But never you mind, join in, you can be a witness to me tracking down my errant wife and my errant horse that she has stolen without my permission and you can witness personally the lesson she will be taught for having disobeyed my royal person and then you may return to Europe and tell all of the royal courts of her behaviour, and I doubt there would be one that would disagree with my actions."

Marques de Draq bows his head low as the King spurs his horse on into a fast canter and he worries deeply about what will happen next.

They ride through meadows, the two dogs in front keenly following the old mare's scent; they pass alongside a field of golden wheat where four reapers pause momentarily, sickles raised and bow their heads to the King. They ride on until in the far distance, Marques de Draq sees the immense, dark forest in the distance. Not a word is said, but he has the distinct impression that the King is immensely and strangely happy, and he worries even more what he will do to Isabel when he finds her.

The King trots through to the small glade, his stallion frothing at the mouth from the hard ride, he dismounts with the two wolfhounds sniffing the ground remembering that they had been here the previous dawn but also remembering their fear.

"You will now all dismount, we will give the horses a chance to regain their breath and then we will lead them through the forest and from now on I want no sound, none at all."

He bends down to the nervous wolfhounds who fall onto their sides as he strokes them, whispering inaudible, soothing words into their ears until finally he picks up the reins of his horse and enters into the dark, silent forest with the two dogs loping in front, sniffing out the old Mare's path but periodically looking anxiously back at him.

Further on, they veer off to the right and bound ahead but the King whistles them back and continues on, for he cannot resist the overwhelming urge to see where he had last seen Mahayla all those years before and his heart quickens at the thought that pray to God, he may even see a glimpse of her and then after that they would double back and pick up the mare's scent as before.

Sir Clifford and Sir Stephen raise their eyebrows at each other, wondering why he is ignoring the path set by the two dogs; when a few yards on Sir Clifford realises that it was almost at this exact spot that the Spaniel had lain wounded the day before. The two wolfhounds with low growls pick up the scent of the Spaniel and something else that they clearly don't like and he knows exactly what that is, as the image of the youth with the strange eyes looms in his mind.

The King stoops down and picks up the discarded arrow, turns to grin back at them, drops it back to the ground and whistles the dogs' on.

Finally, through the trees they espy the glittering surface of the Deep Pool set centrally in a large, almost round clearing, the forest sitting marginally back but surrounding its contours with its dark gloominess. A massive, fallen oak tree, spread-eagled over from the far side stretches in their direction, yet diminishes to an inconsequential spread of thin, lichen covered twigs that hover over the pool's surface. From one of the twigs, the startlingly red sliver of something hangs, the colour so starkly incongruous with the dark, sombre surroundings that they all wonder what it is.

They say nothing however, but watch the King standing still in front of them; they watch him breathe in deeply as if relishing the aroma of the forest. The two wolf hounds stay hidden back in the bracken fearfully looking up at him as if they know something bad is about to happen and he doesn't. He turns to look at them all and upon his face he wears the happiest smile that they have ever seen and they all wonder if he had gone quite mad.

"We are here at the centre of my universe, the centre of all good thoughts..." And then quite unexpectedly his stallion begins to rear and cavort wildly. He has no choice but to mount and still grinning, he reins the stallion in sharply as the wolf hounds growl even more apprehensively.

He turns to face the pool again. A sudden warm breeze skims across the surface, creating soft rhythmic ripples, the tall grasses on the far side whistle as the reedy, high notes of a flute when the dangling red collar begins to swing gently and it is then that the King sees it and he grins widely.

Marques de Draq stands silently back, also recognising the Spaniel's collar and wonders how on earth it had ended up here and why does the King seems so interested in it?

The King pushes his ever prancing stallion forward and calls to the two wolfhounds, pointing over to the red collar, encouraging them to retrieve it; they nervously dance all around the prancing horse, trying to please him with their bounding enthusiasm, but now he shouts out angrily.

"Get it, you foolish hounds!"

They look at each other with nervous eyes and bound forward, the male stops abruptly but the smaller female tears off and wildly leap's forward trying to reach the pool of deep water that she knows that she will never reach and lands into the sucking mud and whimpers forlornly as she is sucked down. The King cries out in his dismay.

"What is this?"

He dismounts from the prancing horse, giving the reins to Sir Clifford and runs swiftly over to the fallen tree and runs along its length until slipping down he mounts it like a horse and stretching out when he nears the dog, grabs her collar and with all his strength battles to pull her up from the sucking mud, staring at her wild, frightened eyes, while all the time whispering down to her,

"Quiet now, quiet now."

Finally, finally he pulls her clear, and pulling her up, dripping with wet mud, sits her on his lap, holding her tightly as she licks his face, he laughs softly and then he sits quite still staring at the surface of the Deep Pool, totally ignoring the red collar that dangles just out of reach.

The strong vision of when he had last swum with Mahayla on that final dawn becomes as clear in his mind as the clear water in front of him and he sees her form slowly rising up from beneath the surface, her red, gold hair, her smile, but he is forced back to reality when the pool begins to bubble with a strange, energy force. The water increases in its turbulence and changes from clear to turbid as clouds of silt rise up from the pool's depths and he begins to feel a strange, thrumming force pounding in his chest,

118

"My Lord?"

The men all hear the tree creaking wildly with his and the dog's weight, but still he sits there as if entranced. Sir Clifford calls urgently again.

"My Lord, you must make your way back."

He then looks around at them, grins and begins pushing his way backwards on his rump, the dog clasped tightly in his arms, until looking down he sees where the shifting, wet mud ends and swinging his leg over the trunk, throws the dog onto solid ground and then leaps over himself. He strides back to them, the muddied wolfhound agitatedly shaking the wet mud from her body but not wishing to be left behind leaves the job half done and follows tail down at his heels.

"I have just witnessed the largest pike I have ever seen, eying me for his supper, would you believe? Thanks be to God that the dog didn't reach the pool, otherwise I fear it would have been a bloodbath if she had."

He points over at the collar.

"Now we will have to consider how to retrieve that...it's a pity we don't have a small boy in our company, for not one us will be able to reach it easily."

They all view the collar, trying to hide their puzzled expressions from the King, not entirely sure for what possible purpose he would want to retrieve it, when from within the silent forest the sharp clicking of wings makes them aware of a Peregrine Falcon sweeping out of the dark foliage at great speed. It flits over to the collar, grasps in its talons, flies over, drops it at the King's feet, sweeps away again and disappears back into the trees. The whole,

119

unbelievable performance had literally lasted for a few seconds only, but each one had clearly seen the bird's bizarre tackle.

Marques de Draq mutters out from the rear.

"This is surely witchcraft."

The King bends down and picks the collar up.

"No, it is not witchcraft, how dare you utter such a thing in my presence?" He turns abruptly, his men and horses part so the Marques stands alone and glaring over at him, he snarls out, "You are the most foul of creatures, your lips open and out pours forth the filth and bigotry from your dark soul. I know you, so beware, you are not in your country now but in mine and I will not tolerate such trouble evoking here."

Because he knows precisely who has sent the bird to his aid, he feels her spirit all around him, he wishes she would show herself, but perhaps she can't for fear of upsetting her tribe, no doubt she has a partner, no doubt she has young and he cries inwardly, "Mahayla."

"The importance of the collar, my Lord?"

Lord Clifford speaks quickly, seeing the wild passion in his eyes and dreading the consequences of many possible wars if the King were to kill the Spaniard outright as he continues to glare over at the ever increasingly, wilting Marques, who head down, mutters, "I meant, nothing my Lord, nothing at all"

"Good, from now on keep your filthy thoughts trapped within and may they increase in their corruptness and rot your innards...Sir Stephen, I owe you an apology, it appears you were correct about the collar."

His men visibly relax at his switch from unbridled anger to happiness. He shows them the front face with the empty sockets and then shows the other side of the collar, grinning widely where they again see nine, empty sockets.

"You see? In the front face were imbedded glass fakes, but imbedded in the inner face, such unimaginable wealth was hidden from my eyes, nine diamonds all cut from a large diamond called Le Diamante Azul."

He turns to glare again at the Marques.

"*Have* I pronounced its name correctly, Draq?"

Draq struggles to show no emotion, only shaking his bowed head miserably.

"Your pronunciation is exemplary, my Lord, but as I have told you before, I know nothing of any of this."

"We shall see. The diamonds that the clever Isabel had hidden within this collar rightly belong to me as her King and her husband, so we will track her down and retrieve them, and track her down we will and if I find that you Draq had any part in it, you will be as dead as she will ultimately be."

He hands the collar to Sir Clifford, takes the reins of his ever, excitable, stallion from him and quickly mounts to again calm the horse.

Sir Stephen looks up at him in concern, part of him is happy that he was correct about the collar but the other part of him is dreading a wild goose chase based solely on the King's suppositions, in this the most formidable of forests, swarming with wolves, wild boar and according to folklore, all manner of other weird and terrifying life forms, rightly called the Unfathomable Forest, for no one had ever attempted to penetrate deep into its depths nor had it ever been mapped.

"But my Lord, how do you know for sure she has the diamonds?"

The King looks down at him in utter scorn.

"Have I not just led you here and have I not just found the collar, and you dare to doubt me? I know she is within this forest riding on *my* horse and she has *my* diamonds so I will not hear any more of your stupid misgivings."

Sir Stephen bows low in submission.

Lord Clifford stands passively looking on, but inwardly dreading that the dog would appear on top of all the other strange events that have just occurred.

"Now let us lead the horses back the way we came and follow the trail that the dogs had picked up on back yonder." But the two dogs begin to growl apprehensively, his horse rears again, the other horses quiver with fear, all aware of the stench of some wild, unfamiliar creature that is silently approaching. The men look in the direction that the animals are staring wild eyed at, when from within the high bracken; an enormous figure silently emerges with the most hideous, bestial features they had ever seen.

They stare in revulsion at his enormous teeth laden, open grinning mouth, and then take in his huge, naked, muscle bound, mud splattered upper body, then his sheathed sword, his strange, embroidered, deerskin leggings and realise that this is a warring creature with incredible strength.

Out of all of them the King is the only one that appears not to be horrified or intimidated when he shouts to the dogs to stop their infernal growling and steadying the stallion, he calls out,

"What are you called, Dog Head?"

The Dog Head takes in his mud, splattered garments and grins insultingly at him as if they are comrades-in arms

"I am called Morgar, and your name Human?"

The King grins back down at him.

"I am commonly known as Edward." His men glance at each other, wondering why he does not say he is the King as Morgar cocks his head to one side, eying him slyly.

"Is there something I might help you with, are you lost, or are you perhaps searching for a young female of your kind riding a white mare?" The King continues to grin at him.

"You are very astute Morgar, do you know where she is?"

"Her exact whereabouts no, but she is within the forest and in the company of a dangerous, renegade Dog Head who we have since banished for helping her and from what I understand they are heading to the Northern Lands."

The King frowns as his stallion continues to dance small skittish steps as Morgar continues to grin up at him. His stallion suddenly whirls around again, wild eyed.

"Tell me Morgar, do you know a Mahayla?"

Morgar glares up at him with sharp, golden eyes as a sudden growing understanding fills his being and he now sees the undoubted resemblance between the Human and Cannin.

Cannin may have the bitch's eyes, but there is absolutely no doubt in his mind that the Human in front of him is his father. Not a vagrant as he had supposed but some sort of nobleman and he is filled with rage that not only does

123

Cannin have the royal blood of the Dog Heads coursing through him but he also has highborn blood. He struggles to control his high emotion and considers how he will answer, until finally,

"There was once a Mahayla, but she died many years before."
The stallion whirls around again, picking up instantly on the King's sudden distress and the bad, smelling creature's evil intent.

"Of what did she die?"
As he whirls back to face him, Morgar sees the expression on his face had completely altered, gone the smiling, bonhomie, good natured face replaced by a hard, chiselled look of anger or possibly distress, he finds it impossible to read his features accurately, but whatever, he now knows he is completely correct in his assumption.

"She died in childbirth, fourteen years ago of your time, she had broken our laws and coupled with a Human, no disrespect of course intended to all of you present," He grins horribly around at the standing soldiers who view him back with utter loathing, hands on swords wanting any command to slice him through as even Draq, stares at him with utter revulsion.

"She was always of a wanton nature, wandering alone through the forest, until consorting with...well you can imagine, no doubt with what you upstanding Humans would call a desperate, low life forms of your species. We had despaired of her for years and knew she would come to a bad end and ultimately she did."

The King, twirls around again on the ever, half rearing stallion. He feels it in his soul, he knows the vile creature is not lying, he knows that she is dead, feeling the utter and complete hatred from the Dog Head towards him, and knows that he had wanted her beyond anything, no doubt promised to him in betrothal and then he imagines the sort of life Mahayla would have had with this vile beast if she had lived.

"What of the child?"

"The boy child survived only for a few minutes after her death, we named him Mongrel, being neither one of us nor one of you."

The King hisses down softly as his men struggle to hear his words.

"Tell me Morgar, was Mahayla to be yours, before this vile specimen of humankind in front of you took away her maidenhood?"

Morgar, unable to control himself, growls deeply in his fury and in his jealousy, how has the Human guessed, how does he know?

"What does any of it matter anymore, she is dead and good riddance, shall I point to you where she died, shall I?"

He turns and points over to the left of the Deep Pool.

"Just over there at the foot of the fallen tree yonder and her son too, the creatures ate their flesh and took away their bones, which is the way it should be, hidden away, so none would ever know that they had ever existed."

The stallion is pulled sharply back and with perfect control it now lifts its legs in a high, prancing style and closes in on Morgar. He stands completely still, slightly taken aback at the changed behaviour of the horse, but then puts his hand to

125

the hilt of his gladius grinning now, relishing that this weak Sapien can do nothing against him, unbalanced with his anger, a full head shorter and no doubt half of his strength... the stallion twirls, dancing out of control again, but without warning, it leaps forward as the King's sword appears as if from nowhere and cleaves his giant head from his body in a vicious sweep. The head falls to the ground; the body continues to stand for a mere second and then crashes forward with a sickening thump.

The extreme, sudden and violent action shocks all alike and in that second, flocks of birds take to the sky from all the tree's around shrieking so wildly that the King's men look up in stunned awe when crashing through the bracken, a fat old female Dog Head pounds over with heavy feet and picking up the head of Morgar by his long plaits, kneels to the ground, cradling the head in her lap, howling and whining as the King, white faced with fury, bloodied sword still drawn, circles around, wanting, needing any excuse to kill her too.

In the dark of the forest, the Dog Heads, having been summoned by Cannin's bird, stand still in shock having witnessed the entire event when the King booms out,

"Silence."

The birds instantly cease their screeching of wild happiness that Morgar is dead, but all the Dog Heads know that their abrupt silence had not come from the order of the King but from the high pitched whistle of the Elder, completely indiscernible to the Humans' ears, but to them piercingly loud and in acquiescence to his high spiritual command, they religiously kneel with their heads bowed in silence.

126

The horses quieten and the two wolfhounds sit as if to attention, Malita continues to cradle Morgar's head but snarls over at the treacherous mud flats in her fury that even in his death, the Elder is still able to command all.

Marques De Draq touches his forehead, rapidly making the sign of the cross, believing now that the King is the incarnate devil, but his men look at him in reverence, knowing this is why he is the King, why they follow him and why they always will. All eyes are fixed upon him when he bellows out,

"I know you are listening to me Dog Heads, understand for my grace only that I have allowed you to remain in my forests, not one of you have ever been persecuted in my reign, I have allowed you to live your own lives in any manner that you choose, because of one, her name being... was...Mahayla."

He nearly chokes in grief at that moment, his head lowers, but then lifts he lifts his head again and shouts out violently.

"If I ever hear her name again been taken in vain, or hear vile, untrue accusations from any of you, I will burn this forest to the ground and every other forest in my realm and turn the land over to crops where you will work and toil, like the despised forms of Human low life that you appear to scorn so much, because I am the King of this land and the only reason you are allowed to exist is because of me, do you understand?" His voice thunders and echoes through the Unfathomable Forest as the water bubbles agitatedly in the Deep Pool.

In the dark of the forest, the Dog Heads remain bowed, totally understanding that their numbers are so paltry in comparison to the vast Human population, that to take on the might of the King of the Humans' would be utter suicide, and now with the shocking understanding that Cannin is his son they know then that his future is no longer anything to do with them. Morgar is dead and they know that Malita will now follow directly after him and so they stay kneeled, waiting silently when true to form she screams out in her fury.

"You have killed my son, my innocent son, you are no king, you are nothing but a murderer and an imposter and for that you will die."

"By whose hand, you foul creature, yours? I think not. You will now join your son so I'm wiped clean of your vile existence, but before I kill you, are there any others of your blood line existing so I may slaughter them all too?"

"My husband, my beloved, lives in the Northern Lands, I dare you, I beseech you, to take him on, but you will not kill him as easily as you did my son with your trickery."

He looks down at her, breathing in and out heavily with anger, but yet with a sardonic smile on his face,

"Ah, the Northern Lands, where it seems everything is running to."

She pays him no heed in her fury.

"My husband is the rightful king, we Dog Heads have the correct lineage, we are the ancient, indigenousness natives of this land, we have been here since the dawn of time, long before you Humans crawled out from the swamps as slithering worms."

She notices that he lowers his head, no longer looking at her, but turns and stares over at the Deep Pool instead and filled with triumph at his deflated anger, she screams even louder,

"You are not the King, you are nothing other than a filthy, disease ridden Human, full of vile unclean spawn, defiling a Dog Head female, so your vile offspring will spawn on and on, diluting our..."

The arrow speeds forwards, enters her left eye as she falls backwards into a great heap onto the ground. He turns to see Sir Clifford lower the bow,

"I apologise my Lord, but I feel she had said more than enough."

He turns back to stare stonily down at her dead body, her hand still clutching onto Morgar's plaits.

"You are right Sir Clifford, as always. I do feel suddenly so weary, now leave me all of you, I must have some time here alone."

His concerned men look over as he bows his head and sits so forlornly on the quiet stallion that they hesitate; he turns to look at them and seeing their distress for him, he smiles reassuringly.

"Go on, I will you meet you where the hounds turned, I will not be long."

They lead the horses away through the foliage, his two dogs stay sitting, watching him forlornly as he dismounts and leads the stallion over to the exposed roots of the fallen tree. He kneels down, kisses the soil and rising up he is drawn to gaze over at the now, still surface of the Deep Pool, tears running unchecked down his face when two white butterflies appear, wings touching, cavorting with each over the surface as for once the Pike lies deep beneath the water and leaves them be.

"I am so deeply sorry Mahayla, but know this; I will always cherish you beyond all others."

He takes the reins of his horse following in the direction that his men had taken, paying no heed to either Morgar or Malita's remains and when he approaches the dense forest, he looks back one final time, to the place where he had loved so passionately and swears he will never forget that this was where he had lain with her and that it was a place of light and happiness.

When he enters the trees, Elsu swoops down and lands on the fallen oak watching his retreating form, the Dog Heads slip away into the deep forest, while the pack of Dog-Wolves lying deep in the shadowy foliage creep forward fearfully but when they realise their former masters no longer breathe, they attack viciously.

CHAPTER FOURTEEN
The path of the wild boar

The wolfhounds eager to please the King now that he is leaving the terrible place of death and the frightening scent of the two dead Dog Heads, tear forward, quickly catching up with his men and again pick up the scent of the mare and dash forward like creatures possessed. His men wait for his approach and all are relieved when he smiles and utters the words,

"Let the hunt begin."

They lead the horses in the direction of the barking hounds until reaching another clearing, where they view the two dogs circling around in a frenzied, activity of action, chasing in one direction and then another, barking excitedly until it becomes clear they have no idea of the way forward. The King stares at the broken down foliage all around them.

"Wild boar and judging from the damage an enormous number. The dogs will never pick up the scent. I think it is best that we return to Elsygne to regroup. We know she is heading to the Northern Lands with the renegade Dog Head, of that I have no doubt, but instead of us trampling like fools through this wilderness, we will bypass all of this far quicker than she can make her way through, and then catch her at the other side where she will undoubtedly appear, because there is only one road to the north and there we will wait."

His men affected by the strangeness of all that had occurred, follow him in their relief as he leads his horse back to the small glade where they all eagerly mount the horses.

Marques de Draq, the last to mount, glares back one more time at the forest and curses under his breath at Isabel.

The wild boar, keep up their endless accompaniment as Cannin keeps up his light effortless trotting, on and on through the broken foliage they have created in front. Isabel astride the mare stares continuously at the back of his head wishing he might say something or give her some form of reassurance, but he says nothing, and she knows that he is not happy with her. Archie runs at his side, keeping up with the set pace quite happily and she feels a pang of jealousy that her dog totally ignores her.

The stench of the wild boar added with the constant, evacuation from their bowels makes her feel more and more nauseous. Her stomach aches and rumbles painfully with lack of food and water, the swarms of flies, wasps and horseflies that surround the boar and the old mare continually attack her and even though she is in the shade of the trees, she is unbearably hot in her heavy clothing.

The more she stares at Cannin the more she begins to loath him, even with his constant running, he appears not to have even broke into a sweat, whereas she can feel rivulets of sweat coursing down her inner legs and whilst the mare's back is so broad, her backside hurts her beyond anything, her inner thighs are chaffed red raw with the constant rubbing and now on top of everything else she needs to urinate.

"Please John, we need to stop, I have to... I need to go into the bushes."

He stops abruptly and walking back stares up at her coldly,

"Why do you call me John? My name is Cannin."

132

She shakes her head at him with a patronising smile, this is now her opportunity to repay him back for his lack of respect towards her and for ignoring her,

"The Pygmae said your first name is John, named so by your mother at your birth, so I presumed that is what you are called. As when I was born, my mother and father called me by my first name which is Isabel and so, needless to say that is the name that I am known by."

He glares up at her,

"My name is Cannin and that is what you will call me."

"No," She says, quite adamantly. "John is your first name and Cannin is your Cynocefaloi or Dog Head name, whatever they may be, I can't even bear to imagine. So I will call you John, as your mother did, because that of course would be completely correct."

Cannin is now even angrier that not only does she know all these things about him but that she dares to insult the Dog Heads. He also doesn't trust her, to hide her stones in the manner that she did says to him that she is of a deceitful and secretive nature.

"My mother was a Dog Head and I am half of one, so I warn you to be very careful."

She tries not to smile at his anger, she knows he wants to ask her more about the strange ritual in the hibernation cave and she guesses that it is one of the main reasons why he is so cold with her. If only he knew that he is now the King of the Dog Heads...obviously the ruler of some primitive, barbaric forest tribe, so she will keep his Pendant of Office hidden safely away until he does what he has been paid to do and then she will offer him the pendant back for the return of all her diamonds. She wasn't in her right mind when she gave them to him before, but now she is, and he will learn that she is of proper royal blood.

She grins at him in her cleverness; but to her surprise he grins back at her.

"If you want to go into the bushes so badly, go ahead, I don't even know why you would ask my permission?"

She nervously looks down at the wild boar that look back up at her, snorting irritably, they have a job to do, which is to escort the King to the northern reaches of the Unfathomable Forest and then to get on with the rutting of the sows and they do not want to be held up by this nuisance of a Human. She looks down at their hairy fat grey bodies and wicked yellow tusks.

"I'm scared to, I don't think they like me very much."

"Ah the truth at last. These friends of mine, that you are so frightened of, that have helped you all along could have killed you at any point if they had wanted to...so feel free to go, but one thing, within this forest you must dig a hole to piss and crappe in and when you have finished you must cover it over with soil, otherwise we will have every wolf in the forest chasing after us."

She finds his crudeness towards her completely shocking, never has she been spoken to in such a way.

Everything is at a standstill but she has no choice but to slip off the old mare, her bladder is full and fit to bursting when she feels even more alarming, dark rumblings coming from her guts.

"I am more than capable of sorting out my own toilette thank you...Archie, come." But to her consternation he stays at the youth's side.

"Dog, go with her and remember *Isabel* do what I have told you to do."

She glowers darkly at him as the boar part at her faltering path through them and when through she runs in her desperation and when she feels she is a safe distance away, lifts her skirts behind a wall of ferns. Archie sits nearby, looking anxiously back in the direction they had come from and she knows he would rather be with the youth. She hisses over at him.

"You are such a traitor, I came here to help you and all you want is to be with him."

She proceeds to pass such a vast amount of urine that she is mortified with embarrassment at the level of noise she's making and then the deep rumbling in her guts intensifies as her embarrassment reaches new proportions.

She calls out, "I do hope you're not listening, John?"

There is no answer; everything is silent, unbearably silent apart from the squelching noise from her guts.

Archie stares at her anxiously, she becomes more and more unnerved, maybe he has left her... but no, he can't have done, she has given him her diamonds for a safe passage through this forest, he had promised her.

"John, are you there?"

Rapidly pulling down her skirts, Archie accompanying her, she stumbles back to see that he'd disappeared with the old mare and the entire herd of boar.

135

"I can't believe that he would leave me like this." She very nearly sobs out.

She has no choice but to follow and picking up her skirts, tiptoes over the broken bracken, staring with abject fear at the dark, shadowy forest all around her, imagining the black wolves leaping out and ripping her to shreds.

She picks up her speed, Archie runs in front until finally she catches up with the rear guard. All of the boars have stopped with the mare standing quietly in the front but to find that Cannin had completely disappeared.

Her fear is insurmountable, she looks wildly round but then loud rustling comes from above and peering up, she catches sight of him so high up in the branches of a tall tree that she pales with fear that he would fall to his death and then what would become of her? A swarm of bees fly alarmingly all around his head, she watches him thrust his arm into a hole in the trunk until pulling out something in his hand, he wraps it in a leaf before slipping into one of his many pouches and agilely descends the tree. He pulls out the leaf package and bowing his head sarcastically, he offers it over to her.

"Break off a small piece."

She hesitates, he proffers it again and she shakes her head.

"You would refuse my gift?" He smiles at her so incredulously that she feels she has no choice but to take it, gingerly opening the leaf package until she reveals a section of honey comb.

Carefully snapping off a piece, eying him suspiciously all the time she hands it back to him and then checks the portion to check to see if any dead bees still lurk in the hexagonal pockets and when satisfied she can see nothing amiss, slips the broken section into her mouth and carefully sucks the sweet, viscous honey, completely convinced that she has never tasted anything quite so delicious. Mouth full, she smiles at him gratefully.

He nods his head curtly before turning away but as the honey comb dissipates she feels something hard in her mouth and spitting it out into her palm, see's to her utter shock that it's one of her diamonds.

"Why have you done this, I could have broken my teeth or worse, I could have choked on it or even swallowed it?"

He turns and grins, his mouth so full of honey comb that she grimaces at the disgusting sight and is even more disgusted when he speaks with the gluey substance muffling his speech and she prays that his teeth will rot in his mouth.

"I have only given back one of your stones to you for showing your gratitude in the acceptance of my gift of the honeycomb, that is all. And, you will be given another of your precious stones for every example of good behaviour you manage until we reach the end of the forest and then, I'm sure they will all be yours again, but whilst I am guiding you through, you will shut up, behave and do as I say, or no more stones."

He trots off again with Archie running at his side, the boar in front heave off sharply and in his wake, he whistles for the horse to stay waiting for her. She slips the diamond into the inner pocket of her cloak and stares after him, completely confused that he doesn't want her diamonds, but of course, an animal like him would have no idea of their worth and then she grins and whispers under her breath,

"More fool you John...Cannin, whatever your stupid name is, because you will now not be getting your Pendant of Office."

She takes the reins of the mare and follows behind but is forced to run as the mare picks up speed to keep up with Cannin's set pace. The rear boar periodically chase almost up to her heels but retreat when the mare lowers her head and clicks her teeth warningly or kicks out to keep them in check and each time Isabel looks at her with gratitude.

Never has she been so frightened or so humiliated in all her life and she finds that she hates Cannin even more than she did the King.

She runs on and on, mile after mile, watching his distant, fair head forever in front, never faltering, until she has had enough.

"Cannin... please stop, I cannot do anymore, please."
Abruptly everything stops. He makes his way back to her, the boar part like a tide with Archie, as always, running at his side.

"Fair enough, we have covered plenty of ground today and surprisingly you have done better than I had thought you were capable of, and hopefully we are many leagues in front of my tribe."

He reaches into his pouch and absentmindedly hands her another diamond, she slips it into the deep pocket of her cloak whilst he looks all around at the trees, the birds and animals are still worryingly silent towards him and he cannot understand why. Not one with give him any information and even Elsu has completely disappeared, no matter how many times he has called for her to appear.

He takes the reins of the mare, stroking her nose for a second and then turns into the deep forest.

"Where are we going now?"Isabel worriedly calls after him.

She now finds that she doesn't want to leave the beaten, safe road of the boar, no matter how stinking and strenuous.

"I'll show you, but no more shouting out, particularly from now on; the wolves will be stirring soon."

At his ominous words, she follows behind as he leads the mare through the bracken into the dark shadows of the trees, but before long, streams of diffused sunlight filter through the leaves above as the forest perceptibly thins. And then she hears the sound of rushing water, her thirst is now beyond anything, and through the trees, the most glorious sight of a fast moving river meets her eyes.

Two heavily whiskered otters, stare at their approach and quickly, hump backed, dive beneath the water and re-emerge on the opposite bank and slink off into the dank undergrowth.

The mare and Archie tear forward and drink great gulps from the river water and unable to control herself she runs forward and drinks the water in the same way, head down like an animal.

Cannin removes his cloak and belts, leaving them on the bank and wades in up to his neck. He gulps the water in great mouthfuls and then dives under. Turning over a rock he grabs a scurrying crayfish and rising up from the water throws it onto the bank.

He dives down again and again, until he has snatched up at least a dozen and with a final flourish, he dives down again and throws out an enormous, twisting Lamprey. He wades out of the river and whistles to the patient boar crowding in their huge numbers on the bank and with an enormous rush of excited grunts and shoves they leap into the shallows until the river is obliterated into a chaotic muddy mess.

Isabel sits back and removing her shoes dips her sore feet into the cool muddy water, regardless. The crayfish lie all around, clicking their small pincers, but she doesn't care, the glistening Lamprey twists and turns next to her, exposing it's open sucking mouth full of dagger teeth but she doesn't care, she doesn't even care when Cannin slices it's head off with the gladius, guts it quickly and doesn't care when he throws the innards to Archie.

Gone already are the days of her dog's special diet, of dainty tit bits from her plate and she doesn't even blanch when her dog, her special dog, devours the grotesque offal with great chomping, swallowing bites.

All she knows is that she is practically dead and even if the wolves appeared now and gulped her down in the same way, she wouldn't care.

She falls back on the grassy bank, feet still within the cool of the water and passes into a deep and utterly exhausted sleep while small ants, antennae raised, explore her tumbled hair.

CHAPTER FIFTEEN
The Dog-Wolves

The smell of smoke and something delicious cooking nearby wakes her finally; she opens her eyes to view the black silhouettes of trees reaching up to a dark, blue sky, like the colour of the deepest sea, dotted with millions and millions of white stars, she focuses in on the two lower, brightest of the stars, wondering at their intense light as she breathes in the cool, fragrant night air. Everything is so still, so peaceful and so entirely beautiful that she wonders dreamily that perhaps she is dead and this is heaven.

She raises her head, and resting on her elbows finds she is lying a few feet back from the rushing river, the mare stands over to her right, head lowered and she guesses she's asleep. Archie lays in a dead sleep directly next to her, she turns on her side and strokes him tenderly, realising that all that had been wrong with him all along had simply been that he was as frightened as her.

She turns her head to look back at the small, smoking pit behind her from where the delicious smell is coming from and beyond that the dark silhouette of Cannin standing upright, expertly stripping the bark from an almost straight branch that reaches to his chest. She watches him curiously cutting notch's in the top with the gladius and insert in a sharp pointed stone and strap it into position by lengths of sinew that appear as if from nowhere.

The shrill cry of some kind of animal erupts the silence from across the river and she shivers, the atmosphere immediately changes and she feels that something bad is about to happen especially when Archie sits bolt upright, growling deeply and the awakened mare snorts loudly.

A second later, Elsu flits through the trees, Cannin listens to the bird's low calls as she sweeps past before disappearing into the darkness. He quietly walks over to the smoking pit, spears out a charred leaf package and brings it over to Isabel.

"Food for you, and no, there are no diamonds hidden within this time, just beautifully cooked lamprey, it is a particular Dog Head delicacy and one which I know you will enjoy."

He pulls off the hot package from the spear and squats down next to her and unfolds the crisp leaves back, as she breathes in the beautiful aroma.

"It'll be cool enough to eat soon, but I want you to remain perfectly still, make no noise and keep staring at me even when I tell you that the black Dog-Wolves are across the river and are watching us."

She stares at him wide eyed in fear.

"They are planning a surprise attack, they know the boar are asleep in the forest behind us and so their intention is to swim over and grab what they can and in the first attack they are aiming for you, or if not that, then the dog as the weakest."

Silence for a second as she sits as still as stone but with her heart guiltily hammering in her chest and she prays he cannot hear, "How did they find us?"

"I think you know the answer to that, but it's not all your fault, they know the boar had helped us before, so they took a gamble and followed behind, sniffing around for evidence until they found it."

"I'm sorry."

"Never mind, it is done now. I want you to eat the Lamprey as if nothing is wrong, give some to the dog and help yourself to more if you're still hungry, but keep busy, stroke the mare, appear unconcerned but don't look across the river."

"But I thought you had scared them away before?"

"The boar did that, not I. I could stir them again, but the Dog-Wolves would just flee and we would always have them following us waiting for the first opportunity to attack. This time I must kill the alpha male outright which will buy us some time while they fight each other to see who will be the next leader and then, hopefully we will be out of the forest. If they were the grey wolves of the forest we would not be having this problem, but the black wolves are hybrids, part dog, part wolf and have been trained by Morgar to attack and kill Humans..

"Who is Morgar?"

She finds she hates the name already.

"Morgar *was* a Dog Head, Elsu has just told me the shocking news that he has been decapitated by a strange Human War Lord in the forest and his mother slaughtered by another of his entourage and so the black Dog-Wolves are on the rampage. All I can say that whoever this warrior is, he must be very powerful to have killed Morgar."

She swallows in her fear at his words; knowing intuitively that the warrior is the King. Cannin strokes Archie for a second and then stares back at her.

143

"I am going to disappear into the trees in a second, eat now and then bustle around, I want lots of activity to keep them focused on you, do you understand me?"

She looks fearfully into his blue, lit eyes and nods her head.

"What choice do I have, I have brought this on us, but I pray you will return?"

"If the spirits allow it."

He rises up, walks past the smoking pit and lies down in the dark shadows as if to sleep. She picks up the leaf package and begins distractedly eating the Lamprey, cold with such fear that she finds it impossible to eat. She throws it to Archie, who swallows it down in one huge gulp.

"Would you like some more Archie?" And standing up walks slowly over to the hot pit and bending down, her back to the river, sees that Cannin has gone, leaving behind his belts and for a fleeting second considers searching for her diamonds, but then she chastens her thoughts and finds herself trembling instead for his safety.

She picks up a small branch and one by one, levers out the hot leaf packages, horribly conscious that behind her and over the short expanse of the river are the Dog-Wolves and somewhere out there in the dark is Cannin and somewhere beyond that is the King.

She leaves Archie to rip apart and devour the Lamprey as she quietly walks over to the quivering mare, deliberately standing in front of her to take her vision away from looking across the river and stroking her nose, she whispers quietly,

"You beautiful horse, thank you for your kindness in helping me, and if I survive I will never forget it. Shall I gather some fern for you to eat, or perhaps I could strip some

144

bark from the trees or perhaps we could do it together? And amble slowly away from the water edge, away from the danger that surely is coming our way..."

The mare knows precisely what Isabel is doing and nuzzles her face gently, but she will not move, angrily conscious of the gathering across the water.

Further upstream Cannin slips into the depths of the cool river and near to the bottom he glides down on the current to where the black Dog-Wolves are gathered, to see the alpha male set off first, paddling furiously against the current completely unaware of the danger beneath him. Cannin raises the spear with both hands, his torch like eyes illuminating its underside and then he thrusts viciously upwards, straight into its belly and kills it outright.

The current pulls sharply and he has to use his entire strength to pull the speared Dog-Wolf through the water towards the bank. Above the surface he can see Isabel stroking the mare. Crouching down in the shallower water he pulls the spear free and quickly grabbing the loose scruff around its neck, rises up, and hauls its heavy head up onto the bank.

Isabel spins around and very nearly cries out at the sight, he grins at her as he clambers out and drags the dead creature by the scruff of its neck over to the smoking pit and then standing upright he growls savagely in the direction of the black Dog-Wolves across the water.

The cries they make are something that she will never forget, of rage, of fear and then of loss and when they have finally finished, Cannin howls the howl of the victor, up into the night sky and as she stares at him, she is more than frightened by his power but at the same time, never has she been so impressed by anybody before in her life.

The wild boar, awakened from their sleep gather silently in their hoards on the periphery of the forest looking on, the white mare rears up victoriously, while Archie sniffs nervously around the Dog-Wolf corpse... and then to Isabel's utter shock, the forest becomes alive with the calls and shrieks of birds and of animals and as she looks at him, she now knows that he is truly a king.

CHAPTER SIXTEEN
The Wild Horses of Lygan

Dawn breaks, Isabel sits comfortably astride the mare, Cannin having already neatly folded his cloak over her broad back. Archie sits quietly next to the mare as Cannin says good bye to the wild boar.

At their grunting insistence, he kneels, head bowed, eyes shut, as one by one they sniff his face intently and then back away and stand silently.

Isabel watches the bizarre performance when her attention is caught by the arrival of a turquoise winged, orange bellied bird that lands on a twig near to her. More and more silently arrive until the low branches are now so full that she looks at them curiously.

The last boar sniffs him and moves off as Cannin rises up, he had heard the Kingfishers arrive but didn't dare open his eyes in case he insulted the boar. He smiles, the favoured birds of the Elder, he has sent his birds in lieu of his physical presence to bid him farewell...he knew his grandfather would not forsake him and his heart soars with happiness that he is leaving the forest for the first time in his life with his blessing. The Kingfishers flit further back into the trees, waiting to accompany him out of the forest.

"Let's go Isabel."

She looks down at the black Dog-Wolf and shudders at its enormous size.

"What of the Dog-Wolf?"

He looks up at her.

"To the victorious, the spoils of war."

He doesn't tell her, that as the victor the Dog-Wolf it is his to devour but without the boar helping him he would never have got to this point and he knows they will be immensely grateful with his enormous gift.

As they head off into the trees, Isabel turns around to see the wild boar closing in and quickly presses her legs against the mare's sides to speed her on, finding that she hasn't the stomach to watch them devour it.

"How much further is it to the edge of the forest?"

"I'm guessing that we should be there by mid morning."

Cannin takes off, Archie at his side, the mare breaks into a high trot with Isabel astride her, desperate now to be out of the forest. The Kingfishers flit from branch to branch ahead and in spite of her fear she finds herself becoming more and more entranced by their beauty.

"What are these birds called that accompany us?"

"Kingfishers."

"A very apt name, that's what you should be called, you are the king, you fished for your prey and you caught it." And she adds quietly, "Please God, I pray, do not let that happen to me."

She feels inside her deep pocket and holds the Pendant of Office tightly in her hand, but how could she possibly expect this youth king of animals to help her against the King of England?

Cannin takes her words as a compliment and grinning runs on with the Kingfishers, glimpses of turquoise wings flitting ahead, he's never investigated the far northern reaches of the forest before and he's more than grateful to them for their kind accompaniment.

Finally the forest stops abruptly, Cannin crawls forward through the sparse foliage and views the great expanse of land ahead, dotted with small scattered dark copses of woods, so small that he considers how he will manage to keep under cover over the open land, until he fixates onto a much smaller minutely moving dark clump in the far distance. He pushes his vision on, a group of around thirty armed soldiers sit on restless horses, he turns his head from side to side, his hearing picking up on the clanking of the horses bridles, he pushing his vision on more, closing in on them to see the foremost tall figure astride a chestnut horse looking through a thin tube, scanning the forest and to his disbelief he sees he is holding a Star Gauge. He mutters under his breath,

"I wonder where he got that from?"

The Human pans the tube over to stare directly in his direction when the midday sun reflects off it with a blast of fierce light as Cannin eyes innocently refract the sun light back from the dark of the forest. The King immediately snatches the Star Gauge back from his eye, nearly blinded and blinking furiously, stares back in his direction with a look of sheer confusion and then with such a menacing, hard look on his face that Cannin retreats further back into the dark foliage.

It's obvious to him now that this cannot be none other than the War Lord and he must have helped himself to Morgar's Star Gauge as a war trophy after he slaughtered him.

And then it comes to him, now he understands why the Elder has sent the Kingfishers to help him; he wants him to leave the forest to seek out the Dog Head King to save them all from this terrible warrior. Isabel stirs restlessly beside him.

"What are you seeing Cannin, is it safe to leave the forest?"

"I think not, there are a group of thirty armed horsemen waiting."

"What are they waiting for?" But she knows as soon she utters the words that it's the King and his men waiting for her to emerge.

"I think to slaughter Dog Heads and as two have already being slaughtered, I think his intention is to slaughter more."

"Show me them, let me see."

"Keep low and crawl forward with me, but don't raise your head; he sees everything."

She crawls forward with him as he points in the far distance. She can see nothing other than flat land, but then something small and dark begins to come rapidly in their direction, closer and closer until she recognises the chestnut stallion of the King.

"Quickly Cannin, we must disappear as quickly as we can, I know him, he is the War Lord you spoke of earlier and he will destroy us."

Cannin looks at her suspiciously.

"How do you know him?"

She cannot lie to him,

"He is my husband and he wants me and Archie dead."

"Why, is it because you have stolen his stones?"

She cries out passionately,

"They are not his stones; they are mine as my birthright, passed on to me by my dead mother. He has everything else

150

of mine, why should he have them as well? He hates me, he drugged me and nearly killed me, he drugged Archie and then brought him here to be slaughtered and if it wasn't for you, my dog would be dead. I beg you; I implore you to please hide us."

The horse thunders closer and closer. Isabel grabs his arm in her panic.

"Please Cannin, he will kill us all."

Cannin removes her hand and turning his head, whistles deep and low back into the forest depths.

The chestnut stallion approaches fast until a few yards from the edge of the forest, the War Lord expertly reins it in as Cannin studies him with interest, he needs to see this warrior that has killed Morgar. The King looks quizzically at the perched Kingfishers boldly staring at him from the low branches, Isabel ducks her head down, shaking in fear as Archie creeps over and lays quivering at Cannin's side.

But Cannin is far more interested in studying the warrior. He takes in his long, fair, straggled hair, his hard yet youthful face, younger than he would have thought, possibly in the late twenties of life. He takes in his size, a good head smaller than Morgar, but powerfully built with wide shoulders and is more than impressed that this Human has managed to destroy Morgar, the largest and most ferocious of the southern Dog Heads. The King, totally aware that he is being scrutinised in minute detail, calls out loudly,

"Dog Head, I know you are in there with my wife and my horse that she has stolen from me. I have been told that you are now a renegade, having been banished by your tribe for helping her, but none of that is of any consequence to me, send them out and you may go in peace."

The mare whinnies at the recognition of his voice with the stallion whinnying excitedly back when he hears the voice of his mother.

The King smiles and whistles his special whistle for the mare to come, but she remains still apart from idly swishing her tail. He whistles again, but still there is no response.

Cannin rises up from the undergrowth as Isabel looks up at him in complete, stark fear.

"She doesn't want to come to you, she's angry at your neglect of her for so many years and wants to remain with me where she is in good company and has lots of exercise."

The King stares into the foliage but can see nothing, but the voice, he realises comes from a youth, a mere youth. He grins widely,

"I had forgotten you Dog Heads have power over animals so she will not come to me unless you tell her to do so."

"No, she is a free animal and chooses her own path. Ask her again, but this time ask her as if you really mean it, that you would love to see her again and you will ride her like you used to do."

The King's grin disappears, the rawness, the memory of Mahayla is still so prevalent in his mind that he falters in knowing how to respond. Cannin calls out again.

"Your reluctance tells me that you do not want her back, that she is too old and no longer of any importance to you."

The youthful voice pierces his soul and he frowns heavily; the Dog Head is correct, painfully correct. Fleeting, sharp memories of his horse come back to him, aged twelve years when she was first given to him, the breaking in of her, the endless hunts, her fearlessness... Mahayla... the many battles where she carried him victoriously...the births of his stallions and then he forgot her.

He stares starkly at the dark forest, he feels he is in competition with this unknown, faceless youth entity, he lowers his head, his emotions rising to the surface and whistles to her like he used to do, with his gladness to see her and then he hears her barging through the ferns towards him as she appears from the dark forest.

He grins at his supremacy over the youth and dismounts from the stallion as she trots over, greeting her son first, heads nuzzling each other and when done she turns her head and looks directly in his eyes and snorts gently. He strokes her nose and breathes into her nostrils.

"I am so sorry that I have neglected you, my most favourite of horses, I will make amends, I promise you."

All reason forgotten, everything forgotten, he speaks his words, meaning them entirely when in the distance he hears his men pounding forward on their horses, he furiously turns to see his nephew at the forefront, the mare snorts angrily and with a quick turn canters back into the forest and disappears. The chestnut stallion whinnies and for a second follows after her, the King quickly lunges forward, grabs the reins and mounts as Sir Stephen hastily pulls up a few yards back.

"I apologise my Lord, I had no intention of spooking her, I simply thought..."

"You thought what? You fool; I nearly, so nearly had her back with me." And then he stops, wondering at his extreme emotion and instantly collects himself at the startled look on his nephew's face and turning back to face the forest he bellows out,

"Enough now boy, send out my wife and the horse. I have no wish to spill anymore Dog Head blood unless I am forced to do so."

His men gather a short distance behind him as Cannin calls out again.

"But like your horse, your wife does not wish to be with you either, she says you have treated her cruelly and the only reason you are here is because you want her stones which her mother gave to her on her death bed."

The youth's accusatory voice is now becoming more than he can tolerate and particularly galling in front of his men.

"They are not her stones, they are mine, everything she possesses, including her body belong to me as her husband."

His voice increases in his fury. "Get out here now Isabel, I've had enough of this nonsense otherwise I shall come in and slaughter both you and the Dog Head regardless of your ages."

Marques de Draq calls softly from behind. "My Lord, may I, as the humblest of creatures be allowed to speak? Isabel is still a child, only just fourteen years of life, she has no experience of the world of men, she is highly religious, pious, she would never intentionally do anything wicked, she is frightened of you, that is all. If you forgive her for running away from you, she will come back to you and if

154

you show her an occasional amount of kindness she will be your obedient wife for evermore."

The King snarls around at him,

"What if I don't want her back, what if I kill her now and her accomplice, in fact, why am I listening to this claptrap from you Draq?"

He unsheathes his sword: the harsh grating sound to Isabel means only death. She raises herself and standing up calls loudly out but in a trembling voice,

"Wait my Lord, I will come, give me time enough to collect my possessions, only the shortest of time, I beseech you."

She holds her hand out to Cannin to say goodbye, but instead he unties the pouch and hands it over to her. She looks at him, her eyes now brimming with tears.

"Thank you Cannin for helping me, I'm sorry that I cannot pay you for all your help, but he will kill us both if I do not give him what he wants."

"The stones are of no interest to me, but I realise the dog cannot go with you on fear of death and the mare doesn't want to return to *him* either, so I will travel with the two of them, their good company is more than enough payment."

Thundering, crashing noises come from the deep, depths of the forest, she stares back,

"What's that noise?"

He grins at her.

"Probably just the wild boar chasing the sows."

She smiles fleetingly, Archie whimpers at her feet and bending down she clasps him tightly.

"Good bye Archie, always remember me."

155

Rising up, she walks over to the mare, strokes her soft muzzle and whispers softly,

"Thank you." And turning away, she walks through the ferns and emerges out into the bright sunshine. On the edge of the forest, she holds onto the stem of a young sapling for support, and in the other hand, she clutches tightly the pouch with the diamonds to her, her legs feeling so weak and shaky that she can barely stand when she sees how they all stare at her.

They gaze coldly at her wild appearance; her tangled black hair, her black velvet clothing smeared with filth, her drawn white face and her body quaking with fear as each one barely hides their contempt for her.

From within the forest Cannin studies their hostile faces, taking in each one in turn, heavy, ugly looking men until he recognises the thin, paltry youth that had nearly killed the dog with his arrow and then almost hidden away at the far back, he recognises the older soldier from before and the only one he notices that doesn't sneer at Isabel.

Isabel glances nervously at the King, he looks at her with derision, even Draq gives her an incriminating, hard stare as if she has done something vile and unclean and then she realises that is what they think of her, that she has sullied herself somehow and not from one of them, not one, is there any hint of kindness or welcome. She walks two steps forward, looks briefly back at the forest and then facing them all again walks one more step and then stops.

Marques de Draq, knowing her so well, watches her faltering strange behaviour.

"Come Isabel, come child." He quickly dismounts from his horse and leads it over.

"Let me help you to mount my horse, I will lead you back, never fear, you are in safe hands now."
She looks at him as if she doesn't know him and cries out harshly.

"Do not come any closer to me...as you are here, my Lord, on account of my stones and certainly not for my well being, allow me to check the *diamonds* in this pouch to make certain that they are all here and for your men to witness that I have not cheated you out of the last of my inheritance."

She shakily tips the diamonds into her hand, kisses them lightly and under her breath whispers, "Good bye."

Stretching out her palm to show them the glittering stones, she closes her hand, walks further forward and then throws them at the King with such unexpected force and passion that his stallion rears up in angry surprise, at the same time the Kingfishers take to the air in a noisy rush, startling the horses at the front causing them to whirl around and half rear.

She turns and runs faster than she has ever done before, straight back into the forest to find Cannin, Archie and the white mare still waiting for her. She smiles in her gratitude, Cannin lifts her up and grinning, places her on the waiting mare. He whistles low, when a heavy black stallion with the longest white mane and tail she has ever seen appears from the shadows and behind him, to her shock are at least another dozen more. Cannin quickly jumps astride the black stallion. "We have to ride hard and fast now, grip on tight and whatever you do Isabel, do not fall off."

They then both hear the King's thundering voice out in the open.

"Find them all, damn you, every single one... a pox on you Isabel, do not think this is the end of this, you are my wife, I will track you down and may God help you when I do."

Cannin twists the black stallion's white mane into a thick rope, holds tightly on with both hands and presses his legs against its sides, it leaps forward, Isabel follows swiftly behind on the mare with Archie tearing next to her with the wild horses thundering behind. The speed they go is utterly petrifying to Isabel, but grimly, determinedly she clings on, her legs clasped tightly against the mares' sides, following Cannin's wild horse crashing through the foliage, leaping decaying logs, on and on until in front, the wild river again. The black stallion leaps into the water, the mare leaps in behind, Isabel, clinging on, shrieks wildly, soaked completely through. Archie leaps in after, Cannin reaches down and pulls him up by the scruff of his neck and holds him tightly against his chest, the other horses crash in behind as all push forward against the turbulent current to the north as Isabel cries out,

"What are these horses? I have never seen any with such long white manes and such long white tails!"
Cannin calls back, happy at her elation.

"They are 'The Horses of the Bright River' or 'The Wild Horses of Lygan, named so after this river. Humans have persecuted them for centuries on account they cannot be tamed. This last herd are the ultimate in warring horses and understandably hate Humans with a passion and the only

158

reason they are helping me is because they fear the might of your husband."

"They would be right to be afraid; do you think he will follow us?"

"Not yet, otherwise I would have been told. The horses are taking us to the source of the river, he won't be able to track us through this water and then hopefully we will be so far ahead that he'll give up."

Isabel crosses her chest.

CHAPTER SEVENTEEN
The two diamonds

"How much longer do I have to wait for you imbeciles to find them? I have only the seven, there are two more."

"But we have searched everywhere...my Lord." Sir Stephen quickly adds in his frustration and as he and all the men inwardly curse Isabel.

Horses' hooves are re-scrutinised, huge men scramble around, heavy knees hurting, unaccustomed to bending like servants, the wolfhounds are again given Isabel's glove to sniff, shouted at to seek, but again head off in the direction of the forest following her trail until shouted at to return. All are disenchanted until finally the King glares around at Sir Clifford who, his head bent low, sits silently on his horse.

"What is this? That you sit so still on your mount like a toad on a rock, do you have dark singular thoughts that you keep from me?"

Sir Clifford raises his head slowly and looks directly in his eyes, "I wonder, my Lord, that you could ever accuse me of any wrongdoing?"

Marques de Draq standing aloof, having been ordered to remain completely still on pain of death, looks over at the normally silent Sir Clifford and is delighted at his bravery in crossing the King and is more than impressed with the menacing chill in his voice.

The King continues to scowl, until finally, "I apologise Sir Clifford, take no heed of my words. But what else can I do, what else, when there are two of my diamonds missing?"

"Perhaps my Lord, because the two you should be searching for are no longer here."

"Is this a play on words, what do you mean, are you saying that that my wife and the Dog Head renegade are more precious than my missing diamonds?"

"I simply mean my Lord, that Isabel must still have the two in her possession which your dogs have repeatedly tried to tell you, a dangerous situation for even with the two she could buy powerful allies."

"You mean the Northern Dog Heads. I do not fear Dog Heads and besides there are only a few tribes left. But I agree with you, I have no wish to ride towards the north, after all I have a kingdom to rule, lest I forget. Let us move quickly now before they get any further ahead."

He turns and stares back at the deep forest and pulling the Star Gauge from out of his boot looks through it and mutters to himself,

"And there she is, still watching me all the while, she will lead me to them, I know she has been sent to aid me."

He slides the Star Gauge back into his boot.

"Mount your horses and let us ride." Elsu immediately lifts up into to the air and takes off in a northerly direction with the King following behind.

CHAPTER EIGHTEEN
The source of the River Lygan

The River Lygan changes constantly in its snaking path northwards. At one section its breadth so wide, so deep and the current so powerful that the wild horses take to the shallows, but the further north they go the river gradually becomes narrower making Isabel stare worriedly through the trees on the banks, the short distance across the water reminding her of how close the black Dog-Wolves were the previous night. But the warm safe sun, reflecting off the dark rippled surface of the water, tells her they are far behind and asleep until dusk comes and by then they will be long gone.

They pass through miles of water meadows, where dragonflies frolic and swans glide by, unruffled by the fast moving herd of horses, through marshland where spotted Orchids grow profusely, until the river eventually becomes a stream, where to either side thick woodland of Alder and Willow grow simultaneously, full of motionless fallow deer that stare so curiously at Isabel that she smiles at their lack of fear of her.

Finally the shallow stream is barely three feet across. Cannin throws Archie down, leaps from the stallion and helps Isabel dismount as all the horses gulp thirstily from the water.

"Come and see the source of the River Lygan."

They walk a few yards on until they reach a small bubbling of clear water coming up from the ground.

"This is the source?" She says, almost disdainfully; she had always imagined the source of a river as a great rushing waterfall falling down from high mountains.

"I have never been here before myself but this is without question the source."And then he remembers verbatim the Elder's words from when he was very small.

"To drink from the source and once drunk, everything becomes as clear as the purity of the water itself and your life changes forever more and you cannot be what you once were."

Isabel stares down at the small eruption of bubbling water, somewhat awed by his solemn words.

"But it's so small, how does it become the wild river that we have travelled up on?"

"I was told the water pours down from the Ivinghoe Hills which we are on the lower reaches of, into a deep cavernous pool below ground until it bubbles up at this point and then it builds in its strength and force fed by smaller waterways along its route as it rushes downhill towards the plains and there it joins the River Thamius that leads to the Great Water."

Isabel stares at his young earnest face, he doesn't know that she herself had come across the Great Water, as he calls it, and had sailed up the Thamius in a vast ship and that all he knows and has ever known is the Unfathomable Forest and realises that this is the furthest point that he has ever been before and she pities him for his ignorance.

"The horses always come here in late August, the sun warms the river too much, so they come here to drink and to cool their blood, preparing for when the temperature drops shortly and winter comes. They will stay here for a few days and then return to the safer, southern depths of the forest where there are no Humans." And then he turns to look directly at her, "Or at least where there used to be no Humans, but who knows now?"

He looks back down at the source but with a faraway look on his face, prompting her to kneel down and pulling her hair to one side she drinks the bubbling, freezing water, his words resounding in her ears...*to drink from the source and once drunk, everything becomes as clear as the purity of the water itself and your life changes forever more and you cannot be what you once were.*

When done, she looks back up at Cannin, suddenly full of guilt at her greediness; she should have waited for him to drink, it is after all his first time to see the source to find that he still stares down at the bubbling water with Archie looking up at him with concerned eyes and again a flicker of anger courses through her at her dog's devotion to him.

"Are you not going to drink?"

"When you have had your fill." He answers quietly.

"But I've finished, I don't want anymore."

But inwardly he is afraid to drink from the source.

"Come Cannin, it's your turn, why do you hold back?"

And then seeing his reticence she wonders anxiously that perhaps she should not have drunk from it herself?

He turns his head back to the south, this is the final point, to drink from the source means there is no going back to his life that he has always known. He mutters outwardly but more to himself than to her as Archie continues to look up worriedly at him.

"I don't know, everything is changing too quickly, I can tell something bad has happened but none will tell me what it is, other than they all push me to leave to go to the north, why? I have asked them all repeatedly, they say it's because of the War Lord, that I must seek help, but I feel something else that they keep secretly from me."

Seeing the fear and uncertainty on his face she rises up and walks slowly over to him.

"Come Cannin, drink the water, if for no other reason than you are thirsty, you and I are the same, we have no kin as such, my father is still alive but barely and soon to die from his ancientness and he sent me here with no thoughts of my happiness to marry the War Lord who hated me from the moment he set his eyes on me. I do not want to live that life anymore, God has sent me to you and you to me, drink from the source and we will leave together."

Still he hesitates, a breeze picks up, blowing down from the hills carrying with it the charged motions of a great brewing storm. He shivers; the mare and the wild horses cease their drinking from the stream, lift their heads and sniff deeply in. He is full of foreboding until he hears the rapid whirring of many wings as the Kingfishers re appear in a great flock and land in all the trees around him.

He smiles, he is being given sanction by his grandfather and now without hesitating he kneels down at the source, palms cupped together and fills his closed hands and bowing his head as if in grace, he carefully sups the water and when he finishes, he whistles out a strange unmelodic tune. The Kingfishers abruptly take to the air with loud sharp calls and flit away through the trees and when they are lost from sight she notices his eyes are almost tearful at their departure.

Her guilt fills her soul at all the trouble she has brought to his life and before she can stop herself, she blurts out, "I have something I must tell you Cannin, it is bad and you will not be happy."

He turns to her.

"I know, you have kept the two stones but that is not a bad thing but a good thing. I go to seek the King of the Dog Heads, he is the same as me, half Human, half Dog Head, he will give me patronage and I'm sure with the gift of one of your two stones he will give you patronage too."

She is completely confused; but surely he is the King of the Dog Heads, she had witnessed his coronation? She feels for the Pendant of Office in her pocket, grasps it, deliberates in giving it to him, then she releases it and fumbles more frantically for the two diamonds and holds them tightly.

No, she will not tell him about the pendant, it and the two diamonds are her only bargaining tools; she will keep all in her possession until she sees what the future holds.

She blushes however, at her deviousness, but Cannin appears not to have noticed for at that moment he abruptly turns around at the sound of rapid, noisy clipping sound of wings coming through the trees as now Elsu appears and lands on a branch above.

"So there you are at last."

He listens to the bird's calls and frowns heavily.

"The War Lord is coming fast across land, somehow he knows the direction we're going in but how would he know that? I feel he is being helped by a powerful force to find us, something so powerful that it frightens me with its strength, we will have to leave immediately."

Isabel shivers at his words but notices immediately how the falcon studies her intently from its leafy perch as if judging her and she feels instinctively that the bird doesn't like her.

It screeches out again to Cannin and then takes off and disappears back in a southerly direction. Isabel finds herself being picked up by Cannin again and placed on the mare's back, he whistles low to the wild horses and sets off again in a light trot through the trees with Archie running at his side. The mare follows behind, the wild horses drink quickly again from the source and follow after. Cannin runs on contemplating the route forward when he realises they are all following, he waits until the black stallion trots up to him, whinnying loudly and then he smiles up at Isabel.

"It appears that The Wild horses of Lygan have decided they want an adventure and want to follow me and even if I refuse they will still follow, I never thought that I would be given such help, I am truly honoured."

"Perhaps because you deserve it, Cannin."

She smiles down at him, but as he turns away, her face darkens with envy, why do the animals and birds adore him so much? She has never had such reverence in her life, even her special dog that she has nurtured since a puppy mostly ignores her now.

And then she chastises herself, she has drunk from the pure source; surely her thoughts should be as pure now?

But what if these are her pure thoughts, unleashed, coming directly from the dark realms of her soul and she rapidly crosses her chest.

Cannin leaps astride the black stallion, reaches down, grabs Archie up by the scruff of the neck and holds him tightly to his chest. The great horse thunders off at high speed, followed by all, the late afternoon summer sky darkens above, purple bruised clouds mass together, the wind strengthens in force whipping through the trees in a frenzy of vehemence.

From out of the woods they ride and as far as the eye can see are great, rolling, grass covered hills, above them the gigantic dark cloud formation sits ominously, as vast and as tall as the highest mountain and with a terrible cracking noise it sends earthwards a great, striking artery of white lightning. The horses gallop even faster, another great streak of lightning close by and then another, the deep rumbling growl of thunder fills the air and then the heavy rain plummets down in enormous droplets.

Cannin has never felt so exhilarated and laughs wildly at the speed of the horses as they tear forward with nothing to hinder their path and for the first time in her life, Isabel too shrieks out with uncontrolled laughter at the stinging rain and her wet hair whipping her face painfully.

On a high ridge, the King and his men look down on the high drama they are witnessing, the gigantic cloud sending down its missiles of lightning and at the speeding herd of horses racing along. The grey rain falls in great torrents onto the valley but strangely all the higher ground including the high ridge they stand on is bathed in the late afternoon sun. The King calls out,

"The judgement of God, see how they are marked by his vengeance." All, and in particular, Marques de Draq, cross their chests avidly.

The King pulls out his Star Gauge and focuses on his white mare, stunned by her incredible speed and equally taken aback by the sight of a laughing Isabel confidently astride her and remarkably keeping her seat without a saddle. He had no idea she could ride so well and he frowns deeply with displeasure.

He stares next at the fair headed youth on the leading black stallion holding some kind of animal close against his chest, expertly controlling the horse by clutching onto its mane with one hand only and inwardly he begrudgingly admires his horsemanship. He glances quickly over the herd of black and chestnut horses galloping behind and only then does he smile.

The heavy rain stops as abruptly as it had started and panning back to the Renegade, he can clearly see now that the animal he holds is Isabel's wet bedraggled spaniel.
He passes the Star Gauge to Sir Clifford.

"Tell me what animal the Renegade clutches to him? Either my eyes deceive me or I have been deceived."

Sir Clifford focuses in on Cannin, somehow he knew it would be the youth with the strange eyes as he also somehow knew it would be the Spaniel tucked under his arm. He very nearly smiles openly at his superb horsemanship and with a struggle to remain impassive he passes the Star Gauge back to the King without comment.

"Any thoughts Sir Clifford, on how it is that the dog has strangely managed to survive?"

"I cannot say with any certainty how it is possible, my Lord."

The King turns then to his waiting men, all bemused by his smiling face.

"Behold the illusive wild horses of Lygan, never in my life did I think that I would be privileged to see one, let alone to see a herd of them. Glory at their speed and at their beauty... archer, kill the Renegade but on no account touch the horses and Sir Stephen, when the Renegade is killed, you will this time successively destroy the animal he holds."

Sir Clifford stares silently ahead and finds himself praying inwardly for divine intervention as the King adds,

"And archer, shoot the Renegade in the head, it is the only sure way to kill a Dog Head, for on any other part of the body they apparently have the most remarkable ability to self heal."

The archer, the King's most expert of marksmen, quickly raises his longbow and fixes his sights on the youth; still just within range and pulls back the taut hemp string, his eyes narrowed with deadly purpose.

High above the falcon hovers but not one notices, and not one notices when she suddenly drops from the heavens with the speed of a thunderbolt, abruptly rearing up in the archer's face, talons outstretched, screeching in fury just as the arrow is released. The falcon flits away, the arrow flies off course by a tangent, Cannin hears the falcon's shrill warning, hears the oncoming arrow, turns swiftly and watches with horrified eyes as it plummets into the neck of the wild horse behind Isabel.

The horses immediately pull up, Cannin throws Archie down and leaping from the stallion walks slowly over to the felled chestnut mare.

The King groans out loud, sickened to his stomach by the sight of the dying wild horse.

Sir Stephen quickly raises his bow and aims the arrow at the Spaniel following closely at the Renegade's heels when the King snarls out.

"Stop, give them quarter for a minute, damn you."

Isabel, with terrified eyes looks up at the King and his men on the high ridge, shaking with fear at the harsh brutality.

"Cannin, they are too close, please, please let us leave."

But he totally ignores her and kneels down at the side of the horse. The King's men watch him pull out the arrow from the neck of the horse, watch him bow his head as if in grief, the wild horses gather all around him and then he is lost from sight. Minutes pass, the soldiers restlessly await for a command from the King when the two wolfhounds begin to whine loudly.

Then they see the Renegade's head rise up, he has clearly mounted again and holding the Spaniel under one arm just as before. The white mare, Isabel astride, abruptly takes off at great speed, the wild horses gallop behind, when they all see the so called dying horse gallop away as fast as the others. The King cries out in his disbelief as Draq again crosses his chest and mutters quietly,

"What kind of kingdom is this? I am surrounded by evil, black forces and I wonder that my Lord allows it?"

The soldier closest to him takes in his words nervously and crosses his chest when the King mutters just as quietly, so that only Sir Clifford hears his words.

"How is that possible, how can it run like that?"And then he remembers to fourteen years back, remembering Mahayla's words to him.

"I am what is called a healer, there are only a few of us left out of all the Dog Head tribes and I am privileged that the gift has passed onto me but whilst I can help all animals, I unfortunately cannot help myself."

"Why, what ails you?"He had asked, in his love struck concerned voice.

"Nothing as yet."She had answered and laughed.

Now he understands why the Spaniel still lives and why the wild horse still lives and his anger boils within him, the Dog Head youth is undoubtedly a healer and now he has become more dangerous than ever before. He screams out,

"I want the head of the Renegade!"

The King's chestnut stallion leaps forward and charges in pursuit as his men follow after.

The herd of wild horses pound on, a good start ahead when on the horizon a double banded rainbow emerges, set against the blue black rain washed sky. Onwards the wild horses gallop, passing seemingly under the rainbow bridge, up the small rolling hill in front and then completely disappear from view. The King and his men force the horses on at relentless speed until reaching the tor of the hill, they stop and look down to the valley below, scanning the landscape until finally comes the realisation that the herd had completely and utterly disappeared.

The King pulls the Star Gauge from his boot, scanning the landscape even more minutely, he views in the far distance a dense black wood, but the herd could never have possibly reached it in the time they had. He turns to look at Sir Clifford but he, as always, looks passively onwards.

He focuses skywards on the hovering Peregrine Falcon above and contemplates ordering the archer to shoot it down, but then he wonders, what is this bird that helps him and then helps the Renegade? And then it comes to him...the Dog Head youth toys with him, plays with him, all are in his command...the falcon does his will, the animals do his will and so does the bitch Isabel...but to what end, why does he do this, surely he must realise who he is? And then he shouts out menacingly, "Do not think you can beat me boy, because none can."

And then he laughs out loud at the absurdity of it all, and laughs even more when he remembers the very real battles he has fought over the years, against vast armies, securing the realm to keep his people safe, to find himself chasing some lone wild youth and his greedy, spoilt wife and all for the sake of two diamonds. He notices that his men want to laugh with him but as they have no idea what it is that he finds so amusing, he quietens down and smiles.

"I apologise for my private mirth, let us camp here tonight, I am in the mood to sleep under the stars, something I have not done for a long time. In the early hours before the first bird call, I want you four." He points at each of his most trusted scouts.

"To track down the enemy, behead the Renegade, bring back my wife with the two diamonds and my horse, I don't care how long it takes you, or how you manage it, just do it and you will find that I will be more than generous in my gratitude towards you."

The four men grin happily at the honour and bow their heads to the King. He is renowned for his generosity and already they can visualise the great wealth and new titles he will bestow upon them.

"And then at dawn I will return to Elsynge because I have already invested far too much time in all this nonsense." Marques de Draq lowers his head, now what will become of him and more importantly of Isabel and the two diamonds?

CHAPTER NINETEEN
Death Valley

The archer heads out as the sun dips below the horizon, the valley already swathed in low lying mist when he espies a female roe deer in the distance and crawling through the long grass, he rises up like a spectre, kills it outright and drag's it back by its hind legs to the encampment.

A fire had already been lit in the midst of the valley, the flesh is prepared and as the humour rises at the strange events of the day, hidden brandy bottles are produced at the King's command, they laugh at his acceptance of the normally punishable crime as he joins in with them, drinking a toast to the recovery of the majority of the diamonds.

They laugh even more with their deep, bawdy voices when they hear the far away coughing bark of a male roe deer, wondering where the female he had chased for so many hours had disappeared to, so that even the King bellows with laughter at their crude allude to himself and Isabel.

The men continue to imitate the calls of the stag with even more wild shouts of laughter as the deer they mimic in a far copse now listens silently, taking in the smell of the burning flesh of his lost desire.

The narrow deep earth fissure, zigzagging like a lightning streak stretching from one side of the valley to the far side, that the King had entirely missed due to its sharp edges being blurred with low stunted overhanging bushes, conceals mid length in its dark depths the still forms of Cannin, Isabel, Archie, the white mare and the herd of wild horses.

175

Cannin climbs up the sheer bank of the fissure and from between the stunted bushes, he yanks a flowering yarrow out by its roots and jumping back down squeezes the juices from the dark, purple, roots onto a dock leaf and carefully dabs around the arrow wound on the chestnut mare's neck, whistling softly to calm her. The blood flows full and dark from the wound, his initial attempt at stopping the loss had been enough for her to escape but not nearly enough to save her and he realises more drastic action is needed.

The soothing anaesthetic of the yarrow roots immediately takes effect and the mare now stands quietly. Cannin reaches into his pouch, removing a long thin bone and carefully removing a fine white hair from her mane, threads it through a narrow slit and carefully stitches the gaping hole. As he stitches away his anger at the shooting of the chestnut mare infuriates him more and more and the insulting mimicry of the roe stag's calls fills him with such fury that the horses snort softly at him to calm.

Isabel, back leaning against the high, mud bank of the fissure, Cannin's cloak on top of her, stares up at the sky completely aware that she sits in wet mud and yet so utterly exhausted that she cannot move from her position.

"Cannin, I hate this tunnel, it stinks of rotting flesh and I'm still so cold, why do we stay here, surely we must be away?"

"We have to stay here or have you forgotten how ill the mare is? If only she had been given a little more time to recuperate, but we were not allowed that because of your husband, so I suggest Isabel that you rest whilst I tend to her."

He stares down at Archie with his blue lit eyes, the dog immediately runs over to her and lies on her lap, she strokes him softly as the extra warmth from his body sends her into a deep, dark sleep.

The banks of the fissure at low level, punctured with the tunnels of the burrowing inhabitants namely foxes, badgers, stoats and weasels are in awe of such a host of enormous herbivores and with the presence of an actual real Dog Head, never having known such a thing for such a long time, that they are scared to venture forth for their night hunting particularly when the wild horses click their teeth menacingly at them to remain hidden when they stick their noses out too far.

The fissure, or Death Valley, so called by all the animals, is avoided by all apart from the burrowing inhabitants and the occasional pack of migratory wolves that use it to travel secretly across the valley to the Black Woods at the far end.

Cannin takes in the stench of the decaying flesh deep within the burrows and almost smiles at what Isabel's reaction would be if only she knew. The thought makes him slightly happier, he waits for another few hours or more, whistling softly to the injured mare when the men's voices become quieter and he guesses now that most of them are slumbering.

He glances again at Isabel and is certain that she will not stir again until dawn; he removes his belts, hanging them from a slender, jutting out dead root of a tree long gone, removes a long, saw like bone from his instrument pouch, clenches it between his teeth and steals away into the darkness with the horses silently watching after him.

As he climbs quickly out of the fissure, two waiting weasels, intent on making mischief for this juvenile Dog Head accompany him for a short while, until he growls at them to disappear and continuing on, he runs light footed through the high mist and makes his way over in the direction of the faint glow of the dying fire.

Closer and closer, the tethered horses are away over on the other side of the encampment and apart from the occasional snort they stand quietly.

The Humans' inert forms, lying in varying sleep postures, heavily shrouded in their cloaks tells him they are all asleep. And then he sees what he has come for, the War Lord, semi sitting up with his head resting on a saddle but fast asleep, judging by his deep and regular breathing. At his bare feet, the two wolfhounds are stretched out happily on their sides and apart from the odd twitch and whimper they are also in a dead sleep, no doubt exhausted from their exertions during the day.

Cannin silently approaches and bending down next to the two dogs places either thumb on top of each of their skulls and presses down gently, staring keen eyed at the face of the War Lord watching for any change in his breathing. After a few seconds the dogs lie completely still as if dead. He stares at the naked throat of the Human and contemplates how easy it would be to cut his throat but he hesitates at the very simplicity of it.

He has to admit to that he grudgingly admires *him* for beheading Morgar, something that he could not have done in his wildest dreams and finds that no matter how angry he is that he cannot kill him.

Banished beyond the sleeping men like a pariah, Marques de Draq's sharp, black eyes glitter in the dying light of the fire at the vision of the crouching youth, praying that this sprite of the night is here as an assassin to kill the King but then he notices disappointedly that he appears to be weapon less.

He should really shout out but then as he stares at the close proximity between the two, he is suddenly struck by how uncannily similar they are, they could almost be related, they could almost in fact be father and son.

He exhales out at the shocking realisation.

Cannin immediately whips around and stares directly at the dark, slumped body of Draq who quickly shuts his eyes and lies as still as a corpse. Cannin, eyes narrowed, frowns but then turns back to the War Lord, inhaling deeply in, and then he grins at the sight of the standing leather boots next to his head.

Now he knows where the Star Gauge is hidden, he detects the merest trace of the hereditary uniqueness of a Dog Head and he wonders who the previous owner of it was? Certainly not Morgar as he had previously thought, but another and he is filled with the sense that it was one that he had known in the past, but who it could possibly be he cannot think.

Crawling over, he puts his hand into the left hand boot and triumphantly pulls out the Star Gauge; he studies the inscriptions and then looks confused just as the King slightly stirs making him leap off like a deer into the darkness. The two dogs immediately rise up, stretch and follow in his wake.

Marques de Draq, smiles his vulpine smile and closes his eyes and dreamily savours the visual information that has just been given to him alone and considers how he could use it to his advantage in the future.

Disappearing into the darkness, the two dogs flank Cannin as he races silently back to the fissure. He whistles for them to stay put at the edge and then leaping down the high bank he quietly bends over the sleeping Isabel and Archie.

"Isabel, wake up." She half opens her eyes and then shuts them again as the piercing light from his eyes pierces hers.

"Cannin, please leave me, I'm too tired."

"I need you to look at this and tell me what is written."

At the urgency of his words, she begrudgingly sits upright and looks at the Star Gauge lit by his eyes like a shining torch and stares at it suspiciously.

"What is that?"

He grins at her.

"A Star Gauge, taken from your husband, he will find that he will not be able to follow so easily from now on."

"What do you mean, you stole it from him, *you* were close to him? I cannot believe you were so stupid to put yourself, Archie and me in such deadly peril, he will track us all down even more now in his anger at its loss, it's bad enough I have kept the two diamonds but to take his war instrument means that we will all surely be dead by dawn!"

"Why do you call it his war instrument? It is simply a device Dog Heads use to study the stars to gauge the weather."

Isabel stares at him incredulously.

"It is *his* war instrument and it is said that is how he wins all his battles."

Now Cannin snarls so angrily at her that she shivers in fear at his fury.

"The Star Gauge or war instrument that you call it belong only to Dog Heads and as a Human he has no right to possess one, particularly if he uses it for warfare. Only the hierarchy of the tribes are allowed them and so he must have either stolen it or killed a Dog Head for it, that is why I took it from him, to find out, I could have slit his throat, but I did not, so tell me now what is written here?" He holds it out to her but his extreme anger scares her and she abruptly bows her head and remains silent. He stares at her furiously, Archie whimpers and the horses stir agitatedly and he realises he has frightened them all and with a softer voice he whispers to her.

"Come Isabel, there are some markings at the base that I don't recognise or understand, they are completely different from Dog Head symbolisation...tell me is it the War Lord's name that is written?"

Isabel hesitates, afraid to look; the last thing she wants is for Cannin to find out who her husband really is, he stares sharply at her with his piercing blue eyes.

"I ask you again, tell me what is written?"

Still she hesitates; he pulls out a dead root from the wall of the fissure.

"Why are you so afraid to look? Take this then and make the Human markings of his name in the wet mud, his first name." He doesn't know why but he knows that is what is written, and then he continues. "Come Isabel, you told me that my first name is John, and that yours is Isabel, now write his."

She takes the twig from him and writes slowly, hesitantly...
E d w a r d

All the while she writes in the mud, the light from his eyes pick up the milky rain water filling in the furrows, turning each letter into burning, white light and she shudders at every significant mark she makes. Cannin compares each mark and when she finishes, he sighs deeply.

She moves forward and stands next to him and reads not just *his* name, but at what is written in Latin afterwards and is completely shocked, her mind reeling with the implications of what it says. Cannin lowers his head.

"It is as I had thought, it is his name clearly written. I have done a very bad thing, it was a personal gift from a Dog Head to him, it is his, I will have angered the spirits by taking it and I must return it to him."

She stands silently, deliberating to tell him the rest when he half turns back and whistles and it is only then that she sees the King's two wolfhounds leaping down the steep bank and trotting towards them as Archie growls low and warningly.

"My God Cannin, you have brought them with you too, what have you done?"

"I was going to keep them with me to repay him for his cruelty, but they can be of use now and return the Star Gauge."

He walks over to the two wolf hounds and bending down hangs the Star Gauge from the male dog's neck, whistles low and when he finishes they immediately leap up and scramble out of the fissure and disappear.

He gathers his belts, straps them on and looks back along the fissure taking in the southerly air.

"Time to go Isabel, dawn is coming fast and so too are more of our enemies."

"What enemies?"

"The Dog-Wolves. I never thought they would leave the Unfathomable Forest, but they have, and are intent on vengeance."

She blanches in fear; he bodily lifts her onto the waiting white mare, leaps onto the black stallion, reaches down to grab Archie, clutches him to his chest, pushes his way through the herd and sets off at wild speed along the narrow, inset course of the fissure as they all follow behind. They clear the valley and then leaping up and out of the steep ravine they pass into the Black Woods.

Behind them and in their wake, the foxes, badgers, stoats and weasels poke their noses nervously from their burrows, sniff deeply in and rapidly retreat into the dark depths.

Further away in the Human's encampment, the King awakes with a terrible start, the horrible dream of the devil wolves still fills his mind and he looks wildly around to find that the usual reassuring presences of his two dogs are not there... he instinctively reaches over into his left boot to find the Star Gauge gone and snarling angrily he leaps up when he sees through the low mist his dogs running towards him, their breath sending out, intermittent small clouds of white vapour and he can tell they are strangely excited. He quickly pulls on his boots, unsheathes his sword and strides towards them.

"Where have you been?" He hisses angrily, the dogs immediately sit obediently, yet looking up at him with fearful, guilty eyes.

"What is this?" He bends down and with a jolt sees the Star Gauge dangling from the male dog's neck. He removes it, scowling heavily in the direction the dogs had come from and hangs it from around his neck.

"Show me."

The dogs take off as he runs swiftly and silently after them, his anger at the Renegade, because it can only have been him, fills him with such passion that all he can think of is to remove his head from his body as he did Morgar. In the distance the dogs stop, heads turning for him to hurry up, he approaches and then peers down through the stunted bushes to see the dark fissure below.

He breathes out, "So clever Renegade this is where you hide." And without another thought, he jumps down into the dark depths, crouching low with his sword held menacingly ready for action, but to find the space completely bereft of any living form as light begins to filter down from the oncoming dawn and he stands up in his disappointment that there are none to kill.

He studies the many unshod hoof prints of the herd of wild horses in the mud then he sees the odd distinctive shod print of his white mare, but any footprints of either the Renegade or Isabel had been trampled to nothing. But then he comes across his name inscribed in the wet mud, still just about discernible and he wonders at the significance of it? Why have they written his name, is it a message to him, perhaps a warning? For a second he is chilled to his soul, the black arts spring to his mind but then his temper rises in its vileness, with the realisation that the Renegade and Isabel childishly toy with him and he growls in his rage.

He calls for the two dog's to join him but they do nothing apart from whimper from above and then he senses there is something not quite right about the situation and with it comes the strongest feeling that he is about to be attacked.

As he stands there, his ears pick up a distinct drumming noise from the north of the fissure and coming rapidly towards him as the very ground trembles beneath his feet. The sound becomes louder and louder, the vibrations increase, he steadies himself, sword raised when from a rounded bend four of the wild horses gallop straight towards him. He lowers his sword and presses hard against the bank of the fissure to allow them to pass.

But the leading chestnut horse espies him and pulls to an abrupt stop only a few yards away and paws the ground angrily, her eyeballs flashing eclipses of pure white as the other three horses stand behind snorting furiously at his presence. He calls out quietly.

"Quiet now, quiet, I will not hurt you."

The mare tears forward unexpectedly at his words, teeth bared, but at the very last second pulls back, shrilling angrily like a horse in battle. He lowers his head at the onslaught, knowing never to stare in the eyes of an attacking creature when his eyes rest on the wound on her neck and he instantly realises that it is the wounded mare from the day before.

He is completely taken aback; the wound is so neatly stitched to be almost nonexistent. Never has he seen such skill, he had seen for himself the thick flow of dark, venous

185

blood gushing from her neck. He was amazed at the time that she had managed to run away but now to find her alive and well shocks him beyond anything he has seen before in his life.

The horse looks down at his lowered head, lowers hers and sniffs his hair deeply. A few seconds pass, he is aware that the other horses now stand quietly and then she presses her enormous forehead against his and pushes him back. A cold sweep of fear crosses him at her strength and he knows she is warning him to retreat or face death. But still he finds he cannot use his sword against her, no matter how hard pressed.

He holds his head against hers as she continually pushes him back as he desperately struggles to stand upright, never has this happened to him before, he is helpless against her will and then she stops abruptly.

He raises his head to look up at her, but she is staring wild eyed beyond him and he turns to see what she is looking at. Dozens of red burning eyes streak towards him from the shadowy depths of the fissure as his terrible dream of the wolves becomes frightening reality.

The oncoming wolves are as black as night and then he realises they are not pure wolves but half dog and by their stealthy fearless approach, he can tell they have been trained to attack and kill humans. They pause momentarily, taking in his scent and know that he is the slayer of Morgar, with hideous growls they creep forward and then he realises that their prey is *him*.

They come closer and closer; he half turns his head and to his surprise he finds the four horses instead of fleeing are preparing themselves to fight the Dog-Wolves and he wonders with a half, bemused smile why they would help him of all Humans? He spins back, crying out his terrible war cry and lifts his sword as they attack. The noises in the fissure echo for miles around, deep growling, tearing noises, yelping, howling and the attacking sound of the wild horses. His men awake in a fright, Sir Clifford seeing the King had gone, bellows out.

"To arms, to arms, follow me."

Swords drawn, they tear across the flat plain in the direction of the horrific noises, Marques de Draq gleefully running behind, when abruptly everything becomes silent and every one of his men fear the worst. They approach the edge of the fissure as Sir Clifford shouts down.

"My Lord?"

To his relief, he calls back up, breathing heavily but clearly unhurt.

"Saddle the horses and return here."

With the carnage done and arms bloodied, the King watches as the few remaining black canines retreat to the south, he turns to face the horses and has the strongest impression that the mare is pleased with him as she snorts defiantly at their retreating forms.

He approaches and lifting his hand she allows him to pass his bloodied hand down her head, and he feels more than honoured that she has allowed his touch. She takes in his scent again, snorts gently and turns abruptly with the other three horses. They thunder back from where they came, and he is in no doubt that they return to the Renegade and he is more than confused.

CHAPTER TWENTY
The Black Woods

Elsu sweeps down through the Black Woods, screeching for Cannin to stop. The horses break from a high gallop to a low trot until they stop beneath a dead twisted beech tree.

Archie leaps down, Cannin dismounts and following Elsu's directions carefully parts a great clump of ferns to reveal an air hole to another underground world of the Minors. He whistles up to Elsu, thanking her, when he hears quite distinctly from Death Valley the whining and growling from the attacking Dog-Wolves with the terrifying cry of the War Lord piercing the air, mingled with the battle cries of the wild horses and he wishes he was there, fighting his own battle. Isabel looks over at him, wide eyed in fear as the white mare and the wild horses stir agitatedly.

"My God, what is all that noise?"

Cannin half laughs.

"Your husband slaughters the black Dog-Wolves and strangely I thank him for it."

"You would thank him? He would never willingly help you or me."

"Nevertheless, he is in his ignorance, I can only think he has been caught in the crossfire, but it's good news because apart from him there is now one less enemy to hound us."

Isabel turns fearfully back in stark terror at the horrific noises and stares through the dark woods to see the light of dawn creep up in small glimpses through the trees and without help from Cannin she jumps down from the snorting white mare and rushes to his side in her fear.

Cannin kneels and whistles down into the air hole as Elsu screeches angrily for him to hurry up but no response comes from the darkness below.

"Please Cannin, let me." Isabel looks fearfully back again, hearing the tremendous sound of angry men and horses now coming in their direction. Cannin stands up and stares back to the south as Isabel pokes her head into the dark air hole and whispers down. All Cannin can hear is her soft whispering of their language and then he hears a deep, but quiet voice call up, as if questioningly. He strains his ears to understand the language but then all is silent, as unseen by Cannin she dips into the deep pocket of her cloak and dangles the Pendant of Office down.

A dim light is lit from below, she sees the dark, small figure tentatively climb the ladder, hand stretched upwards to briefly examine the pendant. The figure abruptly descends as she slips it back into her deep pocket. Silence, but not quite, she can hear faint whispering and then the cavern below is lit up more and the same deep voice whispers up to her. She whispers down her thanks and rising up she gleefully smiles.

"We are most welcome, especially you Cannin."

Cannin stares at her starkly.

"I don't understand, why especially me?"

Isabel smiles more.

"Because they've been waiting for you."

He still looks at her cautiously. She smiles even more reassuringly at him.

"Because of Elsu, of course."

He turns to look at where Elsu had perched to find yet again she had gone. But there is no time to understand why she disappears from him all the time now as they both hear the thundering horses coming closer. He takes Archie under his arm, whistles a low tune to the horses and descends the ladder as Isabel deftly follows behind.

The mare and the wild horses immediately gather together and gallop in a close herd towards the oncoming sound of the fast approaching Humans. They clear the Black Woods, joined by the waiting chestnut mare and the other three horses, abruptly turning like a flock of migrating birds and take off to the east in a blur of black, chestnut, with a hint of white and quickly disappear from view but not before the King see's through his Star Gauge that the horses are rider less.

He pulls his horse to a stop.

"Enough now, let them go, the horses are a ruse. Sir Clifford, how far away is the Earl of Warwick?"

"As the crow flies, I would guesstimate thirty three leagues, a two days hard ride, my Lord."

"Good, that is where we shall go now; you two will ride ahead to inform him that I arrive." He points at two of his men. He studies the rest of his men and then points at another two.

"You two will ride back to Elsynge Manor, the Queen's Ladies-in-waiting are to remain there and by my strictest command are to be treated with the utmost courtesy but on no account are they to leave nor are they allowed any visitors, any trouble, they are to be imprisoned immediately. From there, ride on to London and tell them that on a curious whim, I am in the mood to visit Warwick, but only for the shortest time..." He pauses and then grins.

"Tell them I think it is time that I show my face in the northern realms after all these years, lest they have forgotten me. And you four,"

He now points at the four scouts, "Will enter the woods the Renegade hide's in and make as much noise as you can, day in, day out. You will not find them, Dog Heads are masters of concealment, but it will be enough to unnerve the Renegade and flush the pair of them out of their hiding place and push them on to the north where I will wait for them. You will follow behind but at a distance and let me make myself clear, I now do not want them killed under any circumstances, this is simply a reconnaissance mission and that is all, I have other plans for the Renegade and my wife."

At the rear Marques de Draq sits on his horse quietly, contemplating on how to escape and to find Isabel, after all two diamonds are better than none but almost as if the King could access his inner thoughts, he adds,

"And you Marques de Draq will stay with me and from now on will be under close guard."

The King grins at his furious countenance.

"My Lord... you cannot do this to me, it is tantamount to war between our two countries, I am simply '*ambactia*' an ambassador of goodwill, I do not involve myself in politics, I am merely here as Isabel's representative and for no other reason."

"You are a tyrant, a sneak thief, a potential assassin and war monger, if you were none of these things you would have left by now and returned to Spain remarking to all of my wondrous and happy marriage to Isabel, but did not. You remained and so you are all the things I accuse you of.

191

Be grateful that I do not kill you instantly, because who would know if I did? I could say that you had simply died in a tragic horse riding accident. You have no friends here, no one at all and you only survive because I allow it and I can do whatever I like, because after all, I am the King."

Sir Clifford sitting further back on his horse, smiles for the first time in a very long time.

The King abruptly pushes his horse on and looking up sees the Peregrine Falcon arise up from the Black Woods, he smiles at her presence and rides northwards to Warwick with her leading the way. When they finally reach their destination, she rapidly flies back to the south and he knows who she returns to.

CHAPTER TWENTY ONE
The burning of the Black Woods

Three weeks pass, the King holds court in Warwick and every morning when he awakes, the very first thing he does is to train his Star Gauge on the skies waiting for the return of the Peregrine Falcon, waiting for her to lead him forth.

In the Black Woods, Isabel languidly lies in a sunken, rock pool as gushing warm water continuously pours in through a dark hole set below the waterline near to her and drains away in the far corner, disappearing through a grated hole at the bottom in the far corner. The pool having been hewn from the natural rock is yet of such design and of such device, the like that she has ever seen before and she is more than impressed.

Far above, through a small, round, air hole cut through the rock, she glimpses the outside world, watching as another wind torn bird is snagged away from her vision and smiles that she is down here and not in the harsh, smoke filled air above.

She sinks lower into the warm water, aware the small people keep the furnace below the pool constantly burning to please her constant demands but she knows if it wasn't for Cannin she would not be treated in such a way.

She smiles, such a heavenly place, the Pygmae here, or as Cannin constantly tells her off for all the time...the Minors, are so much more sophisticated than the ones in the Unfathomable Forest, such sumptuous clothes they have given her from their old masters from time forgotten, such wondrous cuisine, roasted duck, venison of such quality she

193

has never tasted the like and such attention to her well being, that it was just like being back in Castile, so much so that she could quite easily stay here forever. But then she glimpses Cannin's dark, brooding, form stride pass, with Archie at his side as always, and as always he glares through the opening to the warm pool with an angry face that builds everyday in his fury at her repose. An angry, trapped animal comes to mind and she's glad there's nothing he can do about it with the menacing presence of the four King's men camping in the woods above.

And then she calls after him as she does every morning.

"Cannin, please come join me."

She grins wickedly, knowing that he won't, he seems to find her nakedness beneath the water completely embarrassing and she giggles in her enjoyment of the power she has over him.

But then quite unexpectedly, Cannin turns back on his heel and marches into the cavern. She cries out in her shock,

"Cannin, what do you think you're doing?"

"We've come to join you."

Archie immediately leaps into the pool with a great splash, the water is turned quickly to filth, the three female Minor's rush over from their crouching down behind the rocks as Cannin sits on a rock ledge and pulls off his leggings. They quickly gather around him, unbuckling his leather chest plate and when removed he bows his head to thank them. They stand waiting whilst he removes his belts and taking them quickly; they lay them carefully on a rock shelf and retreat to hide again, to see what the king does next.

Cannin stands up, pulls off his tunic as Isabel automatically closes her eyes, inwardly fuming that he thinks he can take such liberties. He throws it to the ground and steps naked into the frothing water and sitting on a rock ledge beneath the water he begins to wash Archie and when finished he grins over at her.

"Isabel will you not wash me as I have just washed Archie?" She keeps her eyes shut in her fury.

"I do not wash dogs, that is the duty of servants and you have both tainted my water with your filth."

Her anger is beyond anything she has ever felt before in her life, these two filthy creatures bathing in the same water as her!

"You are just as filthy as us Isabel, we are all creatures of the earth and there is no difference between any of us."

She hears him slip deeper into the warm water and from the sounds she knows he washes his own body.

She wonders if he stares at her naked body beneath the water but clearly not, when again he splashes Archie with water. And then a prolonged silence ensues. She half opens her eyes to find him staring intently at her face.

"I have waited patiently Isabel for you to regain your strength, ready for the next part of the journey. I have to leave here immediately before hibernation starts otherwise I will not gain audience with the Dog Head King until the warmer months return. But as I can see you are clearly physically and in your mind not capable of continuing on I will leave you here with the Minor's, who as you have found will look after you well."

She snaps fearfully at him at this unexpected turn of events.

"I don't doubt that, they understand my commands, not yours, you can't even speak their language." But she worries, in only the last few days she detects the Minor's growing anger towards her and she knows it's because she angers Cannin.

He immediately rises from the water, she rapidly closes her eyes again and hears him clambering out of the pool as Archie leaps out directly behind and she finds herself splattered in droplets from his wagging tail. She hears Cannin pulling on his tunic, more rustling and guesses now that he's pulling on his leggings and then the rapid pattering of the Minors' small feet and then the sound of the leather chest plate being buckled back on.

"One last thing Isabel before I leave, these poor Humans burn their wood steadily beneath this pool for you, their winter allowance, in order to warm the water that you bathe in everyday and soon there will be none left. The creatures above have told me that the Dog Head tribe that used to supply them left many moons ago and I've found out the Minors gather for themselves at night. But they can't while your husband's men lurk above burning all the trees, I have to stop them before there is nothing left and the only way I can do that is to lure them away from here. When I do go, it would be a kindness on your part to help these people gather at night to pay for their generosity towards you."

Isabel opens her eyes as her fury builds up to find him fully dressed.

"You would leave me here as a servant to *them?* And no doubt you will take my dog from me too so I'm left here all alone."

"The dog can stay with you if that's what you want, because in all honesty it will be far easier for me to travel alone."

Archie begins to whimper forlornly when he realises Cannin is leaving and follows after him. But Cannin stops abruptly when the entire tribe of Minors enter into the cavern and drop on their knees, heads bowed all around him.

The cavern is full of their whispering voices; Isabel hears snatches of their dialogue... "The King has finally had enough... It is time he left... Should have gone long ago...She holds him back...We do not like her...She should go too...But she is bad news for him, she hides from him his Pendant of Office?...Why does she?...She means him ill will... Perhaps we should kill her?" At this point Isabel calls out from the rapidly cooling and rapidly diminishing pool, when she finally realises they have abandoned the furnace and the continuous pumping from below and crosses her arms over her naked breasts.

"Cannin, I apologise, please, I will come with you, please do not leave me here."

Cannin studies the small bowed heads below and whilst he cannot understand their language he totally understands that they want her gone and don't like her and want him to leave too but in an altogether kinder way. He turns and looks at her steadily and she finds herself quelling at his piercing stare, until finally, water all gone, he growls out,

"Alright you can come for the short distance, but if there is any more nonsense from now on I will return you to your husband because quite frankly after your behaviour here I don't know if I even like you and if it wasn't for your dog repeatedly ensuring me you're a good Human, I would leave you... but then," he laughs harshly. "I wouldn't wish you on these poor people either."

When he finishes his cold, measured dialogue towards her, the Minors rise up, heads still bowed but she can see quite clearly their happy, elated grins. Cannin points at her and the three females that had been her constant companions rush over to dry her as he leaves the cavern with the rest of the Minors.

All except for Archie who runs over to her with his tail curled between his legs in a high state of anxiety. She looks down at him tearfully,

"Thank you Archie, I knew you wouldn't abandon me." And crouching down, he allows her to hug him, both realising that strange and fearful events will now happen and they have no choice but to follow Cannin.

CHAPTER TWENTY TWO
Return to Fair Isle

Norway and the end of the summer months. The deep fiord lays seemingly dark and still, yet from beneath its surface strong undercurrents push out the ice floes from the melting glacier into the open sea, carrying off walruses and ringed seals on their frozen backs, including the three year old bear on his own small island of ice.

At first, he is unconcerned as he is pushed further out, being far more interested in voraciously chomping on a fish that a startled gull had dropped, but a strange chill wind picks up in force and he is pushed even further out, the tossing sea increases in its dark turbulence and when he looks again the land is so far away that it dawns on him it would be impossible for him to swim back. His alarm deepens even more when the walruses and seals on the nearby floes flop speedily back into the sea and he is left all alone and even the whirling Ivory Gulls above that hate his kind warn him to go back to land.

Within minutes, the chill Siberian wind becomes a freezing, violent force carrying with it the first snows. He cries for his mother, but the shrieking wind increases in its velocity and all she can hear from the land is the odd snatch of his voice until all is gone and she whine's pitifully after him to come back.

The ice floe that he stands on is battered by the vast wind with such violence that he lies down on his side terrified to move. The day passes, night comes but still there is no let up from the snow storm until finally a slight lull in the high wind at dawn allows him enough time to claw down to the blue ice below to find an incarcerated frozen deer, he scrapes lower and feeds on its frozen flesh as the falling snow continues to cover him in its vastness.

Days pass, his ice floe, stiffened and rigid with its thick, top layer of frozen snow pushes ever further to Fair Isle as he lays beneath in a dormant state until the muffled cries of gulls stir him from his comatose, the storm tears off to the Arctic, the sea calms and it is then he smells land.

He pushes his head out from the frozen snow, the stark vision of dark land with high cliffs meets his eyes, seabirds startled by his sudden appearance swoop down, shrieking with anger and he cowers down in the snow again, realising that the sight and smell of the land in front of him is all wrong and he is not where he should be.

Lomond, surrounded by his pack of whining dogs on the shore, watches the lone ice floe bobbing ever closer. He strips off his clothing, whistles to the dogs' to stay put and wades through the shallows until he comes to the edge of the rock shelf and then dives into the deep water below until he swims up and levers himself onto the ice floe. The dogs' sit silently, watching his every movement, desperate for his command to allow them to join him.

Kneeling down he sniffs the surface, taking in the scent of the strange creature but also the stench of the remains of the deer. He stares down in astonishment at the young, brown, hairy face and the small frightened eyes looking back up at him from the icy hole and he growls soothingly.

"The dark beast, the dark beast, beware, beware!" The shrieking birds continue to warn him, until he whistles out to them all to shut up.

He continues to growl soothingly, he cannot understand what the creature is; never having seen anything like it before in his sixteen years of life, but one thing he does know is that the creature is completely terrified.

He whistles to the Kittiwakes to go to his father on the western side of the isle where he knows he swims with a pod of newly arrived white whales and even though he had said that he mustn't be disturbed under any circumstances, the white whales being such timid creatures, he felt sure that this was a big enough event to warrant the intrusion. And continuing kneeling he begins to coerce the creature out until finally with a low growl the bear slowly pushes up through the snow and stands, eyes locked with his. Lomond crawls away to the edge of the ice floe, coaxing him to follow suit.

The bear follows behind and from his kneeling position Lomond dives into the sea and head emerging up and with more soothing growls the bear with a careful, slip into the sea, paddles behind him. The waiting dogs' on the shoreline whine horribly and then bark fearfully at the oncoming beast, but the bear never having met dogs before, pays them no heed, all he knows is that he must follow the comforting creature in front of him.

Lomond waits for the next rolling wave to throw him violently up onto the beach and leaping to his feet, he turns and continues to encourage the bear to him and he smiles to see how gamely it paddles, head up through the heavy waves.

And then, as always, the Wulver appears as if from nowhere and stands next to him. Instantly the dogs quieten, the bear stops paddling and looks up with terrified eyes and whimpers fearfully. The rolling tide pushes him forward, he tries to back paddle, he cries again until the Wulver whistles harshly to it, but still it cries out plaintively.

"A lone adventurer it seems, he has lost his mother, help him Lomond, push him up over the shelf."
Lomond dives immediately into the sea, but the bear watches the Wulver still, he knows this being is all powerful and senses the danger towards him.

The next great wave pulsates forward as Lomond beneath the water pushes up on the bear's rump from behind. Claws extended, the bear hooks onto the rock lip of the shelf and pulls itself up and out and then collapses on the stony beach in a great, bedraggled heap and lies as still as death in his abject fear of the Wulver.

The Wulver in turn looks down at the terrified bear, he knew; he had heard it on the winds from days before, that this would be the day his son would leave him, the reason why he had chosen to swim with the white whales on the western side to put off the inevitable and in the vain hope that he could ignore the howling of the wind spirits. He sighs as deeply as the oncoming tide, he had also promised Lomond's mother that he would allow him to go to the Scottish mainland to find his Human side when he was of age, he wishes now he had never agreed to it and with extreme difficulty he fights the urge to kill the bear in order to keep Lomond with him always and keep him in safety.

But as Lomond leaps from the sea and crouches down by the bear, the Wulver sadly registers the happiness and interest on his son's face, something he hadn't witnessed since his mother had died two years before.

"What is this creature father?"

The Wulver struggles to keep his emotions hidden.

"He is called a bear by the Humans', but one that is highly unusual. He is brown from the Nordic region but also crossed with white from the land of eternal light and is known as a Grolar and when older he will be a force to be reckoned with. Like yourself, there are none like either of you and for that reason he has been sent here by the wind spirits to be your companion."

But inwardly he questions why they have sent the bear to Lomond? And then it comes to him, it can only mean that he is in need of a strong ally on the mainland and that he will be in danger. He hesitates to continue.

"He is a flesh and vegetation eater like the dogs' but his appetite is far larger than theirs and even if I wanted to, I cannot allow him to stay here, there is not enough to feed him with and he will disrupt the careful balance that I maintain on this small isle."

Lomond looks up at him earnestly.

"So are you saying that I take him with me to go and see where my mother came from?"

"I am. The mountains are vast, remote and full of game; it will be a good place for him."

"You do know I shall return." But his eyes return to stare down at the bear, his face glowing with happiness.

203

"I know that, remember all I and your mother have taught you and if you find you have too many troubles on the mainland, remember I will always come to your aid." But even as he says the words, he knows that he won't, for every creature must face their own destiny, including his own son.

"I wouldn't ask you to father, this is my journey, after all I'm two years past being of age."

The Wulver bows his head in acquiescence.

Lomond dresses quickly and helps his father pull the reed covered boat to the waterline. Removing the reeds he finds to his shock the boat already filled with provisions, of sheep fleeces, dried fish, crawling crabs and sheep bladders full of spring water. And then he sees the shark's jaw bone studded with its rows of jagged teeth, his father's most prized possession. Lomond turns to look at him, suddenly filled with guilt and remorse in leaving him on his own.

"I thank you father for all of this."

"You do not have to thank me; it is for me to thank you for all the joy you have given me over the years."

The bear still lies as if dead when the Wulver crouches down and lifts his head in both hands and stares directly into its eyes. The bear begins to bawl and struggles to get away from his hands, but then it growls, teeth bared in an angry snarl. The Wulver releases his hands, the bear rises up, shakes itself aggressively and with one great leap jumps into the boat and growls back at him defiantly.

"The bear is ready now; he will be your talisman as you will be his, the winds are fortuitous, time for both of you to go."

Lomond quickly jumps into the boat, his father pushes it into the waves and diving beneath and with the force of his arms he pushes the boat through the tide and out into the open sea. Lomond takes up the oars and begins to row furiously and when he's far enough out, he lifts the sail and speedily cuts through the heavy waves to the south.

The bear noisily chomps on a crab as Lomond turns to look back to Fair Isle and realises he hadn't said goodbye properly to his father in his haste to leave, but then he thinks why should that really matter, after he's climbed his namesake he's coming back anyway and not just because of the promise that he had made to his mother but because he wants to.

Far beneath the boat, the Wulver follows it's dark shape and whispers as the current of the sea to all within his power that Lomond's voyage to Scotland would be safe and then he sadly returns to his hidden grotto and begins to count the enormous piles of different shells that represent every day of his son's life since he was born. But... what to do... what to do without either of them, why did he liaise with a Human, why did he? And he howls out in his loneliness and in his anger.

CHAPTER TWENTY THREE
The dark underworld

Night falls, Cannin climbs up the ladder and silently slips into the dark woods.

Isabel sits anxiously on the rock ledge of the sunken pool, Archie sits at her feet, both facing the group of silent Minors that stand as still as immoveable stone, guarding the way out of the bathing cavern. She wraps her wool cloak tighter around her body, without the burning furnace beneath the ground the temperature is unbearably low, so much so that she shivers uncontrollably particularly as a hard cold wind blows relentlessly downwards on her head. They had taken her cloak and her clothing she had arrived in with menaces hours before; she knows only to find the Pendant of Office, but did they think she would be so stupid that she would have left it where they could find it? Begrudgingly, only an hour ago they had returned her travel splattered clothing back to her, cleaned to such perfection that they could have been new, the only pleasurable event that had happened all day. How glad she is now to have shed the silk robes they had given her to be wearing again her own proper warm clothing.

How long she has sat, she has no idea and no matter how many times she asks to see Cannin she is met with the same cold, menacing silence, unnerving her to such a degree that she believes that at any second they will rush over and kill her, especially as she sees for the first time they wear belts with long daggers.

She stares up at the air hole, the sky is so dark and she guesses it must late evening, her stomach rumbles painfully with lack of food when suddenly, abruptly she is asked to stand and to follow behind. She immediately rises; her heart hammering in her chest, Archie rises with her and unconcernedly trots after them. She follows behind the group of silent Minors and led through the outer chamber, along a straight vaulted passage until they stop at the mouth of a black tunnel.

"Where is Cannin and where are you taking me?" She asks fearfully in their tongue, but again not one will answer her. They retreat the way they had come but are immediately replaced by another group of Minors that rudely push past her, the leading small figure holding just one burning torch, the ghastly flickering light exposing the dark underworld in front of her.

Isabel crosses her chest, firmly believing that is where she is being taken, but again Archie unconcernedly follows after the Minors, prompting her to quickly catch up with him as they pass into the freezing tunnel.

In the woods above, the four scouts sit a few yards away from the intense heat emanating from the burning, twisted beech tree, felled that morning directly above where Cannin and Isabel had first entered the Minor's underworld.

"The Mission my friends I feel is at an end, from south, to east, to west and to north, we have steadily burnt inwards and yet there is still no clue to where they hide."

"Maybe they've burnt to death. After all, there's nothing left of the animals, I thoroughly enjoyed the charred wolf yesterday, and we've got the last of the squirrels burning nicely, which reminds me, they should be more than done."

He jumps up and with his sword pokes it into the fiery roots of the remnants of the beech tree and stabbing into the blackened body of a squirrel, lobs it over to his comrades.

They laugh as more of the blackened missiles are lobbed over to them until one of them stupidly catches the burnt offering, dropping it immediately, his fingers burning when from the corner of his eye he catches a sharp flicker of white amongst the blackened trees. With narrowed eyes he turns to stare intently over but there is nothing to be seen. And then a sense of something being very wrong begins to inexplicably possess him.

He turns to his comrades.

"I'm beginning to think that we might have gone a bit too far with all of this, my Lord said to flush them out not to burn down the entire woods with everything in it and woe betide us all if they are dead."

"What's spooked you all of a sudden? Stop worrying, didn't my Lord say that we wouldn't find them and that Dog Heads are the masters of concealment? We've done the job we were asked to do, how else could we flush them out? And besides we've prepared the way for crops to be planted here, my Lord will be pleased."

"I am not so convinced."As again the scout catches the flicker of white out of the corner of his eye and drops his voice.

"Quiet now, I think something is approaching."

Abruptly the noise of beating wings of a large bird sweeps over them, startling them all, when they hear the cracking of twigs being broken underfoot by some heavy beast. They stiffen and stare over at the oncoming noise, but still they see nothing as the black smoke from the burning beech tree billows low, obscuring their view until the wind lifts again and then through the dark she appears shimmering like a white spectre. One of them whispers,

"My God, it is her, the King's horse. Quietly now, quietly." They sit as still as stone, eyes averted away from her as she tentatively approaches, picking her way slowly over towards them. They can sense there is something clearly wrong as one of them turns his head minutely in her direction and whispers softly.

"Looks like she's lame, I'm guessing the left back leg."
Their four horses tied further back, whinny softly at her approach, welcoming her, she lifts her head and snorts softly in response and approaches more. The four men can hardly control their excitement as one of them whispers,

"We may not have found the Dog Head or the Queen, but to bring to my Lord his most prized horse will be the ultimate coup."

Another whistles softly in the same manner he had heard the King often do to his precious horses and quietly standing he walks slowly forward with his hand outstretched. The mare hobbles closer still, but on gingerly sniffing the proffered hand she snaps her head away with a sudden angry twist and snorting wildly hobbles back into the shadowy trees. She faces them again, head down, her breath shuddering in and out and they realise she is completely exhausted.

"She'll come to us eventually; she's on her last legs. Slowly does it, we'll spread around her and then close in until there is nowhere she can run to." Another of the scouts' returns to the tied horses and picking up a halter creeps back over with it and without another word to each other, they creep off in different directions and slowly surround her. Their ring closes in ever more but each time they reach out to her she runs further away. Time after time, they are so close to almost touch her but each time she glowers at them with wild eyes and pulls away into the darkness.

 Until eventually one of them whispers out,

"Wait, there's something strange going on here, why is she so terrified of us? She knows at least the two of us, has known us for the last ten years, we're not strangers. I think she is warning of something, trying to lure us away to safety and have any of you noticed that each time she runs from us there's now nothing wrong with her back leg?"

And then in the distance the sudden screaming of their horses pierces the night air as the mare turns abruptly and crashes through the burned trees and vanishes into the darkness.

"Wolves, quickly, back to the horses." Another shouts out,

"But where's the fire, we can't possibly haven't gone so far that we can't see it."

On the brink of panic, they stumble in the dark direction of the screaming horses, swords drawn, but after a few yards they stop suddenly, when they realise they are surrounded by hundreds of glowing yellow eyes indicating the presences of all manner of beasts, from large, to medium and to small. They stand as stock still as the surrounding animals.

"Where have they come from? Form a crucifix, there is something unearthly about all of this."

They stand back to back, swords pointing in turn to the north, the east, the south and the west. Abruptly the horses cease screaming, complete silence ensues when they hear the sound of enormous beasts crashing through the blackened foliage towards them.

"What can they be? This is surely the work of the devil?" They begin to shake in avid fear as the crashing sounds come ever closer. Suddenly the golden eyes disappear as if in a blink of an eye but in their place they can just about see four enormous tall beasts as dense and as black as the darkest night and facing each of their swords head on. There is no sound; each of the scouts become more paranoid, wondering what these silent beings are, not a movement nor a breath commutes to them that they are living creatures until the frightening realisation comes that what they are facing are undoubtedly the dark creatures of hell. The oldest whispers hoarsely, his voice cracking with fear.

"Whatever we do, we must stand upright and keep to the form of the crucifix, swords drawn and never weaken until the dawn rises and the first bird calls, and pray to God we haven't driven them all away. If we falter, if we sway the dark beasts will take us down into the fiery bowels of the earth and there we will stay until the day of judgement."

They then stand rigidly, hour after hour, petrified with fear, staring at those dark servants of hell, swords still lifted, outstretched arms quivering with fatigue until the first dulcet song of one lone Blackbird begins, more join in, such a heavenly chorus that never in all of their memories was there a sound so sweet. The light raises more and to their utter and profound shock the standing beasts in front of them are none other than their four, sleeping horses.

They look to their left and only a few feet away the cold, burnt out remains of the beech tree lie in a great heap and it crosses their minds that how was it possible they hadn't seen the flames if they had been standing next to it all night and how was it possible that such a large fire could have died down so quickly to such coldness?

They look beyond to see the heap of horses' tackle lying in exactly the same position as they had left them a few hours before, including the dropped bridle which they believed had been left God knows where in their flight in the dark of the night.

The whole situation is so strange, so perplexing so utterly bewildering, as if that none of what had happened during the night had actually taken place. Their sense of disorientation is so overwhelming that for several minutes they stand in deep fear trying to make head or tail of it, until the most profound of their thinker's speaks,

"I fear we have been bewitched, taken to hell and brought back again, who knows how long we were down there, the fire up here being so cold, and what entity untied our horses to face us in such a way and why do they still sleep so soundlessly, with hardly a breath and no movement? They have been as bewitched as we have and I for one will not ride them again lest they take us back down to the fiery depths. We have been given a warning, a warning to mend our ways; Our Father has saved us as God fearing folk."

They all bow their heads and say amen.

"We will go back whence we came, back to the Western lands and back to our kin. My Lord engages with dangerous, evil forces and I for one want no more of it."

They all nod in agreement and leave the sleeping four horses, but with old routines not being so easy to shed, they march rapidly off in order of rank and head to the west.

Below, Isabel and Archie continue to follow the Minors through the tunnel, up sharp inclines and down dale where temperature range from freezing cold at the top of hills to so hot in the dales that she nearly faints with the heat. How many miles they had walked, she has no idea, her fear and anger having become parallel emotions when yet again a freezing drop of water lands on her head making her squeal out loud and she feels that she would have no hesitation in killing the missing Cannin if he appeared in front of her now. How could he have abandoned her and Archie like this? But more importantly and far more worryingly, what would happen to them both if he never reappeared?

The flaming torch finally splutters to nothing, as she knew it would, how many times had she warned them that it was about to happen? Sheer, utter darkness pervades but without any warning a crack of white light dazzles ahead as if a heavy curtain had been drawn at one side to allow the dawn in. A dark shape appears through the white light and she breathes deeply in.. Cannin, and silently she pray's to God for his return. Archie tears forward excitedly, Cannin immediately picks him up and holds him under one arm as the Minors gather all around and as she approaches she hears their excited, happy voices...

"You are our king, you are our salvation, you drove away our enemies, we will follow you always..."

But their voices stop abruptly when they see Cannin turn and smile warmly at her approach. She smiles shyly back, not believing herself how pleased she is to see him.

"Tell me Isabel, what words are they saying?"

She notices the Minors stare at her starkly and suspiciously.

In response, she lowers herself down and on bended knees, head bowed, she waits for a few seconds until all attention is fixed on her and raising her head, staring directly at Cannin she calls out in a loud, ringing voice,

"They say you are their king, their salvation, you drove away their enemies and will follow you always... as shall I!"

She lowers her head then until it touches the stone ground in complete supplication. All stare at her, the silence almost unbearable, she waits with bated breath, trying hard not to smile, she will show these small, childlike people that she rules, and there will be no more question of her handing over the Pendant of Office, Archie sniffs in Cannin's ear and he smiles wryly.

"Rise up Isabel, the so called king commands it, and with your recognition finally of my royal status, you are allowed to come with me to the Northern Lands, the only payment I ask for my royal patronage is for you to teach me the Minor's language, but..."

His face darkens, "All fun and games put aside, you will swear now that you will always be my loyal subject."

She remains reposed in supposed mockery as the Minors drop to their knees and bow with her, finally they grin, she has learnt her place.

But a dark fear fills her, how would Cannin know such words, she has never heard him speak like this before?

He sounds so much like the King, the same tonal quality, the choice of words so similarly put; so much so that she shudders and then she sees the letters inscribed on the Star Gauge reflect back in her mind... *EDWARD for you to see ultimately the golden treasure of our union. 'M'*

Head remaining low, she breathes in deeply, could *'M'* be Mahayla's initial, Cannin's own mother? Could it be she rides with the King's bastard but with also the King of the Dog Heads? But then she falters, such supposition, such supposition on her part? But what if it is true? She is the Queen of England, but the Queen of nothing, the King is out to destroy her, she has no choice but to stay with Cannin and if there were a choice between the King and Cannin? She knows who she would choose; he could be so potentially powerful...

She raises her head high; staring into his blue, lit eyes and exhales sharply out.

"I swear always my Lord that you will have my allegiance, no matter what happens in the future."

Cannin stares back at her with such dark emotion that she quenches at his look.

"Now repeat your words in their tongue and do it correctly so they will bear witness to what you say, and remember Isabel, I have no more time for deception and lies, you will always tell me the truth, everything from now on."

She unhesitatingly repeats the words in Latin and when she finishes the Minors leap to their feet and cry out to him in fevered passion,

"Ave Imperator!" Cannin's dark mood changes abruptly at their response and he smiles down at her.

"Rise my most loyal of all subjects. Isabel you are forgiven for your duplicitous behaviour from before, now we will start afresh, comrades in arms as we go to the north either to our peril or to our salvation."

He walks over and taking her hand pulls her to her feet. He smiles warmly at her, for a second she stares at his face and smiles back for she knows everything she had thought is true, there is no doubt in her mind now that Cannin is the King's son, for on his face he wears the smile that the King always gave to his trusted men, the special smile that he never gave to her.

But what can she do, to tell Cannin or not to tell him? But then she realises she has to have more proof, definite proof, intuition on her part is not enough, but where would she find it and to what end if she does?

Cannin bows to the Minors, with Isabel translating his words of thanks and gratitude.

She follows after him through the narrow, rock breach to the misty dawn outside where the white mare and the wild horses of Lygan graze peacefully on the dewy grass when she notices four black horses in amongst them all and one saddled and bridled.

"Where have those black horses come from?"

"They were with your husband's four men, but have decided they would rather join with us and ride freely to the north."

"But what of the four men?"

216

Her heart picks up in fear. The sharp image of Cannin dragging the dead black Dog-Wolf from the River Lygan fills her mind, could he, would he have slaughtered them? Part of her is repulsed and frightened by the thought but another part of her is thrilled, thrilled that Cannin would be capable of killing the King's elite men.

But as if he could read her thoughts he turns and looks at her gravely.

"I can tell that you question whether I have slaughtered them or not, but you need to understand Isabel that I am not like your husband, I only kill to eat, for when I die, all creatures will eat of me, that is the way but also, but more importantly it is against our laws to consume Human's. The four Human's of their own accord persuaded themselves that they no longer wish to follow your husband, that his way is of evil and decided to return to the West Country from where they once came."

"But what prompted them to do that, the... my husband commands such loyalty from his followers?"

"I cannot answer that, for who knows what dark thoughts lurk in the minds of your particular species of Humans?"
What did he mean by her species of Humans?

"Anyway, time for us to leave and for the horses of Lygan, I have decided that they must return to the Unfathomable Forest, already they have been far too exposed to the outer world in their kindness to me and any more exposure would be dangerous for them. The four black horses will accompany us from now on, the saddled horse is for you to ride so we may give the white mare a rest and we will swap accordingly giving each horse a rest until we reach the north."

He whistles to the horses, all heads rise as one, ears prick forward but only the horses of Lygan trot over as Cannin strokes each one in turn and then they turn and head quickly back to the south. Isabel mounts the black horse, pleased beyond anything that she now sits on a comfortable saddle. Cannin mounts another, they quickly ride away, the white mare and Archie running together at the front with the other two horses following behind them as they head to the north west with Elsu hovering above, but only after a few minutes of accompanying them she rapidly flies off to the north.

CHAPTER TWENTY FOUR
The Forest of Arden

The King rises at dawn and studies the skies for the return
of the falcon but again sees only the dark swirling clouds of
the gathering migrating birds.

Still time, thankfully, for him to execute the next part of his
strategy and rapidly dressing he quietly sends for Sir
Clifford.

He had been extremely busy in court matters, the people of
Warwick gathering in their droves, with petition after
petition and he treated all kindly and even with the most
preposterous of petitions, he listened attentively and passed
judgement wisely and fairly. The people of Warwick left
happy and all agreed that he is a fair and righteous King.

But in amongst of all of this, he had gathered the
information he wanted, namely of the whereabouts of Dog
Heads and had found out that in the deep Forest of Arden
only three furlongs away it was rumoured that there was a
tribe. On questioning further it appeared they hadn't be seen
for a long, long time but the King knew that they would all
say that, for to admit they had seen them, would be to admit
they had traded with them, no doubt trading with his deer
and wild boar and a hanging offence.

A quiet knock on the door and Sir Clifford enters alone and
shuts the door behind him.

"Time to go, I want the least amount of attention to us
riding out, pick only five men and no dogs. Any questions,
you will answer only that the King is in the mood for a short

excursion, a brief spell in the open air only in order to clear his thoughts."

The horses are brought and they slowly trot away, until when out of the sight of Warwick castle, the King suddenly spurs his horse into a furious gallop and within the shortest time they arrive at the edge of the Forest of Arden.

"Are you sure you must do this alone my Lord?"

Sir Clifford looks at him anxiously as the King dismounts from his horse.

"I am sure, it is the only way. All of you stay here but if I do not return by the time the sun reaches her highest height then you may come into the forest but by then I'll be dead anyway."

He laughs at the startled look on their faces and removing his weapons, lays them on the soft, mossy ground and disappears through the high ferns. Sir Clifford looks after him thoughtfully but worriedly as the five men dismount and sit cross legged to wait for his return.

"At long last some peace and quiet." The King mutters to himself as he wends his way into the depths of the silent forest and when he thinks he is deep enough in, he finds a mossy knoll and sits cross legged, arms resting on his legs and closes his eyes and begins to feel the pulsating of the forest all around him something that Mahayla had once taught him to do. And the more he thinks of Mahalya, the more he drifts away and even though she is long dead and gone, he calls to her inwardly and conjures up her image as he did at the Unfathomable Forest, rising up from the deep pool, her image, so powerful, unable to sleep at night, her face, her body...

A small breeze ruffles his hair from behind and then he is quite convinced he hears her whispering voice, sending him into a deeper trance but then he hears them above her whispering, the tiny movements of gathering wood ants, the tiny fluttering wings of wrens, the creaking of trees, other small creatures making their way over to him, the dry rasping movements of an adder.

The noises intensify; the forest becomes alive with their sounds. So entranced he becomes that he swears the trees cry out, the skies above cry out, such sounds, such a cacophony of rustling, rapid movements, birds' harshly beating wings, the screeching of a falcon, building to such a crescendo that he feels he ears will burst with the noise and blood would pour forth, he sways backwards, opens his eyes to catch a glimpse of the blue sky through the swaying dark foliage above, darkness again, when abruptly the noises stop, he pulls his head forward to find in front of him stand a large group of silent, sullen, Dog Head males.

He starkly pulls himself back to normality, noticing immediately their weapons of such unusual design and craft, the like he has never seen before, that he begins to think that he would have been wiser to have brought his sword, particularly when he sees that each of them are poised stiffly, erectly, like his dogs' before they are sent in for the kill.

But he cannot be seen to show any weakness and leaps to his feet, noticing with interest that not one flinches with any form of nervousness at his sudden movement, and then he surveys them all minutely, deliberately from his slightly raised vantage point. They stare back at him, golden eyed, until finally he speaks.

221

"You know who I am?"

"We know who you are."

Says one, but he cannot tell which of them had answered, their faces still set in the same, snarling way.

"I seek a renegade Dog Head in the company of a young female of my species riding a white mare." Still they stare at him, until long seconds pass and then a voice growls out.

"We know this."

"I was told by Morgar of the Unfathomable Forest that they ride to the Northern Lands and subsequently told that they seek out the King of the Dog Heads."

He pauses, staring at each again for a reaction, but this time there is no reply.

"This confuses and worries me because as you know I am the King of this land and there is no other. This country has enough enemies from over the great waters which you will know I have quelled in the past but what I cannot have is disharmony and enemies within my own realm."

Still there is no answer, he waits.

"Do I take it then that you support Morgar's father and that he is the King?" He finds his voice rising in anger.

"Luthias of whom you speak, is not our King and we have no wish to create disharmony, we keep ourselves to ourselves, have you ever known it to be any other way?"

He calms down immediately; finally the answer he had wanted, but still he cannot see which of them speaks.

"In truth, I have not, not in my life time and not in my father's life time before me."

"It is well remembered by us that your father was tolerant of our species in allowing us to remain free in the forests."

The same voice echoes over to him again.

"So you will have seen that I have followed in my father's footsteps?"

"For now, but we fear that oncoming circumstances will change your tolerance towards us."

"On my oath, as the rightful sovereign of this land I will not, regardless of any oncoming circumstance change my view. It is for this reason; I have had a treaty drawn up, a formal agreement to protect our alliance forever more."

They point their heads forward and sniff in deeply as if by doing so they can detect the truthfulness of his words. After a few seconds, they stop and stand erect, clearly now more relaxed when they part and through their midst a crouched, ancient Dog Head male approaches, so very old that the King wonders that he can still walk. He waits until the ancient being stands in front of him and reaching into the inner pocket of his cloak, produces a roll of parchment and offers it over but with a snarl it is irritably waved away.

"Not yet, not yet, there are other things you must know and then you will decide your path forward. So listen to my words now and listen carefully King of the realm."

The King narrows his eyes at the ancient being's affront to him.

"As you may know, we are an ancient race and are similar to Humans in many ways, but our life span has always been considerably longer than yours. You may die young but your rate of procreation far exceeds ours, already your numbers are ten thousand fold greater than all of our combined twelve tribes on this island. I mention this because sadly, our King, Sagar, after three hundred long years of ruling us wisely has just passed over to the other side and we know that there will never be another like him."

They all briefly bow their heads, the King does likewise.

"But for the entirety of his reign he simply called himself an Elder. That is what we wish for, to follow his wise doctrine, an Elder for each tribe and no other Dog Head hierarchy. He had a great love for your species and saw that for our survival we should live alongside each other in harmony. It is for this reason that we accept that you are our king and we wish for no other. But this is now where you, our king, must listen so carefully...the majority of the Dog Heads would be happy to form an alliance with you, providing namely that we can still be left in peace to continue in our role as the natural keepers of the forests...would this be part of the treaty?" The King replies immediately.

"Of course, the major part."

The ancient Dog Head stares deeply into his eyes.

"We have heard you are a great warrior and have done us the major service in the decapitation of Morgar, the son of Luthias, but Luthias will never agree to a treaty with you, particularly when he finds you have killed his son. He hates your species with a vengeance, the reason why Sagar banished him to the Northern Lands many moons before. Unfortunately, we have recently received intelligence that he has been amassing the malcontents, the bad strains of us and he now has a large following. He is dangerous, unpredictable and indulges in foul practises against our laws and yours. He is also an accomplished and formidable warrior and takes a perverse and abnormal delight in killing.

Already Cannin, the grandson of Sagar, or who you call the Renegade, rides towards him in his innocence, thinking Luthias will help him and give him sanctuary. He believes that Luthias is the true king but Cannin unbeknown to him, is the last of the true royal blood line of the Dog Heads. He has no idea of this and we cannot interfere in his quest for it was the very reason he was born and he must prove that he is fit to rule. But when Luthias knows who Cannin is, he will slaughter him, the only Dog Head alive that can, being of the next high born family and the next in line to be king." The ancient Dog Head pauses, the King stands still, his mind reeling with all the information he has been given.

"But if by some improbable chance Cannin does kill Luthias then by our laws we can obey only him and not you and you would have to negotiate directly with him as our king and it would be his decision and his alone to agree to a treaty or not. But this is all merely conjecture, Luthias will destroy Cannin, of that we are in no doubt, he is a mere child, parentless, a lost cause and we pity him for there is not one who can help him."

The King nods his head as if in sympathy, but the thought of the Renegade being slaughtered by what he imagines would be an even more monstrous and grotesque form of Morgar nearly makes him laugh out loud and he struggles to keep a straight face. The ancient Dog Head breaks into a horrible, yellow fanged grin.

"I see that you understand. When Luthias destroys Cannin as our true king, the last of the royal line of the Dog Heads, as far as we are all concerned you may kill Luthias in any way you choose, but you must destroy him for only then we will sign your treaty."

The ancient Dog Head turns as if to walk away, but then turns back, looks beyond him briefly with a quick flicker of his eyes and then looks back up at him again.

"One last item, if anything were to befall Cannin and he dies before he meets Luthias, we will join with Luthias as our new king and no treaty will ever be signed, then the bloodshed against your species will begin, something we have never done before and something we have no wish for. A dangerous prospect for you, for already the wind spirits whisper of the re-emergence of the Black Death, perilous as you know to you as a species, but not to us, we are completely impervious to it.

So think carefully about what you do next, your very realm depends on it and one day you may also have to depend on us against your enemies from across the Great Water for even now there is one in your midst that plots against you. We of the tribe Sagittarii have spoken and have been elected to speak for the other eleven tribes; we shall wait expectantly for your success."

They turn away and within seconds dissolve into the ferns, the King stands watching and when the last disappears, he sighs deeply and sits back down again on the mossy knoll, contemplating the situation when he hears a slight rustle above and to his surprise there is the falcon, yellow talons clinging tightly to a thin branch directly over his head so close that he could literally stretch up his hand and touch her. He is strangely gladdened by her appearance and gently whispers up to her,

"My friend... or are you?" He stares at her unusual tackle, the rodent's skull delicately dangling from the cross strapping on her chest, and then he notices how finely stitched the edges of the leather are, as skilfully executed as any of his royal seamstresses are capable of and he knows it is the work of the Renegade or now that he knows his name - Cannin.

He frowns - what kind of youth is it that spends his time executing the needlework of womenfolk? He must be weak, effete but yet, he reminds himself, with that same sewing skill he brought a wounded horse back to life. And then he recalls the youth's powerful words to him, that had stung him so much...your horse hates you, you have forgotten how to ride her, your wife no longer... and then the sharp image of his skill riding the untameable black stallion of Lygan, unbridled, saddle less and then the stealing of his Star Gauge from under his nose and then yet again the return of it around *his* own dog's neck?

As he contemplates, he realises he has totally underestimated Dog Heads, such cunning on an equal to his own, but how could such a disciplined species have hidden itself away for so long and why had they historically chosen not to rule supreme?

"Cannin, what do you do to me?"

He stretches his finger up to the falcon's chest and gently touches the dangling skull of the rodent until it swings back and forth like a pendulum. She remains completely still, watching him attentively as he in turn studies her in the same way. But then his anger rises, remembering the ancient Dog Head's words to him and he growls up to her,

227

"What kind of creature is Cannin? Answer me."

The falcon immediately rises above him, her wings sharply beating and flits away when he realises that Sir Clifford stands beside him.

"My Lord, are you ready to leave now?"

"Why are you here, skulking around like a sneak thief?"

"I meant no harm my Lord, but such time had passed that I became concerned for your safety."

The King leaps to his feet,

"There was no need, I take it you heard it all then?"

"I did my Lord."

"Then let us return to Warwick Castle and prepare to ride to the north."

CHAPTER TWENTY FIVE
Rounding Cape Wrath

Lomond rides on the high wind towards the Orkney Isles and bearing around the west shore through grey choppy waves, he grins happily at the sheer speed. The bear crouches in the bows of the boat steadily chomping away on the crabs until all are devoured and then he begins on the dried fish with Lomond smiling at him indulgently.

Finally, everything consumed the bear becomes restless and nose sniffing up from the bows; braves himself to prop his chin and two giant paws on the prow of the boat to view the accompanying screeching seagulls. He becomes more and more excited at their winged presences, his head swinging excitedly to left and right, snapping with great jaws as they swoop angrily near enough for a bite.

But they are the masters of the sky and tease him unmercifully as Lomond laughs at the bear's great, disgruntled growls each time he misses. Finally Lomond whistles to him to duck back down in the bowels of the boat, not just because his excited leaping becomes more and more exuberant, threatening to capsize them, but when in the far distance he sees a small fishing vessel with two distinct figures on board.

He whistles the birds away, they are bringing far too much attention to his position, he has no wish to meet up with anyone especially having been warned by the Wulver that Humans have a profound dislike and fear of bears.

He changes course until the small fishing vessel disappears from sight and then heads back towards the northwest as the wind increases in strength and pushes the boat onwards, until on the far horizon Lomond sees the towering, sheer dark cliffs of Scotland shrouded with white mist at the summits. At their base, huge explosions of white surf erupt upwards in an endless display of sheer power and his heart quickens with excitement at the deep booming noise. He approaches Cape Wrath, aptly named he thinks, as he battles through the tumultuous grey waves, the crouching bear growling apprehensively. Lomond whistles to calm him, the boat sheering from one side to another, he is sucked closer and closer to the high cliffs but he is used to the wildness of the sea and steers the boat around the peninsula remembering his mother's excited words to him.

"As you approach the first cliffs of Scotland you'll see below the clear surface the ancient hulk of a wrecked ship and it is said that the hold fairly brims with golden treasures."

But Lomond ignores this for he knows his father had gathered the treasure after her death and all is safely ensconced in his grotto at Fair Isle.

"Once you have passed Cape Wrath, you will soon come across the first of the hidden beaches of wonder, unreachable by land and such a stretch of pure white sand will meet your eyes. How I wished I could have disembarked and raced against the boat. But, of course, that was not to be and a silly notion by me on all accounts when I think back now."

He imagines her running swiftly then, as a girl, her long black hair flying behind her, her voice still ringing clear in his head, like yesterday.

But not a silly notion in his mind and steering the boat through the surging tide, he leaps out in the shallows and pulls the boat onto the white shelled beach.

"Come bear, let's run!"

The bear lifts his head tentatively from the bowels of the boat and seeing Lomond running swiftly away, his long black hair streaming behind him, leaps out and follows behind him in a great shambling trot, legs all over the show from lack of use, but the more he runs the more empowered he becomes.

Lomond runs faster and faster, his bare feet drumming on the sand like the quick, excited drumming of his heart, he shrieks up to the sky, firstly as a gannet, then as a petrel, mimicking the calls of all the birds, one after another, until scores of birds lift from the cliffs and swirl above him and the bear for the first time since he had left his homeland growls at the excitement of it all.

Finally at the end of the beach, stopped short by the looming enclosure of cliffs, Lomond tears back, the bear in hot pursuit, and on reaching the boat first, he hauls it strongly back into the water. The panting bear, fearing he will be left behind and with a great growl and a huge jump, surprising even himself, leaps back into the boat. Lomond grins, clambers in and lifting the sail takes off again and follows the rock cliff line until he comes to the next beach of wonder that she had described. And then he hears his mother's voice again,

"Much as I loved the land of my birth, it was a wild place of such ancientness, of such harshness and of such savagery, that sometimes I despaired of it, but, when you least

231

expected it, the sun would appear through the stormy skies and then it became a land of such peace and beauty that you forgave it of its wild ways. But I was glad to leave it all behind then, my family were desperately poor and when that unfortunate young man with a handsome dowry found his way to Loch Lomond from Fair Isle looking for a wife it was agreed by my father there was no future for me to stay, having so many brothers and sisters and me being the eldest."

Lomond looks up at the dark cliffs, wondering what the land that lies above looks like, but before long he reminds himself, he'll see it all in its majestic glory soon enough. Dusk falls and phosphorescence follows in his wake when he espies a dark inlet of water disappearing into the cliff face. He rows the boat through, and to his surprise a great fall of white water cascades down through a hole in the roof of the highest cave he has ever been in. At his and the bear's appearance, the roosting bats hanging from the dark underside of the rock ceiling take off in a great, swirling storm and with high pitched squeals, zigzag around and in a great swirl like black smoke ascend through the hole to become one with the cloudy night sky.

Lomond glides around the fall to the dark recesses beyond, a shingled shelf of dry rock meets his eyes, reminding him of his father's private grotto and tying the boat to a sharp pinnacle of rock he jumps out, holding the boat steady and whistles to the bear to join him. It groggily jumps out, now so tired that he rolls into a ball and falls into the darkest of sleeps. Lomond wraps the sheepskin fleeces from the boat around him and lies next to the bear, just as he always done with his dogs on Fair Isle and gladdened by the company he listens to the muted booming of the waves outside and closer still, he listens to the constant, reassuring sound of the waterfall as he too falls asleep dreaming of golden treasures, insurmountable mountains and deep lochs with strange unknown creatures swimming in the dark depths.

CHAPTER TWENTY SIX
The master farrier

Mounted on the two black horses, Archie trotting in front with the other three horses following behind, Cannin and Isabel keep a quiet leisurely pace through a narrow, sparse copse of woods that gives them a small degree of camouflage, for to the far left and to the far right they can see minute groups of people and horses working in the surrounding fields. The sound of many clipping wings close by disturbs the quiet when a flock of noisy brown sparrows appear through the trees and whirr all around Cannin. He listens to their chatter and chatters back in the same tongue and then as quickly as they had arrived they speed off, swooping high and low in front until they disappear.

"Not long now and we will come to the start of the high country and beyond the first hill that you can see ahead there is a large expanse of woods and we will stop there."

At Cannin's low words, the first for so many furlongs, that Isabel actually starts when he speaks to her. She stares at his set, hard profile always looking forwards and never at her, no matter how much she has tried to talk to him. Ever since they had left the Minors, every bit of fawning and ingratiating in her new role as his loyal subject had not worked and she sulks that he is far more interested in the small, scudding flocks of birds that periodically appear to chatter to him. But then to her surprise he speaks again.

"You know he follows us."

Her heart begins thumping wildly, she immediately turns to look behind her but there is nothing to be seen.

"But I can see nothing?"

"That is because he is a good league back, but he is there and has a large troop of warriors with him"

"But how does he know where we go?"

"I don't know how, but something is definitely guiding him. But what is also strange is that he appears not to be in any great rush to catch up with us and I wonder why?"

At this point another flock of small birds cry out as they sweep past. Isabel watches as they fly up into the sky and circle above and if she had never met Cannin she would think they were just another flock of random birds doing what birds do, namely flying around without purpose.

"So what do we do?"

"We do nothing, I cannot push the horses more, they need to walk slowly for awhile to regain their strength, particularly the white horse, have you not noticed how she hobbles because of the encumbrances nailed to the underside of her hooves? She helped me in the Black Woods to get rid of your husband's four men by pretending to be lame and now she truly is."

Isabel with a shocked look turns back and watches the white mare lifting her hooves painfully and feels a pang of guilt that she hadn't noticed before. But the more she looks the more she understands.

"But Cannin, I know what this is; she only needs to have her hooves trimmed and to be re shod, it is simple enough, we just need to find a master farrier."

With a sceptical frown, Cannin jumps from his horse and approaches the white mare whistling softly and in response she immediately lifts her left front leg and kneeling down he studies her hoof.

He delves deep into one of his pouches, taking out some form of implement and one by one pulls out the nails from her hoof until the iron shoe falls to the ground. He picks it up and looks at it scornfully.

"This is nearly completely worn through. Such a barbaric and cruel practise I don't understand why this is done, look at the wild horses of Lygan do they suffer without them?"

"But Cannin, she is an old horse and throughout her life has only been accustomed to wearing shoes. We must take her to be re shod, especially as we are going onto hillier, stony ground, she will suffer beyond anything if we don't and then will truly become lame. This is my entire fault; I did not think to check her when I took her, my only defence being that I was not clear in my thoughts and actions then."

Cannin ignores her and checks the other horses.

"There is nothing wrong with these horses, your husband has treated her more cruelly than I had thought, so where will we find this master farrier?"

"There has to be one close by, we just need to find the closest village."

Cannin whistles up to two inquisitive magpies perching in the branches overhead, they immediately respond with sharp, loud chattering.

"They tell me there is small human settlement beyond the copse of woods over there."

Remounting, Cannin leads the way out into the open, now totally exposed to the far Humans in the fields. Isabel sees his apprehension as he continually stares tensely over at the nearest group.

"Cannin we have every right to be here, just as they have, they're not interested in us, they are just poor people that work the fields, our biggest foe is my husband and you've told me he's a long way back and we have no choice; we have to do this for her."

"I know Isabel, for it is the only reason that I am allowing this to happen, but already I detect a strange and marked heaviness of spirit from the Humans beyond, there is no joy and no lightness in their actions. Some are fearful of even the breeze for they believe that it carries illness and death on its light breath whilst others channel their fear into such deep unbridled anger that I worry what they capable of."

She crosses her chest at his words but as she looks over to the ridged and furrowed field all she witnesses are horses with sweeping brushes tied from their tails plodding resolutely onwards with the people scattering seeds on the soil behind. To the far side and much further down a team of men with sickles hack down high foliage spilling from the copse that they head towards, but not one seems to notice their passing across the open land.

They reach the copse of woods and enter into the shade of the trees following a dirt track but after a short distance all halt when Cannin whistles softly. Isabel hears scurrying noises through the undergrowth, of small yet clumsy animals, her heart quickens in fear, but the horses stand still, ears pricked forward and Archie wags his tail expectantly when four, tiny children poke their heads through the bracken and smile openly at Cannin. He whistles again, now as a blackbird, now a blackcap, now a warbler, a fieldfare, a redwing, now a mistle thrush, a wood pigeon, a collared dove until the children push through the bracken and stand still, so completely mesmerised by his whistling that even Isabel is caught by the moment when with a rush of wings, each of the birds that he mimics land in the spread out twigs of a tree directly above. The small children, eyes wide, cry out with a mixture of delight and surprise on their faces at their appearance and clap their hands appreciatively causing the birds to flit away in alarm. The children's attention is then caught by the sight of Archie and bounding over they stroke him attentively. Cannin, never having seen young children before turns to Isabel with such a smile that she stops her apprehension at their ragged, dirty appearance and smiles with him.

"He's just like the feel of a rabbit, so soft... he won't bite us I can tell...of course he won't...I know that....ye cannot tell me, I knew it before ye... no, I knew it first."

The old woman crouching low in the bracken, watching on, puts down her straw basket full to the brim of berries, bark and roots and stares at them suspiciously.

How odd that the youth, with the bluest eyes she has ever seen, can call the birds to do his bidding and the children that are normally terrified of strangers have no fear? And there is something about the two of them that strikes her as being highly unusual. The dark haired girl wears expensive clothing, most definitely of noble birth and the fair headed youth, though wearing the strangest of garb has also the bearing of a nobleman and their horses are undoubtedly purebred, particularly the old white mare and by the continuous painful lifting of her hooves she guesses who they are looking for and her heart picks up in fear for them. But why do they ride without an escort?

Everything about their young appearance and manner is so incongruous with their surroundings that she concludes they can only be foreigners from over the great water and in their ignorance have lost their way and with that thought in mind she emerges from the bracken and nods her head as a smiling Isabel and Cannin bow their heads at her appearance.

"Can I be of help?"

"That would be kindness if you are able to; we are looking for a master farrier."

The old woman smiles up at her, so she was right, the girl's accent is clearly foreign.

"There is a master farrier a short distance in the direction you are travelling in, but..." She creeps over to the flank of Isabel's horse, watching to see if the children are listening to her, but they are far too engrossed in stroking Archie.

"I need to warn you," She whispers up to them.

"That he is the most vicious brute of a man and he rules everything about here and you must be very careful of him, I would have suggested that you go on to the next bigger town...but judging from the pain that the old horse suffers from you have no choice but to go to him. Do you know how much to pay?" Isabel and Cannin's eyes meet, neither of them had given any thought to payment. She smiles at their obvious ignorance.

"Show me what you have and I'll tell you how much to give him."

Isabel delves into her cloak pocket and produces a small pouch of coin, pours the contents into her hand and shows her. The old woman shakes her head in disbelief at the amount Isabel has.

"Even one of those nobles is far too much, put them away now and do not let him or anyone else see what you have."

Isabel immediately puts the coins back into the pouch; with Cannin staring at her incredulously, wondering how many other forms of wealth she has hidden about her person. The old woman digs into her own pocket and hands two small silver coins up to Isabel.

"That will be more than enough and do not let him bully you for more." Isabel takes them in her hand and smiles down at her.

"Thank you. I don't know how to repay you for your kindness."

Cannin frowns darkly at Isabel.

"On the contrary, I do know how, Isabel hand over two of the gold coins which I think will be more than a fair exchange for the two coins and for your kind help."

Isabel sits silently, head down for a few moments until nodding her head stiffly, she petulantly takes out two of the coins from the pouch and hands them down to the old woman, who hovers in her uncertainty, not wishing to take the wealth offered to her, as much as all her family could earn in six months.

"I'm sorry, I cannot accept, it is far too much."

Cannin smiles persuasively down at her.

"Come, please take them as payment for your coins and for your help, tell her so Isabel?"

240

"Yes, of course, you must accept." She answers quietly, her face burning with anger at Cannin's interference.

The old woman takes the two coins almost tearfully.

"I cannot thank you enough, such a chance meeting, yet I know you are both heaven sent, but please heed my words, once the horse is shod leave immediately before the men come back from the fields. This is not a welcome place for strangers and I worry for your safety."

She immediately calls to the children who happily run after her, waving goodbye as all disappear again into the woods.

CHAPTER TWENTY SEVEN
Baying Smith

They pass along the track through the copse of woods until they pause at the brow of a hill and look down to the vale below and at the straggled collection of buildings making up the small village of Bayston Hill. Cannin's eyes rest on the first of the buildings set in front and away from the others as a thin trail of smoke rises up from the chimney, the first he has ever seen as Isabel points at it.

"I would say that is the master farrier's dwelling, it's the only one with a chimney. I think it would be wise that we leave the horses here with Archie, I shall mount the white mare with you leading me as if you are my servant...thus we will bring less attention to ourselves."

He knows she still smarts at being forced to hand over her two gold coins to the old woman.

"No Isabel, they shall come with us. Has it not occurred to you that the horses and Archie could be in danger if we were to leave them behind? And as all of them have chosen to come with us of their own free will so we are duty bound to protect them as they would protect us."

"I did not think of it in that way, I apologise. But when we get there, you must let me do the talking. I am used to dealing with servants and you are not."

But even then she knows her words sound ridiculous for who ruled the Minors, certainly not her.

Cannin whistles softly to the horses as Archie at the front, nose to the ground follows a zig zag course down the track to the village while the horses follow behind with the white mare treading gingerly at the rear.

Much higher up, two figures hidden within tall conifers view their downward passage. The King puts the Star Gauge to his eye and focuses in on the white mare.

"My horse suffers and for the Renegade to show himself so blatantly out in the open can only mean he takes her to the master farrier below, so perhaps not such a good healer after all. Interestingly, I see the wild horses of Lygan are no longer with him and instead he has four new horses that look somehow familiar?"

He then views the Renegade's profile, not looking from right to left, only onwards and he has the strongest suspicion with his apparent indifference that the Dog Head knows exactly that he is being overlooked. He then focuses on Isabel, pans away, but then he pans back again, something about her is different, and then he sees quite surprisingly that her hair is dressed and held back and her clothing remarkably clean. But then he becomes bored with her and pans back to the white mare.

"I cannot understand why he doesn't just abandon my horse...I can only think the reason he keeps her is to goad me." He promptly hands over the Star Gauge to Sir Clifford.

"But do you see who he goes to? I recognised the village immediately. Such a bizarre coincidence, of all the farrier's he could have chosen, he chooses one that was once in my employ. Ha, ha, do you remember him, a vicious brute of a man, loyal and stalwart in battle though and uncommonly for such a barbarous man he had the most wonderful ability of calming horses, re shoeing them and at such speed!"

He laughs again at the memory.

"Now what was his name again Sir Clifford?"

Sir Clifford studies the four black horses, not answering straight away, because he is not quite sure how he will tell the King of this next impasse.

"Baying Smith was his name my Lord, on account he bayed like hunting dogs when in battle and so named because he came from here, Bayston Hill."

"Of course, of course, now I remember."

"But my Lord, let us pray that Baying Smith does not remember your white mare because it would not bode well for the Renegade if he does. Another matter though my Lord, please cast your eyes back over the black horses that accompany the Renegade." He hands the Star Gauge back. The King studies the horses in detail and then growls out angrily.

"Why did I not notice this before? He has rid himself of the wild horses of Lygan and has replaced them instead with my own scouts' horses and look how they accompany him like obedient dogs? Why does he do this to me? He takes everything from me, my horse, my diamonds, my wife, he kills my men, takes their horses and I am obliged to sit back and do nothing, a pox on all of this, I will..."

"No my Lord, he is a mere youth, he has not the strength or the prowess to have fought and beaten your experienced scouts twice his age? You are forgetting the power the Dog Head has over animals; look how even your own horse has chosen him over you?"

The King glowers in deep anger and jealousy.

"How have I managed to get caught in all of this, what I have done to deserve this youth's hatred towards me? I loathe him more than the worst of all of my enemies, there is none that I loathe more, apart of course from Isabel, I wish him..."Sir Clifford quickly interjects.

"No my Lord, remember what you were told by the Dog Heads, his very survival is paramount to the safety of your realm."

"So what next, Sir Clifford, inform me what I should do, because I am in a mind to destroy all."

"I would suggest that you send down three of the foragers my Lord and at haste."

Three sleeping dogs lying outside the wooden house lift their heads at their approach, Cannin whistles to them, and quietly they lay their heads back down again and fall back to sleep.

Cannin helps Isabel dismount, the only proper attention he has given her since leaving the Minors and her spirits lift. But then he ignores her again and stares with far more interest at the wooden dwelling, the first he has ever been close to.

Everywhere is silent, not a sound until they both hear the loud breaking snore of someone within. A terrible baying yell, and then the snoring again and then another baying yell, followed again by the most terrific snoring Isabel has ever heard. Archie whimpers in fright, but the three dogs clearly used to the sound, raise their heads wearily and fall back down again. Isabel nearly laughs out loud and for the first time she actually sees Cannin grin and filled suddenly with enthusiasm at his good mood they quietly enter through the open wooden doors to view the most enormous, ugly brute of a man half sitting, half propped up against the far, dark wall, head lolled to one side in a state of unconsciousness with a trickle of snot snaking in and out of his left nostril.

Isabel approaches him with a look of disgust considering how she might wake him while Cannin stands motionless on the threshold and takes in the hanging metal implements, the tall chimney, the dark smoking charcoal in the hearth, and a bench laden with rows of horses' shoes.

Baying Smith opens one eye, as if some inner sense tells him that he is not alone to see Cannin's dark silhouette standing at the open doors, his fair straggled hair lit from the daylight from behind creating a golden halo.

Still caught between sleep and wakefulness, he watches the silhouette turn, the so familiar profile, he hears him whistle softly and the white mare hobbles in, such a welcome sight after all these years that he cries out,

"My Lord, I pray I haven't kept you waiting, I'll attend immediately." Drunk with sleep and ale he staggers up grinning stupidly, Cannin grins back, as the farrier bows his head low.

Isabel fearfully looking from one to the other quickly darts over to Cannin and whispers in his ear.

"Remember Cannin you are my servant, go outside and stay with Archie and the horses, I'll deal with this." Cannin still grinning; shrugs his shoulders and returns outside.

A lurching Baying Smith raises his head, now to find Isabel in front of his eyes; he shakes his head in confusion and blinking furiously struggles to clear his eyes.

"Good day master farrier,"

"Where...where has my Lord gone to?"He asks, his speech still thick with sleep as Isabel laughs lightly.

"My servant is no lord, merely a poor youth and has gone outside to tend to the horses."

He focuses in on her now, his senses coming back to him to see a young girl and clearly high born judging from her manner and rich clothing.

"I apologise my Lady, I swore that I saw...must have been dreaming...I'm fairly done low with exhaustion on account of the time of year with all the ploughing, harrowing and such like."

More like done low with drinking too much, she thinks as she smells the stale ale on his breath even from where she stands.

He looks past her at the white mare and shakes his head confusedly.

Baying Smith, embarrassed now at being caught in this unseemly state and mindful of his high position in the community as master farrier begins to feel a surge of anger at being judged and stared at by this chit of girl who is very clearly a foreigner, and he doesn't like foreigners of any description, even beautiful girls.

He stares at her clothing again and then to his satisfaction he notices the hem of her cloak is filthy and her shoes are worn and equally as filthy as if she had been trudging through fields and what lady trudges through filth?

He begins to grin then; she attempts to smile back, but struggles to keep the look of disgust off her face with the wet snot still hanging from his left nostril in a great vile clump of greenness.

"Hurry now master farrier, I am in great haste to rejoin my party that await me on the brow of the hill. Pray, reshoe my horse quickly so I may join them again."

"Of course my Lady, give me just one moment."

He lurches over to a pail full of water, kneels down and sticks his head in. After a few seconds, he rises up, his hair dripping and Isabel is relieved to see the snot had gone.

But now his voice becomes authoritarian and irritable.

"As you are in such haste to leave, my Lady, I need your servant to aid me, I sent my apprentice off earlier to help in the fields and he won't be back until the morrow."

Isabel stares at him, the smile gone from her face, seconds pass,

"I will get him for you; but you need to understand he is simple in the mind and mute, but in his defence I can assure you he works hard and for his help I can expect therefore to pay you less?"

Baying Smith laughs deeply.

"I think not, you will pay me my full rate because I'm the only master farrier for many leagues and by judging the old horse's lameness she can go no further."

"I see you leave me no choice." With fear in her heart, she walks outside to find Cannin lying on the ground staring up at the passing clouds with Archie and the three dogs lying all around him. Baying Smith tiptoes over and peers through the open door at them and at the four, sleek, black horses.

"Now where have they got all those horses from?"

Isabel kneels down next to Cannin and whispers quietly.

"Did you hear?"

He nods his head.

"Be careful Cannin, I think he means us harm."

"I know, we are also soon to be joined by three horsemen. If by the time you hear them and I have not come out with the white mare I want you to ride quickly away with Archie and the horses and await for me back in the copse of woods."

He leaps to his feet and trails after Isabel to the forge to find the farrier scraping away with a hooked tool at the mare's left back hoof.

"Here he is farrier, treat him kindly, I shall wait outside until you are finished."

"Come then, half wit boy, see what I do."

Cannin grins at him as a half wit and trotting over crouches down and watches his work, but every few seconds he is aware how the farrier lifts his head to scrutinise him.

"You see, you scrape out the muck and, rarely have I seen so much muck, be careful of the frog. See now, how I remove this hard, dark layer, see now the white beneath, that is the way she should be." He looks at Cannin again. His resemblance to the King when a youth is almost uncanny, the only obvious difference being his eyes that are of the most intense blue and which he finds strangely unnerving.

"How could anyone have been so cruel to have left her in this state boy?" Cannin looks up at him again with his piercing blue eyes, yet smiles again as a half wit.

"You see this scar here and this one? This old horse has been in many battles and even if I were not to be paid, I would still willingly do this for the likes of her." Because he knows now, without any doubt that she is the King's horse.

249

The farrier stares at him steadily for a reaction, but there is no change in the idiotic way the youth looks back at him. He then moves from hoof to hoof, Cannin scrambling behind him, watching his scraping away, trimming at the hooves and rasping with a file, until finally he stands up,

"Now for the shoes, you choose one for me; choose one that you think will be the right size."

Cannin jumps up when Baying Smith catches a glimpse of the Minor's gladius under his cloak, the jewels on the scabbard shining provocatively at him.

He narrows his eyes, Cannin turns away, picks up a shoe and hands it over to him.

Baying Smith tries the shoe for size,

"Too small, you truly are a half wit, move out of the way now boy." He walks over to the bench and selects four horseshoes.

"Now these are the right fit."

He works at speed now, hammering each shoe slightly into shape, nailing them into position until finally he stands up, stretches his arms upwards, yawns and then leaps forward and grabs Cannin's upper arm with such a powerful grip that he growls in pain.

"Do not move boy or I'll break your arm. Tell me who you are and where you got this horse from and who is that foreigner girl outside?"

A small, inconsequential movement from Cannin and then shockingly the farrier feels the sharp point of a thin dagger pushed up into his nostril.

"Remove your grip from my arm farrier or I shall with one movement slice your prying nose from your face.

250

Luckily for you I only kill to eat and my laws forbid me to devour Sapien flesh, but there is nothing in my laws to say that I cannot disfigure you permanently, beginning with your nose."

Baying Smith stands completely still, the boy's voice is without question the King's, albeit with a more youthful tone.

"Come boy, I only jest with you, you are too young to be offering such violence."

"Then release me."

"Not until you tell me what is going on here."

The white mare abruptly whinnies to Cannin, Archie barks, his own dogs' bark as Isabel mounted on the black horse, her face white with fear, rides into the forge,

"Cannin quickly now the horsemen are coming, please Farrier let him go."

Cannin growls out.

"Do as she says and release me."

But he holds on grimly.

"I will not, because I can snap your arm in two as quickly as you can slice off my nose."

Cannin ignores him and calls out to Isabel.

"Ride away, go back to our friends, they will you help you."

"But I cannot remember the way?"

"Archie will show you, go quickly."

Isabel reluctantly turns the horse's head and rides off; he hears the quick thundering of the horses' hooves taking off up the hill, when in the opposite direction the sound of the three horsemen comes ever closer and at great speed. The white mare, her brown eyes fixed on Cannin whinnies again and paws the ground agitatedly as Baying Smith watches her from the corner of his eye.

"The mare is very much attached to you it seems, she used to be that way with only one other and I see she has swopped her allegiance over to you, which tells me that you are not responsible for her shameful neglect and that you have put yourself in great danger to bring her to me."

Baying Smith stares down at Cannin's cold blue eyes as animalistic as a wolf's and releases his grip, Cannin slips the dagger from his nostril, tucks it away beneath his cloak and jumping onto the mare's bare back, turns and bows his head to the farrier.

The farrier bows back.

"Will you not tell me who you are?"

"I cannot because as yet I do not know myself."

The mare trots out of the forge, Cannin presses gently on her flanks,

"That is as I had thought."Baying Smith says quietly.

The mare takes off at great speed delighted finally to have Cannin on her back and pounds away.

The King watches Cannin and his horse through the Star Gauge, panning their flight up the hill and in a strangely deflated voice at the sight, he turns to Sir Clifford,

"It seems all is well, he rides away on my horse though whether that is a good or a bad thing I cannot say with any honesty."

Elsu sits way above the King's head, the conifer branch that she clings to swings haphazardly in the high wind when she takes to the air and gliding on an air current she watches all movements below from her lofty position above. She watches the Kings' men stop at the forge and dismount, she watches Baying Smith join them, she watches as they happily shake hands as they renew their acquaintance from when they were all comrades-in-arms in the last battle eight years before, she watches all four turn to view Cannin astride the white mare ride fleetingly away up the hill and she sees Baying Smith smile appreciatively at her speed and then she hears his words on the wind,

"That old horse will run as fast as she ever did now on account of her new shoes, but does she not remind you of my Lord's white mare from years before? When she first came I thought it was she but when I looked closer I realised that of course it couldn't be. But still, the very sight of that old horse awakens such memories and she gladdens my soul."

The three horsemen inwardly agree, but stand impassively for they know; high above the King watches every one of their movements through the Star Gauge.

Cannin reaches the brow of the hill where Isabel, Archie and the horses wait, Isabel, white with fear, smiles nervously at him.

"I knew you would come." He half smiles as they turn to look back to see the King's men chatting and laughing with the farrier.

"Why do they not follow us?"

"They will."

She looks at him in confusion, the mare trots off, she follows behind trying to assess what had just happened.

"But why did the farrier let you go?"

"Only because he realised that I was not responsible for the neglect of the mare." She presses her horse on to catch up with him.

"But did he ask you other questions?"

He turns to her and puts a finger to his lips to quieten her questioning. She follows behind him, somewhat annoyed but then trusts his omniscience, when she too realises there is a deathly silence within the woods, not at all like when they had passed through earlier. Archie sniffs ahead, nose down, ducking into undergrowth back and forth across their path until he stops in front, leg raised, nose held high. A sudden loud raucous cawing, two hooded crows lift up from the overhead branches, Cannin releases the stone from the catapult, the first crow dies instantly and falls into the ferns, Archie immediately darts after it. He aims at the other crow, a sharp twang as it too plummets to the ground and leaping off the mare he lightly runs to pick up the body. He takes the dead bird from Archie's mouth, reaches into his pouch and ties their heads together with a short piece of sinew, hangs the corpses around his neck and mounts the mare. The sheer speed and the skill he used to kill the crows frightens Isabel, as again she realises there is more about Cannin than perhaps she would like to know.

"Why did you kill them?"

"They were warning the Humans in the fields of our approach and plus we need to eat later. We are in a dangerous position and caught in the middle, the three horsemen are now following behind and in front the angry Humans are coming towards us. If I were on my own I could disappear but with you I cannot, so when we come to the open and when I tell you to, we need to ride fast." He whistles a soft tune; the horses pick up their hooves and in a combined light trot make their way towards the daylight ahead.

They reach the open to see the field workers only a short distance away and heading straight towards them. The men view them suspiciously and talk amongst themselves, but both can hear their voices carry over.

"There they are, I knew they'd come this way, Baying Smith will have driven them back to us...Strangers and rich, look at her clothing...But why do they ride without an escort?...And feast your eyes on the horses they have, must be worth a King's ransom...Stolen I bet...They look like foreigners to me...And look at the dog, I've never seen such a dog in these parts before?

Then all are silent but with some unseen and non vocal signal the leading men armed with their sickles make their way over to them, picking up speed until they are half running over the furrows.

In response Cannin bends down and picks up Archie, the horses immediately spurt forward and tear off at great speed, the men seeing their prey escape run after them with blood curdling yells, sickles raised when all of a sudden both Cannin and Isabel hear the bellow of a hunting horn. Further on they stop and look back, the three King's men stream out of the copse of woods, swords drawn and within seconds circle around the group of men as way back, the women and children stand silently with the plough horses and huddle together fearfully. As Cannin and Isabel look on, one of the horsemen waves his sword around his head, points it at them and then points to the north.

Isabel shaking with fear, cries out,

"What does it mean? Why do they help us?"

As she cries out, Cannin looks up to see Elsu hovering high above as exactly at the same time the King from his high position watches her through his Star Gauge.

CHAPTER TWENTY EIGHT
The voyage to the south

Lomond and the bear continue their voyage in the small craft, the light southerly wind pushing them onwards following the jagged coast line of high insurmountable cliffs. The sea is so clear that Lomond can see a huge shoal of schooling fish below and with flashings of silver they whorl and spiral as one until disappearing quickly away and then he sees the black shape of a shark pass beneath his boat following intently behind.

They sail through narrow inlets between bare rock isles where the resting birds watch them pass, all now used to the presence of the bear. Every now again they are joined by leaping dolphins as Lomond listens to the messages from his father and asks them to return his greetings when they pass Fair Isle again.

Such fair weather sailing, on and on, until coming to another white shelled beach, surrounded by high cliffs and now that he realises there is not a Human in sight, he makes no attempt to hide and as dusk falls they pull ashore and he lights a small fire of dried seaweed.

Wading into the sea he dives deep under and from a hole in a rock a gigantic conger eel pokes out its head menacingly at his presence. Seconds later he brings it to the surface; the bear seeing his grappling fight rushes into the water and with his enormous jaws crushes the eel's head and drags it onto the beach, his first lesson in hunting and Lomond is delighted in how readily and proficiently he takes to it.

He slices off a section of the eel and leaves the happily growling bear to consume the rest. With the smell of the cooking eel filling his nostrils he gathers tendrils of fresh seaweed, places them on the fire and sitting down he views the blue whale humped shapes of low lying isles out to sea and smiles contentedly.

A peaceful night and in the first light of dawn they set off across the beach to the deep, freshwater loch behind, drinking their fill and then embarking the boat they head onwards to the south.

CHAPTER TWENTY NINE
The devil incarnate

The dark of night in the deep shadows of a dark spread of woods, Cannin turns back and looks up at the lone, high enormous boulder directly behind him as Elsu perching on the summit surveys all from her high position.

He finally makes up his mind and gathers twigs and small branches and before long a roaring fire is ablaze, for in the distance and on a small wooded hill he sees the War Lord's enormous fire and the sound yet again of wild laughter. Isabel frowns unhappily when he puts on another bundle of dry twigs.

"I'm not sure we should be having a fire Cannin and especially one so big, surely they'll see it?"

"Equally I can see your husband's and if he and his men can enjoy themselves then so can we, besides I don't think the crows will be to your liking unless they are cooked."

She stares up at him, her black eyes full of fear as Archie quivers at the sound of the shouting voices.

"I'm not in the mind for eating, whatever it may be."

"You will change your mind in a short time, besides we have a company of grey wolves closing in, the smell of the horses is driving them to distraction and the fire will hold them at bay."

"Please God not more wolves." She stares fearfully around into the darkness when from further back she catches the golden light from their waiting eyes. Cannin grins at her.

"Don't worry, the grey wolves will not attack us, they are merely being opportunistic that is all. They'll be bored before too long and will go after easier prey."

He begins to pluck one of the crows,

"Here, help me it'll take your mind off their presences."

He throws the other crow over to her.

"Do I have too?"

"Just follow what I do."

With a disgusted look on her face, she nevertheless follows his instructions as they carefully pile the black feathers in a heap.

The night deepens; the King walks a few yards away from the camp with Sir Clifford at his side and both watch the blaze of the fire in the dark distance.

"The Renegade is getting braver and the only thing that is keeping my rage at bay is that he will soon meet his Nemesis."

"I imagine my Lord he has only lit the fire to ward off the wolves, there does seem to be a large number here. But I have noticed he has marginally deviated off his northern course, but I'm sure it is only because he seeks cover from us."

"Maybe he leads us deliberately into dangerous areas with the assistance of his falcon Did you notice that she led us to this point but disappeared as soon as we had arrived here at dusk?"

"I expect my Lord that she has gone only to eat and then to roost, we have after all travelled many leagues today."

The King turns back to view his men happily lounging around the open fire, eating and conversing openly as he had encouraged them to do but now he feels a pang of irritation at their fun. He looks further back and his eyes rest on the shadowy form of a miserable Draq sitting all alone.

"What to do with him, what to do?" He questions himself out loud. His men hear his words but continue conversing as if they hadn't.

The King turns back to Sir Clifford.

"What is to be done with the ambassador? I feel he could be of some use and yet so far I have not thought of a single task he could perform that would be of any benefit to me, unless of course he were to cut his own throat." The men nearest to hear him grin but immediately carry on with their conservations as if again they had never heard a word.

"He has been complaining of illness my Lord, and wishes to see a physician to be bled, but I feel it is all pretence. The men keep away from him; he has convinced them he suffers from gaol fever which he says he caught whilst imprisoned by you at Warwick Castle."

"It would give me enormous pleasure to bleed him myself and bleed him dry...but how could the men believe that nonsense, all knew he was given his own private quarters and given the most wonderful cuisine and the most attention that has ever been allowed of any ambassador and why, I even allowed him to keep his sword!"

Draq keenly aware that the King speaks of him, prompts him to rapidly back away on his rump into the shadowy bushes because he has the certain feeling that if he doesn't leave now he never will. He backs away more, stands up, shaking with nervousness but not one of the King's men appears to have noticed his disappearance. He walks slowly at first, expecting loud shouts, but nothing happens and he quickly trots down the hillside, into the darkness of the woods and heads in the direction of the far off blaze.

The King and Sir Clifford edge further away from the men.

"They want him gone my Lord, he constantly whispers of the devil incarnate that is in their midst and chants to them in the dark hours that if only they would open their eyes, they would know who he is, and the very reason he has been struck down with illness is because he knows the devil's identity. He frightens them and all believe he is a curse."

"And so who is this devil incarnate he alludes to? Of course, of course, he speaks of me when it is *him*." He whips around in his fury, his finger pointing in the direction of Draq to find him no longer there and his men, heads bowed stand as still as statues.

He yells out in his fury,

"Where has he gone? You, you and you, who were supposed to be guarding him, find him and kill him."

The three men immediately pick up lighted torches, for they all know where he has gone to and follow each other in the direction of the Renegade's fire, but after a show of rapid response to the King's fury, they now tread slowly through the tangled undergrowth each praying that the Renegade will kill the ambassador.

Draq trots quickly through the dark foliage, Cannin's blaze a constant luring beacon in the distance. All of a sudden he stops, to the left of him through the trees, he sees fast moving large shapes racing in his direction, he then sees their glowing, slanted eyes and very nearly shouts out when he realises he is tracked down by a pack of wolves.

Picking up a branch, he waves it furiously in their direction; they halt but whine horribly at him. Quickly picking up pace but still brandishing the branch, he now half runs, sweat pouring in rivulets down his face with the wolves following excitedly behind.

The King and Sir Clifford watch down at the three trailing, faltering small balls of fiery globes making their way towards the blazing fire of the Renegade when abruptly they stop.

"Why have the fools stopped?"

Cannin tears off a wing of cooked crow and hands it over to a reluctant Isabel.

"Go on, try it." She tentatively takes a bite and then smiles.

"It's similar to chicken, but stronger in flavour and in truth I have to say I like it." She eagerly eats the rest and takes the breast that he offers her. Cannin throws Archie chunks of meat and when they have all finished, he hands Isabel over a handful of red berries. She eats them all with relish and smiles warmly at him.

"What a truly delicious meal, thank you Cannin."

When without warning they both hear the sudden, loud raucous cry from Elsu, Cannin abruptly leaps up and sniffs deeply in.

"There is one that comes towards us as dark as night and burns inwardly with dark desires."

Isabel looks at him in fear and jumps up,

"Who is it that comes?"

And then Isabel hears Draq's voice in the distance.

"Isabel, I am here to help you, tell the Dog Head that I come in peace." She laughs in surprise and claps her hands lightly.

"It is Le Marques de Draq!"

"You trust him?"Cannin asks suspiciously.

"Of course; he is my father's best friend and my guardian."

She prays inwardly, thanking God, as a vision of her beautiful country with its warmth, beauty and of her perfect life of pomp and splendour fills her mind.

"He's being followed by the wolves; I'll stop them before they rip him apart." Without another word, Cannin slips into the darkness, passing Draq as a shadow, who completely unaware of his fleeting presence stumbles into Isabel's sight, the light from the fire exaggerating his beak like nose and glittering black eyes. She notices that he's drenched in sweat and his normal confident manner to be so changed to almost being furtive; particularly in the way his eyes sweep almost feverously around the small clearing, checking everything minutely. His predatory eyes appraisingly rest on the saddled horse when Archie uncharacteristically begins a deep, rumbling growl in his throat when Isabel, having gotten over her shock at his ghastly appearance now smiles in welcome.

"Archie quiet now, you know the Marques as well as I."
Draq smiles then at Isabel, but with such a hideous smile that she wonders if some terrible thing had befallen him.

"I excuse my appearance, but I have just escaped from the King, he has had me under close guard and I need to move quickly and will have to forego the formal etiquette due to you. But where is the Dog Head?" She looks at him steadily and without knowing why she lies to him.

"He has gone to collect more wood for the fire, I asked him to leave so we may speak freely."

"A wise move, you cannot trust him or anybody else in this God forsaken country. You will quickly give me the two diamonds so I may return to Castile to raise a huge army, and then I shall return, destroy the King and you will rule supreme."

Isabel frowns at his quickly spoken, desperate words.

"But why must I hand over my diamonds over to you Marques de Draq? They are mine and I am extremely displeased that you do not even have the courtesy to address me in the manner that you should have done." She glances past him wishing Cannin would return, but Draq immediately catches her quick eye movement and snarls viciously.

"Be warned Isabel not to put all your lot in with a forest animal and a barbarian, I am the only person you can trust." His voice is now so disproportionately angry that a growing understanding comes to her. She turns and steps slightly away, distancing herself and then turns back to face him.

"I would have thought that you would not insult the so called barbarian in such a way, I would have thought that you would be immensely grateful to him for helping me in the manner that he has and, as yet, I have not heard you offer to take me from here and back to Castile and to my father." With a struggle he attempts to rule his anger by smiling, in what he believes is a reassuring smile but to Isabel it is even more grotesque than before.

"Come Isabel, I cannot take the risk of escaping with you too, it is better that I travel alone and it is better that you stay with the Dog Head until I return."

She pouts now as she did as a child.

"But my father will be extremely displeased that you have left me here and you seem to have forgotten that you vowed to him that you would always care for me?" She notices his agitation grows now out of all proportion,

"I have had enough of this nonsense, you imbecile of a girl, your father as you know as well as I, is old and weak and before I left for England with you, he gave me full powers to make all decisions on his behalf, and so I have decided you *will* stay here and you *will* immediately give me the diamonds."

Draq moves forward a pace, his hand reaching beneath his cloak when they both hear the booming of the King's voice thundering through the trees.

"If you have anything about you Renegade, destroy *him* that comes to you." Draq leaps forward towards Isabel and by the light of the fire she sees the shining blade held low in his hand, Archie tears forward at him growling, when suddenly Draq stops, stands upright with a look of utter astonishment on his face and topples onto the fire.

Cannin emerges from the shadows and puts away his catapult as Isabel stands still in complete and utter shock.

"Quickly now Isabel, we need to be away, your husband's men are very close."

He whistles to the horses who led by the white mare make their way into the darkness of the woods, he picks up Archie under his arm and with the light from his eyes Isabel follows shakily behind, a few steps on when she's hear the most hideous growling noises. She trips forward and clutches Cannin's arm and for the first time he allows it as she begins to weep at the loss of what she had always known.

A few moments later, the three King's men in trepidation approach the fire that was, but now isn't as they pick up the smouldering smell of flesh and wool, the wolves with low growls abruptly cease their frenzied circling around the humped black form and with teeth bared disappear at the sight of the burning torches.

But their rapid, scurrying, departure lifts the crow feathers high up into the air; the men step forward, trying to decipher what they are beholding when their lighted torches pick out the wild flurrying of the black feathers and watch as they settle like a feathered cloak over the humped black shape. They shake with abject horror, when one cries out,

"Behold, behold a sorcerer caught in transformation."

They turn tail and begin running back, the lighted torches flickering erratically when the King bellows down,

"Hold still there, stay where you are on pain of death."

"Sir Clifford, join me, Sir Stephen remain here with the rest of the men, and *all* of you watch the horses."

Sir Clifford takes a lighted torch, the King strides through the bracken, sword drawn until they reach the terrified men.

"What goes on here?"

"Something unearthly my Lord, something so terrible in our very midst, a sorcerer transforming into a crow."

The King growls angrily at them and on approaching the humped black shape, he growls even more.

"You fools, it is only the ambassador, come now and assist me."

The men walk cautiously forward and at his shouting order roll over the smoking Marques de Draq, his face untouched by the fire but with an almost perfect round indentation on his forehead. The King notices his sword still within his grasp and guesses what he was all about. One of the men cries out.

"But you see my Lord, the mark of the devil is upon his forehead?"

"You mean the mark made by a stone delivered from a catapult, an excellent shot; the Renegade is to be congratulated on his marksmanship and for killing the sorcerer before he could become a crow. Good, we are now rid of him and I need to retire for a few hours before the dawn comes."

"But what do about him...it, my Lord?"

"I would have thought it obvious; the ambassador in his stupidity went into the woods alone in order to relieve himself and was eaten by wolves that is all." The three men slowly smile and then break into relieved grins.

"The devil incarnate has gone, praise be to God!"

The King and Sir Clifford listen to the praying voices of the three men following after them. But a part of the King fumes that he had to openly praise the Renegade in front of his men, but he has no choice, he cannot have his men becoming terrified of him as well, for who knows where that would lead to?

CHAPTER THIRTY
Ludlow

Cannin finally stops, he realises that Isabel cannot go any further when her grasp on his arm is rather more now of him carrying her whole body weight and he directs her to the base of a heavy old tree and carefully lowers her down and within seconds she is in the darkest of sleeps.

Through a thin thicket of saplings that border the end of the woods he views the vast, dark meadow beyond and yawning heavily lies down next to her. Archie creeps in between as he covers them all in the ancient Roman's heavy woollen cloak and within seconds they too are fast asleep. The horses gather around and slump to the ground on their sides and with exhausted, loud exhalations close their eyes.

No wolf disturbs their deep slumber, the creatures of the night skirt around and creep off to other parts, everywhere is silent as they slumber on and on.

The rising of the dawn, Isabel wakes and on opening her eyes the first thing she sees is Cannin, still fast asleep, his face barely inches from hers and for once she can look at him in close detail. She studies the small blue veins on his mauve tinted closed eyelids, she studies his hairless face, not even a hint of manly hair sprouting forth, she stares at his cupid bow of pink upper lip and listens to his almost childlike breathing. She stretches out her hand with the most irresistible and passionate urge to touch his face. Her hand hovers over and then she rapidly changes her mind, nestles back down and slumbers again.

Cannin opens his eyes when the first of the Blackbird's warns his comrades of their presences and particularly of the Peregrine Falcon hovering above. Cannin whistles to them that they all come in peace and they flit silently away.

He carefully uncovers Isabel and Archie from the warmth of his cloak, rises up and stretches, Archie follows suit as the sun climbs higher in the east. The green lush valley beckons them all, Archie tears out of the woods, briefly stopping to take great gulps of water from a small brook and after, with high excitement tears forward and springs through the long grass where rabbits, hares and a cloud of birds flee from his exuberant charge. The five horses with excited snorts join in and canter giddily after him, kicking up their back hooves in their joy in being out of the dark woods.

With a shiver at being uncovered, Isabel wanders out onto the meadow and drops to her knees; head bowed with hands pressed together and mutters quiet words. Draq's betrayal of her has lowered her spirits to such an extent that her visualisation of her future and all of her plans seem pitifully weak and unattainable now, for always deep down she had believed that he, her father and the might of Castile would ultimately save her before she would need to carry them out.

Cannin surveys the wild humpbacked blue hills to his left, and then views the valley in front of him, far away he can see small clusters of half timbered buildings and much further in the distance he espies the largest settlement he has ever seen. He scans over to his right as ancient craggy peaks stretch up to the sky where screaming buzzards lift in rising circles as he contemplates the next move.

He looks over at Isabel's lowered head and for a moment listens to her murmuring voice and knows she prays to her spirits and feels her sadness as sharply as a wound.

He whistles to Isabel's saddled mount, a placid black mare that trots over and waits whilst he lifts Isabel from the long grass and sits her astride.

"Come Isabel, I believe it is time that you are who you are."

She lifts her head at his words and stares down at him almost suspiciously.

"I have no understanding of what you mean?"

"I will take you to where you should be."

He points to the far distance in the valley; and for the first time she notices the castle of Ludlow and the surrounding buildings.

"You mean back to civilisation and away from the wilderness, ha Cannin, not such a good prospect for me."

"But with your wealth in the two stones and your gold coins surely you will be able to find Humans that will help you against your husband; he cannot be so powerful that he rules all?"

Tears come instantly to her eyes.

"There are none that can help me in this: I have not a single friend here apart from you. But I have been thinking there is one, I have a close cousin that lives in the land of the Scots, a country where my husband would not dare to cross the border to and where I will be safe and from what I understand it is not so much further on from where you travel to and if you truly wish to help me, take me there before you go to the Dog Head King."

271

Cannin frowns.

"No, I have to go to the king before hibernation starts otherwise I will not gain audience with him until the winter months are over."

She smiles down at him, yet feels a pang of guilt at her duplicity.

"But what is this immediate haste Cannin? I will introduce you to my cousin and she will be more than grateful to you for your kindness in helping me and a chance to meet her good friends who will equally welcome you as my true friend and my true ally. Please, I beg you take me and Archie there...but if you choose not to stay after you have delivered us, then so be it, you could leave immediately before the winter sets in, surely we have time enough for that?"

She stares into his blue wolf eyes, keeping her face dead pan and her heart still. He turns from her, sniffing the wind from the north like a dog and turns back to face her again.

"We may just have enough time and I agree it is far better for you to be with your own kind as it is for me to be with mine."

"Thank you Cannin." She smiles at him again but as he turns to whistle to Archie and the four horses still running wildly about, her face darkens as she contemplates all four things at the foremost in her mind,

The most important, what vile creature masquerades as the Dog Head King? Because it is obvious to her now that Cannin is the true king, proven to her not just because of her witnessing his coronation and not just by the presence of the Pendant of Office in her pocket but by the actions of the

Minors in their total belief in him and all the animals...but a king obviously of only a tiny human sub species? He is worth far more than that.

Secondly she wishes him safe and well as he has yet again saved her and her plan is to keep him with her, even if in the short term it means him being held in close confinement in her cousin's castle because thirdly, there is no question in her mind that he is undoubtedly the King of England's son - albeit a bastard, she just needs time to prove the blood line, for without any other heir Cannin's worth is beyond measure and she is still the Queen of England after all and, fourthly, she admits it to herself, she loves him.

Cannin turns back and grins up at her as the sun rises in its force, his hair turning to gold, she smiles back and again she sees the King's special smile on his face and she basks in the warmth of it.

"Let us away then before your husband catches up, but before we go there is something about his actions that confuse me. Firstly and most strangely he is in no great rush to catch up with us, his men stopped the field workers from attacking us and then he warns us about your guardian and even now he is just over yonder waiting for us to move. It is almost as if he is our escort, although an unwilling one, for even from here I detect his anger and frustration. But to what end, is it simply that he plays with us like a wolf before he and his pack rush in for the kill?"

Isabel looks behind her and is chilled at how not so very far way are the stationary mass of troops, she sees the King fixate on them through the Star Gauge as he turns aside to Sir Clifford, grinning, "There appears finally to be an

273

altercation between the two of them, what a damned nuisance I cannot hear their words."

Isabel turns her head back to face Cannin, studiously trying to keep calm as him.

"I agree there is something strange about his movements, but as I barely know him I cannot answer truthfully what his motives are? But what I have always been told about him is there is no weakness and there is no forgiveness."

"I believe he follows us to find out our destination, perhaps Morgar told him before he was slaughtered where we were going to? Of course, that would make sense, by his very actions your husband has shown how much he hates Dog Heads, maybe his ultimate goal is to kill the king?"

Isabel swallows in fear at his innocent words.

"Even more reason Cannin that we ride to my cousin, because surely the King of the Dog Heads will be fuming that you bring all this trouble to his realm?"

Cannin stands quietly for a moment and with slanted eyes views the waiting King and his troops.

"I have come so far now that I must continue, everything pushes me to go on and follow this path."

"Cannin please consider, there is no need for all of this haste."

"Have no fear Isabel, I will take you to the border first and then continue on my own, but for the time being we will allow your husband to follow us for he has proved he is more than useful as our escort and when I judge the time is right I will lose him and he will not know your path. So not another word, he is already suspicious of why we are lingering."

Isabel bows her head so he cannot read the expression on her face, but inwardly she swears that from now on regardless, she will do everything in her power, no matter what, so that Cannin will accompany her to the land of the Scots and to safety.

At no visible or verbal command, Archie takes off to the north, Cannin leaps astride the white mare, she picks up her hooves and high steps forward, gently breaking into a trot and then into a easy canter following Archie's lead. As she careers forward all follow behind, firstly Isabel on the black mare, the other three black horses directly behind, the King spurs his horse on with his men in tight formation behind but all the while he watches his white mare and such a surge of jealousy fills him and he wishes that it was he who rides her...and then he wonders, was that how he must have looked to his enemies at about the same age as the Renegade when he first went into battle?

The very thought spurs him on, his mood inexplicably lightens, perhaps all of this is not such a chore after all? He can revisit his youth and watch his horse in her newborn glory and recapture an air of what once was...at least for the time being.

CHAPTER THIRTY ONE
The white squall

The continuing noisy hiss of the boat slicing through the dark blue swell, the humming of the wind in the sail and the calls of sea birds are the only noises Lomond and the bear hear as they sail comfortably on and on to the south. So calming are their surroundings that Lomond for once allows himself to indulge in total relaxation.

To their left the dark craggy cliffs continue to stretch up to the sky and to the right they pass huge islands that at times Lomond wonders which is the mainland and which is not, but his sense of bearing carries him on, as his mother's voice continues in his head telling him the way forward.

They pass the isles, back out into the open ocean when a great mass of Herring Gulls suddenly lift up from the rocky crags with shrill warning cries, Lomond whips around to see the monstrous white squall, higher than the tallest of cliffs rushing behind him, the first he has ever seen but he remembers his father warning him not just of their rarity but of their extreme violence.

He speeds away before it hits, the terrific wind pushing him forward with frightening strength, he passes another of the hidden coves and attempts to steer towards it, but he is not allowed and he realises his will is not his own and he is now commanded by the wind spirits.

He runs before the squall, he looks behind again as gigantic waves, far higher than his boat surge towards him with dolphins diving through their turquoise midst, warning him, warning him, but he cannot resist laughing wildly at the sheer, exhilarating speed.

But then he wishes he hadn't tempted fate when he realises the galloping waves are nearly onto him and he quickly reduces the sail before the colossal wind rips it to shreds.

Hour after hour they speed on in their frantic pace to keep ahead of the towering waves that threaten to swamp and drown them, the day passes, night falls, but still there is no let up from the ferocious storm, on and on when Lomond realises he has been completely pushed past the land of his mother and he cries out in his growing fear as the bear lies silently in abject terror.

Finally the sky begins to marginally lighten on the southern horizon and utterly exhausted with the constant bailing out of the rain and sea water and the managing of the tiller that Lomond shouts out for joy when the howling storm abruptly snakes off to the west. It is only now that he can see it in its true perspective and he realises how lucky he is to still be alive.

He steers past a jutting headland to see a raised sand and shingle beach in the distance and dropping the sail, he picks up the oars and begins to row, his arms shaking with fatigue and with the cold with the rain still falling in torrents. The huge heavy breakers carry him forward and smash onto the beach in their fury and with the violent motion the boat is shoved high up onto the shingle.

Lomond climbs out, his head still rolling from the motion of the sea and reels as if intoxicated; the sodden bear jumps out behind, shakes the water from his coat and lopes off to the nearby rocks and drinks rain water gathered in a shallow pool.

With the last of his strength, Lomond dismantles the sail, turns the boat over and rests it's prow on a low, round isolated rock and like a mollusc with an outer shell he shields himself from the last of the rain and the wind when he becomes aware that the bear has completely disappeared.

He looks wildly around in his panic when the bear leaps out of the high turquoise breakers with a dead seal gripped tightly in his jaws and nestling down begins to devour it in his ravenous hunger.

Lomond sighs in relief and whistles to the wind spirits thanking them for his and the bear's survival and for the rich gift of the seal, the sky immediately clears to blue, the rain stops, and in utter exhaustion he slumps down beneath the boat but he can still hear the aftermath of the cries of the wind spirits within the retreating squall telling him that he must help the new king that comes.

"What new king?" He whispers and falls into a dead swoon.

The bear seeing his collapse lopes over, kill forgotten and sniffs worriedly around his still form, when he abruptly lifts his head. He hears strange vocal tones coming towards him and sniffing in the air, rushes back to the seal, picking up its limp form in his jaws and pounds over to the fore dune backing the beach and hides behind the ridge of sand. The strange noises come closer and peering through dense tufts of stiff grey grass he omits a low, warning growl.

The two Benedictine monks, completely unaware of his presence, pass further down onto the beach, the older leading an old donkey pulling a cart with the younger of the two walking slightly in front when they both automatically stop. The donkey takes in the fresh aroma of the bear nearby, but he stands stoically so used to the strange scent of the Dog People that nothing surprises him anymore.

The two monks gravely survey the storm debris made up of corpses of sheep, two dead dolphins, countless dead fish, scores of different species of gulls and the only living creatures are vast numbers of lobsters and crabs that strive weakly to crawl back into the water but, in the midst of all and by far the largest sight is Lomond's overturned boat and they look at the unfamiliar craft in complete surprise.

Brother Bernard quickly walks across the shingle gesturing for brother Firmin to follow with the donkey and cart and almost in fear, he kneels down and peers under the slightly raised prow of the strange boat, his fear turning rapidly to concern when he see the still form of Lomond. He lightly places his hand on the youth's forehead and then crosses his chest. Standing up he carefully overturns the boat and removing his black wool scapular lays it on top of Lomond as the older, obese brother Firmin puffing heavily, joins him.

"This boy has been blown to us by the storm and somehow has managed to survive. It is fortuitous we have found him before they, but even so we run an enormous risk in helping him."

Brother Firmin stares down at Lomond compassionately.

"We cannot leave one so young to *them,* and by the very miracle that he has survived the storm tells me he has been heaven sent to us, I feel he is the sign we have been waiting so long for."

"But I worry they will sniff out his scent and know that we will have taken him to the monastery and will come for him."

"They have not dared yet to enter into our sacred domain and besides once we have placed him in the cart, the only scent they will pick up would be from here and by the time they awake at dusk the incoming tide will have swept away any evidence."

"And the boat?"

The older monk frowns.

"We'll drag it out and sink it into the deep waters but let us move quickly now before any prying eyes see what we are about."

They anxiously look around but strangely there is not a bird to be seen.

They quickly lift Lomond up and with some difficulty place him in the cart, but with a low unconscious growl he rolls himself into a tight foetal position. They tuck the scapula tightly all around him and gather his few possessions including the sharks jaw and place them next to him. Brother Firmin places his hand on Lomond's forehead and shakes his head worriedly.

"We must be quick now; he needs to be next to a hot fire otherwise he will die."

Hurriedly they drag the small craft into the heavy sea; out onto the edge of the reef where brother Firmin holds it tight. Brother Bernard picks up heavy rocks from the sea bed and throws them into the bottom of the boat. Finally the boat, teetering on the edge of the reef, nose dives down into the deep water below and sinks down to the very bottom, never to be seen again. They wade back through the heavy waves and onto the beach, hurriedly gathering lobsters and crabs, the very reason why they had come to the beach in the first place, and load them hastily onto the cart and when done they quickly make their way back to the monastery.

The bear watches all and knows intuitively that Lomond is in safe hands and lowering down with the remains of the seal grasped between his claws, he happily proceeds to devour the rest.

CHAPTER THIRTY TWO
The Pennine Way

Both the King and Sir Clifford watch the Peregrine Falcon hover way above the Renegade and Isabel. Periodically they watch the two far bigger buzzards that follow her attempt to attack from behind but each time she rounds on them viciously and they retreat. The King smiles ironically.

"He takes us to the wilderness or is that the falcon does? I'm beginning to wonder who rules the roost around here, her, me or him. But in truth I am glad we follow this desolate path for I would like to keep this entire business kept as quiet as possible. I have decided to view this all simply as an interlude, a short drama that I must indulge myself in, before I have to return to my interminable duties in London for I'm sure that already my ministers are gathering to plot against me. So we shall get the job in hand done quickly, we will return where no doubt traitorous heads will roll, for such is the life of a king."

Sir Clifford, with a discreet sideways glance, witnesses him yet again lift the Star Gauge to his eye and study the two obsessively as yet again all hear Isabel's tinkling laughter echo back to them on the cold wind.

"I cannot think what she can find so amusing out here, but I swear it is because it is a source of endless mirth to them both that I follow behind like an accursed wet nurse but still, we must keep close for I feel very strongly that the Renegade is waiting for just the right moment to rid himself of us."

Cannin, Isabel, Archie and the horses rise steadily up the fells on a lonely shale ancient tract that follows the vertebral column of the Pennines to the north. Far below the shale flanks to either side of the spine, both companies espy miniature cattle grazing on rich green grass where clusters of stark woods remind them that before too long yule tide will be upon them.

As they climb ever higher, the path now takes them in between rocky pinnacles of limestone and the further they climb, the cold also steadily increases, the time worn limestone pinnacles become more numerous in number until they reach a vast moorland plateau covered in rabbit shorn grass, purple sprouting heather and dying clumps of golden grass.

Small groups of wild sheep munch nonchalantly at Cannin and Isabel's approach and are not even perturbed by Archie and the black horses trotting amongst them but when they see the King and his troops appear up onto the plateau they hurtle away with alarmed bleats.

Cannin turns back and immediately whistles to Archie and the three black horses to rapidly put themselves in front of him, a wise decision for in that very second Sir Stephen and the head archer shoot down two of the sheep not so very far behind them. Isabel immediately spins around at the loud twanging noises and takes in a sharp intake of breath when she sees how close the two dead sheep are to them. Cannin smiles grimly.

"I believe your husband shows us his archers' killing skills in order to remind us that if he so chooses he could shoot us down just as easily."

Isabel immediately glares directly at the King with a look of unbridled contempt, her black eyes boring into his, her unkempt long black hair blowing as wildly as the unkempt mane of her horse. He stares back at her through the Star Gauge and it is then, for the very first time, that he acknowledges her true beauty.

Gone is the white frail pinched look about her face accompanied always with the habitually worn, sour downward turning of her thin unsmiling lips. This new, reborn Isabel is a sight to behold, her upright haughty stance in the saddle, her face and body strangely fuller. And whilst her appearance is bedraggled, he feels her youthful strength and vitality even from where he is.

The realisation of her beauty comes as such a shock to him that in an aside and in a low voice he growls out to Sir Clifford,

"I believe Isabel has found her true calling being nothing more than a vulgar slattern."

But when he finishes, he regrets his bitter diatribe, a sad failing on his part. Sir Clifford diplomatically says nothing in response but Sir Stephen on his other side glares over at Isabel with complete and utter hatred.

The King continues to stare through the Star Gauge and sees a verbal interaction between the Renegade and Isabel, he notices how eagerly and earnestly she listens to his words, she had never behaved like that towards him and when they slowly continue forward with the Renegade sitting on *his* white mare, he struggles to hide his jealousy.

Sir Stephen half glances at him, wondering how he manages to stay so calm when the King, striving to keep his tone emotionless turns quietly to him.

"Let us unnerve them a little, retrieve the sheep but remember, carefully does it."

Sir Stephen turns and nods at the archer behind him; both trot forward slowly at first and then tear forward on their horses at breakneck speed towards the dead sheep as the King sits on his mount, half grinning, while Sir Clifford watches stonily on.

With the sound of the thundering of the hooves of the two horses, Isabel automatically looks nervously back as Cannin continues on, whistling to all to pay no attention and half turns to tell her to come with him,

But her mare rears agitatedly in nervousness at the two horses oncoming speed and Isabel struggles to control her, Sir Stephen and the archer rein in a short distance away, both staring at her maliciously and then she hears Sir Stephen with an exaggerated snarl on his face, hiss out the word,

"Bitch."

She is so stunned at his insult to her, the worst of any insult that could be made towards a woman that she blanches, particularly as she is still the Queen. So this is what they think of her, that she is a doggess, a bitch on heat and they think she lays with Cannin? Her shame is beyond anything that they would think this but even more she feels the shame that they would think this of Cannin who is entirely innocent. The King viewing the scene through the Star Gauge see's Isabel's shocked face and realises that Sir Stephen has clearly said something inflammatory to her.

"Why is it that Sir Stephen cannot seem to follow even the simplest of orders?" But he grins nonetheless.

But in that second Cannin swings around, face coldly impassive, catapult drawn and aims it at Sir Stephen's head. Sir Stephen half grins at him until through the Renegade's long tangled fringe he catches a glimpse of his piercing blue eyes and realises he is staring at the unmerciful face of a killer.

"Apologise."

The Renegade utters just the one word but so meaningfully put that Sir Stephen realises that if he doesn't, he will soon be as dead as Marques de Draq and with enormous difficulty and white with fury at having to comply, he spits out the words,

"I apologise."

Cannin swings around on the mare's back and rapidly fires the stone from the catapult high up into the sky, striking the buzzard directly behind Elsu. The heavy bird plunges earthwards at incredible speed as the King and his men watch in disbelief that a single stone released from a mere catapult could reach such heights and kill a large bird so efficiently and so effectively.

Cannin turns again to Sir Stephen and the archer.

"Retreat back to your position and do not come so close again."

Both turn their horses' heads and trot slowly back to the King, their faces burning with the humiliation of being ordered about by a mere youth and a Dog Head at that, but both having seen his killing skills at close quarters realise that he could have so easily have killed them outright if he had chosen to do so.

The King all the while, hears the murmuring words from his men behind him, praising the Renegade's sheer skill... surely he is as skilled as the archers and he realises then that he must keep his emotions to himself, for he cannot, must not allow his men to pick up again on his utter hatred of the Renegade.

He sits silently in his saddle when he hears the Renegade's strange whistling echoing back to him. The dog immediately tears across the terrain and drags the buzzard back in his jaws, as nearly as big as himself and drops it close to the Renegade. Isabel claps her hands in high excitement and he can hear her praising the dog in Latin. When Sir Stephen and the archer approach, he angrily waves them to one side, still staring fixedly through his Star Gauge while Sir Clifford in attempt to diffuse the King's mood, speaks in a light hearted tone.

"Finally it appears he has found a use for the dog."

The King ignores him, watching darkly as the Renegade jumps down from *his* horse, he watches him kneel and bow his head to the dog and he finds he still cannot resist a snipe.

"He bows subserviently to a dog?"

He then watches him take up the buzzard, tucking it under one arm and leap back on *his* horse, his anger rising again when he sees Isabel smiling at *him* as though love struck.

Why didn't she ever smile at him in that same manner? But then... he admits it to himself, he never gave her a chance and now she has fallen for the Dog Head and it is his own entire fault.

He watches them slowly trot off without another look behind, the falcon flits down and lands on the Renegade's shoulder, the dog runs ahead, joining the waiting three black horses when a white mist descends downwards without warning and they completely disappear from sight. An unfamiliar feeling of panic grips him and he calls out to his men.

"Quickly now, we mustn't lose them."

They quickly ride forward, the swirling freezing mist sweeps towards them until they too are enveloped within and are forced to continue at walking pace. They eventually come to the dead sheep, but by now the mist is so dense that they cannot even see a few feet ahead. The King snarls out,

"Take up the sheep and let us continue."

Sir Clifford frowns unhappily at him.

"My Lord, it would be foolhardy to continue, ahead there are peat bogs and the horses could get stuck or worse. Let us wait here until the mist lifts, the Renegade is caught in this in exactly the same way as we are and he would have to have stopped as well."

"You obviously have no idea what powers Dog Heads have, I would not be surprised if he has prayed to his spirits to connive a way to mask his flight from us and they have obliged him by conjuring up this dense mist."

"But we must be careful my Lord, before long we will come too far more rugged and dangerous terrain, there is one lone trail, with precipitous falls to either side and only enough room for one horse to pass along its back at a time."

"I do not give a damn; we must catch up otherwise we will lose them." He spurs his horse on, for he must find them, the thought of losing his horse...of losing her, and then he realises that it is not just his horse that he thinks of.

His men ride on following the formidable, yet reassuring dark shape of the King and his horse through the thick white mist. There is not a sound to be heard apart from the heavy breathing of the horses and the clinking of their bridles until all are in a dream like state, following him on and on as he rides continuously northwards.

Hours seemed to have past when all of a sudden the King hears the shrill call of the falcon so close by that he stops his horse and peers all around trying to catch sight of her or of anything tangible when in the distance he catches a glimpse of a small yellow glow piercing through the white mist to his far right. At first he cannot understand what it is, he lifts his hand for all to stop, and then he smells the unmistakable aroma of cooking flesh wafting over and unseen by his men he smiles and as he smiles, the mist lifts, to find that he and his horse are teetering on the edge of a deep precipice.

He stays completely still in his shock, luckily his horse remains in a hypnotic state and stays just as still. He views the dark valley far below him and in a strange disconnected way he realises that dusk is falling and then it strikes him like a hammer blow that if it hadn't been for the warning cry of the falcon and the glow of the fire he would have fallen to his death.

He gently turns his horse's head and with a very slight pressing of his thighs against its flanks, walks it away from the edge and back to his anxious men. The mist thins more and taking his Star Gauge, he views the far off small fire burning in a shallow hollow surrounded by a high half circle of rocks. The seated figures of Cannin and Isabel can be clearly seen; the dog in her lap, he can hear her tinkling laughter and a short distance away the five horses stand in a group, heads down and very obviously asleep. He pulls a face in his confusion and wonders what strategy the Renegade is playing now; he could so easily have disappeared, so why didn't he?

"Let us settle down for the night but I think perhaps a good distance away from the edge of the precipice." He laughs and his weary men begin to smile as he adds,

"I believe that God smiles down on us and he wishes us a safe journey to the north. So let us eat."

His men then grin, for they know that it is the King that is smiled down upon, as he always is.

A fire is made, the sheep prepared but all the while he views the soft glow of the far off fire, his men are quiet when they see his deep, reflective mood and when he finally lays down to sleep they follow suit but all notice that he doesn't confer with any of them and more surprisingly not even with Sir Clifford.

CHAPTER THIRTY THREE
The monastery

The bear, having consumed the seal in his gluttony and unable to resist the other delicacies left on the beach by the squall returns to feast, leaving great piles of discarded bones and numerous shells scattered over the shingle beach.

Gulls, Skuas and Kittiwakes join him and a great feeding frenzy begins until the bear so sated with food decides that enough is enough and wends his way back to the safety of the dunes and falls asleep for the remainder of the day amongst the clumps of stiff grey grass.

Dusk is falling when he wakes up with a start, some inner sense warns him that a great source of danger is coming his way, he sniffs deeply and takes in the powerful stench of two unknown creatures and peeping his head above the fore dune he watches to see what they are.

Two trotting Dog Heads with spears in hands emerge onto the beach and kneeling down sniff the droppings left by the donkey from earlier that day as the fast incoming tide sweeps up to them, carrying the discarded shells of the lobsters and crabs that the bear had in his innocence left strewn all over the beach. With low growls, the Dog Heads pick up the shells and sniff them deeply and crouching on their haunches stare suspiciously around and the bear suddenly fearful that he is all on his own realises he had better quickly find Lomond. He quickly lopes through the dunes until he comes across the wheel tracks left by the monks' cart and snout to the ground he rapidly follows the scent of the donkey. Behind him the two Dog Heads stand up and screech to the gulls, but not one bird responds and it is then that they realise strange, unsettling things are afoot.

Lomond opens his eyes to find he is in the small, stone walled room of his dreams which he realises now is and always was complete reality, as the familiar source of light emanating from the burning embers of a fire in a small hearth near to him fills the small space with warmth.

He cannot quite understand how he has ended up in this most strangest of places but he does seem to recall a series of Humans praying quietly all around him with such reassuring and calm voices that he would drift off... they would come and they would go but in the interludes when he was left alone the wind spirits would sneak in through the gap under the wooden door and whisper to him of his duty to the new king.

He lies still for a moment but becoming aware of how overly hot he is, he furiously kicks off the sheepskins covering him to find, to his shock, that he is stark naked. He sits bolt upright but then he espies his clothing carefully draped over a wooden bench next to the fire alongside the heavy shark's jaw bone. He leaps up from the straw pallet and as he dresses, the approaching softly spoken voices of the Humans that had prayed around him come towards him.

"I do say he has indeed been heaven sent to us how else could he have survived the wrath of the white squall?"
Lomond peers through the bars of his door to see a group of six standing men wearing long, black gowns, all of different sizes in girth and in height, but all of a considerable age.

"But we have all seen he has the same affliction as the Dog People, how many times have we seen their tracks on the sandy stretches of the beach at dawn? He has exactly the same webbing between his toes so how do we know that he is not one of them and has been sent into our inner sanctum to kill us all?"

Brother Firmin shakes his head disappointedly at the normally affable brother Winfrid.

"You are wrong, he is not one of them, not only does he not possess their bestial features but he also wears the garb of the people from the Northern Isles, and I believe, I most firmly believe, he has been guided here by God to relay his message to us. How can you explain his consistent calling out, over and over again that the king comes, what else could his words possibly mean? He is the sign, I know he is the sign that the people will come back to us."

"His words are just fever ridden gibberish; you are reading far too much into all of this brother Firmin."

They all stand silently for a second, heads bowed, all unaccustomed to arguing amongst themselves and deeply unhappy that they have been driven to do so, when to their utter horror they hear the most terrible bawling of some unknown creature coming from the outside accompanied by the sound of the gates being shaken violently. Brother Winfrid, white with fear points his finger to the outside.

"The beasts have come to get us, I told you they would, now what do we do?"

Lomond opens up the door to the cell and pads quickly past them,

"It is only the bear wishing to be with me."

Their faces are shocked at his sudden well appearance, shocked that they had forgotten to bolt the door to his cell

293

and so shocked that they have no choice but to follow behind and as Lomond follows the cries of the bear, he whistles a low sound like a strange kind of bird and the terrible bawls subdue down to low whimpers. The monks are astounded that he finds his path so easily down their long convoluting passages to the outside and even more shocked to see the huge, standing hairy bear with long white claws grasping the upright rails of their iron gates. At the sight of Lomond, the bear's lower lip quivers emotionally and he growls to be let in.

Lomond turns quickly to the monks.

"You must let the bear in, he says they are following his scent from the beach and will soon be here."

None of them have any doubt of whom he is talking about, but before any of the other monks can answer, brother Firmin runs over and rapidly unlocks the iron gates, the bear rushes through in a great hairy explosion and bowls Lomond to the ground in his happiness to see him, the other monks step back in fear when Lomond calls out,

"Quickly lock the gates."

Brother Firmin locks the gates, Lomond disentangles himself from the bear and they all retreat and hide behind a great stone wall a few yards on from the entrance gates. Lomond with both hands holds the jaws of the bear shut to cease his growls, the monks crowd behind him fearfully and if they thought the bawling of the bear was frightening the noises they hear now are utterly terrifying, sounding exactly like a pack of wolves, the air filled with their growling, yelping and howling and the sound of their bodies crashing against the iron gates, and now they know what the villagers had had to endure for the last twenty years and they bow their heads in their shame that they hadn't had the courage to have helped them more.

Lomond listens intently to the horrific noises when abruptly the noises cease, apart from low menacing growls and he turns to the monks.

"They are fearful of entering in here, they believe this is a place of great power, hence their extreme anger and frustration. But they are offering threats that if you do not hand over the bear immediately they will take out their vengeance on the Humans in the village. I had better go and speak to them and explain that the bear is with me and not with you."

The monks stare wide eyed in fear at him, that he can understand their noises must surely mean he must be one of them, that is apart from brother Firmin who smiles at Lomond, everything he has believed about the youth is now proving to be true.

"How is it that you can understand them?"

Lomond smiles back at him.

"Because I am half of their strain and the other half of me, on my mother's side, is the same as you. My name is Lomond and I and the bear have been carried here by the wind spirits so that soon we may offer assistance to the new King that comes."

Brother Firmin smiles again and bows his head to his youthful words.

"I am pleased that I now know your name Lomond, my name is brother Firmin, but I have to ask, who is this King that you speak of?"

The terrible howling begins again in earnest and Lomond has to raise his voice.

"The wind spirits say he is the King of the Dog Heads...I had better go quickly and speak to them, their anger is now out of all proportion and I fear for what they will do next."

He releases his hands from around the bear's jaws and walks out from behind the stone wall, the bear immediately shambles behind him, brother Firmin follows behind the bear and then the other monks not wishing to be left alone and palms quickly put together in prayer walk at the rear, their hearts pounding in fear.

The terrible howling subsides at Lomond and the bear's approach, the monks stand further back when they see that behind the gates are enormous, dark hulking shapes and numerous pairs of golden, lit almond shaped eyes and the flashings of yellow teeth.

Lomond stops when he is a few feet away and stands quietly; the vicious growling begins again spewing such profanity and hatred towards the monks that if they could understand he knows they would be in even more fear than they already are. The bear growls back agitatedly, Lomond whistles to calm him, which results in the Dog Heads quietening when they realise that the youth standing in front of them understands their tongue. Lomond waits for a moment and then he calls out.

"I will not speak to you in any other tongue but Human for I know you can speak it."

He stands quietly again, angry growling and snapping noises ensue until the deepest and most menacing voice the monks have ever heard growls out.

"You will give us the Grolar bear, he has trespassed on our land without our permission and has eaten of our particular delicacies and so he must suffer the consequences of his actions."

His foul breath stinking of rotting carrion reaches Lomond's nostrils and he knows they want the bear to not only eat his raw flesh but that they all covet his thick fur coat and he shudders inwardly of what they would do to him if they got their hands on him.

"The Grolar bear and I are under the protection of the wind spirits and we have been brought here by the force of the white squall at their command."

Silence apart from deep sniffing noises as they take in his words and his scent. And then the deep voice becomes more cautious and in turn more suspicious.

"Who are you and why would the wind spirits send you here?"

"We have been sent to pay homage to the new king when he soon arrives and are at his command." Terrible barking laughter ensues so that even the monks realise they laugh in derision at Lomond's words until finally there is silence apart from deep collective sniffing noises when the deep malicious voice growls out again.

"The Mongrel will be dead soon enough so you have come on a wasted journey and besides no Dog Head can help him, it is forbidden."

"It is forbidden for pure Dog Heads, but as I am half of your strain and half Human, I am not governed by your laws and can choose whatever strain I'm in a mind to support and I'm in a mind to support the new king, for after all we are the same." More deep fearsome growls as the monks palms together, begin again to murmur their prayers.

"We do not recognise your scent, you have no blood of ours, you lie." The voice shouts over the monks' prayers, but now Lomond growls menacingly with the bear joining in and then he speaks again in the Human tongue.

"If I were send to my father now of your insult to me you may be assured that his wrath towards you in refuting his blood coursing through my veins would result in all of your deaths so I suggest that you leave now and await for the arrival of the new king and let us see what will be."

Another voice now from behind the gates, far higher pitched than before and with a whining, ingratiating tone in the pretence of being subservient, howls out,

"But why do you not tell us the name of your father?" Other voices join in, mimicking the words.

"Come give us the name of your father."

Lomond turns and walks towards the monks and with enormous relief they see he has a huge smile on his face and his eyes strangely lit almost from within. But regardless, they are so enamoured at his courage that a great surge of strength courses through them as the cries continue to call out. Lomond turns to face them again.

"But surely you must know by now who my father is, or have your senses been so corrupted and so diminished by your vile life style that you cannot recognise him in me?"

Now there is complete silence at his insult to them, they sniff in far more deeply than they had done for years and growl between each other and then it comes to them... and without another sound they rapidly turn tail and lope silently off into the night.

The monks bow to their knees in their relief and now pray loudly, Lomond leaves them and with the bear following closely behind he makes his way back to the cell in his exhaustion, collapses back onto the straw pallet with the bear lying next to him and wishes that his father were with him.

But he cannot ask him, this is his journey but even so he worries that he has the strength to fight against this terrible enemy. He falls back into the deepest of sleeps while the wind spirits as small breezes cavort around his head, whispering in his ears of their commands of what he must do when the new king arrives from over the high mountains.

Back at Fair Isle, the Wulver paces relentlessly up and down the round pebbled beach as more and more of the sea birds fly from the south with their shrill calls, telling him of all, the dolphins leap through the waves chattering belligerently and for the first time ever he contemplates leaving his kingdom, but he knows he will never get there in time even if he were to grasp the fins of the fleetest of the dolphins.

He growls out to the wind spirits, they gather quickly around him apologetically, soothingly, caressingly...But what choice did he give them, how many times had they asked for his help? He has left them with no choice, no choice other than to use his son, of course only half of him, but surely one half is better than none?

"You have forced me into this position, now I know why you sent the plague ship here, everything done so meticulously, so carefully planned to make me to do your will, well now that you have forced me to be involved, you will now do my will."

Of course, of course, they whisper, anything the great, the mystical, the legendary Wulver wants is his... he only has to ask?

"Then I ask for this."

CHAPTER THIRTY FOUR
The cattle drovers' caves

A dark and stormy dawn sky greets the waking eyes of the King and his men, they rise up quickly, all viewing the Renegade putting the saddle onto another of the black horses. He helps Isabel to mount and then leaps onto another and with a shrill whistle of some description of bird, he leads on, all follow behind in a single file with the white mare accompanied by the dog at the rear.

Hurriedly, urgently they gather themselves together and follow after, the King with the Star Gauge to his eye again,

"Now I understand why he took my horses, it was all in order to have a fresh mount every day, he knows that ours will soon become jaded with no fresh supply available and then he will surely lose us. But what I still do not understand, cannot understand is why he didn't disappear when he had every opportunity to do so?"

Sir Clifford, riding at his side, glances quickly at his stern face.

"Perhaps as you have always thought my Lord that he sets out to goad you, to lead you on?"

With the Star Gauge still to his eye he stares at Isabel's windblown long black hair from behind, watches her hand pull the hood over her head until her face is lost from his sight which he finds annoys him almost as much as her quiet servility in following behind the Renegade as if she were his chattel.

"I believe you are right, for what other reason could there be?"

They follow after and soon come to the thin trail with sheer falls to either side that Sir Clifford had warned of earlier. The Renegade without hesitation follows its course and in single file all walk behind, the King and his men follow after as high treacherous winds buffet them all relentlessly, not a word is said but all are strangely glad they follow the sure footed course of the King's white mare in front and the lightly trotting dog.

With the high winds, now comes down the rain until again the visibility is only what they see a few yards ahead, but then the falcon appears in front, sodden wings heavily beating and the King and his men follow, listening to her calls as she leads them on until finally in mid afternoon they pass onto another plateau of purple sprouting heather but surrounded by high rock formations with the open gaping mouths of dark caves in abundance. The skies clear in time for the King and his men to see Cannin aim his catapult at a swift moving mountain hare, they watch in fascination as the creature falls to the ground away in the distance as again the dog tears over to retrieve it and yet again he hears his men whisper appreciatively of his skill.

The King turns to Sir Clifford and growls out the first words since the morning.

"If it were not for the Renegade and his damned power over my dogs they could have been with us and would have been a lot more useful than that runt of a dog, another grievance that I hold against him. Pass me your bow and one arrow, archer."

Sir Stephen glowers behind his back that he had not been asked.

The archer quickly passes him the bow and an arrow in surprise, the King turns and aims to his right into a veil of low hanging mist, his men exchange glances and all wonder if he had gone quite mad. The arrow is released, seconds pass, nothing happens, all stand silently in embarrassment when finally they hear a loud, startled grunt and the sound of some creature thumping heavily to the ground. He passes the bow back to the archer and growls around at two of his men.

"Retrieve it." They immediately canter away into the mist as the King watches Cannin and Isabel dismount soon after and lead the horses into the mouth of one of the larger caves and he guesses they are stopping for the night.

"We will stay in the last cave we just passed; I believe these are cattle drovers' caves and with any luck we will find they have left peat for us to burn, the Renegade is wise in the choice of location for it is so perishing cold." And then he laughs out loud.

His men ride back to the deep cave and on entering find a huge stack of dried peat and before long a fire is burning, the horses are tethered at the opening to the cave when exuberant cries call out from his men as the male red deer is dragged in with the arrow sunk deeply into its forehead. Such a good omen at the King's prowess with the bow that their spirits lift as he openly grins at them.

"I have not told all of you before, the reason why we follow the Renegade and the Queen and even now I cannot speak freely, suffice to say that my hands are tied and I cannot do as I would like. Their survival though, particularly the Renegade's is of the utmost importance and will be until we reach the Northern Lands and, feelings put to one side we will escort them, whether they like it or whether we like it, until they reach their destination. When they have, I will then inform you of what we will do next. But until then, we will use our proper senses; I do not want to hear again of devils, faeries, will of the wisps, goblins and the dark forces. You are, and have always been, as my chosen men the elite and whilst I appreciate we have not been in a war for eight years, we must never forget our huge successes then and before that. We have never been influenced by fanciful notions and we shan't now. We are a hard fighting force and from now on that is how we shall behave and I include myself in this. Are there any questions?"

They all shake their heads but each one inwardly questions why he does not speak of the powers of Dog Heads?

"Good, the Renegade will be up at the crack of dawn, so let us surprise him and be ready before he is."

CHAPTER THIRTY FIVE
The gathering of the gulls

"Lomond, the strangest sight is to be seen, brother Firmin says you must come."

The elderly Brother Rayvan calls softly through the bars of his cell being far too nervous to enter in, for he is still entirely unsure of the sleeping Grolar bear. Lomond rises up and without a word groggily follows behind him; the bear opens one eye, stretches and quickly shambles to catch up as they wend their way along the stone corridors and back towards the outside.

Brother Firmin, brother Bernard, brother Wigbert, brother Eddmar and even the dubious brother Winfrid smile warmly at Lomond's approach as brother Firmin rushes over to him and grasps his hands.

"Thank you for coming Lomond, I know you are still in need of rest, but I felt certain you would be happy to witness the most unusual and awe inspiring sight that we have ever seen and we know it is because of you."

And so said, he opens the heavy wooden doors to the outside, beckoning him to follow, they pass alongside the heavy stone wall which they had hidden behind in the early hours in the morning as Lomond looks up to the darkening sky and realises dusk is soon to fall. They round the end of the wall to see perched on the gates and all along the high, outer walls of the monastery vast numbers of differing species of sea birds.

At his and the bear's appearance their many differing voices scream out passionately, the screeching chorus piercing his ear drums to such an extent that he covers his ears, however the bear with great excitement lopes over to the high walls and rising up on his haunches growls appreciatively. The monks become more and more concerned at Lomond's indifference to the great bird gathering and stare at each other in confusion until suddenly Lomond uncovers his hands from his ears and lifts his arms skywards and all the birds abruptly quieten. He lowers his weary arms, whistles a few sharp notes and the birds in their masses take to the air and fly away.

Brother Firmin in great agitation cries out.

"But Lomond for them to come here, here of all places, says to us brethren that huge changes are happening?"

"I apologise for what appears to be my seeming indifference to this gathering, but I am still so weary. You are correct in your assumption, the sea birds have swopped allegiance over to us. They will no longer spy for the Dog People who have treated them cruelly. They say they are too greedy, they take everything and because the Grolar bear generously shared the spoils from the squall with them they will now join with us and will serve the new king when he arrives.

And so I apologise again, I must lie down to gather my strength before the king comes, but I ask, before I do and if it would not seem to be too forward, if I might be allowed something to eat, for the bear's great growling, gurgling guts, packed so full from his avarice, that I have had to listen to for hours, the reason why I have not managed to sleep fully, plus his continual boasting of how much he has managed to consume has in all honesty driven me to either never eat again or gorge myself as he has. But in truth, I am so weak now that some morsel, any morsel would suffice and perhaps some water."

At his great speech, the monks are mortified at their negligence towards him and they usher him along. But as brother Firmin opens the door to the refectory to allow Lomond through the bear pushes past the monks, nearly bowling them to the ground which forces Lomond to growl so angrily at him that he stops in his tracks.

"He may not come in brother Firmin, he has ate so much I wonder that he can even walk, we will leave him outside because I can assure you what he will void soon will not be to your liking." The monks look at each other with absolute horror; not so much about the droppings, but a bear prowling about unsupervised would only result in one thing, for in their mind's eye they have a vision of him eating their last and only donkey, their one heifer and the few chickens. Lomond catches their looks.

"Is there something amiss?"

Brother Bernard bows his head.

"We have no wish to offend you or the bear, but we are concerned that his appetite may pick up again and he may be tempted to eat our very limited numbers of live stock."

"Please be assured, he will not be able to eat anything for a good many days. We will leave him outside for that is what he is used to and besides he will make an excellent guard."

They enter into the refectory and the door is firmly shut on the bear, he growls unhappily for a few minutes and then becoming bored he decides to familiarise himself with his new surroundings.

"We are honoured to have you as our guest Lomond, it has been such a long, long time that we have had company. We are a monastery long forgotten, not just because of the isolation of where we are located from the rest of the country, and not just because we have historically been plundered by marauders from over the border from the land of the Scots...I beg that I do not offend you with my words?" Lomond shakes his head at brother Firmin, being far more intent on devouring the lobster on his plate as the six monks sit together on the opposite side of the wooden table and stare at him intently when he notices that he eats alone.

"But I feel that I offend you, will you not eat with me?"
Brother Firmin smiles over at him.

"We have set times to eat and must wait a little longer for our supper and your needs are far greater than ours, for we do try to maintain the doctrines of our faith even though with best intentions we are sadly remiss these days. But please allow me to continue if I may?"
Lomond bows his head.

"Twenty years ago, our numbers here were greatly reduced as were the villagers when the plague swept over us. We lost many of our brethren and have been reduced to the number you see in front of you. We sadly lost our Abbot at that time and by unanimous decision by all present and as his deputy I have taken over the position, until God willing we are once again remembered by Westminster." Lomond stops eating and views them across the table and feels their sadness and desolation and in an attempt to make them feel better and before he can help himself and against what his father had always told him, he speaks out.

"I too know of the ravaging of the plague, my mother's family were wiped out by it and she was the only one that survived hence I came into being."

The monks would like to ask him more, but the very thought of asking who his father is, would be so indelicate that they collectively stare down at the table and Lomond instantly realises that he has embarrassed them.

"I apologise brother Firmin, I have put you off your train of thought, please continue."

They raise their heads to see that Lomond's eyes are lighting up by degrees and turning to the dark windows they realise it's time to light the candles and wonder again at being so remiss. Brother Bernard as the youngest excuses himself and quickly returns with a large brass candelabrum. brother Firmin waits until the candles are lit before continuing.

"Thank you Lomond for listening to our woes and now that brother Bernard has rejoined us I will continue. At precisely the same time as the plague took hold the Dog People or Cinbin as the locals call them, arrived and moved into the ancient burial mound nearby.

At first, not one of us realised their evil intent but only after a few days they began to take the livestock from the villagers with menaces and as you can imagine, with their fear of these creatures the villagers handed over everything they asked for but not before too long, a very strange relationship developed between them all."

At this point, Lomond ceases eating and takes a sip of his wine and nearly chokes never having drunk anything quite like it before.

"What kind of strange relationship are you talking of?"

"The strangest kind of relationship, one of the men on death's door covered in the terrible sores took it upon himself to go the burial mound asking for the pagan God's to save him, for this is what they had always done throughout time long before we established the monastery. He was ushered in and was never seen again. From then on, the villagers convinced themselves that the Dog People were of the ancient God's and laid the sick and the dying at the entrance as all disappeared.

They believe the burial mound is the portal to the afterlife and when they saw that the Dog People were not affected by the plague and in their ignorance, they began to worship them as deities. We tried to persuade them of otherwise, but they would not listen as even now the ritualistic sacrificial offerings continue. Every month the villagers supply them with an offering of live stock but on the winter solstice they are expected to pay homage with human flesh. The plague victims ran out a long time ago and so the villagers have been handing over their old people and sickly babies to keep them happy. Fortunately, or perhaps not so fortunately, Yule or the winter solstice is almost upon us, the only relief the villagers get until spring for this is when the Cinbin hibernate and to all is a day of great celebration.

But we are frightened of what the villagers will be able to offer up now for there are no old and no sick this year and we know the Cinbin will not be satisfied with just livestock, they will demand a human sacrifice, and whoever this human sacrifice is, will die the most horrible of deaths."

Lomond finishes his lobster and looks up at them.

"How do they die?" All the brethren notice, that surprisingly for one so young he is not in the slightest bit perturbed by what he has been told so far.

"We were told by one of the frightened old men of the village before he disappeared years before that when the winter solstice comes, heralding the shortest day and the longest of nights, the sun rises up from the horizon at dawn and for the only time of the year, blasts through the gap above the eastern door into the central chamber of the burial mound. At that very point the top of the sacrifice's head is sawn off and the live brains eaten. They then slit the throat, drink the blood, after that they rip the sacrifice apart and devour it. There is much more that they do but of such abnormality and of such atrocity that I cannot bring myself to speak of it."

When he finishes speaking the candle light flickers erratically as if some ill wind stirs within when at exactly at the same time the bear growls so menacingly from outside that the monks' turn their heads apprehensively to look out of the window. A chill silence ensues and the monks wonder if they have put too much trust in Lomond when they watch him sniff in deeply and his eyes glow even more intensely than before.

"I thank you for the food brethren, I'd better go and see the bear, he tells me *they* have just thrown over some delicacy for him to eat but he says that it is tainted and not fit for consumption, thankfully he hasn't touched it but only, I feel, because he's so stuffed."

311

The monks look uneasily at each other with many forebodings as Lomond gets up to leave, when brother Firmin feels duty bound to ask him if he would need help.

"Perhaps we could accompany you Lomond, if you think we could be of any use?"

Lomond stares back at them and sees for the first time the stark fear on their faces.

"Yes, I would be glad of your company for this is a strange land that I find myself in and you can be a witness to the horror that we will undoubtedly find outside."

Rising quickly, yet shaking with fear they follow behind Lomond, out through the door, and follow his lit eyes until they come across the hulk of the bear standing over a whitish object on the ground.

Lomond crouches down next to him and sniffs in deeply.

"It is carrion from a Human and obviously not to their fancy being several months old, but it has also been laced with some vile substance, no doubt to kill off the bear."

At his stark words, the monks step ever closer in their horror, they don't want to, they fear to, but they know they must see what it is and as they close in and lit by Lomond's eyes, they see the gnawed, yellowed foot of a human male, but in their minds what is more horrific, is not just the sight of the foot or where it had been snapped off from the tibia and fibula but the sight of the yellowed split toe nails still attached to the bone phalanges.

They cry out in their fury at the abomination and drop to their knees.

"Mercy for his soul, we pray o Lord, mercy for his soul."

But as they cry out, the air is suddenly full of the most hideous yelping, howling and cackling laughter from beyond the monastery walls abruptly silencing the monks.

Lomond rises to his feet and stares at the gates when the yelps, howls and laughter carry off into the distance until there is silence apart from the bear's low angry growls. Lomond turns back to the monks and helps the elderly brother Firmin to his feet, noting how they all shake and he realises then they are too old and too fearful to cope with anything more.

"Come brethren, rise up now; do not allow them to alarm you they will never enter into here. Their anger is channelled at me and the bear and they are warning us that we will be next if we dare to go out of the gates. Now, and far more importantly we must dispose of this foot in case some unwitting creature eats of it, but what to do with it I wonder?"

His quiet strength fills them all with shame at their cowardice and quickly it is suggested by them all that the best way would be to burn it. Brother Eddmar accompanied by brother Wigbert courageously trot off to a small wooden shack and return with a spade and a stout stick. The brethren gather around Lomond, all trying to hide their revulsion as he carefully pushes the foot onto the spade with the stick and with them showing him the way; he carries it gingerly over to a small stretch of wasteland and tips it onto the remnants of an autumn fire with the bear quizzically watching on. Kindling is placed on top, Lomond takes out two stones from his pouch bends down and striking them together, creates a small spark which in turn ignites the kindling and before long there is a fierce, stinking blaze. The monks begin to pray and Lomond bows his head as he listens to their words.

"O Lord, who art ever merciful and bounteous with thy gifts, look down upon the suffering souls in purgatory..."

Lomond shuts off their voices, paying more interest in the tears trickling down their old faces and he finds him pities them beyond anything. Finally they stop and stand silently looking over at him and he realises they would like him to speak.

"I thank you brethren for your kindness to me and to the bear, but I'm afraid we must retire until the dawn comes.

I bid you all a pleasant sleep, for with the new day, new beginnings are about to happen for us all."

He bows his head and walks away with the bear at his side.

The monks watch after him and cross themselves with more conviction than they had done in such a long time.

CHAPTER THIRTY SIX
The chapel of light

An hour before dawn, the King and his men are ready to ride. They silently mount their horses and wait in formation ready for the appearance of Cannin and Isabel to come from the cave and in their increasing boredom the men's attention steadily becomes more taken by the falcon gliding majestically above.

As time slips by and behind the King and Sir Clifford, some of the men cannot resist to half smile and jocularly wink at each other, all imagining why it is taking them so long to appear from the cave as Sir Stephen sits motionless on his horse and pretends not to notice.

The long minutes go past as the horses begin to pace agitatedly with the King watching the cave mouth, his face hard set when the dog appears followed by three of the black horses and trot off to the north. Seconds pass, but to him it seems a long, indeterminable space of time when finally they appear, Isabel riding his white mare and the Renegade on one of the black horses and without a single look in his direction they trot away.

The King seethes inwardly at their casual indifference towards him, knowing full well that the Renegade is entirely aware of his presence. He puts the Star Gauge to his eye and scrutinises Isabel, focusing in until he can see every windblown hair, for in his mind he cannot banish the vision of the two wrapped in each other's arms in the dark of the cave. He takes the Star Gauge from his eye and without looking around he growls out,

"From now on there will be no hidden chat, no sly glances or any other form of innuendo and the first that even thinks or attempts it, I will personally slice off his head, you have all been warned."

And from then on there is not a sound as they all wend their way onwards to the north as the cold wind pushes them relentlessly from behind.

On the straw pallet, lying alongside Lomond, the bear rolls to one side and with a great grunt rolls himself back and growls directly in Lomond's face, his breath so hot and so stinking that Lomond is forced to open his eyes.

"Alright we will leave now as you clearly leave me no choice."

The bear leaps up and stretches, Lomond quietly rises, still dressed and momentarily pauses to look at the heavy shark's jaw bone and then picks it up.

They wander along the dark corridors until finally reaching the great wood doors to the outside and as Lomond opens them, a stark, cold dawn greets their eyes. They walk to the outer gates, Lomond pushes slightly against them, but they are still locked and so no chance of slipping away unnoticed. He props the jawbone against the high wall next to the gates and stands still for a moment, head cocking from one side to the other trying to locate where the monks are when he hears the sound of praying voices coming from somewhere behind deep walls. They follow in the direction of the voices until coming to another set of huge dark wooden doors and pushing through Lomond stops suddenly on the stone threshold and gasps, the enormous space is comparable exactly in height and breadth to the sea water cave that he and the bear had slept in on their way down, but with such a difference, as huge red stone columns flanking the nave ascend to the dark timber ceiling with the light of dawn filtering through high up stained glass windows filling the space with such an ethereal quality of light that he is completely awestruck.

At the far eastern end, a window in the shape of a flower allows more light in, picking out the white clothed altar below. In front of it the six monks' face each other sitting on low wooden benches, three on one side and three on the other and are so absorbed in their prayers that it is not until the bear growls out and crosses the threshold they had thought themselves to be completely alone.

But before Lomond can stop the bear, he noisily passes a vast stream of urine, the monks turn around with horrified eyes as brorther Firmin abruptly rises up.

"No, no, he is not allowed to enter in here, make him leave Lomond, he must not, cannot enter into our sacred place, he has no soul, no soul, make him leave, I beg of you."

The other monks rise up as Lomond stares back at them coldly and whistles to the bear, who now realising he has done something very wrong lopes back and sits next to him.

"I have done as you have wished brethren, he has come back to my side but I wonder that you would be so harsh to him, for how would he know as a wild creature that he is not allowed in here? And I also beg to differ with you, for it is my known understanding that all creatures possess souls."

The monks quickly come forward when they realise they have upset him.

"We apologise Lomond, we have no wish to upset you or the bear. Of course he may enter, of course, but he must refrain from using the chapel as if he were outside." When he sees the monks' extreme distress, he quickly relents.

"I accept your apology, but I feel we have outstayed our welcome here, we bring too much trouble to your gates and I think it is best that we leave."

This causes the monks to now look anxiously at each other, as brother Firmin once again becomes their spokesperson.

"But Lomond, have you any understanding of what awaits you outside the gates? We beg of you to reconsider, whilst it is common practise for the Dog People to sleep during the day, it isn't always the case, they will come out of the burial mound if they have a good reason to, in particular when the marauding cattle thieves used to cross Hadrian's Wall. They slaughtered all that came, another reason why the people are indebted to them, so please avoid the village otherwise we will fear for your safety for even as monks we are not allowed to set foot there anymore but even more importantly please do not go anywhere near the burial mound."

"You still do not seem to understand that I and the bear are protected by the wind spirits and you have no need to worry on our behalf, but I thank you for your concern."

Seeing that he is still utterly determined to go, they accompany him to the gate as Lomond picks up the shark jaw and hangs it over his shoulder like a great scythe, brother Firmin pretends not to notice but as he turns the key in the lock he turns to stare directly at Lomond's face with high emotion.

"I know you do this in order that we might not suffer any more distress and so I thank you for your sensitivity towards us. But if you change your mind you and the bear will always be welcome here, regardless of how it might affect us... take great care Lomond and remember you will be in our prayers."

Lomond smiles and bows his head but as he and the bear walk away a sudden, shocking realisation comes to brother Firmin and he calls after him.

"Lomond, I beg you will forgive that I intrude too much, but is your father, could it be, could it be that he is the one that is called the Wulver?"

Lomond turns back, nods his head and carries on.

The monks watch after him until he and the bear disappear.

"I know we should not acknowledge that such a creature as the Wulver exists, but the people of the Northern Isles believe in him totally, they call him the wolf head, the immortal spirit." And then he sighs deeply.

"I have always thought that the people are only primitive in their beliefs because of their lack of education but as we have witnessed with our own eyes there is much we do not understand. Let us return to the chapel now and pray for Lomond, the bear and for this new king of the Dog People that comes and continue to pray day and night to make up for all the years where we have been remiss."

CHAPTER THIRTY SEVEN
Azenor's mantle of flight

With sea gulls whirling above, Lomond and the bear make their way to the distant stone village.

There is no sign of life, no smoke from roofs and if Lomond didn't know better, he would say the village had been abandoned long ago. But then he picks up the sound of grunting hogs coming from somewhere within and walks on until he approaches the first of the stone buildings and stops at the start of the stony track separating the line of dwellings and knows instinctively that behind the closed doors, frightened yet angry Humans hide themselves from him and the bear. He senses they have been warned that he and the bear are dangerous creatures and must not be entertained in any shape or form.

He continues on, staring at each building in turn, searching for something, he does not know quite what, when his eyes meet the green eyes of a flaxen haired girl, possibly of his own age or maybe younger staring directly at him through a low window. She immediately ducks down, her heart hammering in her chest. Lomond walks on as if he hadn't seen her, somehow realising the danger towards her if she had been seen to have clearly looked at him, but the image of her face remains clearly in his mind, for never has he seen such a look of despair and of such forlornness and he contemplates broodingly why that should be?

As he disappears along the stone track with the bear loping at his side like a great dog, the girl rises up from the earth floor, feeling such high strange emotions and recalling his black eyes, like the limpid eyes of a seal, her most favourite of creatures, wonders who he could possibly be and where had he come from?

She looks over to her long white feathered mantle that the upright skeleton propped against the wall wears patiently for her until it is time, lovingly started when she was born by the womenfolk of the village as every year, more and more tiers of feathers are sewn expertly around the whale bone ribs.

So nearly completed now, her mantle of flight, soon she will be able to soar with the gulls and if she so chose she could swoop down and swim with the seals for she will be one with the elements, part of them, the most supreme, the most admired, the godliest of all creatures. She will be able to dive down into the deepest of seas, rise above the highest of mountains, fly wherever she wants, she needs no sustenance she has been told, she is of them, told as soon as she could understand, that she is their chosen one, but sometimes she ponders as she grows older and understands more, if she is of them, which is her father and where is her mother, for the Cinbin are all males?

She puts the question, one dark winter day to her many mothers from the village as they busily sort out the best of the feathers lying at their feet.

"Your father is the highest one. Your mother, one of us, unfortunately died at your birth, being far too weak and too fragile to live after the carrying of you, for you have his blood coursing through you, the blood of the strongest. You are destined to go to great heights, such heights, he has assured us, and that is why you are the chosen one."

They neglected to tell her that after *he* had coupled with her mother viciously, cruelly and without consent, and as soon as she was born, her mother was taken to the barrow before the dawning of the winter solstice and was not seen again. But two months on and at the end of hibernation, *they* had brought the skeleton to the village and whilst it was never mentioned out loud, all knew it was her.

The five Cinbin that had brought the skeleton passed on the instructions of how the baby would be nurtured until she was of age and of the making of the mantle. They mentioned no name for her, referring to her only as the spawn and so after much secret debate in the daylight hours and amongst them all, she was named Azenor - the name meaning testimony or evidence, the only defiance they had ever shown against their masters.

In blissful ignorance, Azenor spent her childhood in momentous happiness, the women of the village were all her mother and adored her above their own children, she was stroked, caressed and kissed at the slightest of ills. Even the bad tempered men of the village, who were viciously cruel to their own children, winked and smiled at her as she skipped along, the chosen one, the flaxen haired one, the one that will soar above...but then she turns back to the sea bird cloak...they had always told her that it was to be made of the finest of white dove feathers, but what she sees now is a hard, unyielding, encapsulation. She pulls a face, and dipping into her pocket pulls out the single dove feather that had fallen in swirling elegance at her feet from only an hour before, that had fallen from the dove that had swept over from the bad place, the place of the black monks, the evil ones but nevertheless she had slipped into her clothing before any of the Cinbin had noticed. They being far too busy growling at all of them to hide in their dwellings, to remain silent and under any account not to look out, for the black monks' missionary is nearly upon them with his human eating bear.

She stares critically over again at the stiff, unyielding mantle and wishes that it was made instead from dove feathers, just like the one in her hand that they had always told her that it would be, the feathers' heaven sent, the wings of doves when yet again the memory of Lomond's dark seal eyes stare into hers.

But then she pulls herself together, of what use are the feathers of doves? Only the sea birds survive through the harsh elements with their tough feathers, doves cannot dive into the deep water and view the seals swimming beneath and more importantly the sea birds eat the weak doves, eat them all, devour everything and she falls to the earth ground and hugs herself in a great passion because very soon, so very soon she will go to the promised place.

When Lomond and the bear clear the village, the bear following the scent of the dog people avidly and yet reluctantly, they both stop to view the high, rounded, enormous burial mound in the far distance, looking very much like an innocent green hillock. But from even where there are, they both take in the stench of rotting carrion while above the sea birds glide above silently for they have no wish to alert the Cinbin of Lomond's approach.

As he walks over the flat plain he sees the many marks of their giant, webbed feet and calculates their numbers exceed well over forty and he finds it interesting they make no attempt to cover their tracks, in fact so much so, that a great path of their toing and froing between the ancient burial mound and the village is visible and clearly had gone on for a long, long time. And he frowns then at their departure of the natural path, the carefully chosen one, but then of course what predators do they have? They rule supreme, they are the predators and none are safe, not a single Human or any creature.

He finally approaches the large door crudely made from driftwood and guesses they had fashioned it themselves and the huge stone that had obviously once covered the entrance had been tossed to one side. He then follows the contour of the mound until coming to the western entranceway and realises that this one is not in use. There isn't a door, but instead large round boulders partially block the way in and he surmises it wouldn't be too difficult to unblock it.

Looking now in a northerly direction, he sees the high border wall that the monks had told him of and decides it is the perfect vantage point, from there he will be able to see everything, the mountainous range from where the king will come from the south, the burial mound and bearing to the right the village and further along, the dark outline of the monastery set against the perfect disc of the grey sea and so now all he has to do is to wait.

CHAPTER THIRTY EIGHT
The lone monk

"My Lord!"

The shout and the sound of drumming hooves coming from behind causes the King to rein in, he turns to look back as one of the rear guard canters towards him.

"What is amiss?"

"Way behind my Lord, there is one that follows us, and has been doing so since dawn. At first, it seemed harmless enough, a lone monk riding on a donkey, but every time we looked back he was riding the poor beast as if it were a Destrier and has been beating it something cruel to keep up which we all thought a strange practise for a black monk, being how they love all creatures... but what makes it even more suspicious to us now, is that when we stopped to challenge him, he immediately hid from sight." The King frowns as this intrusion but seeing that the Renegade and Isabel are not so far in front, he turns his horse's head quickly.

"Sir Clifford continue on, I will rejoin you all shortly."

The troops stay in their position until he rides past them and then they carry on. The King and the soldier ride back until stopping on the crest of a small hillock.

"Down there, my Lord. He disappeared by that far rock that looks like a fat toad."

The King lifts the Star Gauge to his eye and pans in, picking out every deep crevice in the rock face and then he sees small clouds of mist coming from behind the rock clearly from the monk's exhalations.

"Yes he's there, but we don't have the time to ride back down and the weather is rapidly changing for the worse, perhaps he is a cellarer and has innocently been to a local market and carries his goods to the monastery that Sir Clifford tells me is further along?" But then he frowns... a monk riding at such a height, in this weather and the monastery in the valley below, why would he?

"However keep a close eye and if you see him again report back to me. Now let us catch up with the others before we are swamped in this mist rising up from where he hides, and if indeed he does follow us, it will soon be impossible for him to do so."

They quickly catch up with the troops; the King nods his head to the rear guard and rides back to his position at the front as again he lifts the Star Gauge to study Isabel. He knows that he is being overly obsessive, but he pretends to all that he is only studying his white mare, which in truth he is to a certain extent as every now and again in a low voice to Sir Clifford, which he knows his men can hear, he remarks on her outstanding prowess for such an old horse, she could almost be as she once was.

Not one of his men say a word but inwardly they all see how Isabel has changed too and apart from Sir Clifford, they stare after her just as eagerly as the King, as even now Sir Stephen views her in a different light.

For she is their shining yet dark light, not once do they see her shudder from the high cold wind or the sweeping rain storms, they admire how she expertly rides on, without a whimper or a cry, on and on, and like the King they resent how the Renegade has managed to control her, resent what they believe he does to her at night.

The next dawn, all set off again when the King notices Sir Clifford staring constantly over to the western hills and picking up on his right hand man's inattention to his total being, his brow furrows.

"You look thoughtful Sir Clifford, does something ail you?"

"No my Lord, I was only thinking of how close I am to my ancestral home of Brougham Castle, not even a day's ride from here. I wish I could see it again even though I know it will be in a sad and sorry state having been neglected for so long."

"Ah Brougham Castle again, I know I have kept you from it, but if I allowed you to go back, what would I do, you would never return and who else can I rely on?"

Sir Clifford bows his head.

"But let us see, when this business is settled satisfactorily, I will give you enough wealth to restore it to its former glory, how does that suit you? But only of course, on the understanding that if I ever need you, you will immediately come to my aid."

Sir Clifford, without being able to stop himself, beams outwardly, such an unusual sight and so rarely seen, that the King smiles back.

"I don't know how to thank you, my Lord."

"No it is for I to thank you. What do you say when we finish our business we ride back that way and see what needs to be done?"

Sir Clifford bows his head happily.

More days pass, the Renegade always selecting where they camp down for the night and always a clever decision with shelter in caves and water in abundance for the horses but for some inexplicable reason when the King awakes that dawn he begins to feel uneasy at the very easiness of it all. He studies the falcon above and as he studies her constant reassuring presence, she abruptly cries out and flies off at great speed to the north and in a questioning tone he turns to Sir Clifford.

"This is the first occasion she has left him since we passed up onto the high hills way back; I wonder if it is something of significance?"

At the same time Isabel turns to Cannin.

"Where does she go to?"

The King sees Isabel turn to the Renegade with a look of suspicion on her face and whilst he cannot lip read, he guesses that she also finds the falcon's departure peculiar, he watches as the Renegade turns back to speak and wishes that he could lip read.

"She goes forward to check out the land ahead, for very soon we shall come to the land of the Scots." But Cannin's face seems troubled and she wonders why?

"I do not wish to cast aspersions, but do you completely trust her?"

Cannin turns and gives her such a hard stare that she immediately lowers her head.

"But of course I trust her; I have known her my whole life, why do you say this?" She keeps her head low almost fearful now to continue.

"I don't know, I just feel that sometimes she is a double agent, playing both sides."

She waits for the angry retort but strangely he says nothing and half turning her head she sees him look ahead with piercing, searching eyes.

The King lowers the Star Gauge with a small smile on his face as Sir Clifford turns to look at him.

"We are nearly at the most northerly point of your realm my Lord."

"Good for soon he will die."

Immediately Sir Clifford snaps back at him.

"My Lord, only God chooses ones fate, but putting that to one side, once we reach the brow of the hill in front, you will see the land flattens down to a great plain, to the west is the sea and in the far distance is the ancient wall that separates your realm from the land of the Scots and as far as we can go." But the King having heard the disapproval in Sir Clifford's voice finds his temper rising.

"It is obvious that you have some sympathy for the Renegade which I could if I chose, find traitorous, particularly as I have promised you to restore Brougham Castle."

"I am very aware of that my Lord, of what you hold over my head but I admit truthfully that I have reservations about this entire business and I would be a liar if I spoke otherwise."

"What reservations? He has stolen from me, he has consistently mocked me and for that he will pay the price with his life."

"I am not sure my Lord, if any of these things you accuse him of he has done with malice in his heart against you, for all I see and have witnessed is a lone youth that somehow and inadvertently has been caught up in matters that are none of his making." The King is now so angry that he spits out the words,

"What matters do you speak of that are none of his making?"

"From the very start my Lord, did he choose that the dog be taken to the Unfathomable Forest; did he know that Isabel would follow after? I think not. There is a very strange business going on here and I pity him, for as the ancient elder of the tribe Sagittarii said, he is parentless, not one can help him and he is a lost cause."

"Never speak to me in this manner again, if it were not for your constant loyalty to me over the years I would order your instant death, but take it from me now, Brougham Castle will stay in ruins, for you have hurt me Sir Clifford, wounded me to my very soul."

"So be it my Lord." He bows his head sadly, as the King, uncharacteristically, vents his anger out on his horse, kicking its flanks furiously and spurts ahead. His men follow behind, each in turn staring wide eyed with shock at the dejected Sir Clifford as even Sir Stephen shoots him a brief look of sympathy. When they have all passed, he looks over to the west and in his mind's eye, he sees the restored castle and then he sighs, for he knows now it will always be in ruins...for a mere second he considers making his way there anyway...but no he cannot, for the promise he once made to the old king on his death bed.

Trailing behind he slowly follows, sickened by the thought of what will surely happen to the youth next. Further back but closing in fast, the black cowled monk follows on the exhausted donkey when at exactly the same time, many furlongs back, two monks discover the naked corpse of their missing brother at the bottom of a deep gorge.

CHAPTER THIRTY NINE
The falcon's mission

Beyond the burial mound the undulation of Hadrian's Wall is the most prominent feature on the landscape stretching from the west to the east as far as the eye can see, until it disappears into mist.

High up in the ruin of the watch tower, Lomond and the bear have a commanding view of the landscape and all along the ancient wall to either side they are accompanied by hoards of silent sea birds silently scrutinising the land and sky just as keenly as they do.

A tiny black speck appears from the southerly hills rapidly coming in Lomond's direction and he recognises the sharp tipped wings of a Peregrine Falcon, there is no deviation from its headlong course and to his mind he feels intuitively it is on a mission. He breathes in the sharp frozen air and exhales out, the falcon is surely the sign that everything is about to happen.

Elsu flits over the great plain, circles around the burial mound looking for a way in when she espies a gap up above the main entrance. She swoops down, lands carefully on the stone lintel, peers down the dark passageway and lifting in the air flits along until flying up into the void of the massive central chamber and up to the high corbelled roof. The earth ground below is littered with sleeping Dog Heads and all around the circumference of the massive chamber are the openings to much smaller chambers, packed full she can smell, of even more Dog Heads.

The high smell of fresh and old carrion also wafts up to her, so delightful to her senses that she is almost tempted to swoop down amongst the many dark huddled sleeping forms cradling their varying forms of prey and help herself, but she can't... but how tempting to pick at their prey?... but no, she reminds herself...nothing must deviate her from her course. The sharp, clicking noise from her wings echoes loudly all around, a few of the Dog Heads growl irritably, semi conscious of the fact that no bird has ever dared enter into their domain before but groggily in response hold more tightly to their gnawed bones and fall back to sleep. She realises more drastic action is needed and omits the most piercing, sharp shrill cries and with their sleep cruelly shattered, they furiously leap to their feet and with lit golden eyes watch her circle above. Now they listen to her cries, she circles around one more time and then flits along the dark passage to the outside, rising up into the air, shrilling furiously and flies back to the hills as rapidly as she had arrived.

Lomond watches her fly away and grins, the challenge is on, the new king is only a short distance away. Within the chamber, the Dog Heads howl like wolves and he can hear them even from where he is and hears their great excitement.

A short while after, ten of their number emerge out of the entrance way and lightly trotting, loping, then trotting again make their way to the village and Lomond wonders why? But he doesn't have to wait too long when he sees the flaxen haired girl mounted on a huge bull emerge from the village. Clearly nothing is going to plan when he hears the cries of the distraught womenfolk of the village, some wailing inconsolably, others screaming out as they words carry over to him on the still air.

"But we are not ready yet, Azenor is not ready yet, she has had only half of her draught...why do you rush this, why do you do this...This has been planned since the day of her birth, you are not even allowing her to wear her mantle that we have lovingly made for her all these years...She is the chosen one...Why are you spoiling this for all of us?"

One of the women attempts to put herself in front of the girl and the bull but is cruelly picked up by one the dog people and tossed to one side as effortlessly as if she were a small bird, her head smashing onto a low lying rock and Lomond sees her skull is split open as blood spouts out high into the air.

Now everything is silent, there are no more cries, the women stand motionless watching Azenor riding slowly away on the bull, surrounded by the Dog people who grinning wildly, look back at the women and growl out their hatred towards them and then laugh wildly in derision. But Lomond is more fixated at the sight of the flaxen haired girl, semi naked, clothed only in a small white tunic, there is something so strange about her, the way she sits so still, her face devoid of any movement or emotion, her green eyes staring straight ahead and her white flesh already mottled dark purple with the cold. He growls out in his anger and it is only then that the Dog people turn to look in his direction and stop, clearly perturbed by the hundreds of silent sea birds lining the ancient wall. They whistle out to them, but not a bird stirs at their command and then pushing their eye sight on, they see Lomond in the dark of the watch tower.

334

He is implacable in the way he views them back and they begin to talk loudly amongst themselves so he can hear every word.

"Remember we have been told to ignore him, the wind spirits protect him and the Grolar bear" They all growl with laughter.

"But not for long, he has made a costly mistake to say openly and arrogantly that he is at the command of the new king...None can help *him* that comes, he will be dead by sunrise...The new king, our king will command everything then, all of the spirits, of the wind, of the water, of the trees, all will do his bidding. And then what will he do, with no father to protect him? He is only the half, he has no power... after sunrise, the wind spirits will turn on him and the Grolar bear and rip them both apart and we will feed on their entrails." And then they laugh at their lies, deep growling vicious laughter, because they know he has heard everything.

They whistle to the bull to continue, eyes still fixed menacingly on Lomond up high as the girl Azenor sits still on the bull's back like a frozen effigy of who she once was. Lomond picks up the shark jaw and runs his finger tips over the many pointed teeth and inwardly seethes.

CHAPTER FORTY
The return of the falcon

They begin to rise up the last hill, the pink clear afternoon sky and the presence of an enormous low yellow sun belie the time of year and if it wasn't for the sharp cold and their misty breath it could almost pass as an autumn day.

Isabel looks at Cannin apprehensively as he continuously rides onwards with Archie tucked under his arm. Archie stares forlornly at her and she begins to feel that something is not quite right.

"Have we not left it too late Cannin to rid ourselves of my husband, he is so close behind now that it frightens me?"

Cannin smiles at her with the warm, special smile of the King and she immediately relaxes.

"Everything will be resolved soon, you are not to worry. We will stop shortly where Elsu waits for us."

Isabel looks up to see Elsu's dark silhouette flit down from the pink sky and land on a sharp rock as her shrill screeches fill the air. When she finishes Cannin whistles two short shrills back.

"Time to dismount now Isabel, Elsu tells me when we reach her, we will see the most wondrous sight."

The King and his men stop abruptly on the flattened tor of the hill directly behind when they see the Renegade and Isabel dismount. The King puts the Star Gauge to his eye and pans in on the motionless falcon sat on the sharp rock next to the edge of a precipice; he pans down to the green plain below and sees the grey sea to his left, the monastery, the small village and then over to the right he sees the burial

336

mound and beyond that Hadrian's wall, the most northerly he has ever been.

"The falcon has returned, something tells me Sir Clifford that events are about to happen."

There is no response, he turns to his right and finds to his surprise there is no Sir Clifford. He looks wildly around and behind him.

"Where is Sir Clifford gone to?" Sir Stephen bows his head.

"He is at the rear my Lord."

"What is he doing there? Tell him to pass up on up here immediately."

He puts the Star Gauge back to his eye and watches the Renegade sit down, his legs hanging over the edge of the precipice and he wonders what he is all about? To tempt fate in such a way is foolhardy, reckless and he feels the strongest urge to tell him to move away from the edge and back to safety. But then he knows the only reason he thinks this is out of complete and utter selfishness but even so he find his heart hammering alarmingly in his chest when he remembers how close he was to the edge of *his* precipice.

He is glad then when Isabel approaches Cannin, she stands back from the edge but looks down, he can see in complete fright and by her gesticulations urges him to move back, but he does nothing but sit there still staring at the view below, he doesn't know why but he has the strongest impression that the Renegade would have no compunction about leaping off.

But then he sees the Renegade turn and smile up at her, such a warm smile as yet again he feels a pang of jealousy at

337

their intimacy, the dog creeps over to his side, the Renegade puts his arm around him as he too views the scene far below, panting heavily and clearly in a state of high agitation. His white mare is not so foolhardy though thankfully, nor are the four black horses as they graze happily further away. He finds Sir Clifford at his side again and smiles broadly at him.

"Well there you are, lurking so far behind, what has come over you?"

Sir Clifford bows his head, his face hard and grey and the King then feels such a pang of guilt at his harsh words and the obvious affect they have had on him, his most faithful of men.

"I apologise to you Sir Clifford, my passions run too high, this entire business...of course I will restore Brougham Castle, you know always I keep to my promise, will you forgive me?"

Sir Clifford stares directly into his hazel golden eyes.

"I forgive you my Lord."

For what choice did he have?

"Good, so there's an end to it, let us be friends again and see what they are all about." And he immediately puts the Star Gauge back to his eye again and studies Isabel.

CHAPTER FORTY ONE
The coming of age

"Cannin, I would prefer if you would move away from the edge, I cannot do this for you if you sit there, I fear for your safety and for Archie's."

And of my own, she says inwardly, peeping over the edge of the precipice and then back to view the King and his mounted men staring in her direction.

"There is nothing to be frightened of Isabel, see how calmly Archie sits next to me now and besides I have to sit here otherwise they will not come."

"Who will not come?" She asks nervously.

"You will see, now do my hair as I have asked you to do."

And seeing that he has no intention of moving, she kneels behind him and tries to find a way of removing the four long pheasant feathers plaited into his tangled matted hair without hurting him.

"Why do you have these feathers' in your hair?"She frowns at the entanglement and guesses he has never brushed his hair in his whole life.

"They were plaited into my hair by my tribe, such a while ago that I can hardly remember when, possibly when I was very small. They are the tail feathers of male pheasants given to me by them as a gift. They symbolise the power of healing, perseverance, confidence and of forgiveness."

Isabel listens to his words as he continues on, imagining his life as a small wild creature that she soon forgets about the edge as she carefully tries to remove the feathers, Archie lies down at Cannin's side and falls into a deep sleep, the King watches and after a short time yawns loudly.

"Dismount, I feel we are going to be here for a long time." All dismount, the horses begin to graze, he and his men sit on the tor of the hill watching on as the deepest feeling of relaxation washes over them as Isabel tends to the Renegade's hair.

The pink sky above, the golden sun, such peace, the most peaceful they have felt since they had begun on this strange journey which seems an age ago now. Some of the men fall asleep but the majority stay awake watching on.

Isabel having finally removed the feathers begins to section the Renegades' long straggled hair and plaits each length tight to his skull and when she finishes the King turns to Sir Clifford.

"I have heard that the Dog Head males have their hair plaited when they come of age, which would make our Renegade fourteen years old." He grins then; all this fuss to his appearance will soon be for nothing.

But shockingly and without warning, the peace is shattered when an enormous Golden Eagle suddenly appears up from the void, wings flapping so noisily and yelping so shrilly at the Renegade that everyone present believes he is under attack. Isabel in complete terror cowers down behind his back, the King and his men jump to their feet and watch to their amazement as the Renegade stretches up and calmly pulls out the longest of the eagle's tail feathers. The eagle hovers over him, the Renegade bows his head when the giant bird flaps off and soars above. Another eagle flies up from the precipice yelping just as loudly. The Renegade follows the same procedure, and then another arrives, until in total six eagles circle in the pink of the sky directly above, but it is only the King that notices how the falcon sits still on her rock and he has the strongest feeling that she controls all and then he notices his horses, particularly the white mare, heads upright, stand completely still and the only ones that seem affected by the bizarre sight are he, his men and Isabel.

Cannin, his head still bowed but with Archie's heavy head now in his lap, calls quietly out. "Isabel, take each of the feathers that I pass to you and firmly push the quill of each into my six plaits." He passes one over as she quickly does as he asks, her hands trembling at the strange behaviour of the eagles.

"But why have *they* brought their feathers to you, what can they possibly mean by it?"

"Hurry now we must do this before the sun sinks below the horizon." She quickly takes another and gazes up at the sky at the circling eagles, reminding her of the Griffin Vultures of Castile.

She begins to poke the quill up another of his plaits but her hands shake so much that she nearly cries out in her frustration.

"Calm now Isabel, there is nothing to be agitated about."

"But you still haven't told me why the eagles have given you their feathers? I feel something terrible is about to happen and why do you not allow me to plait them into your hair like the pheasant feathers and so they stay put?"

"Something terrible has happened. The eagles have just informed me that my grandfather has passed to the other side at the very start of this journey that I began with you. Such sadness to me in the manner of his death and such sadness that all was kept silent from me but they inform me that it was his dying wish that I would only be told now when I had reached this point, ready for when the sun rises for the winter solstice. The eagles know I am far from my tribe, so they give me the gift of their feathers to not only mark my belated coming of age ceremony but also to grant me physical strength, courage, vision, new dimensions of perception, spiritual awareness, victory but overall to give me spiritual protection."

"But spiritual protection from what, what do you mean?" His words frighten her so much that she looks back in anguish to the King with all his men watching keenly over and she wishes someone could help her.

"Now you have done Isabel, stand well away from me and join the horses and say not one word, otherwise you will spoil the ceremony."

He carefully lifts Archie's heavy head from his lap, whistles softly into his ear and pushes him off, Isabel retreats fearfully back to the horses; Archie joins her when he stands slowly up, right on the edge of the precipice, arms down by his sides staring downwards, while the King, Sir Clifford and the men watch with ever increasing anxiety.

Seconds pass as if he is contemplating something, when he slowly lifts his arms to the skies and screams out the most awesome cries they have ever heard and within seconds all manner of birds rise up from their hidden positions in rocky cliffs as if they had been waiting all along for this moment, the sea birds sitting on Hadrian's wall scream over, until the sky is full of crying, screaming birds, circling around, their sounds so piercing, so awe inspiring, that they all cross their chests in fear.

In the valley below the villagers rise up from within their dark stone houses and for the first time in years cross themselves, the monks cease their singing for a second but then carry on with fervour, Lomond grins, the bear growls happily as do the Dog People within the burial mound but for quite another reason as they continue quite unconcernedly to carefully sharpen their weapons as they had done all day since they had last seen Lomond. Finally when the screaming of the birds finally stops, they attack the bull with frenzied glee using their freshly sharpened blades and hack it to pieces.

Azenor, discarded and forgotten about, lies in a small wretched heap, hidden in the dark of the western passage still drugged by her draught and remains completely oblivious to it all.

CHAPTER FORTY TWO
The escort

The sun disappears below the horizon and exactly at that point the birds fly off until there is not a single one left in the sky and then complete and utter silence ensues, not a sound or a whisper of a breeze is to be heard from sky or land. Such a deathly silence that the King, Sir Clifford and all the men continue to watch the Renegade, for what else can they do. They watch him sit back down on the edge as if totally exhausted, head bowed as Isabel walks over, kneels down and wraps her arms around him from behind and so they stay in that position until the light from the dying sun completely disappears until replaced almost immediately by a huge white moon. The King mutters out in his jealousy,

"Such high drama, all because he knows that we watch him." But his words sound hollow and unconvincing to all.

But such a clear night, none can sleep, no fires are lit and not a word is spoken as all sit waiting, for what they do not know, but they all know whatever it is will be happening soon.

Not one thinks of eating or drinking, the horses stand as still as statues looking down to the valley below, the hours slip by when from the east, the sun way below the horizon still lights up the sky to a pale muted gold when they hear the first of the howls piercing the absolute silence. The horses stir agitatedly and whinny sharply, Archie whimpers at Cannin's side, the howls increase in volume until Isabel who had fallen asleep, her arms still around Cannin, her head and body slumped against his back stirs slightly as he continues to sit upright looking down at the valley with lit eyes.

"What are those strange noises Cannin?" She lifts her head, her voice still heavy with sleep.

"Pay no heed, rest for a little while longer." But the howls increase in volume coming closer and closer, so loud now that she sits up in fright.

"But what are they; they sound like the Dog-Wolves?"

"No, not the Dog-Wolves, they are only the Dog Head King's lieutenants coming to welcome me and to escort me to him."

And then she cries out.

"But Cannin, you promised you would escort *me* to the land of the Scots first and then you would seek out the Dog Head King afterwards, you have betrayed me!"

"No, I have not Isabel. I have brought you to the land of the Scots as you had asked, it is just over yonder."

But now the howling creatures are almost now upon them.

"I don't want to look at them, I don't like the sound of them, what can I do, what can I do?"

She looks wildly around and then she sees them approaching in the vivid light of the spectacular moon, such dark loping creatures, eyes shining gold, with great canine teeth and of such growling size that she cowers down in her fright and clings herself around him

"Please Cannin, do not go with these creatures, they are evil, they are not what you think they are."

"I have to go with them. I will not be able help you anymore Isabel, you need to return to your husband for protection, go to him quickly before they get here."

345

"But he hates me, he will never help me!"

"He looks at you now in a completely different light I promise, go now, the horses will accompany you and give him back the two diamonds. Do this for me Isabel the only thing I have ever asked of you." She looks around again as they come ever closer with their wild yelping howls.

"I *will* go to him and I *will* beg him to help you."
Cannin smiles at her with the warm smile of the King.

"I need no one's help but you must go quickly now."

He quickly lifts her up onto the white mare's back and she hurtles off in the direction of the King, Cannin whistles and the four black horses canter after and then he whistles for Archie to follow but he stubbornly remains.

"Go now Archie otherwise they'll eat you alive and I will not be able to stop them."

Archie trots off as Cannin turns to face them, but only for a short distance when he hides in a grassy hollow and watches on.

The King takes the Star Gauge, ignoring Isabel's approach with the horses and focuses directly in on the approaching five Dog heads' features.

"They're nearly onto him, big heavy old males, ugly looking brutes, armed to the teeth and not unlike Morgar in size, I fear the Renegade does not stand a chance, I wonder how many more there are? For even with those five, we will have a battle on our hands after his death. Here, take the Star Gauge Sir Clifford and close in on them, but do you not find it strange that the Renegade has no facial likeness to Dog Heads, you could almost believe that he was one of us?"

Sir Clifford pans in on the approaching beasts and then shifts his attention onto Cannin's profile standing resolutely and he feels sick to his stomach.

"Yes, my Lord, it is very strange, perhaps he is not all Dog Head?"

The King frowns at his words but then taking the Star Gauge back focuses in on Isabel's beauty and smiles warmly. Sir Clifford seeing his attention had shifted away slightly nudges him.

"I beg pardon, my Lord, but they are with him now."

All watch as the five Dog Heads bow down sarcastically to the Renegade and now they are up close, all see how very young and how very small he is in comparison to their great bulk.

"Greetings from Luthias, oh king, grandson of Sagar and son of Mahayla, we have been sent to escort you. But first you will show us the Pendant of Office, then you will remove your cloak and your belts in order that we may carry them for you as is fitting."

Cannin bows his head and pulls the cloak back over his shoulders revealing the Pendant of Office around his neck which they all stare carefully at, he then removes his cloak and his belted sword and hands them over.

The King pans onto his chest.

"He has some type of pendant hanging around his neck, almost like a golden whistle, but why is he handing over his sword, what is he supposed to fight with?" And for some inexplicable reason he finds his temper rising.

"And the other belt, oh king." Cannin takes off the belt but then removes one of the pouches, holding it in one hand as he passes over the belt. They view Cannin dangerously now and growl deeply.

"You will hand over the pouch."

"I cannot, it is a gift for Luthias from his son Morgar that he requested that I must pass onto his father personally. It is for him only."

"You will hand it over."

"I will not, I am your king and you will do as I say, now take me to Luthias, I am anxious to make his acquaintance, it has been a long journey."

They stand menacingly for a second and then grin horribly.

"Come then oh king, let us proceed."

Cannin follows two of them whilst the other three follow behind and the one that holds his cloak and belts throws them unceremoniously over the edge of the precipice and catches up. When they disappear over the brow of the hill, Archie skulks his way through the long grass, over to the edge of the precipice and looks over, the belt with the pouches lies curled on a small jutting out shelf of rock just below him.

CHAPTER FORTY THREE
The belt of pouches

The King and Sir Clifford stand silently having witnessed the throwing over of his belts and the cloak and say not a word, for each knows by that very act that the Renegade is doomed. Isabel comes closer, nearly with them when the white mare shrilly screams out and rears angrily, the four black horses follow suit and the King knows she is warning him. He turns slowly to see the crouching forms of two more Dog Heads on the outcrop of rock at exactly the same level as his head, merely a leap away with their golden eyes glaring directly at him.

"Ah Dog Heads, I am glad you are here, we have been searching for an age to find your whereabouts."

"You are trespassing on our land; you do not have permission to be here."

The King smiles broadly.

"I warrant that we do not have permission, but we have heard that Luthias your king is wise and all powerful and we come to pay homage to him and if it is entirely possible would like an audience with him."

"He is presently too busy on other matters, but I will tell him of your presence but who shall I say that visits him?"

"Tell him that a poor human of no consequence would like an audience with him that is all."

But the two Dog Heads linger staring at him with piercing, suspicious eyes as the King's horses all now rear and whinny in fear, sensing their increasing hostility.

"But it seems as if you are all warriors, why is that?"

"We simply bear arms for it appears this is a dangerous country to be in. There is no safety anymore have you not noticed yourselves how dangerous it is..."

Eyes now forward, he stares appreciatively at Isabel's oncoming beauty when he hears the slashing noises and the dying guttural growls from the two Dog Heads coming from the rocky ledge and when all is silent, the white mare trots up with Isabel astride, followed by the black horses.

"Isabel, how glad I am to see you."

The King smiles his special smile for the first time at her and she finds herself feeling uncomfortably flustered and confused at his warmth.

"I thank you my Lord for receiving me but I beg for your help. Cannin is in the most desperate of trouble, they take him to kill him and I know you have the power to put a stop to it, please help him for he is entirely innocent."

She abruptly stares over to the shadow of the dark rock aware of the sound of a sword being sheathed when Sir Clifford appears suddenly and walks over to the King's side. She nods her head to him, he bows back and then she notices how all the King's men scrutinise her, pushing each other to get a better glimpse of her and she wonders why?

"I am afraid Isabel that I cannot help him, my hands are tied."

"But my Lord at his request I have brought back your horses and the two diamonds, which he said that I must return to you." She slips off the white mare, bows her head and hastily delves into the pocket of her cloak.

"I was wrong to have kept them my Lord, he never wanted any part of them."

350

"Keep them Isabel, I no longer want them."

And then she cries out and furiously delves into the pocket again and then falls to her knees in her anguish.

"The Pendant of Office has gone, he should have been wearing it and now I have lost it, what have I done, what have I done? They will surely kill him now."

The King looks quizzically down at her.

"What is this Pendant of Office?"

"He was given it at his coronation that I was a witness to, it is the symbol of the king, but he doesn't know, he has no idea that he is the true king and now he goes to the imposter who will kill him."

"What does this pendant look like?"

"It looks like a golden whistle with the snarling head of a wolf or a dog."

"Isabel, he was wearing it when he went with them, I saw it myself through the Star Gauge."

Now she cries out.

"So he knew I had it the whole time, he knew and yet he still helped me and Archie, he must have taken it when I was asleep, this makes everything even harder to bear, so much harder that I know not what to do?"

Tears stream down her face.

"I cannot live without him, I cannot, I love him, he is my brother, he is my son, please my Lord you out of all must help him!"

But now the King looks down at her with such rage that she visibly quells.

"You love him? He is your brother, your son? What is this mad gibberish that you say to me as your husband and your King?"

She now looks up at him fearlessly, her black eyes boring into his as her anguish turns to anger.

"I say to you that I love him as a brother and I love him as my son, for that is what he is to me, he is my son through marriage."

The King now strides forward and with one hand viciously pulls her up by her hair and holds her face in front of his.

"You would dare to concoct such falsehoods in order that I help your lover? I have no son, the one that I had died at birth fourteen years before."

"No, no my Lord, Cannin is not my lover, how could you insult him in such a manner? He is your son, born of you and of Mahayla, his first name is John, your middle name, named so by Mahayla. His Dog Head name is Cannin named so by Sagar, his grandfather. Look at your Star Gauge, what do you think Mahayla's inscription means or would you wish for me to decipher it for you?"

He continues to hold her viciously, snarling into her face, his voice breaking with his high emotion.

"I know what it reads, for it is mine. I will kill you for these lies, these suppositions." And then she spits out at him.

"Then do my Lord, for I have no reason to live anymore, for he is the only friend I have, the only one that has helped me. But before you kill me, let me tell all present what the inscription reads and see what they make of it."

And before he can stop her, she cries out,

"*Edward* for you to see ultimately the golden treasure of our union 'M'-'M' is for Mahayla and the golden treasure of our union is Cannin, your own son."

The King throws her to the ground and pulls his sword from the hilt in a vicious sweep and puts the point at her throat, as she, half laying and half sitting grins up at him, daring him. The King's men are now deeply unhappy, he hears their deep voices mumbling behind but he doesn't care, a pox on their judgement on him when Sir Clifford walks forward.

"Come now my Lord, enough is enough, we cannot have two such young people die at the same time." But the King still keeps the sword point at her throat when Archie appears through the long grass dragging Cannin's belt of pouches and drops it at Sir Clifford's feet, looking up at him with fearful yet dangerous eyes and he realises the dog will attack if not treated kindly.

Sir Clifford lowers himself down on bended knees, extremely painful old knees these days and smiles at him.

"Here now my Lord is the dog, see what he brings."

The King half looks over, glares back at Isabel and then turns again when he sees the Renegade's belt of pouches.

"The dog brings this to us for a particular reason and if we are all to remain calm he may allow us to look within the pouches where I warrant we will find something of significance."

The King scowls doubtfully but immediately the high tension lessens.

Sir Clifford stretches his hand out and strokes the dog's head.

Archie sits and then Sir Clifford removes all the pouches as one by one he unties them. The King lowers his sword and comes forward to look, Isabel crawls over, the men crowd around, all with a morbid desire to see what he had carried in his pouches.

Sir Clifford empties the first pouch as a curious selection of bones fall out, clearly instruments or weapons of some kind, one of the bones looking like a thin dagger. The next pouch houses his catapult and a few stones, more small bone instruments fall from the other two pouches but when Sir Clifford empties the last one a single folded leaf package tumbles onto the grass.

The King looks scornfully down at the objects.

"A sad, pitiful reflection of his short life, a few bones, a catapult and some dried up old leaves, hardly the wealth of a King." Isabel begins to weep but Archie growls willing Sir Clifford on.

At his prompting, Sir Clifford carefully picks up the leaf package, placing it in the palm of his hand and gently endeavours to unfold it. But by the very touch of his fingertips the dried leaves crumble to nothing and he is left holding a small, round, gold coin on a chain; he studies it with furrowed brow and then looks up at the King censoriously.

"But where would he have got your seal from my Lord and why would he carry it about with him?"

The King takes it in his hand and turns ashen white, the memory flooding back to him of when he gave it to Mahayla over fourteen years before and hanging exactly on the same chain.

He paces around now, clasping the seal tightly in one hand and in the other he drags the sword behind him as his thoughts run amok. But then he stops short and looks savagely around at them all.

"He must have found it, no doubt rooting around in Mahayla's bones and in my infantile son's bones, such desecration, such utter desecration, I cannot bear it."

And dropping the sword he falls to his knees.

Sir Clifford rises from his kneeling position painfully.

"No my Lord you are blinded by your hatred towards him, how is it I and everybody else can see his uncanny likeness to you and how is it that you cannot?"

The King turns his head and stares over at the pile of small bones and viciously shouts out,

"I cannot acknowledge such a thing, I cannot accept it, it is all a lie, those small bones are no doubt the bones of my infant son and he carries them with him like a trophy as he does my seal."

Sir Clifford walks over to him, seeing the distraught, pained youngster that he was after his mother and then his father had died.

"I am sorry my Lord, you are entirely wrong, they are not human bones, but clearly the bones of small animals. You cannot now refute the evidence that the Renegade or Cannin is your son. You can choose as is your right to not acknowledge that he is your bastard son but you cannot deny his existence. But anyway what does any of it matter anymore? Your problem will be gone soon enough when Luthias slaughters him."

Isabel rises to her feet now in confusion.

"But how is that you know the name of the imposter king?"

"We have known ever since we stopped at Warwick, my Lady. We were informed of Cannin's quest by the Dog Head tribe of Sagitarrii from the Forest of Arden. Cannin has to destroy Luthias, the next in line to be king in order to retain his kingship but he has an impossible task ahead of him. We have been told that Luthias is an accomplished, formidable warrior and is considerably older than Cannin, so much older, that Cannin is a mere babe in Dog Head years. But the most important issue is this, so that everyone present here understands, Cannin *has* to kill Luthias himself, none can help him, not us or any of the tribes of Dog Heads."

Isabel whispers now, more to herself and to Archie, who sitting at her side claws at her dress at her distress.

"I cannot understand all of this, does this mean that Cannin has always known this was his fate?"

As at the same time, the King whispers out, "I cannot accept the enormity of this, it is too much bear, I am destroyed, I am utterly destroyed, Mahayla, please forgive me, forgive me!" Sir Clifford looks down at him harshly.

"Come now my Lord, let us follow his path down to the great plain and finish off what we set out to do."

He turns to the crowd of surrounding men.

"The King's son will be slaughtered, of that there is no doubt and as you have all heard now we cannot involve ourselves, but after his death we will slaughter all of the beasts that have taken him and not one must be allowed to survive in the name of John, Cannin, son of Edward and of Mahayla, grandson of Sagar, and the last King of the Dog Heads."

The black cowled monk hiding behind the rock with the two Dog Heads lying at his feet with slit throats turns away having heard enough.

The King keeps his head lowered, manically biting the insides of his cheeks until the blood flows rich and full in his mouth when his white mare walks slowly over to him and nuzzles his forehead and then he stands up, his face altered from utter despair to a harsh, menacing coldness.

"Saddle my horse."

His men are not sure which horse to saddle, but Isabel makes their minds up when she walks over to him and the white mare.

"May I ride her my Lord?"

He briefly looks at her and nods his head, to her chagrin Sir Stephen rushes over and lifts her on, but as she looks down at him all she sees now is a frightened youth and forgiving him, she nods her head and when mounted gestures for him to pass Archie up to her.

Sir Clifford barks out orders, and whilst he waits for the horses to be saddled the King puts the Star Gauge to his eye and watches Cannin and the five Dog Heads enter onto the green plain below, he scans on to see the falcon circling over the enormous burial ground and now he knows where he is being taken.

CHAPTER FORTY FOUR
The King of the Dog Heads

Stretching along Hadrian's Wall, the sea birds have resumed their perch, their numbers increased tenfold by the addition of rarely seen migrants from far off continents.

In the dark of the watch tower, Lomond and the bear view Cannin's approach with two Dog Heads in front of him and three behind and he wonders where the other two Dog Heads that had left earlier had disappeared to?

As Cannin nears, Lomond is struck by his young age and seeming indifference to his predicament, noticing then that he is weapon less carrying only a small pouch and he frowns, at that very point Cannin looks up, scanning along the walls, taking in the huge numbers of birds until his eyes rest on Lomond and the bear.

Their eyes lock, Lomond bows to him and for a brief second Cannin smiles back in response and calls out,

"Your name stranger?"

"My name is Lomond and this is the Grolar bear and we are here at your command."The Dog Heads growl angrily at the exchange but do nothing else and Lomond senses that deep down they have a fear of the new king.

"I thank you for the sentiment, but do not linger here, please return to where you have come from and at haste."

Cannin bows his head and carries on. The driftwood door is opened up and Cannin is ushered into the eastern passage and the door is shut loudly.

Lomond picks up the shark's jaw and with the bear following they clamber down the broken sections of the ancient wall until leaping into the deep ditch at the bottom. Hidden from view they tear along until coming to the western end of the mound and climbing out of the ditch they make their way to the disused entranceway when all of sudden the most terrible growling and yelping ensues from within as he hears their jubilation howls at the new king's soon to be death.

He takes the opportunity with all the noise to roll away two of the top boulders blocking the entrance and climbing over followed by the bear he passes into the stone passageway and nearly gags at the stench of rotting carrion. He gingerly treads over raw bones of all sorts of beasts including to his disgust, the remains of Humans.

By this point the Dog Heads have whipped themselves up into a frenzy, their voices magnified out of all proportion coming from what he can see in the distance is an enormous central chamber.

The new king stands in the centre of the space surrounded by many more of the beasts than he had first calculated and guesses now there must be at least twenty more than he had thought and for a second he swallows in fear but then he sees a small white figure sitting up against the stone wall halfway along the passageway, her head tucked between her knees, and he realises it is the girl Azenor.

He walks along, propping the shark bone against the wall next to her and lays his hand gently on her shoulder, sickened that her bare arms had been smeared with animal blood. She slowly raises her head at his touch and looks up at him in such wonderment, for what she had wanted to happen, had prayed to happen is now reality, he sees her lit eyes and realises to his shock that she is the same as him.

She stretches up and throws her arms around him and for a short while he holds her tightly all the while whispering in her ear. He releases her arms and removing his sheepskin gilet hands it over to her and growls quietly into the bear's ear, they quickly run down the passageway and back to the outside.

She follows behind the bear, down into the ditch as he takes her back to the watch tower and when hidden within they look out across the vast plain to see a large troop of soldiers galloping down from the hills. She looks to her village, but all is silent and not a soul is to be seen and finds herself torn between homesickness and complete hatred of them all when rounding the headland a huge ship comes into view, sails furled, and to her mind it is like a great bird sweeping over the water.

She has never seen anything like it before in her life, no sea vessel ever as large has sailed so close to the shore before but the bear growls deeply in fear at its approach and lies down on his side in abject terror. She bends down to stroke him, her eyes still fixed on the ship and she imagines with relish the fear on the villagers' faces when they see it and, when they see the troop of soldiers coming ever closer.

Lomond walks slowly along the passageway, shark jaw in hand and tucks himself in an enclave and watches on, not one has detected his presence, but he has the strongest feeling even if he were to walk amongst them he would be ignored for the only thing they are interested in at the moment at least, is the death of the new king.

The growls, howls and high yelps turn now to low subservient whimpers when from a low chamber a head pokes through, so grotesquely huge and so grotesquely ugly, that he shudders at the sight. The stooping Dog Head enters into the central chamber and standing upright rises to such a height that the new king looks like a small child, but he notices with interest that the new king doesn't lift his head in fearful awe but looks steadfastly onwards as if at some goal of his own and he finds he admires him more than anything. But then the deep voice growls out, the most menacing and chilling voice that Lomond has ever heard.

"Welcome Cannin, grandson of Sagar, son of the whore Mahayla and the son of a degenerate Human, at last you arrive to do battle."

Cannin bows his head.

"I thank you Luthias for this meeting, but before we do battle..."

Great howls of howling, growling laughter erupt at this point, for to do battle he needs a weapon and he has none.

"I am in need of a weapon, for your lieutenants have taken my sword and all I have is my bare hands, which does remind me, I have a gift for you from your son Morgar."

Luthias bends down and sniffs in deeply and detects the scent of his son as Cannin dangles the pouch in front of him but then he picks up something else now, something distinct and so beguiling that he begins to salivate.

"Morgar told me that you would cherish this above all else, apart from me of course as the kind bearer of the gift."

More yelps of laughter greet his words at the thought of how Luthias would indeed cherish his flesh afterwards.

Luthias closes in now, taking in even deeper sniffs in his excitement, Cannin holds the pouch out further when Luthias snatches it viciously away from him but his nails are more like claws and Cannin realises he cannot open it.

"Allow me to help you Luthias, my fingers are so much smaller than..."
He peers around studying the claw like nails of the other Dog Heads.

"Than your entourage, they may damage the gift but more importantly Morgar said that this was for you only and for no other."
Luthias glares around now and growls deeply at them all to remain still.

Cannin takes back the proffered pouch and deftly unties the leather cord, opens it up and tips the contents to the earth floor.

The immediate release of the fungi sends forth its powerful pungency into the air; Luthias immediately drops to the ground and crawls forward drooling almost like a starved wolf.

In complete fascination, Cannin steps back watching the effect of the fungi on him as the others begin to let out low growls of jealousy.
Luthias snarls at of all them to remain silent, hovering over the fungi and bending down delicately picks up a section with his enormous teeth and begins to chew. After only a few seconds such a look of euphoria spreads over his grotesque features that Cannin cannot help but smile. He stares at Cannin all the while he chews and then bending down again he greedily devours the rest until all is finished and kneeling

362

up, he grins yellow fanged at him as the sense of euphoria intensifies, as the well remembered heat rises through his body accompanied by the great surge of aggression that fills his mind and body. He agilely leaps to his feet seeming even taller and larger than before and draws his sword in a great flourish.

"Now I am ready to do battle."

Cannin bows.

"I am ready too, please pass me a sword."

Luthias grins even more as his aggression reaches to such heights that he could slaughter a thousand Humans with just one swipe of his sword.

"If you haven't brought a sword with you then it is entirely your own fault, it is well documented in the Articles of Kingship that you must choose your weapon of choice and bring it with you and so I have taken it that you have chosen to fight me with your bare hands."

Behind the Dog Heads, Lomond goes to go forward, shark jaw clutched in hand, incensed with such anger when he finds his arm clenched with a vice like grip from behind and turning viciously around he is completely shocked to see his father who immediately puts his fingers to his lips.

Cannin smiles grimly.

"Now I understand why my grandfather banished you, you are not fit to be a king."

At his words, Luthias now burns alive with his anger, he begins to spasmodically shake and convulse, his eyes blur with rage and then he roars out,

"You have killed me." He drops his sword and falls to the stone ground and shakes uncontrollably. Cannin walks over and looks down at him pityingly.

"Not I Luthias, but your son Morgar. He should have, and more importantly, you should have remembered that the 'Destroying Spirit' must be gathered fresh in the dawn and consumed immediately otherwise it builds up in toxicity and added to the amount already stored in your body from years before, I am sorry to say your last meal has become your final one."

Luthias's heart beats erratically for a second and then stops. A ghastly silence prevails; the Dog Heads sniff in his last dying breath laced with the smell of the toxic fungi, totally bewildered by this completely unexpected turn of events that for a second they have no idea what to do and Cannin realising he must now take the initiative calls out loudly.

"It would appear that I am now officially the King of the Dog Heads, not a role I take lightly but I have never been given a choice. So lay down your arms now and let us speak of how we can move forward."

They now glare at him with evil intent; they unsheathe swords and point them at him as the first Lieutenant growls out,

"We refute your kingship for you did not slaughter Luthias with your own hand."

But then a deep voice calls out from behind.

"He did exactly that, his weapon of choice that he brought with him was the fungi and so you will now accept him as the king."

They turn around as the Wulver pushes his way through with Lomond. The bullish, gigantic first lieutenant looks him up and down when a sudden understanding comes to him of who he is and begins to look at him apprehensively.

"And so it is the great Wulver, not seen for the longest of time, the great Wulver that has finally been forced from his rocky island kingdom to aid his mongrel child." But even his caustic words come out nervously when all of a sudden a great hammering on the eastern door begins, the noise echoing all along and then the noise of the door being smashed to pieces as a great body of men barge their way in. At exactly the same point the sun rises up from the sea and blasts through the open entrance door setting the eastern passageway and the central chamber on fire with its intense light. The Dog Heads lower their swords in complete shock as the King and his men march towards them bathed in the golden light. A great sense of foreboding hits them, reminding them all of what should have been happening as the sun entered, namely Luthias devouring the Mongrel and the spawn's brains, heralding the start of his reign as the new king.

Cannin watches the leading dark silhouette marching down the eastern passage towards him, his golden hair lit like a halo. The King enters into the central chamber, sword drawn with Sir Clifford behind and his men behind him.

He stops and looks arrogantly all around, taking in the scene and calculates he has a shortfall of at least forty men. He looks over at the Wulver and Lomond standing alone and bows his head to them, knowing intuitively they are not part of the rest; they bow back and then he walks over to Cannin and looks down in revulsion at the corpse of Luthias.

"Well there is no doubt in my mind that *was* the malcontent Luthias for never have I seen such a resemblance between father and son, the same hideous looking heads and I would know because I had the most enormous pleasure of slicing off Morgar's head in the Unfathomable Forest."

He laughs harshly at the low snarling from the Malcontents.

"I take it that it was you that achieved Luthias's death Cannin?"

Cannin nods his head in complete and utter shock, not being able even to look up at him.

The Wulver calls out.

"I and my son Lomond are witnesses to the king's defeat of Luthias."

"And are there any here that refute that he did? If so let it be known now." The Dog Heads say nothing knowing that they cannot lie with the Wulver watching over.

The King grins maliciously around at the Dog Heads, listening to their deep growling complaints for not only is Luthias dead but so is his son as all realise now whose father Cannin's is, for the resemblance is just as uncanny.

The King lifts his head high and in a cool, clear voice booms out,

"As none have stood forward, I proclaim John, Cannin, son of Edward and of Mahayla, grandson of Sagar officially the King of the Dog Heads, confirmed by me, Edward, the King of England and Cannin's legitimate father. He will rule alongside me controlling all the forests within my realm. I have had a treaty drawn up to that effect and when he chooses in his own time to sign it I would be greatly honoured, if he chooses not to, then so be it, it is his decision." Cannin lowers his head, struggling to hide his emotions.

The King then looks over at the Wulver and at Lomond.

"Before I continue, I will excuse the two of you from the following proceedings and ask you to leave forthwith; but I thank you both for the support of my son."

The Wulver bows his head to the two kings as does Lomond, they both bow back but as Cannin lifts his head he smiles directly at Lomond, a strangely mixed smile, one of extreme happiness but then tailing off into almost a smile of ...Lomond cannot make out what, but in his mind something fatalistic. They make their way along the western passage to the outside, Lomond feeling strangely deflated and bereft, not quite believing that the adventure had actually come to such an abrupt end as he again pictures Cannin's tragic smile.

CHAPTER FOURTY FIVE
The battle to the end

They pass out into the daylight, when the Wulver stops and looks up to the sun.

"In a very short while, the sun will rise higher and cast the burial mound back into darkness again and that is what the Malcontents wait for, they know they already heavily outnumber the Humans and with the added advantage of rendering them unseeing they will slaughter them all and devour each one. When the darkness comes I shall go back in to aid the Humans and I want you to go to the eastern entrance with the bear and wait for me."

"But I would like to help?"

"You are far too young to take on such a foe as these, go quickly now, there is hardly any time left."

In the central chamber the King deliberately takes time to study the sullen mob in front of him, calculating which one to fell first, all as big as each other but his eyes continuously flit back to the brutish, first lieutenant. They stand as if obediently for the longer he takes; the better it is for them.

The King's men stand just as quietly in the eastern passage and watch just as intently when the King looks to Cannin and seeing his dropped head speaks lowly to him in an aside.

"With your permission Cannin, may I proceed?"

Cannin nods, so wiped out with such emotion and with such fatigue that he can barely stand upright as the King bellows out,

"I shall now proceed to tell all of you the law of this land. I will not suffer malcontents, war mongers and enemies within my realm and so I will now carry out the letter of the law in all its force, you are all sentenced to death." He grins, they snarl back and raising his sword upright and without warning throws it like a lance into the head of the first lieutenant and rushing over pulls it out with a great yank and bellows out, "Go only for their heads and slaughter them all." And so the violence begins.

Isabel having been left alone outside in the supposed care of the tethered horses, had followed with Archie right from the start as the King and his men had entered with the golden light of the sun. They had slunk, from giant slab to the next, hiding behind their rounded edges and had witnessed it all. She stays where she is when the King attacks, his men charge forward, their war cries so terrifying that for a second she falters and then she sees Cannin picking up the dropped sword of the dead lieutenant obviously going to join the affray and she cries out in her fear for his safety.

"Cannin, Cannin please don't..."

And then she disappears back into the mouth of the passage as if snatched away by a giant hand, Archie tears towards Cannin, barking furiously as the slaughter goes on all around, his voice lost in the great growls and shouts of violence, but Cannin catches sight of his brown and white patches from below, turns to see the dark elongated shadow stretching into the central chamber of a black clump rising and falling as if in a violent struggle.

He runs into the passageway, the sun blasting in his face, he raises his sword when he sees the kneeling, hooded figure behind Isabel, hand around her throat, throttling her to death whilst the assailant's other hand furiously fumbles in her cloak pocket. Isabel stares at Cannin in terror, eyes bulging from her head, when the cowled figure pulls his hand out from the cloak pocket and raising up a clenched fist screams out triumphantly and as he does so, the hood falls back to reveal Marques de Draq's savage contorted face, the round indentation on his forehead ominously dominant as he continues to coldly throttle Isabel. But then he becomes aware of Cannin striding towards him and with huge reluctance releases his hand from her throat, Isabel falls forward, struggling to breathe as Archie tears forward barking furiously.

Draq casually slips the diamonds into a hidden pocket beneath the scapula, stands up and as Archie nears, kicks him viciously in the head where he falls to the ground and lays completely still.

Watching Cannin coming ever closer with his sword pointing at him, Draq reaches from under his scapula and pulls out his sword, steps back a few paces, turns to look back at the daylight to freedom and in that moment decides to flee.

Cannin reaches Isabel, lays the sword on the ground and squats down in front of her and lifts her face up between two hands and smiling reassuringly, gently begins to massage her neck. She begins to breathe a little easier.

Cannin turns to look over at Archie's still form with such a worried look on his face that Draq looking back, stops short, his anger rising that the Renegade ignores him totally, ignores what he has just done, far more concerned with the welfare of Isabel and the dog - what a pity he did not show that same level of concern after he had felled him with the stone from the catapult and had left him to be eaten by the wolves. Yes, he appreciates that he could have killed him outright if had chosen to do so, so why didn't he?

The Renegade is now breathing into the dog's nostrils as the dreadful, fearsome battle continues in the central chamber. Draq looks back, not one notices him, he carefully retraces his steps, his dark shadow stretching before him. Isabel still struggling to breathe sees the dark shadow creeping over the earth ground next to her, a terrible stain abruptly stopping. She turns suddenly to look up, her eyes terror struck when she recognises Draq. He lifts his sword, hands held high, the sun lifts higher abruptly casting the burial mound into darkness, Cannin immediately kneels upright and worriedly stares towards the central chamber, and it is then that Draq strikes, downwardly thrusting the sword to the left side of the spine, a clean thrust, without a hint of bone thwarting its passage into lung and heart and inwardly he congratulates himself on his killing skill.

Draq pulls out the sword, wipes it clean on the black wool scapula and walks away to the outside as if nothing had happened. Cannin stays upright, unseeing but listening still to the great battle, he hears the King bellow out, "Do not falter, go for their lit eyes, kill them all."

Isabel tries to shout, she cannot, crawls over in front of Cannin and kneeling, holds him upright, the palms of her hands against his chest but even as she looks into his eyes she sees the last pinpoint of internal light go and his head falls heavily onto her shoulder. She remains as she is, propping him up, whispering hoarsely into his ear,

"Please Cannin, please do not die, you will live, I know you will."

And then she sees Archie's still form lying next to him and croakily screams out,

"Assassin, assassin, stop him that flees, stop him, please God, somebody please stop him." And then her head rests down on Cannin's shoulder as she weeps inconsolably.

But not one hears, the battle too loud, too vicious, Draq walks to the lit entrance door smiling, he now has the choice of the best of the horses instead of that wretched old donkey and knows precisely which horses he will take, picturing the four black horses in his mind's eye when three figures appear in the entranceway and partially block out the light. One a youth, the other a flaxen haired girl and the third, he realises, is a bear, but all young and hardly a threat.

He continues to walk forward raising his sword aggressively and waves it at them to allow him to pass.

But now he sees the black haired youth holds some sort of scythe like weapon in his hand and remains challengingly where he is as the girl moves to one side and the bear to the other.

Draq runs forward with a terrible war cry. The youth remains motionless, Draq swipes to kill, when he feels to his complete and utter shock that the weapon the youth holds is now stuck into his head with what feels like a thousand teeth buried in his skull. He falls to his knees screaming in agony, the youth pulls it from his head with shocking strength, but still he feels the excruciating pain at the shark's teeth imbedded in his skull when he feels gigantic jaws crushing

372

his neck from behind and he knows he if doesn't remain completely still he will die.

The bear drags him weightlessly out of the passageway onto the grass outside, holding on grimly and then rests his heavy body on him so he cannot move an inch as Lomond and Azenor stand guard over him. The tethered white mare and all the horses scream out agitatedly, the sea birds scream over ahead, such terrible screaming echoing into the central chamber that all fighting stops.

The King steps over the corpses of the Dog Heads, sees the Wulver emerge from the dark shadows with a raised sabre grasped in his hand, realising then that it was he who had turned the battle to his favour, aware that some great power was hacking and destroying from behind, he bows in gratitude to him, the Wulver bows back and then looks up the eastern passage to the dim light of the outside and points his finger.

The King stares where he points to, and half running, half walking approaches Cannin and Isabel, but before he even reaches them he knows that Cannin is dead. He looks at Isabel straining to keep Cannin upright, walks behind and lifts his dead weight up from under his armpits and holds him upright. Sir Clifford marches up, his face a grim mask,

"My Lord, let us take him to the light so we can see what can be done."

Between the two, they pick him up, Isabel bends down and strokes the still form of Archie and then trails behind, her eyes so blurred with tears she doesn't notice the six eagle feathers lying discarded on the earth ground. They lay Cannin's lifeless body on the grass outside where Sir

Clifford kneels down, struggling to retain his normal impassivity.

"Let us turn him on his side, and see what the damage is."

The King gently rolls Cannin over, staring down at his heavily bloodied tunic as Sir Clifford begins to undo the leather straps of the chest plate, Isabel helps him as hope begins to rise in her soul.

"I know you Sir Clifford of all men can help him, I know you will be able to."

The King's exhausted and bloodied men file out of the burial mound and gather around as Sir Clifford rips away Cannin's tunic and examines the wound and then he sighs heavily.

"I'm afraid my Lord, my Lady, there is nothing that can be done. He is dead, a fatal wound."

The King leaps to his feet and standing up, looks wildly around, utterly bewildered.

"But who did this, who did it?"

Isabel cries out in her fury.

"It was Draq. He attacked me from behind, took the two diamonds from me all the while throttling me to death, he kicked my dog in the head and when Cannin came to save us, he fled but then crept back and killed Cannin from behind, for all he was doing was trying to save Archie. And now Cannin is dead, dead simply for helping us like he has always done."

She bows her head down and then she screams out, wild eyed.

"I shall kill Draq with my own hand, where is he?"

From behind the King's men, Lomond calls out,

"We have him here."

She rises up, but on such shaky legs that the King's men look pityingly down at her.

"One of you give me a weapon." She glares around but all stand silently, heads down, until she screams out,

"I said one of you give me a weapon."

The King nods his head, as Sir Clifford solemnly hands her a dagger, the men part as she walks through them, her face now a mask of pure unadulterated hatred, over to where the bear holds Draq down. Lomond whistles, the bear releases his jaws, leaps off and sits between him and Azenor as all watch silently to see what Isabel will do.

"Rise up and face me Le Marques de Draq so you will know that it is I that kills you."

Draq lays still for a few seconds more, but with a small chuckle, rolls over and sits up to face her, blood running now in even greater rivulets down from his head and openly grins at her.

"You know you will be a traitor to your own people if you kill me Isabel, you will not be forgiven."

She spits out at him.

"These are my people here, all of these; you are the traitor so prepare to die."

"I warn you Isabel, my death will be on your conscience for ever more."

"No it will not, by the law of tallon my retaliation is justified, alas though, the mere punishment of just cutting your throat is not equal to all of your many crimes..."

She sobs then.

"But, at least, I have the satisfaction that you will be judged in the Hereafter."

She comes ever closer; he guesses then she will not do it when he sees how her hand trembles.

"Come Isabel, do not do something that you will regret, I am soon to die of my injuries anyway or they will kill me, either way I am doomed."

"Ha, is this your disgusting way of attempting to make amends to me?"

"It is."

"You liar, for even now I know you contemplate a means to escape."

She hovers over him, the blade poised at his throat, he smiles beseechingly up at her and then she slices viciously, deeply across, drops the dagger and falls to her knees. All watch silently as she crawls back to Cannin and rolls him onto his back so she can no longer see the evidence of his death.

The King kneels back next to her, staring down at Cannin's face and catches a glimpse of what he must have looked like when he had first met Mahayla and it occurs to him that he doesn't even know the colour of his son's eyes. He gently opens Cannin's eyelids to reveal Mahayla's vivid blue eyes staring sightlessly up at him and then he weeps.

CHAPTER FORTY SIX
The ship sails

The sunlight mutedly shines through the high stained glass windows of the chapel basking the body of Cannin on the white clothed altar in a soft diffusion of light. About his neck and nestling on his naked chest the Pendant of Office and the King's seal glow golden.

The King and Isabel sit side by side on a bench in front, hands held, heads down as Isabel prays, her whispering words almost like a child's.

"I thank you God...I thank you for taking Cannin into your great care, where I know you will..."

And then she sobs again as the King holds her hand even more tightly.

Beyond the confines of the monastery, enormous arduous activity is in task, all following the King's only order he had uttered before he had passed through the gates with Isabel at his side and Cannin's body in the monks' cart.

"Clear the burial mound of the Malcontents and include the traitor Draq in this. I want no evidence of their bodies, of weapons, personal artefacts, nothing, dispose of all, so it will be as if they had never breathed and walked on my soil. All other ancient relics, bones, carrion you will leave. You monks,"

He looks down at them, all shaking with such emotion that they struggle to stand still...they were told of the new Dog Head King's death by Lomond, shocked to find out his heritage, but even more shocked they would be receiving both the King and the Queen of England in their humble

377

monastery and with the corpse of the King's bastard son. Years ago they would have considered it an outrage, but not anymore.

"Will bless the spot where my son was murdered, Sir Clifford show them where. After, I want the two entrances to be completely blocked off as they had always been and by my law let none trespass in there again, I thank you all." He gravely bows his head, all bow their heads back to him as Sir Clifford and the Wulver take control.

The King's men ride to the village, the people forced out of their stone dwellings, the men stony faced and at first a great wailing from the women but when they all see Azenor survives with Lomond and a great bear as company they hurriedly harness donkeys to carts as the clearance of the burial mound begins. Lighted torches are taken in where the King's men can now clearly see the cruel evidence of the Malcontents rule and struggle not to gag at the atrocities, battlefields they have been in, but what they witness now is beyond their comprehension.

The Wulver supervises all within; carefully laying ancient bones back in the position they had once rested, with such meticulousness and with such careful detail that all the men become happier and what was to them the most hideous of tasks now becomes almost enjoyable when he picks out bones and tells them from what period in history they had come from. He sorts through and through with the brethren assisting him and even when the last of the Malcontents are carried out, the King's men return, where he shows them the ancient bones of extinct birds, of mountain hares the size of sheep, the elongated canine teeth of enormous cats and all manner of bones from other ancient creatures. So entranced do they all become that even the villagers come in, fearfully at first until before long the central chamber is full as he picks up bone after bone. Finally he ends and beams around at all of them.

"And as the King of this realm has wisely said and quite correctly, that this burial mound belongs to the ancient people that built it and must never be misused, desecrated or entered into again." Sir Clifford smiles, having watched the Wulver's extraordinary skill in turning a vile situation into something so positive and knows he could never have done such a good job himself.

The Wulver bends down and with his two giant hands carefully picks up a large bundle of cloth at his feet with something clearly wrapped in it and cradles it in his arms as if it were a babe.

"So with your permission Sir Clifford,
Sir Clifford bows his head.

"Let us leave and block the entrances forever more."
When they are all outside, the King's men begin lifting up the great portal stone with heavy grunts when the Wulver turns to the brethren.

"Please take this dog to the Queen and tell her there is no permanent damage, he merely sleeps now."
He hands the heavy bundle over to a surprised brother Firmin. Sir Clifford walks over in amazement and pulls back the cloth to reveal a sleeping Archie.

"At least there is one good thing that has occurred this saddest of yule tides, but I swear the dog was dead, how did you manage to save him?"

"It was not I, the new king breathed life into him before he was so cruelly struck down...such healing skills, I bow in deference to him."

A strange, yellow sky lowers down then, with the hint of foul weather to come; the villagers look up and without being ordered all hurriedly transport the remains of the Malcontents to the plague ship, the men carrying them up the gang plank where Lomond and Azenor roll them into position, the women bring up the weapons and put them in another great pile until finally the last two to be carried on are Luthias and Draq. Draq is carried up, but the villagers gather around Luthias staring at the corpse with such fear that the Wulver steps onto the gang plank and thunders out,

"Bring him up now, quickly does it and lay him on top of this pile here, and do not keep turning to the King's men to do this for you, they have already done more than enough."

Sir Clifford and his men stand further back; watching on, so exhausted they can barely stand.

The bear growls deeply and aggressively, prompting four of the village men to pick Luthias up, struggling to carry his huge weight.

"Quickly now, before long the light will fail."

For even as he speaks, the sun sinks nearer to the horizon, setting the yellow sky alight as if on fire. They dump Luthias on top of Draq and run down the gang plank as the Wulver looks sternly down at the villagers.

"Today is your festival of yule tide, bring out all your fatted calves and suckling hogs and share your feast with the King's men to show your gratitude towards them for their deliverance of you all."

He bows his head to all, the sun sinks lower towards the horizon and the ship becomes a great black silhouette comprised of masts and limp sails.

Sir Clifford smiles exhaustedly.

"Let us retrieve the horses and make camp."

They wearily stride off, back to the burial mound and gather the horses; the villagers return to their cottages strangely elated and prepare for yule tide and the monks retire to the refectory.

The King and Isabel still sit in the chapel, hands still held looking over at the altar when the golden light through the high windows mutes down.

"I have been pondering all this while Isabel, on what to do next with Cannin and I have decided that it is entirely right that we take him back to his mother, back to where he was conceived and to where she lies, for there he was born and there he lived for nearly all of his short life and to me, such a blessed place. Would you agree?"

Isabel smiles at him.

"I would totally agree, I cannot think of anything better."

"Let us retire then, for we have a long journey tomorrow."

They both stand and walk over to Cannin again, Isabel bends down and kisses his forehead.

"Until the dawn Cannin, we will see you then."

They leave the chapel and quietly shut the door behind them, the King puts his arm about Isabel, she leans against him and they make their way to the monks' guest quarters and lying on the great bed, arms around each other they fall asleep, overcome with grief and exhaustion.

The moon rises up from the sea, a perfectly round enormous disc, illuminating the many sails of the plague ship as it gently sways rhythmically in the light breeze with the lone bear on the decks standing guard over the dead.

Outside the monastery gates; a great fire is lit, courtesy of the villagers as food is brought over to the King's men. Archie lays on brother Bernard's lap in the refectory, quietly accepting small pieces of chicken, the other monks take flasks of mead to the King's men where they and all the villagers sit quietly waiting patiently for the high tide and the easterly wind that the Wulver had told them would come, waiting for the plague ship to sail away with its rotten cargo, far out to sea where the dead would be fed to the sharks.

But the Wulver does not want the easterly wind yet, he will summon the wind spirits when the time is right, what he requires now is a calm sea and the light of the full moon in order to carry out the most delicate of procedures he has ever had to perform.

In the Captain's great cabin spanning the entire width of the stern and on the wooden dining table in the centre lays Cannin's outstretched body. The white intense light of the moon glares through the open windows illuminating the space with Elsu perching on the sill of one of the windows keenly watching Azenor. She finishes plaiting Cannin's hair with the six Golden Eagle feathers now firmly in place and nervously moves to the side of the table as Lomond on the other side smiles encouragingly over at her.

At the foot of the table, the Wulver dripping wet and wearing only a loin cloth holds a striped sea snake by the base of its head in one hand and stroking it gently with his other hand, soothingly hisses to it in its own tongue. Azenor stares wide eyed in fear at the sight of the highly venomous snake and cannot imagine what the Wulver intends to do with it.

"Now Lomond and Azenor, we must move quickly before it is too late. Lift the king until he sits and his legs are over the end of the table and hold him upright."

They do as he asks, sadly aware that his body is already stiffening perceptibly and his skin colour even in the last few minutes is becoming whiter with purple marbling spreading alarmingly over his back and torso.

The Wulver approaches and holds the snake's head directly over the open wound and hisses gently. The snake opens its jaws and spits directly into the gaping slit as Azenor struggles not to cry out. The Wulver quickly takes the snake to the open window and returns it to the sea and rushing back, places his thumbs on Cannin's spine and with hands outstretched massages slowly downwards whistling a strange tune. He looks up at Azenor's terrified eyes, realising what she been through herself and smiles gently at her and then at Lomond.

"I have to stop the internal bleeding and the sea snake's venom will clot the flow of blood. But I am still very concerned for the king, he has gone into the Dog Head Torpor or acedia and his spirit is trying to leave his body. We cannot allow that to happen, he must live to rule. Already he cries out to join his mother and his grandfather in the spirit world but they do not want this and remain silent towards him, so I must animate his spirit to stay in the only way that I can." He stops massaging and rushing around to Cannin's front, places his head against his chest and listens carefully.

"Good, the blood flow is stemmed and the Atre Torpedus is making his way to us even as I speak. Azenor I wish you to move in front of the king and continue to hold him upright. Lomond please take up the rope harness."

He rushes again to the open stern windows and peers down at the sea with Elsu watching with him. Azenor takes hold of Cannin carefully, his head resting on her shoulder and turns to Lomond and whispers fearfully,

"But what does your father mean by the Atra Torpedus?"

"The Atra Torpedus is... it is what you would know as the Black Torpedo." Her eyes widen in horror.

"But he is the scourge of the dark depths, the death charge, he is a killer, none must go near, even the great sharks will not approach him."

"We must trust to my father, he is the only one that can bring the king back to life, because I know already that he feels it is too late."

The Wulver suddenly cries out,

"He comes, quickly now Lomond."

They pull the pull harness up Cannin's arms, looping it under his armpits and over his shoulders. The Wulver bodily picks up Cannin as if he were a small child and lowers him down into the dark depths with the stretch of rope and when he cannot see his body anymore, he wraps the end of the rope tightly around his arm.

"Now we must let him do his will, it is for him to choose the path, I can do no more."

Lomond and Azenor are not sure whether he speaks of the king or of the Black Torpedo, but in that moment he looks at both of them anxiously, the first time that Lomond had ever seen him look so worried.

"I pray you both to look only to the moon for the king's rejuvenation and think of nothing else." Azenor clutches hold of Lomond's hand tightly trying to banish the menacing image of the ray from her mind.

Smooth, sleek and black, the elusive mammoth ray, the largest ever seen in these waters, softly, almost idly flaps his soft pectoral fins towards Cannin, his nearly round black disk shape terrifying all as even the great sharks and the Orca's disappear quickly into the gloom.

Closer still, he views Cannin's listless body through two tiny eyes on the upper part of his body, viewing his plaited hair floating upwards like the tendrils of a jellyfish and then he sweeps over, wrapping Cannin in his soft black embracing wings and chest to chest sends forth his deathly lightening charges one after the other. Never has he had such freedom to do so, a totally captive prey when from above Elsu takes to the sky screeching loudly, so very loud that he can hear her terrible cries from the depths and it is then he feels a deep throbbing beating against *his* chest...the Human's heart is pounding against *his*? It becomes stronger and stronger and even more powerful, this should not be happening, he releases his soft, winged grip when Cannin's eyes open, lit with such burning intensity that he turns quickly away and makes his way down to the ocean bed and buries himself in sand until completely hidden.

Elsu hovers above as the Wulver and Lomond pull Cannin up from the sea and carefully lift him back through the window and carry him over to the table and removing the rope harness, they lay him down as Azenor covers him with the Wulver's great cloak. Cannin stares at the three of them with confusion and tries to speak, the Wulver rests his hand on his forehead, smiling down at him,

"Welcome back, King of the Dog Heads, all will come to you in time, go to sleep now." The Wulver's hand rests more heavily on his head; warmth spreads throughout his body until Cannin lets out the deepest of sighs and closes his eyes.

"Now let us put the king on his side so he may breathe easily. Azenor stay with him and make sure he stays covered. Lomond come with me, we must prepare to set sail."

The wind spirits gather in force, small breezes at first, collating as one and sweep over the great plain, rustling the stark winter grasses until building in strength they rise high above the fire and sweeping over they fill the limp sails of the plague ship.

The King opens his eyes suddenly and sits upright in the dark of the chamber; Mahayla's dream voice still whispering softly in his ears..."The only truly effective way to kill a Dog Head is to wound them mortally in the head for on any other part of the body they have the most remarkable ability to self heal."

"Isabel quickly now, come with me."

He leaps off the bed, she quickly follows and both run to the outside, along the gravelled courtyard to the chapel doors, he flings the great doors open; the moon shines down through the flower shaped window leaving its imprint on the altar cloth, burning pure white, but Cannin is no longer there. They both run now to the open monastery gates, a short distance away a great fire burns and the men quietly sitting around it, the King looks to the sea, the great ship's sails billowing out as the easterly wind pushes it swiftly out to sea, he bellows out,

"Cann...in...n." His startled men jump up, he puts the Star Gauge to his eye and pans in on the small black speck above the ship, the backdrop of the white moon marking her winged presence to such prominence that he laughs wildly and hands the Star Gauge over to Isabel.

"You see her Isabel, you see her, he lives, he lives."
Isabel looks through and when she sees Elsu, she screams out,

"Cannin please, please come back to us."
But she knows he will not.
The King sees her distraught face and puts his arm around her.

"He will come back to us in time Isabel, for you must understand he now has his own kingdom to rule and neither you nor I can help him with that task."

The ship sweeps around the headland and heads out to the open sea, sea mile after sea mile until the Wulver whistles to the wind spirits for calm. The high winds immediately drop to a whisper as the Wulver turns to smile at Lomond.

"Well Lomond, we now have the inescapable task of unburdening the ship of this lot...hard strenuous work but so entirely pleasurable."

Between the two they firstly pick up Luthias, the Wulver's great strength coming into play, taking far more of his enormous weight than Lomond and dump him over the side. Next Draq, the snapped off shark's teeth still firmly imbedded in his skull follows directly after.

On and on they toil, the bear rolling bodies and heads over to them as they throw them over the side, the great white moon impassively shining down until finally all the remains of the Malcontents are incarcerated in the deep waters where the creatures of the sea feast avariciously on their flesh.

Lomond is so utterly exhausted that he squats down on his haunches, breathing heavily in and out, when he notices the enormous piles of weapons and groans outwardly.

"But what of their weapons?"

The Wulver grins.

"I shall keep them for the king; they may be of use to him one day. Such skill was used in the making of them by the Pygmae, it would seem a shame to abandon them to the ocean bed. Now let us sail to the sea Loch of Fyne where we will all disembark and make our way on land to Ben Lomond, where you can finally climb to the summit my son, as was always your intention."

CHAPTER FOURTY SEVEN
The parting of the ways

Standing on the snow covered summit of Ben Lomond, they view the majestic panorama made up of far off hills as below the great blue waters of Loch Lomond stretch into the far distance. Lomond breathes in the freezing air and smiles so happily that all three smile with him.

"This is where my mother came from and now that I have climbed to the summit, I am entirely contented to return to Fair Isle, you will come with us of course Cannin?"
He turns then to look at Cannin, still so pale and ill looking that he worries for him.

"Thank you Lomond, I would like to and I do solemnly swear that I will see you again but, lest I forget, it appears I have a kingdom to rule and must acquaint myself with the tribes in my realm first, which I fear will take a length of time. But time enough I pray to the spirits for my father and for Isabel to become properly acquainted...as it should be."

The Wulver stares intently at his dropped head and his sad smile with such compassion that Lomond and Azenor look back from one to the other in confusion. A small silence when Cannin now looks up at the Wulver.

"But there is one request I would ask, if I may? I am aware from what you have told me that the Grolar bear would not be a welcome addition to the small population of Fair Isle and if all are happy I would like him to accompany me to the south. I am in need of a strong companion and I cannot think of one better than him."
The Wulver bows his head.

"Thank you my Lord, you do us the greatest of services in taking him with you. He is young yet but he promises to be the greatest of bears but please always remember if you are in need of more aid you only have to ask, for you know where we will be."

Cannin smiles then and bows gratefully to the three and makes his way southwards, down the great mountain with the bear at his side. All three continue to watch his small desolate figure, still wrapped in the Wulver's cloak until he and the bear disappear from sight and with a great cry the Peregrine Falcon sweeps over their heads and follows from above.

Lomond turns to his father and Azenor.

"I feel he is totally alone apart from the falcon and the Grolar bear, I would not want to be him at his age with such a huge responsibility in front of him."

The Wulver looks to the south.

"Within the mortal form of the falcon is the spirit of his mother and she will never abandon him. Yet his task is enormous and even though he is the undoubted king there will be many that will resent who his father is. But he has no choice; he chose to live and therefore chose to rule. Having said that, I do pity him, for his rule will not be easy."

THE END